HE WOULD CONQUER HER BODY AND
WIN HER HEART

"Edlyn, give to me." His hand rubbed her neck, then her scalp, in slow hypnotic circles.

Her eyes had closed, but she saw with his vision. Her ears had failed her, but she heard her own faint denial. She felt his triumph as he kissed her deeply, then his frustration as she let him do what he would with no attempt to reciprocate.

He gathered her closer when there was no closer, tangling his legs with hers, pressing his knee between and high until the pressure brought familiar sensations, then new urgings. She fought to deny them, but he moved insistently, insidiously.

"Feel me," he crooned. " 'Tis Hugh who holds you, who pleasures you. 'Tis your old friend, your new lover . . . your future husband."

D0037126

Books by Christina Dodd
Candle in the Window
Treasure of the Sun
Priceless
Castles in the Air
Outrageous
The Greatest Lover in All England
Move Heaven and Earth
Once a Knight
A Knight to Remember

By Catherine Anderson, Christina Dodd, and
Susan Sizemore
Tall, Dark, and Dangerous

Published by HarperPaperbacks

A Knight to Remember

✥ CHRISTINA DODD ✥

HarperPaperbacks
A Division of HarperCollinsPublishers

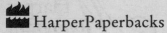

HarperPaperbacks
A Division of HarperCollinsPublishers
10 East 53rd Street, New York, N.Y. 10022-5299

This is a work of fiction. The characters, incidents, and dialogues are products of the author's imagination and are not to be construed as real. Any resemblance to actual events or persons, living or dead, is entirely coincidental.

ISBN 0-06-108488-3

Cover illustrations by John Ennis

First printing: January 1997

Printed in the United States of America

Visit HarperPaperbacks on the World Wide Web at
http://www.harpercollins.com/paperbacks

❖ 10 9 8 7 6 5 4 3 2 1

To my AKZ sisters:

Rhonda Day, Juli Goetz, Marian Hardman, Ann Holdsworth, Kathy Howell, Sharon Idol, Jessica Kij, Sheila McCarn, Bobbie Morganroth, Susan Richardson, Rebecca Easterly, Suzanne Bartholemew, Julie Mulvaney, Deborah Schlafer, Sherrill Carlton.

Thank you for your unending support and enthusiasm. God was looking out for me when Sheila wrote that letter.

1

**Medieval England
Wessex, Spring 1265**

As Edlyn leaned over to fit the key into the lock, the door creaked on its hinges. Confused, she stared at the widening aperture. The wood around the lock hung in splinters, and only the half-light of dawn had masked the damage from her unwary gaze.

Someone had broken into the dispensary.

She took a hasty step back along the graveled path in the dispensary's garden. The recent battle had brought many men—wounded men, frightened men, desperate men—to the abbey's infirmary, and she knew better than to linger alone in their vicinity.

As Edlyn prepared to run, she heard the sound of labored breathing. Whoever had shattered the door remained inside, and judging from his anguished sounds, he was hurt. She hesitated, unwilling to let anyone suffer, yet knowing she should seek one of the monks for assistance.

Before she could make her decision, an arm snaked around her throat. Jerked hard against a sweaty male body, she kicked wildly. Something touched her cheek, and steel glinted at the corner of her eye.

A dagger.

"If ye scream, I'll slit yer throat from gullet t' gizzard."

He spoke the Norman French of all English noblemen, but his common diction and grammar made it almost unintelligible. Nevertheless, she understood him only too well, and in the soothing tone she'd perfected through the days and nights of tending the ill and wounded, she answered, "I can safely guarantee my silence."

The man's grip tightened. He dragged her up until her toes dangled and she gagged from the pressure on her windpipe. "Aye, a woman'll lie always t' save herself." He shook her a little, then the pressure loosened. "But ye won't betray me if ye know what's smart."

She sucked in air, and her gaze roamed the inside of the walled herb garden and the dispensary. She needed one of the nuns. Even the prioress, Lady Blanche, would have been a welcome sight. But the sun had scarcely risen. The nuns were still at Prime. Next, they would break their fast, and only then would they disperse to their duties in the refectory, infirmary, and gardens. Edlyn's survival depended on her own quick thinking—as always. "Are you looking for food?" she asked. "Or medicines? We have many men who have come from the battle seeking—"

The arm tightened brutally, and she clawed at her captor as red suns exploded behind her eyes. Then he dropped her like a savaged puppy. She hit the ground hard.

Putting his foot on her stomach, he leaned over her and pointed the dagger at her chest. "What makes ye think I came from th' battlefield?"

She resisted panic and pain as she tried to think

how to reply. Should she tell him he smelled of blood, filth, and brutality? She didn't think he wanted to hear that, but then she didn't understand how her hard-won peace could have been shattered so cruelly. "Men come here seeking our help," she whispered. "I thought you might have been one of them."

"Not me. I'm not wounded."

"Nay, I see my mistake now."

She saw more than that. An ugly, squat man, her attacker wore a leather jerkin and carried nearly all the weapons that had been created to destroy mankind. Blood smeared his arms and under his chin, but most of it, she thought, wasn't his. He stood too firmly and had proved his strength only too well.

Beneath his leather cap, his wide brow creased as he frowned. He was nothing but some knight's manservant, trained to fight and hurt and kill, and she would wager he did all with supreme confidence. But something confounded him now, and again she tried to sound encouraging as she asked, "How may I aid you?"

He glanced around, then back down at her. "I got someone in there. I want ye t' fix him."

Praise God. Edlyn could scarcely see for relief. This muscled monstrosity wasn't going to rape her. He wasn't going to kill her. He just wanted help for his master or his friend. She'd tasted fear before, and only now did she recognize its metallic flavor on her tongue. "Wounded?" she asked.

He hesitated, then nodded abruptly, as if even that had given too much away.

"He would be better in the infirmary. Let me take you—" She tried to raise herself on her elbows, but the point of the knife suddenly threatened again.

"Nay! I coulda done that by meself. No one must know . . ."

"That he's here?"

"Aye." The man spoke grudgingly. "If ye tell, I'll slit yer throat from—"

"Gullet to gizzard," she finished. "So you've said. But I can't help him if you won't let me off the ground."

He still hesitated, then took his foot off her belly and extended a hand to help her up—and to maintain control of her. "In there." He jerked his head toward the dispensary and stood behind her as she entered.

Outside, the rising sun had begun to illuminate the landscape. Inside, the stone walls blocked the light and the small windows spitefully admitted only the faintest rays. Edlyn opened her eyes wide, trying to locate the source of her troubles.

"He's here on th' floor." Reverence laced the servant's voice. He shut the door, then knelt on the dirt floor beside a man-sized length of metal and rags. "I've brought ye help, master," he whispered. "She'll make ye well."

No response, no movement, no sound. Edlyn feared this master must already be dead, and she balanced on the balls of her feet, ready to flee at the moment despair struck the wretched oaf.

Then her captor groaned in unconcealed anxiety. "Master . . ."

Before she could change her mind, she laid a hand on the servant's shoulder. "Move aside and let me see what I can do."

The servant shuddered under her hand, then leaped to his feet. "If he dies, ye die."

He snarled, but her sharp edge of fear had been dulled. Her captor was, after all, only a servant afraid for his knight, and that made him less of a monster and more of a man. Rebuking his arrogance, she answered, "Your master is in God's hands, as are we all. Now move aside."

The servant stumbled back, and his gaze settled on the cross over the door.

"Open the oven and stir up the fire. I need light." Edlyn knelt beside the prone warrior. A closed, battered helm cupped his head. His surcoat had been removed, and chain mail swathed his chest, legs, and arms. His man freed the embers from their blanket of ash and laid kindling to encourage the flames, and in their light she observed blood oozing through the iron rings. She untied one lacing on the side of his chain-mail hauberk, but found the other one severed and flapping loose. The fallen knight's opponent, she guessed, had slipped a lance through the laces. The force of the blow had ripped them open, then the point of the spear had torn the flesh. With a grunt, she moved the heavy hauberk aside and stared in dismay at the blood-soaked quilting beneath. "Give me a knife," she demanded.

"Not likely," came the surly answer.

"Then you cut off his padding," she said, impatient to see the wound on the knight's belly.

Her captor knelt beside her. "This padding is an aketon." With unsteady hands he cut away the tattered remains of the breeks and shift. "An *aketon*, ye stupid bitch. It protects me master from blows t' th' armor. Don't you know anything?"

She knew more than she wanted to, but she didn't admit that. Instead she said, "It may protect him from blows to the armor, but it has done nothing to preserve his flesh."

Then the servant laid his master bare and Edlyn

sucked in her breath. "God preserve him." She dropped back down on her knees and stared, too afraid to even touch the white ribs and torn muscles that gleamed through the tattered skin. "You need someone more experienced than I to tend this."

"Ye do it," the servant insisted. "No one but ye."

"Why would you condemn him to my incompetent care when across the square lies an infirmary? I'm the herbalist," she declared firmly. "I don't nurse the wounded. I only apply poultices and recommend medicines."

He looked her over, his eyes thin squints of hostility. "I hear how ye talk. Ye're a lady, an' ladies know how t' physic their folk."

"Some of them more competently than others."

"Make it better." The cold point of the dagger touched her cheek again. "Now."

So he wouldn't even talk about it. That meant, she supposed, the wounded man was one of Simon de Montfort's rebels and the servant feared the prince's men would find his master and kill him. It made sense, but she'd seen men die of wounds like this. She'd seen them live, too, but only under the experienced care of the nursing nuns and their trained servants. She glanced at the dagger out of the corner of her eye. She should have run while she could rather than let compassion sway her.

Instead she had stayed and committed herself to doing the job at hand. She had to—she had more than herself to think of.

Standing, she moved steadily through her dispensary while the servant watched her. Inside the compact building set in the middle of the convent's herb garden, the walls were lined with shelves. Dried mushrooms hung on strings from the rafters. A long table ran the

length of the room in the center, and at one end stood
the clay oven.

"What's your name?" Edlyn asked.

"Why?" The crouching man fingered his dagger.

"Because I don't know what to call you." Edlyn
opened a wooden box and scooped a handful of dried
yarrow into her stone bowl. Picking up her pestle, she
ground the leaves into powder and said, "And I want
you to build up the fire to a full blaze."

"Why?"

She wanted to snap at him, but she understood the
suspicion he felt—plus he still clutched his knife. "A
patient as severely wounded as your master should be
kept warm. Also, I'll make him a poultice when I'm
done sewing him and that will help draw out the evil
humors of his blood."

The man mulled that over, then rose and went to
the small stack of wood beside the hearth. "Not much
wood here," he said.

"The woodpile's outside."

"Huh. I'm not leaving ye here alone with him."

"As you wish." Adding just enough water to the
leaves to make a paste, Edlyn placed the bowl atop the
oven to warm, then gathered supplies for the job at
hand and arranged them on a tray. When she stepped
to the side of the table near the door, the servant followed, dagger at the ready. It irked her to be so mis-
trusted, but it didn't surprise her. This was the harvest
of violence: men who couldn't trust and who couldn't
be trusted. When she returned to the wounded man,
she said, "You'll have to put that away. I shall need
your help."

The dagger wavered for a moment, and she looked
at the ugly face of her captor. "Why hesitate? You can
kill me at any minute with your bare hands."

"That's truth," the man acknowledged, and he slipped his dagger into its scabbard.

"Bring me water," she commanded. "It's there in that pitcher."

"What do ye want water fer?"

His constant suspicion irritated her, but she held on to her control. She'd been trained to keep control, to hold her temper and keep her emotions hidden, and for her it seemed as if that training had been just for this moment. Losing her temper could cost Edlyn her life, so she infused a tone of command in her voice. "So I can wash the wound and see what I'm doing. Please do as I require for your master's sake."

The calm assumption of authority worked. The servant rose and brought the water silently.

"Open the door," she said, trying out her new supremacy. "I need more light to see."

He ignored the request and instead crouched beside her waiting for more instructions.

With a sigh at her lack of success, she began to work. Fortunately for the unconscious man, the sunlight had strengthened outside. She could see as she tucked pieces of skin together and sewed them with crude stitches of sheep gut. All through the long treatment, the servant assisted without questioning. He wasn't cowed so much as he was just reverting to his training—when a lady spoke, a servant obeyed, even when the servant held the upper hand. For now, the two were united for this one cause. Later, Edlyn knew, they would be enemies once more.

Sometime during the long process of sewing the patient's flesh, Edlyn became aware he was awake. He had been senseless, she would swear it, but now his muscles tightened when she probed and he stopped the moans that rose each time she pierced his flesh with a needle. He was either very brave or aware, even in his cocoon of pain, of the need for secrecy.

Remembering her own warrior-husband's complaints when he was ill, she thought it must be the latter.

She began to speak to the knight in a low voice, trying to reassure him. He had, after all, lost consciousness after being wounded and returned to it now in a strange place. "You're at Eastbury Abbey," she said, "about ten leagues from the battlefield where you were wounded."

His muscles relaxed as he listened to her, and she knew he understood. But his voice, when he spoke, startled her. "Wharton?" he asked, his deep voice reverberating in the depths of his great helm.

Edlyn cast an ironic glance at the newly named servant, and she could have sworn the ugly man blushed. "He is here beside me."

"Who . . . you?"

"My name is Edlyn."

The warrior flinched violently beneath her hands.

"Did I hurt you?" she cried.

And Wharton snarled, "Ye hurt him, ye clumsy cow."

"Nay!" the warrior exclaimed.

She could hear each labored breath the warrior drew, and she held her own as she wondered if he would lash out at her in pain.

Slowly the wounded man relaxed. "Go on. Finish."

Off to the side, below the warrior's range of vision, she saw Wharton pull his dagger.

"Be more careful," he warned.

With trembling fingers, she concluded her stitching and examined it carefully. "I suppose I'm done." She didn't know what to do for those places where the skin had been totally removed, and she didn't like the way scraps of it puckered beneath the pull of her sutures. She wished for one of the nuns or even one of the fat-fingered monks who served the infirmary. Then it occurred to her that the warrior might be more reasonable than his servant, and she said to him, "I have no skills at this, but your man insisted I do what I could for you. If you would allow me to seek help at the hospital—"

"Nay."

Edlyn recoiled from the force of that single word. Not that the warrior had been loud; quite the opposite. That one softly spoken word had simply proved him to be a commander, accustomed to unquestioning obedience.

She would give it to him, too, as long as his henchman remained between her and freedom. "As you wish," she answered. She stood, stretching the kinks out of her legs. "Wharton brought you here, and if you can lie still a little longer, I'll be done and you can rest."

Wharton bounded to his feet. "Where are ye going?"

"The poultice," she reminded him. "Why don't you remove his helm while I finish preparing it? He'll be more comfortable."

"Not likely," Wharton retorted.

"He needs to breathe," she argued.

Wharton flushed indignant red. "Ye just want t' look on his face an' betray him."

The big knight spoke. "Do it."

Wharton dropped back to his knees and reached for the helm. Deliberately, Edlyn turned her back and busied herself with stirring the poultice. After all, she didn't want to provoke Wharton.

Behind her, the wounded warrior said, "Water."

Freed of the helm's confinement, his voice rumbled

like a great ocean wave breaking on the rocks. Edlyn thought it matched the size of him.

"Aye, master."

Wharton rushed to the pitcher, but Edlyn stopped him. "Give him this." From the shelf above her head, she brought down a bottle and uncorked it, then poured a cup full and handed it to Wharton.

He sniffed it suspiciously, then wrinkled his nose.

Anticipating his question, she said, "'Tis spring tonic. It will give him strength."

With a grimace, Wharton carried it back to his master.

Half turning, Edlyn glanced at the prone figure as she tested the warmth of the herbs on her wrist. Even without his helm, he was unrecognizable. Of course, how could he be otherwise? Beneath the hollow metal headgear he wore a chain-mail coif that swathed his neck and head and revealed only the dim oval of his face. She watched Wharton slide his arm under the knight's head and lift it with the greatest of care. The warrior drank, and Wharton seemed to know without being told when his master was satisfied.

They'd been together a long time, Edlyn realized, and Wharton's devotion was nothing less than complete.

As Wharton lowered his master back onto the floor, he shot her an infuriated glare, and she spun back to her work. Sorting through the basket that held her clean rags, she selected a soft linen to use as a pad and returned to the outstretched figure of the warrior. She kept her gaze down, hoping Wharton read humble submission in her stance, and knelt at the warrior's side. With her fingers, she smeared the green paste across the pad, then placed it over the wound. Only then did she risk a closer glance at the warrior's face.

Sweat, dirt, and blood had mixed and congealed on his skin, creating a mask of battle horrors. Edlyn released her pent-up breath in a rush. "Look at him! His own mother couldn't recognize him."

Wharton grinned, cheered by the news.

"Wash my face," the warrior said. "It itches."

The grin disappeared, but Wharton reached for the wet cloth without question.

Edlyn caught his wrist. "First he needs to have his armor removed, and most of the aketon." She ducked under the table and brought out a pallet, stuffed with straw and covered with tightly woven wool. "If we could undress him, then roll him onto the pallet and pull him into the corner by the oven, he'd remain warmer."

Wharton stared at her, patently unconvinced.

"'Twould be easier to conceal him," she added.

Wharton glanced at the corner by the oven. "There's a table."

"We'll move it." Wharton still seemed unconvinced, and she said impatiently, "There's nowhere else in here to hide him."

"Keep everyone out," Wharton answered.

"I can't do that. I dispense the herbs and potions for the infirmary."

Wharton stared, recalcitrant.

"Men will die if I don't!"

Wharton might have been made of stone. "I don't care about th' other men."

The warrior again interrupted. "I do."

Wharton's indignation subsided, and Edlyn sighed in relief. "Besides," she added, "if I try to keep the nuns out, they'll be suspicious. Now let's remove the armor—"

"The coif first," the warrior said. "Remove it."

His lips tightened as Wharton eased off the chain-mail headgear. Each movement pained him, Edlyn realized, and the links caught in his lank blond hair and tugged at his scalp. Wharton muttered apologies as he worked, but the warrior uttered no reproach to his servant. He simply lay still and panted softly, and when he could he said, "Now my face. Wash it." Wharton took up the wet cloth again, but the warrior said, "Nay. Her."

Startled, Edlyn found herself the recipient of a scowl from Wharton and a damp washing cloth.

She didn't understand it. The two men had been so protective of the warrior's identity, and now the warrior took the chance she would identify him by demanding she clean his face.

And the possibility existed she *would* recognize him. When she had been the countess of Jagger, legions of knights and noblemen had visited, seeking favors and offering support. They'd all vanished when Robin had been killed, of course.

She held the cloth and looked down at the filth-encrusted face of the warrior. Had he perhaps recognized *her*?

"What are you waiting for?" he asked.

She didn't answer. She just bent her head and smoothed the cloth over his forehead.

A broad forehead, fair but marked with the creases of experience. Then the area around his eyes, where she saw wrinkles that came from squinting against the sun. Too, she saw hazel eyes that watched her closely.

She hesitated, her hand poised above him. What did he behold in *her* face that so interested him?

Wharton snatched the cloth from her and rinsed the grime and blood from it, then shoved it back into her fingers.

The dark smudges had successfully camouflaged the warrior's features, changing the shape by creating false shadows. His cheekbones, she discovered as she washed, were high and sharp and matched his out-thrust chin. Before a series of breaks had mutilated his nose, it had been a blade of bone. His lips, even when not swollen and bruised, were generous, the type a young girl would dream of kissing.

Her hand began to shake as she stared.

A young girl might well see this man through an infatuated gaze. She might fall headlong in love with him and imagine in him every virtue. And if that young girl had to go off to be married to a man old enough to be her grandfather, she would carry his image before her like a shining icon. For years she would think he, and only he, was the man who could excite her passions.

She would have been wrong. Wrong about so many things. And now that young girl had grown up, and now she would pay the price for her foolishness.

Aye, she recognized him. How could she not? Not even the ravages of time and distance could disguise this man's masculine beauty.

Thrusting the cloth at Wharton, Edlyn wiped her palms across her skirt as if to wipe away the stain of touching him. "Hugh," she said in a cold, clear voice. "You are Hugh de Florisoun."

2

"*And you are Edlyn,* duchess of Cleere."

Dear God, Hugh remembered.

Hastily, she stood up and moved away from him. "I was the duchess of Cleere. I am not any longer."

He waited for her to identify herself and, when she didn't, said, "Your duke died."

"He was an old man."

"And you remarried?"

She didn't answer; she only turned her face away from the eyes that observed her too closely. Years ago, she would have given anything for Hugh to look at her that way, or in any way.

Now it was too late.

Her disquietude only seemed to amuse him, for he mocked, "You *are* still Edlyn, I hope."

"You may call me Edlyn," she answered.

"Lady Edlyn?"

He probed like a badger after a rat, and she didn't relish being the rat. "Just call me Edlyn."

His interrogation would have gone on until she told him what he wanted to know, or until she said something she would regret, but he turned his head to rest his ear on the dirt floor, then announced, "Someone approaches."

Wharton drew his dagger so quickly she had no time to step away. "Get rid o' him," he said to her.

"Wharton, put it away." Hugh's voice sounded fainter and more weary now that he realized he wouldn't get the information he wanted from her. "Edlyn won't betray me."

His certainty humiliated her. Had he seen evidence of her infatuation for him all those years ago? Did he think it so deep she would still protect him with her life?

She snorted. Only two people existed for whom she would sacrifice so much.

The point of the dagger jabbed her side. "I'll personally see t' yer death if ye do betray him," Wharton whispered.

She'd been mortified and bullied enough. Control snapped. "Get that away from me." She knocked his arm with her fist, and her attack so startled Wharton he dropped the knife. "And don't you ever point it at me again!"

On the ground, Hugh chuckled. "That's my Edlyn," he said in a patronizing tone that made her want to pound him senseless. "You always were spirited."

"I am not *your* Edlyn." Then to Wharton, "And I am not in the habit of betraying anyone who comes to me for succor or sanctuary." With a final glare at both the speechless servant and his amused master, she turned on her heel and stalked to the closed door.

She swung it open on its leather hinges and stepped into the garden just as Lady Blanche and her toady of a servant approached the door.

"Lady Edlyn! Lady Edlyn!" Lady Blanche's

squeaky voice matched her diminutive height. "We need some syrup of poppies at once. We have a noble lord in pain."

Once, long ago when Edlyn had been the greatest lady in the neighborhood and the patroness of Eastbury Abbey, Lady Blanche's rosy apple cheeks and bow-mouthed smile had pleased her. She had thought Lady Blanche to be a dear, sweet nun dedicated to the fulfillment of her holy vows.

She knew better now. "Do you speak of Baron Sadynton?"

Lady Blanche stopped in the path. Adda halted behind her. Their identical glares made Edlyn aware, once again, of their shared heritage. "Are you questioning my judgment?" Lady Blanche demanded.

"Never." Edlyn lied smoothly. "Nevertheless, the noble lord will have to suffer, I fear." She pulled the door shut behind her. "As I told you yester morn, we have used all our syrup of poppies."

"Tut, tut, my dear." Lady Blanche trotted forward, pressing too close to Edlyn for comfort. "We know you keep a reserve for emergencies, and this is an emergency."

"But I am glad you and your servant came by." Edlyn nodded at the woman who stood behind Lady Blanche. "I need someone to carry firewood for me."

If anything could have chased Lady Blanche from the premises, it should have been this threat. Adda devoted her life to creating comfort for Lady Blanche, and Lady Blanche insisted Adda reserve her strength for just that purpose.

To Edlyn's surprise and dismay, Lady Blanche only nodded genially. "Help Lady Edlyn, Adda."

Adda's glare might have shriveled a lesser woman, but Edlyn had more to worry about than a simple scowl.

Like a wounded man stretched out on the floor of the dispensary.

Like a knife-happy Wharton.

Like the scandal Lady Blanche longed to perpetuate in Edlyn's name.

"Let me show you the wood I require," Edlyn said, stalling for time.

"Wood is wood." Lady Blanche took Edlyn's arm and tried to lead her toward the dispensary while Adda walked with dragging feet toward the woodpile.

Edlyn had frequently mourned her lack of height, but she was taller than Lady Blanche and she dug in her heels now. "Wood is not just wood," she answered. "Not to me. Oak burns slow and sure. Pine burns quick and hot. Walnut burns—"

"I know," Lady Blanche said sharply. "What has that to do with anything?"

"An herbalist must prepare her tonics at just the right temperature."

"Please, Lady Edlyn, don't pretend with me." Lady Blanche's mouth formed a deprecating moue. "We both know you're not an herbalist. You're only a dispossessed noblewoman living on the abbey's charity."

Edlyn's fury, already stirred by Wharton, easily ignited again. "I endowed this abbey."

Lady Blanche began to tremble like an ash leaf in the wind of indignation. "A fine endowment that requires such a payback. You bring the taint of your treason here to stain our reputation. If I were abbess here—"

"Lady Corliss is abbess here, and long may she endure." Edlyn's devout prayer came from the heart. Never had Lady Corliss uttered a reproach when Edlyn had fallen from patroness to supplicant. She had been the vessel that had carried Edlyn through the turbulent seas of despair, and Edlyn worshiped the abbess.

As did Lady Blanche. Her pursed lips softened as she echoed, "Long may she endure." Then her small eyes, pressed like raisins into the dumplings of her cheeks, sharpened. "As prioress, it is my duty to protect the abbess from undue aggravation, and you, Lady Edlyn, have proved to be nothing but a disappointment."

"Lady Corliss said that to you?" Edlyn didn't believe it, but even the suggestion hurt. Hurt because she knew it was true. She'd struggled this last year, building on her natural talent to become a competent herbalist and to be of use to the abbey. But always she knew she took another's place, and that added to the misery that crept on silent feet into her barren bedchamber every night.

Lady Blanche had struck a telling blow, and she followed it with a stab to the heart. "Lady Corliss is too kind."

This day, Edlyn decided, could not improve enough to become bearable.

Wrapped in triumph, Lady Blanche trotted back up the walk and out the gate.

Edlyn glanced at the dispensary and prayed the two men hadn't heard the bitter exchange. Hugh would want to know everything about her situation, and she didn't intend to explain. Not now. Not ever.

Stiffening her spine, she reentered the dispensary and halted in surprise. Hugh had disappeared, as had Wharton and all traces of armor. Edlyn blinked. Had worry and distress finally snapped her hard-fought hold on sanity? Had there been no wounded knight, no threatening servant?

But nay, the bottle of spring tonic remained open on the table, and a bloody rag had been shoved behind the wooden boxes where she stored her dried herbs. The table by the oven had been moved along the wall, and the mat had disappeared. Looking closely, she saw the marks on the floor where Wharton had dragged the pallet with Hugh's body weighing it down.

In a flurry of activity, the men had done as she suggested and moved to the best hiding place in the room.

"At least someone is showing good sense," she said as she swept toward the oven.

"To whom are you speaking?"

With a squeak, Edlyn turned to the door. At first she believed Lady Blanche had returned. Then the short figure moved into the room, and Edlyn saw the branches piled high in her arms.

Adda. She'd forgotten about Adda. How foolish of her to think she had routed Lady Blanche when she'd only repelled the first guard.

"I was speaking to myself," Edlyn said.

"Ah." The one syllable rang rich with significance. Adda thought Edlyn touched.

"Let me take the wood," Edlyn said.

Adda swung it away from Edlyn's reaching arms. "Where do you want it?"

The woodpile stood in front of Hugh's hiding place, and the logs, as Wharton had observed, had dwindled down to almost nothing. "Right here in front of the oven," Edlyn instructed.

Adda's gaze swept the area, then she walked forward until Edlyn gave way. "Don't!" Edlyn said sharply, sure Adda's nosiness would earn her the point of Wharton's blade.

Dropping the branches atop the measly twigs that marked the woodpile, Adda said, "Don't, indeed. You've made an incredible mess of the dispensary, and Lady Corliss will hear of it."

Frightened and incredulous, Edlyn stared into the corner. Her basket of rags had been dumped. The rags had been arranged to look like clutter, and the upended wicker covered more than one questionable lump.

Quick thinking on someone's part. It wouldn't fool anyone with the eyes to see, but Adda shared everything with her sister, including myopia.

Edlyn used the edge of her wimple to dab an outbreak of sweat on her forehead, but she wasn't about to allow this toxic imitation of Lady Blanche to reprimand her. "My dispensary is none of your concern, but you make it so, no doubt, so that I will release the syrup of poppies to your care. It will not happen, so return to your mistress and report your failure."

Adda leaned forward until her nose almost met Edlyn's skirt. "You have blood on your apron."

Edlyn glanced down. Blood did indeed stain the apron she wore to protect her thin wool cotte, and she brushed at the marks futilely. "I went to the infirmary at first light," she said. "I must have touched one of the men."

A falsehood, easily traced, but Edlyn never had lied well. "I couldn't sleep," she added hastily.

"The result of a burdened conscience, I suspect." Adda gloated at her own striking rejoinder.

"Get out." Edlyn spoke softly. She didn't realize it, but her voice carried the same element of command that characterized Hugh's. "Get out and don't come back lest your insolence tempt me to the sin of speaking ill of one of God's servants."

"And whom might that be?"

Edlyn walked to the door and pushed it wide. Gesturing to the out of doors, she said, "You." She watched Adda skitter out the door and up the walk, cackling like an offended chicken all the way.

Then she shut the door with a bang. The noise cleared her head; she had to regain control.

Wharton rose from the corner and brushed the clinging rags off his body. Glowering, he fingered his knife. "I told ye t' keep them out."

"And I told *you* that was impossible." She stared as he cleared the rags from the long metal-clad problem stretched out on her floor and wished fervently they were anywhere but here. "Remove his armor," she said. "He needs to rest comfortably, and he can't do that trapped in a pile of rusty metal."

"Rusty?" Wharton squawked.

"Pile?" Hugh sounded as insulted as his servant.

Pleased to have offended them, she said, "He needs a gown." She stared at Wharton. "I don't suppose you brought one?"

"I beg yer pardon, m' lady. I forgot it in th' rush o' battle."

Wharton's weighted sarcasm made her blithe. "It'll not be easy to find one that's long enough for him, but I'll look in the infirmary." She skipped out of the door before Wharton could stop her, and for the first time since she'd seen that broken latch, the tension that blocked her throat eased.

What had she done in her lifetime to deserve trials such as these? She had hoped the worst was over; she had prayed for tranquillity and a release from the unrelenting grief. Lately, she'd thought God had heard her prayers. Obviously, that had been nothing but false hope.

She stepped from the herb garden and into the large open square on which all the abbey buildings stood. From here she could see the nuns' dormitory, the infirmary, the barns, and the visitors' dormitory where she slept. In the center, both spiritually and physically, the church stood, towering over everything, embracing all within its reach.

A flock of the abbey's sheep nibbled on the grass beside the great stone steps that led up to the sanctuary, and one of the less noble nuns fed three grunting pigs the scraps from the kitchen.

On the far side of the church, across the road and with its own small square, the monks lived and worked as an addendum to the abbey. To the nuns went the traveling nobles and the ill; to the monks went the vagrants and the lepers. Everyone had his place.

Everyone, that was, except Edlyn. She didn't need Lady Blanche to point that out. She felt the deficit every day, and as she walked across the square, she wished she belonged somewhere. Anywhere. She'd been mistress of her own home for too many years to easily adjust to living under another's jurisdiction, regardless—

"Lady Edlyn."

Edlyn spun around at the beloved voice.

"You were far away." The abbess tucked her hand into the crook of Edlyn's arm and urged her to walk on toward the infirmary. "Won't you come back to us? We treasure your gentle wisdom."

Lady Corliss smiled at Edlyn, and Edlyn's spasm of guilt almost bent her in half. Lady Corliss didn't deserve such a betrayal. This lady, so tall, so regal, always sought Edlyn out, always spoke of Edlyn's expertise with an admiration that soothed the sting in Edlyn's soul.

"You look so troubled, my dear. Is there something with which I could help you?"

Aye, Edlyn wanted to say. *Tell me* what *to do about a wounded warrior and his hostile man-servant.*

"If you're troubled about refusing Lady Blanche the syrup of poppies, pray do not. You were right, and so I told her when she came to me." Lowering her chin,

Lady Corliss looked at Edlyn from below gray brows. "I know you think I don't see the way Lady Blanche treats you, but I do, and I have taken steps to correct it. She didn't appreciate my reprimand, of course, and swears she'll prove your perfidy, but as I told her, Lady Edlyn is an innocent soul, much wronged."

Edlyn's guilt gained weight as Lady Corliss spoke. "Not so innocent," she muttered.

"Your little sins cannot justify the great iniquities that have plagued you." Lifting her hand, fingers together, Lady Corliss indicated the church. "Of course, who am I to decide? Nevertheless, I have prayed that your burdens be eased and the world shown the truth of your kind and honest ways, and lately I have sensed God's own grace smiling on you."

Lady Corliss had been praying, Edlyn had been praying, and their combined prayers had produced a wounded knight hidden in her dispensary. She had sworn not to tell, but Lady Corliss led an abbey of twenty-two noble nuns and their servants with a mixture of diplomacy and insight. What harm would it do to tell her? Edlyn wanted to so badly. "What if . . . what if I sinned horribly? Would the Lord's displeasure manifest itself on the whole abbey?" Edlyn waited breathlessly for the reply.

"You're not a child, Lady Edlyn. You know the Lord doesn't work like that. He gives to some, takes from others, for no reason we earthly beings can easily comprehend. Yet if one thinks very hard, sometimes one can discern God's plans." With a satisfied smile, Lady Corliss said, "Think on it. When Lord Jagger died, may he rest in peace, the income you used to found the abbey and nurse it through its early years ceased abruptly. We had to prove ourselves able to provide food, clothing, medicines. And, praise God and all the saints, we were able to do so. What happened to you was a tragedy, but for us it was a welcome revelation." She squeezed Edlyn's arm. "You'll see. Somehow everything is for the good."

Edlyn bent her head and scuffled her feet in the dirt. "But this is not like that."

"Would you feel better if you told me?"

"I have sworn to keep it secret."

"Then you must do what you think is right. You have a conscience. You'll make the right choice." The infirmary door stood before them, and Lady Corliss said, "Enough of that. What is your mission now?"

Do what she thought was right. Edlyn stumbled as she said, "I need a . . . gown."

"What kind of gown?"

"Like we use for the sick men."

Lady Corliss didn't hesitate. "Wait here." She disappeared into the infirmary and came back with a gown of rough brown weave. "Here. Now go and do God's work."

Edlyn walked away, and when she looked back, Lady Corliss waved, then walked toward the church.

"She's probably praying for me again," Edlyn muttered. She should have felt even guiltier. Instead, she felt relieved.

She didn't want to return to the dispensary, but she couldn't allow herself to consider. She just marched down the garden path and into the hut to find Wharton glaring like the toad he was.

"Where have ye been? Th' master's in pain!"

"Is the patient stripped and washed?" she asked.

"Washed?" Wharton sounded scandalized. "In his condition?"

Edlyn stepped around the oven and smothered a gasp. Hugh had been stripped completely, and if anything, he looked longer and meaner than he did in armor. The bruising and the thin film of mud formed from dust and sweat made him look as if he were Adam himself, created from the clay of Eden.

"Wash him." She thrust the gown at Wharton. "Then put him in this. I'll prepare something to help the pain."

She didn't stop to see if he did as she instructed, but her skin remained whole and without dagger wounds. Pushing a stool over to the table, she stepped up and rummaged around on the top shelf close to the thatch. From behind the other vessels, she brought out a small corked glass bottle and allowed herself a grin. From the bottles on the table, she plucked three, then in a cup she mixed their contents to her satisfaction.

"He's washed an' in that pitiful excuse fer a gown."

Wharton might have been more surly, but Edlyn didn't know how that could be possible.

"Good." Cup in hand, she climbed over the woodpile to Hugh's side. "Mayhap, Wharton, you should bring in more wood. A large pile would help disguise Sir Hugh."

"'Tis *Lord* Hugh now," Wharton said proudly.

With only the faintest hint of sarcasm in her tone, she said, "Of course. I should have realized a warrior as great as Hugh de Florisoun would have won a title by now."

"He's th' earl o'—"

"That's enough." Hugh still maintained enough authority to silence his servant in mid-sentence. "Bring the wood."

"What if someone sees me?" Wharton asked.

"Tell them you're a mendicant at the abbey. 'Tis impossible to recall all who come and go here." Edlyn knelt beside the fallen hero. "And leave the door open so I can see what damage you did when you moved your master."

"I had t' hide him!" Wharton opened the door.

Edlyn wasn't in the mood to be fair, but Hugh reassured him.

"Did well, too." Hugh's voice sounded fainter now. He waited until Wharton's footsteps faded, then said, "Hauling wood hurts his dignity as my man."

"His dignity could use some adjustment." Now that Edlyn could see the gown, she admitted Wharton might have a reason for being disgruntled about it. The sleeves hung only to Hugh's elbows and the hem struck him at the knee. Edlyn would have to lift the hem to examine the wound, and she should have just done it when Hugh lay naked. It would have been less intimate than this undressing. But she hadn't thought of that then; she had only wanted to get him covered.

"Don't be alarmed. I'm going to look." She kept her voice steady and soothing.

"Don't you be alarmed," Hugh answered.

But when Edlyn jerked her gaze to his face, his eyes were closed.

He had handsome features: strong and full of masculine beauty that had always made women pant after him like bitches in heat.

She snorted. She'd already had that disease, and like someone who had suffered from smallpox and lived to tell about it, she couldn't get it again—and she was only stalling. She had to check that bandage.

Lifting the gown, she focused on that one thing. Hugh's move onto the pallet had loosened the linen strips, and she adjusted them to fit tightly once more. She lowered the gown and allowed herself a small smirk of self-congratulations. That hadn't bothered her a bit. Her hands were hardly shaking.

She lifted his head and placed it on her bent knees. "Drink."

He drank, but a bit of the precious liquid oozed out of the corner of his mouth and he choked a bit as he swallowed.

She would have to hold him higher next time.

Taking the rags, she started folding them. He watched her steadily as she worked, and when he spoke, she flinched at his curiosity.

"Edlyn, why are you living in a nunnery?"

"Maybe I've taken vows." She kept her gaze on her hands as she folded.

He laughed softly, then closed his eyes as a spasm of pain struck. "I don't think so."

Offended, she said, "What? You don't think I'm virtuous enough?"

"I think those two vipers"— he gasped for air— "who visited made your status clear."

"I don't think you ought to talk anymore."

His fingers tangled in the skirt of her cotte. "Then tell me."

He was starting to drift but fighting against it, and she subdued her instinctive rebuff. She did, after all, hold the power in this situation. "Lady Blanche and Adda might have been twins, so alike are they in temperament and appearance."

He struggled to open his eyes. "Don't care about them."

"Lady Blanche's mother was singularly unappreciative when presented with her husband's child by her maid so soon before Lady Blanche's birth."

"Tell me . . . you."

"I think Lady Blanche drank bitterness from her mother's tit, and Adda absorbed it from the moment she was put in Lady Blanche's service."

"When I'm better . . . "

"Both girls were placed in the nunnery at the age of seven to get rid of them."

"Edlyn . . . "

"And they move from abbey to abbey as they make themselves unwelcome."

Hugh's faint snore stopped her. She slid the folded rags beneath his head, but he didn't move, and she grinned in open triumph.

Wharton's voice sounded from behind her. "He's going t' wake someday, ye know, an' he'll get those answers he wants."

Gathering the bottle and the cup, she faced Wharton and his armload of wood. "Not from me, he won't."

Wharton knelt to place the logs on the pile. "He always gets what he wants."

"Then it's time he learned differently." Stepping well away from Wharton, she returned the bottle to its hiding place and put the stool away again. "I have work to do."

"How long will it take him t' get well?"

Edlyn realized that wasn't what he wanted to ask. He really wanted to know if Hugh would get well, and she didn't know the answer to that. She had prescribed the most effective medicine she knew. "Pray for him. Perhaps in a fortnight he'll be well enough to sit up."

"Pray fer him." Wharton's despair sounded clear. "Isn't there more I can do?"

"Let him sleep." She stared at the long log of a man in the rough brown garment. "When his fever rises, bathe him with cool water."

"That'll kill him."

"Not as long as he rests by the oven, it won't. It'll keep the fever from going too high." She frowned at the filthy clothing Wharton had stripped from Hugh. "I'll have to hide this. It's clearly a warrior's aketon, and a large warrior at that." Picking up the pieces, she wondered what to do with them, then stuffed them behind the large jars of oil and wine on the floor. "He probably won't wake until tonight, and then you should give him a drop from the bottle you saw me hide." She pointed her finger at him sternly. "But only a drop, or he'll drift away and never return."

Terror made Wharton's eyes bulge. "Ye do it."

"I can't. I sleep in the guest house, and there's a monk who questions all who come and go in the night."

"That monk'll do as he's told."

"Nay." She tried to soothe Wharton's alarm. "You take good care of your master. This, too, you can do."

"Ye."

When Hugh woke, he was aware of only two things. He was hot. And he had to be silent.

A beast gnawed at his side, cutting its teeth against his ribs and seeking the softer meat of his intestines. Its warm breath seared him and he wanted to push it away, but he dared not move. He had to be silent. Everything depended on his silence. Wharton's safety. His own safety. Edlyn's safety . . . Edlyn.

Edlyn? Consciousness nudged at him. He hadn't thought of Edlyn in years, and she certainly couldn't be here now. Not in a nunnery. Not working like a common peasant. He was delirious. He had to be.

"Drink this."

His dream Edlyn knelt beside him. She lifted his head and pressed it against her bosom, then placed a cup to his lips. He drank greedily, then turned and nuzzled her breasts.

She put him down rather hastily, jarring his aching head. He heard Wharton's voice harp and scold and opened his eyes to reprimand him.

He didn't see Wharton. He saw his dream Edlyn leaning over his side, forcing the ravenous beast to cease its dinner. But it might turn and rend her, so he said, "Careful."

He said it clearly, but she didn't seem to understand. "What?" She leaned close to his face. "Did you say something?"

Her breasts. He remembered resting against them, and now he could see them. Her shift had been negligently tied, and her wrap gaped at the neck. She looked as if she'd just been roused from bed.

He would take her back. Reaching out, he cupped her breast through the material. "Mine."

His dream Edlyn disappeared from view then, and he closed his eyes. She must be quite a woman, because just laying his claim on her wearied him. Then she started working on his side again, and energy surged through him. He woke to touch her, but when he reached out, he touched coarse material and heard Wharton's raspy voice. "Master, what do ye require?"

Sleep. He required sleep, so he could dream of Edlyn again.

3

"How are you going to get me back into the dormitory?" Edlyn desperately needed privacy to regather the shreds of her composure.

Hugh had tried to suckle on her like a baby, and while she could delude herself that his action had been nothing more than a sick man's attempt to return to the comforts of childhood, nothing could change that elemental gesture of ownership he had made afterward.

"Mine." He had cupped her breast through her wrap and her shift and said, "Mine." And it hadn't been a tentative touch, either. He had grasped her firmly and rubbed his thumb across her nipple with such certainty she'd had to reassure herself she was decently covered.

"I don't want ye t' go back." Oblivious to her discomfort, Wharton stood with his feet apart and firmly planted on the dispensary floor. "I want ye here if he needs ye."

"I am not mistress of this abbey," she said. "I must conform to the rules or be banished. Before the sun rises, I am to join with any other guests and together we make our way to the church for Mass."

"Your soul'll not miss Mass one day."

"This is an abbey. They don't see it that way, and anyway, that's not the point." Exhaustion and frustration made her slow. "I must be seen coming from my chamber, or as the only full-time resident not bound by holy vows, I must explain my absence. And since no one saw me leave, it will be difficult to explain."

"What do ye do that they're so suspicious?" Wharton demanded. "Have ye a lover ye visit?"

Unwittingly, her gaze went to Hugh, and she jerked it back to Wharton when he laughed.

"As ye wish, m' lady. Ye'll see, that monk's still snoring at his station an' we'll slip right past him."

She hoped so. She prayed so. Abbeys were obsessed with two things: salvation and sin. Nocturnal wanderings would automatically be assumed to be sin. She would be required to explain her actions, and how could she do that?

As she followed Wharton through the garden and across the abbey yard to the guest quarters, she kept her head down and her hood up, and with every step she trembled with fear. She'd been out in the wide world for a brief time, living hand to mouth, never knowing where the next meal would come from or whether the next place she begged at would be her last.

So many cruelties. So many horrors. They had scarred her. She *had* to get back into her room without discovery.

"Keep close behind me."

Wharton spoke softly, so softly she wondered if he comprehended her fear.

"Take off yer shoes." He paused in the overhang of the guest quarters while she did as he instructed. "If th' sleepy one wakes, I'll distract him while ye slip past me an' down th' hallway t' yer room."

She didn't like the way that sounded, and she didn't trust Wharton. "Don't hurt him," she warned.

"I don't hurt ol' monks," Wharton answered scornfully.

He swung open the door that led to the entry, and Edlyn wondered briefly how he had opened it in the first place. When one wanted admittance, one knocked and Brother Irving looked through the high, covered peephole. If he liked the explanation given for entering the guest quarters, then he took the key from his belt and unlocked the door.

But Wharton, it seemed, made his own rules. Somehow he'd entered the guest quarters without Brother Irving's knowledge and found Edlyn's cell without instruction. Wharton was the resourceful sort.

Through the open door, the sound of Brother Irving's lusty snoring made a welcome din in Edlyn's ears. Wharton gestured for her to stay, then slipped inside the small, cold entry room and covered the single candle with his cupped palm. At his signal, she crept inside, her gaze never leaving Brother Irving. He still sat as he had when they stole past the first time—in a tipped-back chair, his chin resting on his shallow chest.

She released her breath in slow increments. Brother Irving hadn't seen her leave and he hadn't seen her return.

The guest quarters had been built as a long hallway with the doors of the cells leading onto it and the entry breaking it in half. The women slept in the right hallway, the men in the left hallway. Because of Edlyn's status as a live-in dependent on the abbey's charity, her cell was at the end of the right hallway. The candle in the entry never cast its illumination all the way to her door, and when the dusk had settled and she walked the hall alone, she imagined the ghosts of her past walked with her. That always made her run, but she couldn't do it now. Not with Wharton trailing behind her.

Anyway, if the ghosts were smart, they would be afraid of Wharton.

Putting her hand on the door, she turned to her shadowy escort. "Lord Hugh should be well enough until morning." Because she knew how sounds echoed along the stone walls, she spoke as softly as possible. "Don't come to get me again."

Wharton paid her no heed. Instead he gave the door a push and followed it as it swung in. "I'll give ye a light."

"A light?" She scurried in after him. "I don't have any candles."

"I do."

The darkness was less intense inside the room. The window was high and small, just as in the other buildings of the abbey, but except in the coldest weather Edlyn kept it open. She welcomed the moonlight, the starlight, and the light of dawn. She welcomed any kind of light. Earlier when Wharton had leaned over her body to waken her, she had screamed a little—only because he seemed part of a nightmare and only because she couldn't see his face. But she thought she had successfully masked her discomfort. How he had seen through her pretense and why he moved now to dissipate her fear, she didn't know.

He struck a spark and as the wick caught, she thought of something else. "*Where* did you get a candle?"

Laughing coarsely, he placed the light into a pewter holder he pulled from his pocket. Then he looked around the cell. Here he would see the bare truths that governed her life.

He did, too. His gaze had encompassed everything, then he looked at her with pity—the kind of pity that made her soul shrivel.

He placed the candle on the table beside the bed and he left on silent feet.

Tucking her wrap around her, she sat down on the bed and put her shoes on the floor where she could easily reach them in the morning. She slid between the covers, snuggled down, and stared at the yellow flame as hard as she could until she blinked.

Then when she looked around, she saw it all.

The tapestries on the wall. The fine rugs to protect her feet. The constantly burning fire on the hearth. The furs on the bed.

How dare Wharton look at her with such pity? What other lady had such sumptuous riches?

She blinked again. The grand furnishings vanished, leaving only a bare room with stone walls. A narrow rope bed covered with rough wool blankets. A rickety table with a wooden water bowl. And two pallets, folded neatly and stacked in the corner.

She blew out the candle.

"Don't let him die. Ye can't let him die." Wharton's words skidded out of him, each lurching with panic. "He's my master."

"I know." Edlyn washed Hugh's hot, wasted body with a cloth dipped in cool water. Her gritty eyes searched for a flicker of improvement, but Hugh remained motionless. For four nights now he'd lain like this, his head resting on a pile of folded rags, while she had tried everything she knew to bring his fever down and relieve his infection. Nothing had worked. Nothing.

Wharton had tried everything he knew, too. He had shouted, threatened, bullied, and prayed. Now he pleaded, wiping at the tears that leaked from the corners of his eyes. "I beg o' ye, m' lady, bring him back t' health. There is no one t' replace him."

She looked away from Hugh's emaciated form and observed Wharton, pale even in the golden light of the oven's open door. "Go out," she said compassionately. "Breathe the night air."

Wharton had reached the breaking point, it seemed, for he took a last look at Hugh and plunged out of the door. She heard his footsteps as he ran, seeking solace away from this house of putrescence, and she was alone. Alone with a man who wouldn't live until dawn.

She shouldn't care. He'd caused her no end of trouble. She'd been awakened every night by Wharton sneaking into her room and dragging her down here. She'd lied to the people who sheltered her. She'd been surly with the nuns, barring them from the dispensary and shoving her herbs out the door. She'd spent all her time fixing poultices and decoctions, depleting the last of her stores as she wrestled with death for Hugh's soul. Yet when she looked at him, she couldn't give up. She remembered him. He had been part of her youth. The largest part of her girlish dreams had resided in him. And she couldn't let that end. For herself as well as for him.

"Hugh." She leaned forward so her mouth touched his ear. "Hugh. Come back to me."

He didn't move. He showed no change.

Rising, she walked to the long table against the wall. There in a line stood her boxes, each wooden box marked with the name of the herb within. She pulled them forward and lifted each one. Bitter rue. Piquant savory. Strengthening sage. Pungent thyme.

Common herbs. Herbs used to cure and purify. They didn't work. They hadn't worked. She had tried. Turning, she looked at the still, bare body stretched out on the floor behind the oven. Then she put her elbows on the table and cupped her forehead in her hands.

She didn't know what to do. All the jingles she'd ever heard from all the old wives ran through her head.

Borage leaves chopped fine with yarrow,
Brings the poison forth tomorrow.

That wouldn't work. She'd tried it.

Lady's mantle you will pick,
Spread it thick.

She'd tried that, too. Stupid old wives.

Twitch the tail of the dragon,
Pluck it from its lair.
Prick it with a virgin's nail . . .

Oh, this was so stupid. Dragon's blood was just a root. It wasn't good for anything. And she wasn't a virgin.

Moonlight and springtime,
Magic of old . . .

Superstition. Her hands shook. She didn't even know where to look for the stuff.

Under the sacred oak . . .

She remembered all of that poem. *All* of it. She didn't even know when she'd learned it, but it made her faintly ashamed. Ashamed she remembered. Ashamed she even considered trying it.

Then she heard the silence again. Silence pressed down from behind her. No sound of breath. No sound of movement. No sound of life. Hugh was dead, or would be. What difference would it make if she tried one of the ancient spells?

Whirling, she ran out into the garden. The moon changed the familiar landscape to one of stark shadows and eerie shapes. The oak tree in the corner by the stone wall was thick with darkness. Nothing grew under there. The shade clung to the ground; sunshine couldn't penetrate. At night, it was positively spooky. If she believed in fairies, she would be frightened.

Of course, it was a fairy cure she was thinking of trying, so she had better be respectful of the wee folk.

"I hail thee." Her voice sounded loud in the night and she lowered it to a whisper. "Ancients, I come for dragon's blood to heal one of your favored ones." Foolish, to greet an imaginary race in hopes of appeasing them. "You blessed him in the cradle, giving him the gifts of strength, beauty, and wisdom." She placed one foot just in front of another and moved toward the darkest part of the shade into another world. "Help me cure him now." Her breath rasped, her hands trembled, and she knelt close to the trunk. She should have brought a trenching tool, but she hadn't thought of that and she wasn't about to creep back to the dispensary. She wouldn't have the nerve to try again if she did. Using her fingers, she dug blindly, searching for the tuberous roots that stained skin bright red and, it was said, shrieked when torn from the ground.

She didn't hear any shrieking, so she must have done something right. The roots came up easily. She didn't know how many she needed—after all, her guide was a silly song, not a recipe—but she pulled until she had an apron full. Stupid, fruitless endeavor, but she was desperate.

Standing, she crept back out of the deep shadow. She sighed with relief, then hurried toward the dispensary. After a pause, she turned toward the oak and whispered, "My thanks, wee ones."

A gust of wind rustled the oak leaves, and she almost tore off the door getting inside.

Ignoring her racing heart, she tumbled the roots onto the cutting board and heard the silence again. "I'm hurrying," she said. "I'm hurrying." She picked up the knife and brought the biggest root into cutting position. But when she touched the iron to the plant, she hesitated. The fairies didn't like iron. But how? She looked at her fingertips, already stained a rusty red, and at her nails, dirt packed into the cuticles, and started tearing into the roots. Long strands clung to her skin, and blood—no, juice—dripped onto the board and sank into the old slashes left by the knife.

"Funny," she muttered. "I would have thought dragon's blood was green."

With the strands gathered, she walked to the oven and threw the pieces into the pot of water she kept steaming there. "I should recite a spell . . ." But she didn't have to. A scent filled the air, like strawberries growing in the sun or water lilies in a tranquil pool. She stared at the pot, breathing deeply as the smell cleared her mind and gave her a strength she hadn't imagined. Then she jumped. She didn't need the help. Hugh did. Wrapping a cloth around the metal handle, she took the pot off the oven. She set it beside his unconscious body and waved the steam toward his face. "Breathe," she urged. "Breathe it in."

Did it help him? She couldn't tell. The dim light told no tales.

Not knowing exactly what to do with this liquid dragon's blood, she tipped the pot over the bandages on his side and let it soak in. Then dunking her finger into the fluid, she touched it to her lips. It didn't taste like anything. It didn't numb her or make her breath grow short. It just had a thin, tart tang, so she dipped the cloth into the red fluid, then dribbled it between Hugh's slack lips. He didn't swallow, and she realized with a panic he would choke on it. Lifting his head, she rubbed his stubbled throat as if he were one of the sick cats that hung around the barn. "Swallow," she commanded. "Swallow. Hugh, swallow it."

His Adam's apple moved, but only because she coaxed it, and she didn't know how much of the liquid had reached its destination. Still she waited, hoping the dragon's blood would work its miracle, but he remained motionless. A sudden rush of tears surprised her; she must be tired to put so much faith in a useless herb. Nevertheless, she wrung more liquid into his mouth and again rubbed his throat until he swallowed.

"Hugh, listen." She spoke urgently, trying to pierce the mists that shrouded him. "You've got to come back. It's warm here. There are people who love you."

He didn't move.

"Well, not people, but Wharton." He gave no indication he heard, but she continued. "He's dedicated to you. I don't know what you've done to deserve that, but somehow, somewhere you've made yourself a hero in his eyes." Tonight there was only Hugh, and she scooted a little closer to him, bringing his head onto her knees. Leaning down, she spoke into his ear. "I'm sure a large number of women miss you. Nice women. Ladies."

She'd always thought the promise of women could

bring a man back from the dead, but she'd never put it to the test before. She was wrong, it seemed, so she gritted her teeth and did what she had sworn never to do again. She cradled him against her chest.

He needed her now. He had wandered too far into the cold lands, and she wanted to infuse him with a sense of her warmth. In the instinctual act of a mother who had calmed babies with the sound of her heartbeat, she cradled his head so it rested against her chest.

He wasn't a child. Nothing could make her think that. He weighed too much. His length stretched out too far. Muscles, not baby fat, delineated his body. But as he burned her with the heat of his fever, she felt a tenderness that must have its origins in maternal custody. She stroked his hair away from his forehead, trying to give him comfort, to be as close as possible so he wouldn't be alone.

"*I'm* waiting for you here."

She blinked, then looked around. Who'd said that? It couldn't have been her. She would never confess such a weakness.

"But why not?" Again the sound of her own voice surprised her. "Who'll hear me?" She patted Hugh's cheek, rough with his unshaved beard. "You won't remember, will you? You scarcely remember me at all."

A twinge of discomfort impinged on her confidence. He had, after all, known her face even in his first wounded agony. But now he was not just wounded but savagely ill. Dying, unless she could somehow make a difference.

Little wisps of steam rose from the dragon's blood even as it cooled, and the color darkened to a ruby, glowing as if it shed light. It called to her, and she once again dunked the rag into the dragon's blood and dribbled the liquid into his mouth. It stained her fingers, and she sucked them dry.

Rambling now, she asked, "Don't you remember how, when we were young, I used to trail around after you? I adored you. I loved you. You were so tall and strong and so handsome I used to waste time just looking at you when I should have been spinning. Lady Alisoun would scold me. You're the reason I still can't spin an even thread." She chuckled, remembering the joy and agony of that first love. "I always knew you would succeed in your every endeavor. Something about you—the way you strode about, so sure of yourself, the way you rushed to embrace every challenge— made me sure if you would notice me, you'd take me on a journey to the stars."

Memories spiraled up at her from a hidden place in her mind, and her smile faded. Oblivious to the weight on her arm, she caressed the shell of his ear. "You didn't notice me. Then one day—do you remember a village woman by the name of Avina?" She laughed without humor. "You ought to remember her, unless you've swived so many women she's lost in the dust of nostalgia. You used to meet her in the barn. I would think you could have hidden a little better, but I suppose everyone knew to stay away. Everyone but me." Disgusted at the stupid girl she had been, she dipped her fingers into the pot of dragon's blood. After all, if the dragon's blood was a restorative, she needed it, too, and she rather liked the taste.

"Want some?" She asked as if he could hear her, then with her fingers stained red she rubbed the juice on his gums, his teeth, his tongue. Over and over she repeated the action. "I noticed you would disappear into the barn every evening, and so I climbed up into the loft with the idea I would drop down on you and surprise you. Only I was the one surprised. You and Avina put on the most amazing performance. She showed you everything you needed to know to make a woman happy. She showed you many things I never knew."

She pretended to listen to him. "I shouldn't have watched, you say? I should have hid in the back of the loft until you were done? You're right, of course—you have the look of a man who's always right. But you see, I couldn't turn away." Tilting her head back, she closed her eyes. "You looked so enthralled! You dedicated as much concentration to those lessons as you dedicated to anything that interested you. I watched and watched until . . . well. I wanted to hate you then. Instead I spent my nights imagining how it would be in your arms. In my mind, I've spent years in your arms, and the pleasure you have given me has been . . . "

A suction on her fingers stopped her ramblings. She froze, not understanding for a brief moment. Then opening her eyes, she looked down. Hugh's lips were wrapped around her fingers as he sucked vigorously. And his eyes were open.

4

His voice sounded like the bleat of a newborn lamb. "If you touch me again, I'm going to rip your heart out with my bare hands."

Edlyn swirled in a circle, unaware of the herbs she had scattered in her flurry. Had Hugh spoken? Had last night's administration of dragon's blood performed a miracle? Wharton, crouched beside his master and changing his bandage, blocked her view of Hugh's face, but before she could rush forward, Hugh spoke again.

"What's wrong with you?" He snarled in a whisper. "You're getting me all wet." His tone changed to one of disgust. "Oh, God's gloves, Wharton, you're crying!"

"Oh, master," Wharton stammered, his voice quivering through tears. "Oh, master."

"You dolt." Already Hugh's voice sounded fainter. "I'm going to beat you into dough."

Wharton crept backward, groveling like a worm in the face of his master's displeasure, and Edlyn felt the sharp prick of annoyance. Wharton had proved his devotion to Hugh over the last dreadful days, and now Hugh's first words were nothing but bombastic threats.

"Don't worry, Wharton," she said. "He can't beat you into dough. He can't even lift his arms." She walked forward and stood over Hugh. "Can you?"

Those hazel eyes looked up at her without a sign of recognition, and she almost laughed aloud with relief. He didn't remember last night. He didn't remember those mortifying confessions she'd made while under the influence of that fairy juice.

Not that she wasn't grateful to the fairies for their remedy. Last night, she'd almost fainted with a combination of joy and dismay when he'd looked up at her, and when she realized his fever had broken, she'd cried as pitifully as Wharton did right now. But why didn't that silly rhyme tell of the effect of dragon's blood on the unwary nurse?

She hadn't thought of her fascinated scrutiny of Hugh in the throes of passion for years. Seeing him like that had embarrassed her then. The pretending she'd done afterward embarrassed her now, and she found herself saying in an overbearing tone, "We're awake and cranky, no doubt, but I wager we feel better, don't we?"

"You ripped out my guts."

He sounded hoarse, and reluctantly she knelt and lifted his head onto her knee. She didn't like being so close. The weight of his head, his heat, the silk of his hair reminded her too much of last night. Pretending normality, she placed a cup to his lips. "I didn't rip out your guts. I sewed them back in."

He drank greedily and gasped when he finished. "I'm hungry. Why have you been starving me?" he asked.

Remembering all the times she and Wharton had coaxed broth into his mouth and down his throat, she wanted to hit him. He acted like a typical man who'd been ill. Angry at those who'd saved him, impatient with his own weakness, aware only of himself.

Yet he wasn't typical at all. His gaze lingered on her breasts as if he recalled touching her, then his eyes lifted to her face. He *observed* her—an uncomfortable feeling when one has bared one's miserable soul. Placing him back on the rag pillow as rapidly as she could, Edlyn said, "You were wounded. We thought you would die."

For the first time since he'd recovered consciousness, he seemed aware of his injury. His hands curled, his fingers searched, and he touched the edges of the mat as if that would help develop substantial recollections. "Wharton brought me to an abbey." His gaze swept the room. "I've been hidden in the dispensary."

"That's right," she said, trying to encourage him.

Again he looked at her. "You're the healer." His forehead crinkled as he groped among his fevered memories. Then it smoothed, and with a great effort he stretched out his fingers and touched her skirt. "You're . . . Edlyn."

Holy Mother, he remembered! But did he remember from that first day when Wharton had brought him in? Or did he remember from last night? Her mind buzzed and fretted, and she made a production of examining the bandage over his wound.

"You're Edlyn from George's Cross," he insisted.

It would hurt him when she removed the bandage, she thought. Regardless of her care, it would hurt.

Then she felt a small tug on her skirt and looked up to see him still watching her.

"At George's Cross," he repeated, "you were the daughter of a baron."

He wanted an answer, and she nodded reluctantly. "And you were the son of a baron."

"You learned a lady's duties under the instruction of Lady Alisoun."

Her mouth quirked. He seemed lost in harmless old reminiscences. "You learned a knight's duties under Sir David."

"You were a proper girl, gentle and kind, as befitting a ward of Lady Alisoun's."

He *didn't* recall her confession of the night before, or he wouldn't have said that. She hurried to speak and cover her relief. "You were the best warrior in all of George's Cross, as befitting a student of Sir David's."

He closed his eyes as if the effort of reminiscing had tired him. "We were children together."

Children together? Is that all he remembered? Curiously, that angered her, and she shot him a glance of such scorn it should have cauterized his wound. But actually, it helped to be so angry, for someone had to peel that bandage off his wound and Wharton had proved unable to deliberately hurt his master, even for his master's own good. "Prepare yourself," she said.

He opened his eyes again and realized what would happen, then nodded weakly.

She eased the clinging linen off the forming scab.

He arched his back as if she'd burned him. Wharton handed her the jar of ointment she'd used every day to combat the infection, and she hurried to spread it with her fingers. Deep sighs of relief shuddered through him, and she was glad. Glad he'd returned to consciousness. Glad she had the skill to relieve the pain of recovery.

When she had bandaged him, he looked at her deeply, and she bore the examination proudly. She wanted him to realize the girl she had been had grown up, gained skills, and saved his life. He opened his mouth to speak, and she straightened her spine.

"You look the same," he said. "Pretty as ever."

"Wharton." Hugh laid on his side on the pallet and in a rich voice spoke persuasively to his servant. "You'll need to leave before the sun rises much higher in the sky, or someone here might recognize you."

Like a she-wolf guarding her pup, Wharton squatted beside Hugh. Setting his jaw, he looked annoyed. "I don't like leaving ye here day after day in th' hands o' that woman."

From her place at the long table, Edlyn looked at the ceiling as if her much-needed forbearance would appear through the thatch. That woman, Wharton called her. She'd saved his master and protected his own life, and he resented her more bitterly than ever before. It was, she suspected, because Hugh so clearly wanted to spend his time alone with her.

She didn't want it, Hugh did, and so she tried time and again to tell Wharton, but Wharton wouldn't listen. As far as Wharton was concerned, his master was perfect, so the fault must lie in her.

Hugh indicated nothing but courteous regard for his servant when he said, "Lady Edlyn has taken good care of me, Wharton, and as you well know, I will need you here and awake tonight to help me."

"To help you what?" Edlyn asked idly.

Wharton began, "T' help him—"

"—In case I'm stricken with illness," Hugh finished with glib assurance.

Edlyn looked from Wharton's angry, guilty face to Hugh's smooth one and wondered what they were hiding.

"Guess I'd best be leaving then." Wharton rose and

shook out his legs. "I'll be tramping about in th' woods."

"And gathering information?" Hugh asked.

"From any chance-met traveler," Wharton agreed.

Again they were sharing a secret, keeping something from her, but she didn't care. She'd dealt with little boy intrigue before.

Nodding and bowing, Wharton backed away from the long prone figure behind the oven. Then with a sneer at her, he slammed out.

Hugh scarcely waited until Wharton had cleared the door before he began his attack. "Your duke didn't live very long."

Edlyn stared at her hands as they sorted dark green leaves into brown wooden boxes. "Two years," she answered, hoping that would satisfy his curiosity but knowing it would not.

"Two years. Not long at all."

She could feel Hugh's gaze; it made the muscles in her back contract as if she were braced for the stab of a knife. Funny that she suspected Hugh, seemingly so calm, of being more dangerous than the volatile Wharton.

"Was he a good husband?"

"He was a dear." Edlyn didn't know if it was the dragon's blood or pure bloody determination, but once Hugh began to heal, he healed rapidly. He wanted to rise, insisting he needed exercise. Knowing it was too soon, she refused to let him but wished him gone nevertheless. Healing, he was a presence in the dispensary—rather like a lump in her throat that strangled her but was impossible to dislodge.

"A handsome man, and true?" he asked.

She gave a crack of laughter, then submitted to temptation and walked to his side. She told him she had to attend to her duties, but she would be glad to listen to him as he talked. But he didn't talk. He continued his interrogation, and occasionally, with her mind on the mixture of herbs before her, she said too much.

Now she stood, hands on her hips, and looked down at him, relishing the inherent domination of her position. "I was less than a gnat for you when we lived at George's Cross, was I not?"

If it affected him that she stood while he reclined, he hid his chagrin well. Instead, he watched her with those fathomless eyes and said, "I remember you well."

"Do you?" Never in the last days had he given any indication he remembered that confession she had given while under the influence of that wretched dragon's blood, and her early panic had eased. Now she squatted and looked him in the eye. "Then you are a foolish man. I married a duke so old the ceremony and the celebration after brought him to his knees with a pain in the head and a paralysis of his body. He was kind to me, but he never even completed the role of husband."

"He never bedded you?" Again he showed no emotion.

She hung her hands over her up-thrust knees. "He attempted to, and we told his family he had succeeded. He didn't wish to have his inability revealed, and I feared they would strip me of my dower portion when he died."

"Did they?"

She smiled, a mere curving of the lips. "They tried."

Her duke's treacherous children had tried to throw her out without a pence, and when she'd fought for her dower, they tried to have her killed. It hadn't been easy. It hadn't been pretty. But she'd won the money and the lands stipulated in her marriage contract and ascertained the thread of steel in her backbone at the same time.

Now Hugh looked at her as if he saw into her past, at the struggle she'd been forced to face at the age of seventeen, and she recognized the balance between them had shifted. He'd been lying behind this oven for just one day less than a fortnight, and for the first time since he had woken to find himself in her care, they spoke not as patient and caretaker, but as man and woman.

With a faint gasp, she turned her head away and stood, then fled back to her herbs.

Behind her, she heard him say, "Marriage to your duke proved to be a prosperous union for you."

Plunging the pestle into the mortar filled with dry leaves, she ground them into dust. He didn't understand. He didn't know how frightened she had been. Or else he didn't care. God grant him the delicacy to allow this conversation to die.

An imbecilic hope, for he immediately asked, "Do you plan to take your vows as so many noble widows do?"

She dropped the pestle into the mortar. It clattered on the smooth stone bowl and a poof of green dust spun through the air. To cover her clumsiness, she crossed to the oven. She shook the long-stemmed plants she had placed there to dry. The faded leaves rattled, and a few of the yellow buds fell off. With an exclamation of satisfaction, she whisked them over to her table.

She shouldn't answer, but she already knew his methods. If she didn't reply now, he would ask the question again later, and still later, until he'd worn down her resistance. So she said simply, "No vows."

"Why not?"

"They won't have me." It was a plain statement of fact.

"Who keeps you from it? Is it that woman who comes every day to badger you? Or her wretched servant who watches when she should not?"

For a man who remained hidden under rags whenever she had a visitor, he saw remarkably well. "Lady Blanche has no influence here, although she would like to have." Edlyn sighed. "No, 'tis I who have too many duties to fulfill in this world ere I could ever enter the cloister."

"If God calls, surely earthly duties must be dismissed."

"God has not called."

She heard him say something, she didn't know what, then he covered his eyes with his arm. Because he was tiring? Or to hide his expression from her? She watched him suspiciously.

"How long has it been since the death of your duke?" he asked.

"I was fifteen when I wed him. I was seventeen when he died. And that was eleven years ago."

"What a tight-lipped, suspicious woman you have grown to be!" He lifted his arm, and she saw the exasperation he usually concealed. "You tell me nothing."

"Why should I?"

"Because I wish to know."

"As if that matters!"

He ignored that, and using bluntness as he would a broadsword, he slashed at her discretion. "How many other husbands have you had in those eleven years?"

Incensed that he believed he had the right to pry, determined to put him in his place, she answered him as bluntly as he had asked. "One."

He struggled to sit up.

She watched, her chin thrust forward.

"Where is he now?" he demanded.

"He's dead."

He must have expected that, for he placed his next query without pause. "What was his name?"

"You'll know it, I'm sure. He was no doubt a comrade of yours." She turned back to her work and flung words over her shoulder. "His name was Robin, earl of Jagger."

"Robin . . . earl of Jagger?" His voice was hoarse with anguish and fury. "Are you taunting me?"

She stopped work and frowned at him. The raw distress in his voice echoed in her ears, and she fetched her bottle of tonic. It would, she thought, ease the rasp in his throat, but as she knelt beside him, she knew she lied to herself. He hadn't reacted as she'd expected at all, and she wanted to know what he meant. "You've talked too much." Pouring the putrid thick brown potion into a cup, she shoved it into his hand. "Do you need me to hold you while you drink?"

As offensively as possible, he said, "I need you to vow you'll keep your silence until I am well away from here."

She reared, stunned by his attack. "I've kept it this long! Do you think I would tell the nuns what I've done? That I've kept a man alive in the dispensary without their knowledge?" Her gaze raked him from head to toe. "And such a man. A *warrior*."

"What's wrong with a warrior?"

"My husband was a *warrior*. A great warrior. I can't believe I've risked everything—shelter, food, a safe place to . . . " She inhaled and leaned close enough for her breath to touch his face. "I risked my security . . . for another *warrior*."

He watched her warily, as if they were talking at cross-purposes and he were as confused as she. Picking his words with care, he said, "Robin, earl of Jagger, died last year in the service of Simon de Montfort."

"Die? He didn't die." Her cheeks burned, and hot tears filled her eyes. "He was captured by the earl of Roxford, dragged through the streets like a common criminal, and executed."

"As a traitor to the royal prince."

She met his gaze boldly, but her hand crept to her heart. "'Tis a fate you might avoid."

"Avoid?" He frowned. "You think *I'm* a traitor to the crown?"

"Aren't you?"

"I am not!"

She'd heard that before, and she answered him with just as much conviction. "Aye, that's what Robin said, too. He said he was no traitor, but a defender of the rights of the barons against the king's tyranny." Her mouth curled in contempt. "Prince Edward didn't see it that way. Simon de Montfort captured the king last year, and he drags him around like a pawn in his dangerous game. He uses the king's power to make decrees, and Prince Edward would do anything to free his father. So when the prince's commander sent Robin to London, Robin hanged by his neck until he was dead. The prince confiscated all of Robin's lands and wealth. And as a lesson to others who might rebel against him, the prince threw Robin's wife and his children into the dirt to live or die as best they could."

5

Hugh enunciated his words as if Edlyn were hard of hearing. "I am not a rebel against the king."

"Of course you're not." She smirked, just for the pleasure of aggravating him. "That's why Wharton was frightened you would be discovered. That's why you're content to hide here until the other soldiers are gone." She gave up on sarcasm and went right to the point. "You're afraid Prince Edward's troops will discover you and take you to be executed." She took a quivering breath. "Like Robin."

"That is not true."

"Then why don't you call for your companions? Why don't you consent to go to the hospital where the nuns could care for you?"

"I can't be seen lying helplessly. There are assassins—"

Who did he think he was? The commander of the royal troops? She covered her mouth to contain her laughter.

Solemn-faced, he studied her. "You've made up your mind, haven't you? There's no talking to you, is there?"

She shook her head nay.

"Very well. But Edlyn, countess of Jagger, you should be shy of judging all men by the same stick."

He was sulking! The man she thought so impervious had his lips pressed tightly together, and Edlyn experienced a surge of triumph. All men were the same—little boys who demanded respect while failing to earn it. Treating him just as she would Parkin or Allyn, she drew him onto her knee and said, "Here. Drink this."

His hand rose to push the mug away, then he paused. "Would you like to know the other reason why I refuse to go to your hospital?"

"If you wish to tell me," she acquiesced gracefully.

"Because I always knew you were the only one who could cure me."

He laid his hand over hers, pressing her palm into the smooth side of the horn cup. The calluses on his palm scraped her, and he rubbed his fingers in small circles over her skin.

His voice deepened with sincerity. "Even when death pressed close, I heard your voice talking and felt your strength flow into me."

"Heard me?" She almost choked.

"That's why I have been drinking vile things, wearing mashed weeds on my wound, eating pap, and hiding myself in a pile of rags whenever anyone comes close to the dispensary." He brought her hand, and the cup, to his mouth and drank. "Because you tell me to."

She wrinkled her nose. He'd heard her? Heard her? When?

"Is something wrong?" he asked. "You look like you bit down on a bug."

"I . . ." She scrambled for a likely excuse. "This tonic *does* stink."

"It tastes worse." He finished the cup and released her at last. Contemplative now, he asked, "You were thrown out of your holdings with nothing? You and your children?"

"Aye." She wanted to move away, but she had to find out. "Did you understand my voice when you were close to death?"

"That's not important." He dismissed her question without curiosity. "How many children?"

"Two boys. And I think it's important."

"Do you?" She had caught his attention, and he stroked his chin. "How interesting."

By the saints, she didn't mean for him to think about it! "Probably not important." She tried to smile. "Two sons, Parkin and Allyn. I didn't know what to do when the prince's troops came and put us onto the road with nothing but the clothes we wore."

"The prince's troops. Did they hurt you?"

"Rape me, you mean?" Unwillingly, she remembered that dreadful day. "Nay. The knight in charge had strict orders, and he followed them." With scorn and haughtiness. "Throw me and anything that hinted of Robin's possessions into the dirt." She'd stood there among the pile of flags and tapestries marked with Robin's crest and held the boys' hands. "Prepare the castle for its new lord."

"Who was that?"

"I have not heard the prince has awarded Jagger to anyone yet."

"I know where he won't award it," Hugh said.

An odd thing to say. "Where?"

"To any of the lords who support de Montfort." He suddenly seemed to taste the tonic. "Give me something to clear my tongue."

She was glad to change the subject and helped him

back onto his pillow. Wrapping a strip of padding around the clay pot warming on the oven, she brought it to his side and lifted the lid. The scent of herbs wafted into the air, bearing more than a hint of . . . meat?

Suddenly alert, he lifted his head. "What's that?"

"Broth," she said, grinning. "Wharton snared a rabbit and cooked it in a stew."

He craned his neck and stared into the pot. "Where's the stew?"

She understood him perfectly. "You can't have pieces of meat yet. Your stomach's not ready."

"Nonsense. I'm starving on that porridge you've been shoveling into me."

"I'm lucky to get that for you." She dipped the spoon in the broth. "Do you want this, or not?"

He wanted to argue.

He wanted to eat.

He ate.

As she fed him, she said, "'Tis a great sin, not sharing the food with which God has blessed us. The others in the abbey long for meat also. But I didn't think I could claim *I* had snared the rabbit in the royal forest while out looking for herbs."

"Couldn't Wharton have explained *he* snared the rabbit?"

"They already eye him with suspicion. Not that we don't get vagrants hanging about the abbey, but your Wharton has an unusually rough edge to him, and they see him only in the dawn and the twilight." She liked the way Hugh ate, quickly, savoring each drop, yet determined to let every spoonful settle before taking another. "He's protective of his identity."

"Aye." Hugh looked grim. "There are many who would recognize Wharton and betray him for twelve gold coins."

That made her squirm yet again. She tried to keep faith in what she thought was best, as Lady Corliss had instructed, but were there those who would wreak havoc on the abbey for sheltering these two men? Had she brought disaster on them all?

In a voice that sounded amused, he asked, "Are you really so inept the nuns wouldn't have believed you could trap a rabbit?"

"I am not inept at all! But taking a rabbit from the royal forest is poaching, and our abbess takes a dim view of such dishonesty," she replied.

"You could tell her it died at your feet."

"I can't lie to Lady Corliss. She looks at me so calmly through those blue eyes and—" At the memory of that kind gaze and the disappointment a transgression brought, Edlyn shuddered. "Nay, I can't. Anyway, I really wouldn't know how to explain I needed an extra helping to bring to the dispensary."

He nodded, understanding that. "So what happened to the rest of the rabbit?"

"Wharton and I ate it." She waited for him to snarl at her for her selfishness.

Instead his gaze swept her. "Good. You look like you could use a meal."

A jab of gloom surprised her. She remembered a time when Robin had spent a whole day just gazing at her naked body, stroking her, admiring her. Her body was the best he'd ever seen, he claimed, and her body had been the one chain she thought would keep him bound to her.

Silly woman that she had been. His boundless delight in her physical appearance had never faded, but nothing chained Robin. And now Hugh looked at her without interest and called her skinny.

It was stupid to care or to let Hugh's consistent indifference dig at her. After all, what had the man done but ignore her childish infatuation and go on with his life?

Reaching into her bag, she brought out a crust of bread she'd saved from her own meal and dunked it into the broth, then transferred it to his open mouth.

"Mm." He closed his eyes and sighed as if tasting paradise.

Then he opened them, and she knew he had focused on a new problem.

"How old are your sons?" he asked.

"They have both seen eight winters."

"Twins?"

She gave the answer she always did. "Two boys as alike as you would ever see."

"So rare that both children survived birth."

She didn't answer that.

"'Tis time they were fostered." He spoke briskly.

She answered in a like tone. "They have been fostered. Our abbot from the adjoining monastery has taken them under his wing, and even now they travel on their first pilgrimage."

"A pilgrimage?" His brows lowered, and he chewed the new sop of bread thoroughly before he replied. "An abbot? You have placed them with an abbot?"

His incredulity galled her. "Who else would you suggest?"

"For the earl of Jagger's sons? They should be pages in a knight's household."

"They don't want to be in a knight's household." She pointed the spoon at him for emphasis. "They want to be monks."

"The earl of Jagger's sons want to be monks?"

His voice hit a note she'd never heard him use before, and she answered defensively, "They do."

"A waste! The earl of Jagger was one of the finest fighters I ever met. Why, he almost defeated me!"

He jumped and glanced at her sideways while animosity swept her. "At one of the tournaments he frequented, no doubt, while he left me at home to raise money for his battles and raise his sons for the future."

He took the bowl from her and blotted the last of the broth out of it with the remaining bread. He handed her the bowl.

She clutched it tightly and urged herself to stand, to put distance between them, to ignore him as the shallow pig deserved to be ignored. Instead she remained as she was and said, "You give me advice on how to raise my sons, but how much do you care for their fate? They are *my* boys, kept by me and nurtured by me. To you they are only a whim to interest you as you lie there, and you are subject to whims which are nothing more than itches. You scratch them, you're done, you forget. But if I allowed you to, you would twist my whole world around for those itches, and when you had scratched and forgotten, my world would still be askew."

"I am not so capricious!"

"All men are capricious. They have the power, why shouldn't they be?"

He took a breath and when he spoke, he used the voice of reason. "It is not capriciousness which makes me realize that any sons of the earl of Jagger will be fighters. I knew Robin, Lady Edlyn, in the prime of his life, and I felt the power of his blade. I saw how his men worshiped him and how the ladies . . . well." He cleared his throat. "You say his sons want to be monks. Perhaps, but perhaps if shown a different path, they would find themselves more fitted to knighthood."

"Robin *died* in the prime of his life." Her heart almost stopped its beating as she remembered the lively, handsome, heroic man and realized he would never again walk this earth. "I want more than that for my sons."

"But what do they want for themselves?"

"They are eight years old. They don't know what they want." She stood and placed the bowl in the bucket with her other dirty dishes. "Other parents set their children's feet on the path which they must follow all their lives. Why do you think I'm less capable?"

"Perhaps your father could give you advice."

He hadn't answered the question, she noticed. "My father doesn't even know where we are."

"Why not?"

She opened the bag she had taken with her into the woods that morning and shook the plants and roots out on the table. "I haven't sent him word—nor has he sent to ask. When I married the first time, I was one of five girls. My mother gave birth to two more after that, all to be married or placed in a nunnery, all to be given some kind of dowry. I helped purchase husbands for three of my sisters, as I was expected to do." She sniffed the mandrake root, then continued calmly, "Nevertheless, I hazard my father would not welcome me back into his home, disgraced as I am."

"A sad state of affairs," Hugh rumbled.

"Not at all," Edlyn answered. "You were born to a family as poor as mine. Would *your* parents welcome you home again?"

"Nay, but I'm a man grown!"

"Too true." Had he detected her sarcasm? She doubted it. He was too much of a man to ever conceive a woman's thoughts. She was a woman grown and as accomplished as he in her endeavors. But they were not a man's endeavors and therefore worth little.

It irked her, the way men plunged through life, assuming their way was the right way, secure in the world they had created especially to serve their own needs and wants. Women had to try to fit into that world, to understand their men's thoughts and desires. If a woman failed, she was punished *by* her man. If a man failed, a woman was punished *with* her man.

"Perhaps Sir David would consent to give his opinion," Hugh said.

He sounded more hesitant now. Maybe he was reading her after all. She could imagine the frown that puckered his forehead, the way the light hazel of his eyes deepened to green, the serious turn of his mouth.

She could imagine all that, and she cursed herself for that imagination. Why did she know him well enough to forecast his reactions? Oh, aye, she had spent hours as a girl studying him—his firm lips, wide with the promise of sensuality, the way his blond hair swept back from his face, how his eyebrows habitually lowered as he faced the challenges before him.

But she'd forgotten all that! It had been years ago. She did not, damn it, did *not* carry his image like an icon in her mind.

Which led her to another less than palatable thought. If she wasn't remembering him, then she'd been observing him here in the dispensary. Observing him not as a patient, but as a man worthy of attention. She didn't believe she'd been doing that. Yet here she was, prognosticating how he would act and react.

She hated this about herself. It was like thinking she had been cured of an infection only to find it lingered still in her veins.

"I hope you're mumbling that I have a good idea." Hugh didn't sound as if he believed that.

Separating the trefoil, she stacked it into a pile and began plucking the crimson blossoms. "When I lived with Lady Alisoun, she and Sir David treated me with the greatest kindness. I have nothing but respect for their opinions, but I fear I am unable to apply to them for anything. It would not be acceptable to me."

"Your pride is not seemly in a woman."

Her hands clenched into fists, and the scent of spring clover assailed her. Opening her hands, she wiped the smears of red from her palms. In a low tone, she said, "My pride is all I have, and it has sustained me for a very long time now."

"You're too independent."

"Whose fault is that?" Her movements jerky, she stretched a thin cloth over the table and dumped the blossoms onto it.

"Mine, perhaps."

She almost didn't hear him, and she didn't understand what he meant anyway.

He said, "When this war is over, I will have several estates to go with my title. I could foster your sons then."

She couldn't believe it. She couldn't stand it. Hadn't he heard one single word that she'd said? Was her determination so easily brushed aside? His offer demonstrated the truth of her thoughts—that men created war for the love of fighting and struggled against the civilizing influences of wife and home. When faced with the thought of two boys—boys he had never met—becoming men of peace, Hugh endeavored to save them as surely as the saints endeavored to win a sinner's soul. She managed a polite tone, but the undercurrent, if he cared to hear, swept through dark and dangerous. "My sons have had too much disruption in their lives already. I am their mother. They will stay with me."

Gathering the corners of the cloth, she lifted the trefoil. He tried to speak, but she walked past without giving a sign she'd heard and carried the flowers outside. In an area safe from the wind, she knelt and spread them to dry. In the winter they would provide infusions against fits of coughing.

In the winter, Hugh would be gone.

For the first time in her life, she longed for winter. Kneeling down among the herbs, she pulled the few weeds that threatened the comfrey. Last winter had been her first at the abbey. It had been very long, very dull, very cold. She'd longed for the spring as never before, but spring, with its easier travel and its rich landscape, had carried war on its temperate winds. Battle had come too close. The wounded had depleted her stores. A few of the rougher soldiers had threatened to sack the village, and in fact a gold chalice had disappeared from the church.

It took a desperate man to steal from God, and the experience alarmed the nuns. Edlyn thought it frightened the monks, too, untrained as most were in the art of war. Lady Corliss had suggested Edlyn curtail her ventures into the forest until the countryside had settled once more. Edlyn had explained that the season for trefoil was brief, and the leaves from the coltsfoot had to be collected now before they lost their vigor.

What Lady Corliss didn't understand was that Edlyn needed to escape into those woods. There, no one watched her, no one mocked her for what she had been and what she had become. She could discard her shoes, hike up her skirt, and with a free conscience hunt for medicinal herbs, all the while breathing the air of freedom.

Of course, one time she had had the uneasy sense of being watched. The hair on the back of her neck rose, and she heard the crack of a branch beneath a man's shoe. When she'd run into Wharton, bloody from skinning the rabbit, she'd been daunted until she recognized him. Then she'd been embarrassed, and he had enjoyed that.

Still, he had denied following her, and she was left with the fear of having been someone's prey. After that, she had kept a stout oak walking stick close by her side.

She stood. Why was she worried about an imaginary presence? She had two big worries of her own.

She started toward the door when a drop of water struck her cheek. Looking up, she sighed in disgust and relief. Disgust that she had to bring the trefoil in again. Relief that the rain would set the new plants she'd placed in the garden.

She gathered the blossoms and walked back toward the door. As long as Hugh de Florisoun lived in her dispensary, she would have no peace.

He scarcely waited until she crossed the threshold before he said, "I mean for you to come, too."

"What are you talking about?" She feared she knew, and she dumped the cloth of blossoms onto the table before she gave in to temptation and threw them at him.

"I'll foster your sons, and you will live with us."

She had trouble catching her breath. "*Live* with you?"

"I will be good to you, Edlyn."

"Good to me." She tapped her foot, irritated and insulted.

"I'll need a woman to tend the house, and you know how to do that, and right well, too." He dredged up a charming smile—clearly he was used to getting his way. "You'd like that better than this task of digging plants out of the dirt and having to boil decoctions for strangers." He spoke matter-of-factly, as if he knew what she liked and what she didn't.

"I would?"

"Of course you would," he said confidently. "Edlyn"—he held out his hand, palm up—"you and I would be an invincible couple."

"A couple of what?"

His hand dropped and his brows lowered. "A *married* couple."

Panic hit her, twisting her stomach, making her want to retch. "Married?"

A tinge of irritation colored his tone. "What did you think I meant?"

"Not married, that's certain." Never married. Never again.

His voice rose. "You thought I would propose you stay with me as my mistress while your sons looked on? You thought I would take advantage of your lower status to dishonor you with a suggestion of impropriety?"

She subdued the panic and let irritation sweep her along. "In the past, I have not been impressed with any man's integrity in the face of a woman's misfortune."

In a surge of fury, he rose to his feet. "I am Hugh de Florisoun. I am the living embodiment of chivalry!"

"Sure you are." It gave her great satisfaction to layer her words with derision. At the same time, she hustled toward him and wrapped her arm around his. "Now lie down before you start bleeding."

"You doubt me?"

His knees began to shake, and she answered

hastily, "I don't doubt your honor, Hugh. Now let me help you to lie down."

"I offered you marriage in all seriousness and in solemn belief in the justice of my suit"—he sank to the floor, dragging her with him—"and you mock me?"

She eased him around until his rump touched the mat. "'Twas my mistake. I *have* seen men who live by the code of chivalry." She guided him back toward that hated pillow. "But not for a long, long time."

She had her arms around his shoulders, one hand supporting his head, just as if he were a baby—or a lover. She should have grasped the simple truth—that he hadn't lived so long or prospered so well by not seizing opportunity when it manifested itself.

In a tone heavy with sensuality, he whispered her name. "Edlyn."

When she looked down and caught the expression on his face, she knew she was in trouble. She had presented herself on a platter.

Should she drop him and run? Or should she tend to his well-being? She'd worked too long and hard to drop him, but that confident expression he wore irked her. She got him within a finger's width of the pillow and let go. Her action was not enough to hurt but enough to give warning she wouldn't be easy.

She tried to jump back. He already had his arms around her, and he used that off-balance position to tip her forward and onto him. She collapsed on his chest and he groaned.

"Serves you right," she said, struggling to elbow her way up. "I don't want this."

"Be ruthless." He just kept blocking her, expending as little of his precious energy as possible while she exhausted herself. "Hit my wound."

She couldn't do it. She wanted to so badly, but she

just couldn't take him back to the edge of death. Instead she balled her fist and tried to hit his face. He caught her by the fingers and gripped. She struggled, and when she flagged, he grasped the back of her head and held her still for his kiss.

He tried to use his tongue, and that infuriated her all over again. Who did he think he was? Her long-lost love?

Well, he should have stayed lost.

And who did he think she was? A lady of easy virtue?

Her tight-lipped resistance must have given him the message, for he let her pull back her head. She tried to scramble away again, but he handled her with great care, rolled onto his good side, and tucked her half under him.

He was so calm, so deliberate! How could a man who'd been so near death just a few days ago restrain her, a healthy woman? A little alarm worked into her voice as she struggled. "This . . . is . . . not . . . right."

"I'm just going to kiss you, and that is right between couples who have pledged to wed."

"I've made no such pledge."

"You'll see the good sense of it soon."

He said it as if it were the truth. As if her objections meant nothing. As if she were nothing but a silly lady who needed a man to tell her how to live her life! Worse, he probably believed it, the dunce.

With one thigh anchoring her down, he controlled her. He got rid of her wimple first. The covering slipped easily off her head, and his fingers caught in the fine, straight strands that had escaped her braid. Holding the braid aloft, he stared at it.

"Stop that!" She grasped his wrist.

He looked at her, pressed between the floor and his

body. "I remember seeing this, all unbound, in the light of a fire, and seeing you, too, wearing nothing."

"I wore something! I wore a—" She stopped talking.

Too late. Satisfaction curved his mouth, and she snapped, "What else do you remember?"

He didn't answer. He just leaned forward and brushed her lips with his. She kept her eyes open, and when he lifted his head, she said, "First you try to sweep me away. Then you try gentleness. What's your next tactic?"

She must have betrayed an emotion better concealed, for he replied, "Gentleness will do what I wish."

She tried to stiffen even further, but she knew he was probably right. The loneliness of the abbey echoed in her soul. Oh, there were always people around, but in a place where flesh equaled sin, the residents spurned touch. Her sons hugged her, of course, but she couldn't help but remember Jagger Castle. She missed the impulsive embraces of the girls she fostered, the respectful kisses of greeting she gave her guests. Most of all, she missed the body embraces she shared with her man, and this unwilling response to Hugh had to be nothing more than a sequestered soul reaching out to the nearest human for contact.

Either that or she was as wicked as Lady Blanche intimated.

Hugh's forearm lay beneath her head, and he watched her with a fascination she knew to be unwarranted. His regard made her want to squirm, but she held herself still and said tartly, "What are you looking at, knave?"

"At the lady who would be my wife, and—dare I say it?—the woman who saved my life."

An unwilling warmth softened her. "'Twas the grace of God."

"Aye, and He used you as His instrument." He stroked her hair. "Should I not be privileged to rescue God's instrument from the despair of poverty into which she has fallen?"

Her goodwill evaporated. "I'm doing well on my own!"

"Ah, aye." He glanced around at her beloved dispensary. "Very well indeed."

She knew what he saw. The low ceiling, the dirt floor, her carefully tended herb boxes: what was this place when compared to a castle with glass in the windows, a wooden floor strewn with rushes, and tapestries on the walls? Yet because of her previous generosity, she'd had an abbey to come to instead of needing to resort to the streets to support her children. It had been as the priests said—the Lord rewarded good deeds. What Hugh saw when he looked on her was a woman who had fallen on bad times. She thought of herself as a woman who had done well with little.

She voiced a woman's universal complaint. "What asses men are!"

He didn't answer that. He only brought her head to his and kissed her again. Little kisses, nibbles that gave her a taste of him. She didn't want to know about him and kept her teeth clenched, but his tongue darted through her closed lips and she had a sample of him anyway.

The billows of his breathing lulled her as his chest rose and fell against hers. She *was* hungry for human contact, it seemed, for she found herself inhaling with him, exhaling with him.

"Open," he whispered. His beard had grown to a soft pelt that caressed her chin, and the sweet scent of him titillated her desires.

Plastered so closely against him, she felt his heart pulsate against her breastbone, and the beat over-whelmed her own natural rhythm to sweep the blood through her veins.

"Edlyn, give to me." His hand rubbed her neck, then her scalp, in slow, hypnotic circles.

Her eyes had closed, but she saw with his vision. Her ears had failed her, but she heard her own denial. She felt his triumph as he surged into her mouth, then his frustration as she let him do what he would and made no attempt to reciprocate.

He gathered her closer when there was no closer, tangling his legs with hers, pressing his knee between and high until the pressure brought familiar sensations, then new urgings. She fought to deny them, but he moved insistently, insidiously.

"Feel me," he crooned. "'Tis Hugh who holds you, who pleasures you. 'Tis your old friend, your new lover, your future husband."

"Nay."

"So faint a sound!"

He mocked her, but benignly. His hand—how many did he have?—wandered over her throat, her shoulder, along the length of her torso to her hip and rested heavily there. So aware of him, she could even imagine the pain of his wound. She fought the merging of two selves into one. He was an enchanter to so absorb her into his bones and his bloodstream.

"I feel your passion," he murmured. "So long denied, so hungry and demanding." His knee moved. "When you respond—"

Preservation made her answer, "Not going to."

He stopped moving, stopped breathing, and remained so motionless her eyes opened and fixed on him.

She had seen him unconscious. She had seen him in pain. She had seen him recovering. She had seen him curious. She had never seen him determined, but she saw him that way now.

His level gaze held hers. His wide mouth slashed his face straight across. In a voice all the more convincing for its lack of emotion, he said, "I'm not going to leave you alone. I'm not going to let you get away. I will hold you until you respond or until both of us perish of hunger and thirst."

She wanted to tell him it wasn't possible. Someone would come looking for her. And lovers didn't really die in each other's arms, regardless of the romantic fables.

Yet looking at that hunting-mastiff expression he wore, she thought it just seemed easier to give in. Then it would be over, she'd be free, and he'd have his manhood back.

After all, that was what this was about, wasn't it? A woman had defied him, and his fragile male pride had been shattered. Although he didn't look shattered. He looked patient, and that was worse. She didn't want to surrender, but she'd done a lot of things she didn't want to in her life. That was, after all, a woman's lot.

Resigned, she lifted her head off his arm and pressed her mouth to his.

"More."

His lips moved against hers, and she told herself again she was resigned. But her hand had curled into a fist. Instead of using it as a weapon, she propped it under her head. With the other hand on his shoulder and her eyes wide open, she kissed him with her lips, then her tongue.

He opened for her easily, a studied contrast to her earlier resistance. But of course he would—he was getting his own way.

Resigned. She was resigned.

Breaking the kiss, he asked, "Has no one taught you better than that yet?"

"What do you mean?"

"There's more to this than stabbing a man with your tongue."

Before she even thought she said, "But I'm so good at that."

"Only when you talk."

At some point, she must have put some space between them, because he pulled her close again and rolled her onto her back. She didn't like the way he rose above her, dominating every space, but she was resigned to giving him his own way.

"Close your eyes," he instructed.

She obeyed.

"Relax."

She tried.

"Good, now learn."

It was the kiss she'd dreamed of all those years ago. Intimate. The roughness of his tongue lapped at the tender tissues of her inner cheeks.

Passionate. His hands roamed her body, touching places so long untouched she might have been a virgin once more.

Playful. He nipped at her until she responded with a fight. Then he wrestled her into submission and kissed her some more.

She'd never before met a man who liked to kiss. When women talked, they agreed that kissing wasn't pleasure for a man. Kissing was only waiting until the woman indicated her readiness to mate, and if the woman didn't indicate readiness soon enough, then the man quickly suppressed the kissing. That had certainly been Edlyn's experience.

But not with Hugh. Hugh kissed her mouth, her neck, each sharply angled plane of her face, and then her mouth again. He didn't try to take off her clothes. He didn't act impatient when she wanted more. In fact, he held her off with as close to a smile as she'd seen from him and said calmly, "I knew I could make you respond."

Resigned? Had she thought herself resigned? She wasn't resigned! She was angry. Abruptly, deeply furious. His smug comment did what nothing else had done. He had relaxed, the whoreson, and she brought up her knee so fast he didn't have time to even attempt defense. One good strike, and she stood above him while he writhed on the floor.

Livid, panting with rage, she said, "I've already buried two husbands, but I'll make an exception for you. If you ever touch me again, I'll bury you before I ever wed you."

6

"*A warrior should never* exalt in his victory, Wharton, before the enemy is completely disarmed." Leaning heavily on the long table, Hugh made his way around the dispensary.

"Ye are wise as always, master." Wharton danced around him, holding his arms out like an anxious parent with a toddler. "Don't ye think it's time t' sit down?"

"'Tis a lesson I've had taught to me before, but never has it been illustrated as thoroughly as was done this day."

"She's a cruel woman, t' have unmanned ye so," Wharton said fiercely.

"Edlyn is a warrior-woman and worthy to bear my children." Pausing in his perambulation around the room, Hugh spoke to Wharton in direct disapproval. "And she is your future mistress, so you will speak of her accordingly."

Wharton wrestled with the concept of a woman with the power to direct him.

"In sooth, what she did and what she said did not matter. She gave me a great gift." Hugh took a breath.

"She proved to me all my parts are functioning and I am going to live."

"Women are good fer that, at least," Wharton agreed. "Ye've been up longer tonight than last night, and last night longer than th' night before. Shouldn't ye rest now?"

"My strength returns every day tenfold." Cautiously, Hugh pushed himself away from the table and lifted his arms. The skin pulled but not unduly. Edlyn had taken the stitches out the previous day, and even she had seemed stunned by his improvement. "Let us not forget, Wharton, Lady Edlyn's herbal skill brought me back from the dead."

"Don't say that, master." Wharton shivered. "'Tisn't natural."

"I remember," Hugh insisted. "I was lying there behind the oven. I couldn't open my eyes. I could barely breathe. Then I smelled something, and it smelled like . . . like the odor of a fresh destrier before battle, or like chain mail when it has been oiled. I wanted to breathe it in. I wanted to grow strong on the odor." He clenched his fist, and his gaze grew distant. "Then the bandage became soft and warm, like well-rubbed leather, the kind I have my gauntlets made of."

"Ye were dreaming, master." Wharton's assurance faded as Hugh turned his glare on him. "Weren't ye?"

"I know a dream, and I know reality, and this . . . this was both." Hugh considered. "Or neither. But it was real."

"Aye, master." Wary and confused, Wharton asked, "What else happened?"

"Taste. I could taste it."

"Taste what?"

"Taste her."

"Lady Edlyn?" Wharton scrambled backward.

"She thrust herself into yer mouth while ye were sleeping?" He thought. "Or whatever ye were doing?"

"Of course not, you dolt. It wasn't like that at all!" Wharton was a loyal servant, but sometimes his ignorance amazed Hugh. Yet trying to explain seemed hazardous at best. "Flavor burst on my tongue, a flavor such as I've never tasted before. I wanted to savor it. I wanted more and ever more. And I knew it was the flavor of Lady Edlyn."

Wharton shivered. "'Tis ungodly what ye're saying. Has she bewitched ye?"

Slowly, reserving his strength, Hugh moved toward the door. "For what purpose?"

"Ye say ye will wed her."

"So I will." Hugh caught the jamb and swung the door wide to let in the night.

"'Tis not necessary. Ye can have her fer less than that."

Jolted, Hugh remembered how Edlyn had doubted men and their honor. "What is your thought?"

"There's none here t' compete fer her. Just take her!"

Carefully, so Wharton would never suggest such a thing again, Hugh turned to his man. "That would be the act of a knave, indeed, and I will slit the throat of any man who suggests I am a knave."

Wharton's eyes bulged, and he audibly gulped. "Of a certainty, master. I meant that ye have no competition, so ye may wed her as ye wish."

"I thought you meant that." Hugh smiled, but he kept his gaze level and icy. "Although there is no competition for her, the lack of competition doesn't lessen my appetite."

"But . . . why her?" Wharton couldn't hold in his cry of frustration, right from his wizened heart. "Why do ye wish t' wed her?"

After due consideration, Hugh decided Wharton deserved some explanation. "She is in desperate straits here, and I feel a sense of responsibility."

Wharton freely gave the benefit of his advice. "Give her money."

"But I need a wife."

"A young wife," Wharton countered.

"An experienced wife, one who can manage my estates with a sure hand until I have learned everything a mercenary knight needs to be a noble lord."

"Aye, a wife should be of use to her husband." Wharton easily comprehended that. "But she talks ugly t' ye."

"I will sweeten her disposition with myself." Indeed, Hugh looked forward to that.

"She doesn't want t' marry ye."

"So you think Edlyn is a woman who knows what is best for her?"

Wharton's reaction was automatic and unthinking. "O' course not!"

Hugh hid his half-smile. "Nor do I. She is an exemplary woman, but she's only a woman, and she'll only be happy when she accepts the guidance of a man. Men are, by definition, the wiser gender."

Wharton clearly itched to argue, but how could he? Every word Hugh said was true. Wharton bobbed and bowed, and satisfied he had squelched his servant's little insolence, Hugh stepped outside.

Outside. He hadn't been outside since the day of the battle. He'd been stuck in that stuffy dispensary, dying in slow degrees until Edlyn had worked a miracle. And she *had* worked a miracle. He remembered little of his illness, but he remembered that.

Now the stone wall around the garden protected him from anyone who might be out so late. The night air smelled as sweet as freedom, and he squinted up at the sky overlaid with clouds. The rain, more than a mist yet less than a shower, wet his face. He had heard it on the thatch earlier, but knowing and experiencing were two different things.

Fearing to leave his master out in his weakened state, Wharton shuffled out to stand beside him. Wharton hated water of all kinds. He said it would kill a man to drink it and wither his cock if he washed in it, so Hugh took a fiendish delight in keeping him wet.

"Lady Edlyn seems rather"—Wharton trod carefully in view of Hugh's previous displeasure—"different than yer usual fare."

"How so?"

"She's old."

"Twenty-eight, if I did my numbers correctly, and handsome still."

"Ye deserve a virgin in yer wedding bed."

"Deserve?" Hugh barked a laugh, then held his side until the pain faded. "Did I deserve to almost die?"

"Nay, master!" Wharton coughed pathetically, trying without words to indicate the dreaded lung disease that would afflict him if they remained in the mist any longer.

Hugh ignored him. "Deserve has nothing to do with the trials and rewards of life."

"If ye take Lady Edlyn t' be your wife, I know which she will be."

"A trial?" Hugh walked a little farther into the garden. The night was as dark as any Hugh had ever seen. The clouds blocked all light from the stars. Unlit and silent, the abbey waited for the dawn.

The scent of burnet warned him he'd wandered off the trail, and he moved hastily back on the hay-strewn path. Edlyn, he knew, would not thank him for crushing the new plants that she'd sown. "Aye, she'll be that. The world had not yet tested the Edlyn I knew at George's Cross, and she looked at me with an adoring countenance. This Edlyn will fight—she has fought—for what is due her."

Wharton followed Hugh, staying carefully on the straw to avoid the mud. "Fighting's not attractive in a woman."

Hugh had agreed with Wharton at one time, and that time had been only a fortnight previously. Now it seemed long ago, and he didn't understand Wharton's hesitation. "What good is a woman who can't defend what is hers?"

Driven beyond courtesy, Wharton said, "She doesn't like ye."

"She's a challenge," Hugh agreed.

"She doesn't care fer invalids. She thinks a man flat on his back inferior t' a man who stands steady on his two feet."

In the safety of the darkness, Hugh allowed himself a smile. "I thought of that, but I can't believe it. She is so sensible, so matter-of-fact, so strong, she must be able to recognize strength in others."

"She is strong." Wharton obviously considered this to her detriment. "She lifted ye when ye were unconscious."

"That's not what I meant, but aye, she has strong arms and good hands." Her nails she kept short, the better to work with. Her long fingers and blunt palms were capable and expressive, and Hugh had found himself watching those hands and wondering whether they would be capable and expressive when she thrashed beneath him on a mat or in a bed.

"Ye like 'em delicate," Wharton reminded him.

"Delicate doesn't interest me now." Dismissing his

former requirements, Hugh finger-combed the beard on his jaw as he thought. "I have the strength, and she doesn't seem to know the role I have taken in the management of the kingdom, so her indifference must have its origins in another source."

"When she knows who ye are, she'll snuggle up fast enough."

"You think the widow of the earl of Jagger will want me?" Hugh laughed without humor. "She'll spit on me when she discovers the truth."

"Mayhap." Wharton sounded cheered. "Why, if that is true, ye'll not convince her t' wed ye."

"She doesn't have to know before the swearing."

"Ye've got t' give yer name."

"She knows my name. She doesn't know my title." He could almost feel Wharton jump as the idea struck him. "And I would take it ill if she discovered it too soon."

Wharton mumbled something as his relish faded, and Hugh took a breath. His plan seemed riddled with hazards, but as always he rose to any reasonable challenge. He hadn't reached his present pinnacle by seeking fights in every cobweb-laden corner, of course. He planned his campaigns with meticulous care, then fought with wild abandon to win.

He was in the planning stages now. He would fight later. And he would have to fight, he was sure. Wharton might dismiss Edlyn's resentment. Wharton might imagine she would find contentment with his money and his position, but Hugh didn't think so. Hugh recognized the barriers she had erected and gave them his proper respect.

Nevertheless, he lived to knock down barriers.

"This whole affair smacks of madness," Wharton said.

Hugh knew what Wharton meant. Hugh liked women, but they'd always been easy to leave. Give him his sword and his destrier, and he would be happy. "Maybe it's the onset of age," he suggested. "The compulsion to sow my seed and see it grow before it's too late."

"Young virgin," Wharton said under his breath.

Hugh heard it, of course. "Lady Edlyn can bear my children, and she's proven her fruitfulness. Ah!" He slashed the air with his hand. "Enough discussion."

Edlyn showed him no wiles. She was as far from a coquette as any woman could be. It wasn't the compulsion to breed that drew him to Edlyn, it was Edlyn herself.

He suspected the nuns all wore the same thing Edlyn wore—a shapeless cotte over a well-tied shift. The holy women probably prayed their rough clothing would discourage lustful thoughts from the men in their infirmary, but in Edlyn's case, at least, it didn't work.

How could it? She had a body that would make an angel discard his wings. Burned into Hugh's mind with the fire of fever was the memory of her breasts, the golden skin of the firm mounds, the soft nipples begging to be stroked. Whenever he saw those now-covered breasts, he observed avidly, seeing the way they lifted the material, the way they flowed when she lifted her arms to reach something from the top shelf.

Her breasts alone had healed him.

Her waist and hips had performed their own miracles. She had a way of walking that challenged him. He'd never met a woman with talking hips before, but sometime, somewhere, Edlyn had acquired them. *Rise!* her hips commanded. *Come and capture me.*

And of course he did rise, although not to his feet.

He hadn't seen anything of her legs, but he knew the challenge must originate there, between them. After all, he had been lying on the floor, and from there he could see her ankles at any time. Strong ankles. Slender ankles. Ankles that were connected to the rest of her and to the feet she so often bared for his enjoyment. Aye, Edlyn didn't seem to think bare feet were arousing, but every time she slipped off her shoes and padded around the dispensary, it made him think she had performed the first step of intimacy with him.

She had a nice face, too.

But those eyes . . . if he were a superstitious man, he would be stringing garlic and hoping to ward off the curse of those green eyes.

And she did curse him. That he never questioned.

"When ye heard her while she was healing ye— what was she saying?" Wharton asked.

"Something about our childhood together." Hugh frowned. "Something about . . . a barn." He shook his head. "The exact words escape me."

"Long as it wasn't some witchy incantation," Wharton retorted.

"Not that. Never that." Hugh was firm. "She did say something important, nonetheless. I'll think of it, don't worry."

"Can we go in now, master?" Wharton asked. "I can hear th' fairies awhispering under that oak."

"I don't hear anything."

"Ye never hear anything." Wharton sounded peeved. "Ye're blessed by th' fairies, that's why."

Actually, Hugh did hear them. Slight voices that could easily be mistaken for the rustle of leaves. But he never admitted *that* to anyone.

"So can we go in?" Wharton did a good imitation of a man about to expire from wheezing.

"Soon." Hugh stared at the darkest corner of the garden where he knew the oak stood. Slowly he moved toward it, keeping to the paths as best he could. The fairies whispered of enchantment; he countered with logic. "A brush with death brought me here, and I found a childhood comrade in dire need. She saved my life, and I'll rescue her from the wretched circumstances into which she's fallen. You'll see, she'll be grateful to be living her old life once again. I recognize the hand of providence in my life, and her appearance here could be nothing less."

The mist on the leaves sounded like laughter.

"Providence?" Wharton snorted. "Th' hand of th' devil, more likely."

Wharton's insistence incensed Hugh, and he responded in the manner most likely to silence him. "I do not understand why you, a man of war, speak so slightingly of a mere woman. One would almost suppose she had won a victory over you."

"'Tis not true! Did she say so?"

Wharton's quick reply told Hugh much, yet as he stepped into the deepest shadow beneath the tree, he knew he could not allow Wharton to continue to speak of Edlyn with such disrespect. In spite of the dark, Hugh turned and looked at the faithful Wharton to impress him with his displeasure. "Who she is and what she has done to you is of no interest to me. All I care is that my manservant will treat my wife with the respect due her. You, Wharton, seem unable to comprehend this, despite my repeated warnings. Perhaps it would be better if I found another servant."

"Master!" Wharton must have dropped to his knees, for his voice slithered downward. "Ye wouldn't leave me?"

"Not willingly." Hugh stepped forward so he loomed above Wharton. "So I will have your sworn word you will protect and defend Lady Edlyn as you do me."

"Master . . . "

Hugh didn't care for the whine in Wharton's voice, and he stepped back.

"Master!" Wharton crawled forward. "I swear, I swear."

"On what shall I have you swear?" Hugh wondered. He knew his manservant, and not much impressed Wharton as holy.

"On a cross?"

"I think not."

"In th' church?"

"Not effective enough."

"On yer sword?"

"We're getting close." Hugh stuck out his closed fist. "On me. Put your hand over mine, Wharton, and swear fealty to Lady Edlyn on my life."

Wharton's hand trembled. His voice trembled. But he swore while kneeling in the mud beneath the oak.

"Once again, Wharton, you show your wisdom." His man stood, subdued and obedient, as he should be, and Hugh leaned wearily on his shoulder and turned back to the dispensary. "Let us make our plans to capture the elusive Lady Edlyn."

Edlyn squinted into the morning sun as she scanned the open road for travelers. Specifically, for a monk and two boy-children trudging at his side. But the rutted, narrow track remained empty, and she turned toward the dispensary with a sigh.

When the monk had suggested he take Allyn and Parkin on a short pilgrimage, she'd been enthusiastic. The task of tending two tireless eight-year-olds in an abbey stretched her imagination and her resources, and she looked forward to the peace of solitude. And she freely admitted she had enjoyed it. She also missed her sons more than she ever thought possible, and she wanted them back.

Putting her hand on the gate to the herb garden, she hesitated to open it. Before her lads came home, though, she wanted Wharton and his wretched master gone. She hadn't slept well last night because of Hugh. Because of his kisses. She worried that she'd hurt him too much, then she wished that she'd struck twice as hard. The scoundrel. He had been insulted when she thought he would take advantage of her lowly state to make her his mistress rather than wed her, then he had taken advantage of her weaker muscles to kiss her!

Why that even rankled, she didn't know. She'd had enough experience with men to have taken their measure. Nevertheless, she'd slept too long and missed Mass, and Lady Blanche had glared when they'd met in the square.

Shutting the gate behind her, she turned—and gasped. Hugh rose out of the patch of thyme, his long legs steady. "What are you doing up?" she demanded. She hurried between the paths, her feet crushing the herb. Then she saw the ruddy color in his face. Clearly, his energy the day before had been no fluke. He was well, or soon to be. She slowed. "Get out of the beds, you fool, you're crushing the plants."

He rebuked her, his voice slow and measured. "That is no way to greet your betrothed."

"We are not betrothed."

"Then let us go now and remedy that state."

She cocked her head and examined him. The ragged growth of his beard had been shaved clean, baring the lines of his cheeks and chin. He wore clothing, not the robe she'd confiscated for him. Hose and boots and a knee-length tunic with laced-in sleeves. They fit him and were of fine workmanship, a further indication of his success. She found her mouth set in petulant lines and tried to smooth them from her face. After all, why should it matter to her if he'd won a title and the lands he'd always longed for? She, more than anyone, understood how temporary were the trappings of wealth.

"Will you not go to the church and have them read the banns?"

He said it as if it were her last chance to do as he wished. If he were giving up his pursuit, that should surely please her, but somehow she expected more tenacity from Hugh. "You are a warrior. I have no wish to be betrothed to you."

He moved so quickly she had no time to run, and she found herself wrapped in his arms. It reminded her of yesterday and made her angry all over again. "I didn't expect to see you standing so soon after that blow I gave you." A slight shudder shook him, and that satisfied her need for respect.

But he said, "I never underestimate my opponents twice."

A warning, and she took it as such. "I never use the same tactics twice."

He inclined his head. "I will remember. My thanks for telling me."

Stupid, she railed at herself. As if he needed help with his schemes.

He quelled her attempt to withdraw. "You left too quickly yesterday."

"Not quickly enough, I'd say," she answered.

"I would have shown you more." He pressed a tender kiss on her forehead.

"You showed me quite enough." She tried to slither down out of his grip, desperate to get away, to get him inside. The high stone wall around the garden might shield them from watching eyes, but anyone could walk through the gate. . . .

He followed her down. She'd sprouted these plants through the late winter, cherishing them through the last cool nights until they could be placed in the ground, and now this big oaf wanted to roll in them. "Let me up," she said. "It's muddy."

"It rained last night."

"I know that!" Did men take instruction to be aggravating, or was it bred into them? "And it smells like a stew down here."

"Um." He lay on his back and drew her over him. "The stew of love."

She couldn't help it; she half laughed at his poor analogy. "You'll never be a poet."

"I'll never be a lot of things, but I *will* be your lover, my lady." He pushed off her wimple. "And soon."

It was getting to be annoying, his habit of removing her hair covering, and she snatched at it. He tossed it away and went to work on her braid. She was still irate about the night before, but she had to work to maintain her animosity. He seemed different this morning, pleased with himself and frolicking in the sunshine.

In the sunshine. "We have to go inside," she said. "Someone may come by and see you."

"Um." He buried his face in a handful of her hair.

"Hugh, please."

He blew the strands away. "I like it when you beg me."

"Then I beg you. Let us go in. I'll help you."

"I don't need help. I'm almost well."

"Aye," she said doubtfully. She didn't know how that was possible, but she couldn't send him on his way just yet. "The nursing nuns come first thing for their medications, you know that, and—"

Catching her chin, he brought her face down to his and kissed her. It wasn't the nice kiss of the night before, but a bruising kiss, oddly forceful and not in the spirit of playfulness he had previously displayed.

When he let her raise her head, she touched her lips. "What did you do that for? It hurt!"

He didn't answer but stared at her. "Your mouth is swollen."

"I would suppose!" She didn't like his expression; triumph mixed with a rather attentive regard.

Then he rolled her onto her back, one way and then the other. First the straw on the path stuck through her clothing, then her shoulders and hips mashed the small thyme plants and sank into the damp earth. "Have you gone mad? What is wrong—" She heard voices outside the wall, and they were moving this way. "Listen!" He grabbed at her waving hands. "We've got to get you to your feet."

He held her when she would have scrambled up. Just held her.

"Hugh." She tried to extract her fists. "Hugh, you—"

Wharton's voice suddenly boomed out. "There they are!"

And Lady Blanche said, "I told you, Lady Corliss!"

Still held tight against Hugh, Edlyn twisted

around. A great mass of eyes stared at her in shock, horror, and ill-concealed glee from the garden gate. Half the nuns. Some of the monks. Lady Blanche and Wharton. Baron Sadynton. And the abbess, who stood fingering her beads.

7

"I did nothing wrong." Edlyn sat on a bench in the middle of the square and repeated what she'd said many times since this mockery of an inquisition had begun. Every nun in the abbey, every monk in the monastery, every servant, every peasant, and every patient who could hobble stood assembled in a circle around Edlyn and her accusers, and Edlyn imagined the circle was closing.

"Then why do you have mud and straw and green marks on your back?" Lady Blanche looked around, her mouth pinched in triumphant disapproval. "That looks like evidence of wrong to me."

"Because he"—Edlyn pointed at the decorous Hugh sitting across from her—"tried to make it look as if we'd been fornicating in the dirt, that's why. But I tell you, we haven't!"

Lady Corliss sat in the high-backed, cushioned chair that the servants had brought from her room. The abbot stood at her shoulder, lending his authority to the proceedings and his advice should Lady Corliss ask for it. She didn't. She said nothing. Not that she believed Edlyn, not that she didn't; just nothing. She let

Lady Blanche and her wretched servant weave tales of Edlyn's misbehavior without changing expression.

Lady Blanche giggled, high and long. "Why would this man go to such lengths to ruin your reputation?"

It was going to sound stupid, but Edlyn had sworn to tell the truth. "Because he wants to wed me."

From the front of the circle, Baron Sadynton called, "Why would he buy the cow if he's getting the milk for free?"

A gust of jeering laughter from the crowd almost blew Edlyn off her bench, and she struggled with her mortification. She hated the lord. She'd deprived him of his syrup of poppies, and now he took his revenge, relishing it.

A group of men—warriors, for Edlyn recognized the breed—stood back and to one side, watching the proceedings wrapped in a grim, intent silence. Had word spread across the countryside that entertainment was to be had at Eastbury Abbey? Was she to be so disgraced that all of England knew of it? Had she done so badly here that no one would speak for her?

Hugh rose to his feet, and the group of strange men moved closer. "I have begged Lady Edlyn to marry me, and what she says is true. We have never known each other as man and wife. Always have I honored her."

Was his measured testimony supposed to remedy her anguish? He'd destroyed the new life she'd worked to build from the ashes of the old. He'd deliberately put her in the position of having to depend on him, a man and a warrior, to rescue her.

"Who are you?" Lady Blanche asked. "How did you come to our abbey?"

"I was wounded, and the battle still raged. My men fought valiantly still, so my servant brought me." Hugh pointed at Wharton.

Why didn't anyone ask why Wharton had led her pack of accusers to find her in Hugh's arms? No one jeered Hugh. They all respected him—because if they didn't, he had the ability to thrash them. They respected him because he had dishonored her and was still willing to marry her. She'd always known life wasn't fair, but right now, the inequity of it struck her across the face.

Hugh continued. "Fearing for my life, he hid me in the dispensary and forced Lady Edlyn to keep silent and care for me."

"How could he make her keep silent?" Apparently, Lady Blanche wasn't afraid of him, for she smirked at him in disbelief.

Hugh looked at her. Just looked at her.

Until she grew afraid. Until she developed the same frightened respect the others afforded him.

Then he said, "Wharton, tell the lady what you did to Lady Edlyn."

Wharton stepped out of the crowd and into the focus of attention. For the first time since Edlyn had met him, gone was his bravado. As she glared at him, he shuddered as if she'd given him elderberry to clear his bowels. "I held a dagger t' her throat."

"While she remained in the dispensary," Lady Blanche chirped. She might have momentarily let Hugh intimidate her, but she had no such compunction about Wharton. "But when she left the dispensary, she could have told one of us."

"I woulda hunted her down an' killed her."

Lady Blanche tittered. "As if she believed that."

Wharton swung his head toward her and bared his black and broken teeth until Lady Blanche lost both color and audacity.

Edlyn experienced a flush of exultation, then one of

the monks stepped out from the crowd and she sagged. Brother Irving, the monk in charge of the guest quarters, cast a sorrowful glance at her and waited until Lady Corliss nodded permission at him to speak. In a gentle voice, he said, "Lady Edlyn has been sneaking out at night."

No one said a word, but all gazes turned back to her. The group of strange men exchanged glances, and Edlyn held on to the bench with both hands. She would not leap to her own defense. She would not.

"Where has she been going?" Lady Corliss asked.

"I worried about her, so I followed her," Brother Irving said. "She went to the dispensary."

Edlyn lost her struggle to maintain some dignity and bounded to her feet. "I only went when Wharton came and got me. Four nights! And why didn't you say you were awake?"

Brother Irving cleared his throat. "I am not of noble blood, my lady. My father's a baron, and I dare not speak out of place."

Edlyn intercepted a disgusted look from Lady Corliss. She knew Brother Irving would be replaced as doorkeeper.

"Adda has something to say, too." Lady Blanche pulled her stepsister out of the crowd. "Don't you, Adda?"

Adda jerked her arm out of Lady Blanche's hold. Sullen lines marked her face. "Nay. I have nothing to say."

"What do you mean?" Lady Blanche cried. "Don't you want to tell them how Lady Edlyn lied to you about the blood on her apron?"

"Nay."

"What about the things you saw when you spied in the window of the dispensary?" Lady Blanche peered into Adda's face. "Tell them about how Lady Edlyn held the man in her arms and gave him comfort."

"He was unconscious." Adda glared at Lady Blanche. "He didn't even know."

They'd been fighting again, Edlyn realized. Adda's resentment for Lady Blanche occasionally bubbled over into the daily dealings of their lives. When Lady Blanche proved too querulous or demanded too much, Adda stubbornly refused to cooperate and a kind of war ensued.

"You saw them kissing one day." Lady Blanche leaned forward and shook her finger in Adda's face. "Tell them. Tell them, I say!"

"You made me stay out in the rain to spy on them." Adda's voice rose. "I'm not telling anything!"

Lady Blanche reached out and grabbed Adda's wimple and a handful of hair and jerked. Adda went down on her knees with the pain, then twisted around and bit Lady Blanche on the leg. Lady Blanche fell. The crowd closed in, shouting encouragement as if they were fighting dogs.

Edlyn again thanked God for helping her make the decision she'd made eight years ago. It was the right one, she knew.

Lady Corliss didn't say a word; she just walked over to the two older, dumpling-shaped women and stood above them. With last-minute hissing, the women halted their combat. Lady Blanche tried to stand and stumbled on her own hem, and Adda laughed nastily.

"She started it," Lady Blanche said. "You saw that, surely."

Lady Corliss remained quiet.

"You're better to your laying hens than you are to me." Adda got to her feet in slow stages.

"My laying hens are valuable," Lady Blanche retorted. "Which is more than I can say about you."

Lifting her hand for silence, Lady Corliss waited until the two women fixed their attention on her. "It would be better if you were separated until Saint Swithin's Day."

Betrayed into insolence, Lady Blanche said, "You can't do that. Who will care for me?"

"You'll both spend the time in isolation and in fasting," Lady Corliss answered. "Neither of you will want for anything, for there is nothing you will be permitted to want."

If ever Edlyn had wanted her revenge for the slights and insults, she had it now. The cherries in Lady Blanche's cheeks faded as she thought of the days of loneliness and hunger she faced. And Adda, who showed an inbred skill for nosiness, looked only slightly less dismayed.

"For the rest of you," Lady Corliss spoke to the crowd, "there are chores to be done and patients to be served. Please tend to your duties." Every person there bulged with curiosity, but she conceded little when she said, "I will handle this matter alone."

Abbot John stepped forward and spoke in her ear. She answered in equally low tones. He nodded, then turned to the crowd. "Didn't you hear Lady Corliss? Disperse at once."

They grumbled and glanced back longingly, but they did as they were told. All except the warriors, who moved to one side and waited.

Abbot John stared pointedly at them. "Well?"

Who were they? Edlyn didn't like the way they seemed to be of one mind. And when they responded to an unseen signal and moved suddenly out of the square, she liked it even less. They were like birds who flew in formation behind their leader and swerved when he swerved.

She glanced around. But who was their leader?

Abbot John seemed not at all concerned. Probably he'd already inquired about their purpose, and for that reason Edlyn quieted her curiosity. After all, she had more pressing problems than the rumors these travelers would carry with them.

"You two," Abbot John said, indicating his own personal manservants, "carry Lady Corliss's chair inside."

Moving swiftly, the servants obeyed, leaving Edlyn, Hugh, Wharton, and Lady Corliss alone in the square.

With a graceful wave of the hand, Lady Corliss summoned both Edlyn and Hugh, and without waiting to see if they followed, she proceeded toward her office inside the church.

Edlyn hesitated only an instant, then walked after Lady Corliss. She heard Hugh speak to Wharton, telling him to meet the men and go back to the tent, and she wondered briefly at that. What tent? When had he acquired a tent and for what purpose?

Then she stifled her inquisitiveness. She didn't care anything about Hugh. If he had a tent, perhaps that meant he would pack it up and leave.

Gathering a handful of her skirt in her hand, she lifted it to climb the church steps. She squeezed the material into a wad of damp wool and thought, *Hugh leave*? If only she would be that lucky.

His boots sounded behind her, the expensive leather soles thumping on the stone, and she half hoped he would try to take her arm. Not because she needed the assistance, but because she wanted to ram her elbow right into his stomach.

He didn't touch her.

The quiet of the church only fractionally calmed her turmoil. No matter how Lady Corliss decided this case, Edlyn knew a great change had ripped her life apart. As Lady Corliss seated herself behind the rough-hewn table, Edlyn slipped into one of the chairs opposite and tried to take comfort in the fact she belonged here. Hugh did not.

But when he sat in the other chair, she could discern no discomfort in his expression or his pose. The wretched man was at ease anywhere, and that provided her with one more reason to dislike him.

From the way Lady Corliss gazed at him, Edlyn thought perhaps she didn't like him either. "Who are you?" Lady Corliss asked.

"My name is Hugh de Florisoun," he answered readily enough. "I have won a barony and an earldom, with lands enough to support a wife and family, and therefore I beg you for the hand of Lady Edlyn."

He was so smug, sitting there protected by his wealth and his titles, that Edlyn couldn't bear to look at him. With her gaze fixed rigidly on Lady Corliss, Edlyn snapped, "She doesn't have the right to give my hand in marriage."

"Lady Edlyn is right." Lady Corliss sat straight in her chair, her spine not touching the back.

"Did she not, when coming to live in the abbey, vow to obey your dictates?"

How had he known that? Edlyn shot him a glare and saw him relax with a smile. He *hadn't* known it. Not until she'd confirmed it with her fulminating glance. She had better learn to watch herself around him, or her life with him would be—

Nay. The battle wasn't over yet. She wouldn't admit defeat so soon.

"What her vow means, my lord, is that Lady

Edlyn must obey my dictates or be thrown from the abbey. It does not mean I have the right to give her hand in marriage."

"Only that should you command her to and she refuses, she will have to leave." Hugh nodded in satisfaction. "I see."

"That is why I have brought you here to speak to me in private." Lady Corliss obviously disapproved of his confidence. "To see if it's necessary to take such a drastic measure."

"She is compromised," he said implacably.

"I will do what I believe to be the will of the Lord God. It is He whom we must please this day, Lord Hugh, not you and not convention."

Clearly thunderstruck, Hugh watched Lady Corliss from beneath lowered brows. Without a doubt, he had believed he had enforced his will, and he hadn't expected to hear that the situation remained in God's hands.

Mollified by his silence, Lady Corliss said, "Lady Edlyn, tell me everything that has happened starting with the moment you found Lord Hugh in the dispensary."

Edlyn obliged. From the moment she'd seen the broken lock to this morning when she'd been discovered rolling in the dirt with Hugh, she told everything.

Well, not quite everything. She didn't tell about the dragon's blood and how she'd thanked the fairies for their cure. She didn't confess she'd reminisced about the sights and sounds of the barn at George's Cross. She didn't tell about the heat of Hugh's kiss and how much she'd enjoyed it, and she didn't tell how his arrival had awakened something in her, something she thought was dead.

She didn't tell any of those things, but Lady Corliss sensed them anyway.

When she finished, Lady Corliss leaned forward, folded her hands on the table before her, and asked Hugh, "Why did you do these things to discredit Lady Edlyn?"

"I had no wish to discredit Lady Edlyn," he said with evident sincerity. "I only wish to marry her. She is alone. She needs a man to protect her."

Edlyn snorted. "Now there's nonsense if I ever heard it! I grew up as the chattel of first my father, then my husbands. See the protection they've given me."

Hugh took her hand in his before she realized his intention. "I will not fail you."

She jerked and twisted her wrist, trying to get free. "Only when I was forced to fend for myself did I find any security. A security which you have destroyed, I might add!"

He let go of her wrist, and she looked down at the mark his grip had left and rubbed it. Only out of the corner of her eye did she see him stand, and even then she didn't expect him to scoop her up into his arms. She squawked and flapped. "What are you . . . ?"

Sitting down in her chair, he settled her in his lap. He clasped his arms around her waist and held her firmly when she tried to leap to her feet. In that firm, measured tone that so annoyed her, he said, "I will not allow you to escape me, nor will I let you hurt yourself trying."

She tried to elbow him, and he moved her so her back rested against his chest. Grabbing each of her wrists in his opposite hand, he pulled them tight so they were wrapped around her own waist.

"We'll sit still now," he said.

Her legs dangled. She kicked at him, but her soft leather slippers made no impression, and he retaliated with a sharp nip on the shoulder. With a cry, she tried to swing around, but he held her helpless.

"Sit still," he reiterated.

Sit still? On his lap? With her legs resting one on each of his and her rear nestled against his crotch? "I don't have any intention of making you that happy." She tried to wiggle down but succeeded only in moving so she slumped on her spine. His hands, with her wrists still trapped, rested tight under her breasts. She felt stupid and squirmed up again. He helped her, adjusting himself and pulling her close into the same position she'd been in before. Now, however, his lap had developed an uncomfortable bump—long, hard, and impossible to ignore. "Just let me go," she muttered.

"I don't ever intend to let you go." His breath caressed her neck as he spoke. "But most certainly not now. The sight that would be revealed is not proper for a nun's eyes."

Edlyn froze. Lady Corliss. She'd been so involved with wrestling with Hugh, she'd forgotten about Lady Corliss. She'd forgotten about dignity, she'd forgotten about anything but the need to get away from Hugh before he made her want to stay. Her eyes burned with embarrassment as she looked across the table and saw the abbess observing her in the same manner she utilized when observing a patient. Trying to salvage the situation, Edlyn said, "See how ill he treats me?"

"Well, Lady Edlyn." Lady Corliss smiled faintly. "Your lips *are* swollen, and you have a most becoming color in your face." She rose. "You will let me pray for an answer to this dilemma."

She moved no farther than the window that overlooked the square, but she withdrew so completely into prayer she left Edlyn and Hugh alone.

Edlyn had seen Lady Corliss pray before. She was familiar with the warmth of holiness that permeated the air, the fragrance of joy, and the sense of blessed peace. Hugh was not, and he watched keenly as the abbess communicated with God. The result of that prayer, Edlyn knew, would be final, and Edlyn prayed, too. Prayed in a frantic jumble for freedom and for assistance.

But when Lady Corliss moved away from the window, she didn't go to her seat again, as Edlyn expected. She came right to Edlyn. Extracting Edlyn's hands from Hugh's grip, she held them firmly and Edlyn's hopes plunged.

In the tender tone of a mother speaking to her daughter, Lady Corliss said, "I believe that this lord is the answer I have prayed for."

"He is not!" Edlyn's objection was instinctive and accompanied by an attempt to stand—an attempt Hugh easily thwarted.

"Protesting against God's will does not make it less God's will." Lady Corliss seldom rebuked, giving this chiding all the more weight. "I believe it is God's will that you wed this man."

Forgetting where she sat, Edlyn slumped, then straightened again when he rubbed her back.

"Then the Lord remains at my side." Hugh chuckled, well pleased. "I pray to the Lord He continue to hold me in His favor."

His complacency sat ill with Lady Corliss, and she looked straight at him. "God does not take sides, Lord Hugh. He does what is best for us, His children. And I cannot approve of the manner in which you have wooed this gentle lady."

Beneath her, Edlyn felt Hugh's whole body reject Lady Corliss's admonition.

Lady Corliss continued. "Such reckless disregard for her reputation and her peace of mind speaks ill of the man who would keep her as his life's mate. Once damaged, a reputation is not easily repaired, and the fragile trust Lady Edlyn might have shared with you, Lord Hugh, lies shattered at your feet. It is up to you to mend both, for you, with your disregard for the conventions of courtship and kindness, have broken them."

Edlyn could tell he didn't like that. He didn't like any of it. Probably what he really hated was that a woman reproved him; he surely didn't care whether he'd destroyed Edlyn's reputation and her trust. He just wanted his own way and got it by any means he could.

"Nevertheless, Abbot John is prepared to call the banns. They'll be called three—"

Hugh interrupted. "I don't have time for banns."

Now Edlyn stiffened. He'd just been given as ruthless a reproach as she'd ever heard Lady Corliss give, and when she offered him his own way, he claimed it wasn't enough.

Yet he gave an explanation, which was more than she expected. "I've been too long from the battlefield, and I need to claim my new lands before autumn. I need to go as soon as possible."

"I'm not going without my children," Edlyn said. About this, she allowed no room for debate.

Lady Corliss was more concerned with the validity of the marriage. "Banns are necessary. I would not have you discard Lady Edlyn and claim an improper ceremony."

"Then call them three times today and let us wed before the sun sets." He stood, depositing Edlyn carefully on her feet. "Else I'll take Edlyn with me without the ceremony."

Lady Corliss hesitated, then bowed her head. "It shall be as you solicit."

Taking Edlyn's chin in his hand, he leaned toward

her. "Stop glaring at me like that. Our marriage will be propitious, you'll see. Now be a good lass and get cleaned up for our wedding." He straightened and dusted his hand over her head. "You still have weeds in your hair."

"I do hate you." She said it flatly, with the intensity of one who had never laid claim to such emotion before.

He heard it, she guessed, because he blinked. "But why would you?"

His obtuse confusion made her want to scream, but she didn't. She controlled herself enough to answer, "Because you think you're doing right."

He corrected her. "I *know* I'm doing right."

She did scream then, just a little. How could she talk to a man like this? He was even more pigheaded than Robin, and she hadn't thought that was possible.

Robin. She stilled and drew a painful breath. "I won't say aye."

"What?" Lady Corliss asked.

"When?" Hugh looked confused.

"At the wedding ceremony. I won't agree to become your wife." Both of them stared at her stupidly, as if she were some tame house cat who'd suddenly spat in their faces. "I've done that already—been the wife of a warrior."

"Of course you have. Who else would you wed?" Hugh demanded. "A man of the cloth?"

He didn't understand. He'd never understand, and she would just weary herself trying to explain, so she added, "You're rebelling against the king, and I have no wish to be branded the wife of a traitor again."

Lady Corliss gazed at him from top to toe as if she could discern the slant of his loyalties by his appearance. "Are you a traitor?"

For an answer, Hugh walked to the huge Bible that sat on the corner of her desk. Putting his hand on it, he said, "I swear I am not a traitor to the king."

He was staring at Edlyn, but Lady Corliss answered. "That's that, then. You'll have to wed him, Lady Edlyn."

Was he a liar as well as a scoundrel? Edlyn would have said yes only a few moments earlier, but Lady Corliss had a fine sense for those who lied, and she had readily accepted Hugh's vow. *Was* he a traitor? She didn't really care. "I will not," Edlyn said. "He's a *warrior*."

If Lady Corliss understood Edlyn's statement, she showed no indication. "Wed him or not, you cannot remain at the abbey. Your presence has created dissension and turned our thoughts away from our service to God."

Edlyn's guts squeezed tight with pain, but panic drove her. "I've been on the road before."

"And your sons will have to remain here, safe from your influence."

Briefly, Edlyn fought comprehension, but when she understood, she cried, "You can't take my sons!"

"But I can. They are already under the care of our monks, and a woman such as you cannot be allowed to raise children."

Lady Corliss didn't believe in Edlyn's disgrace. Edlyn knew she didn't. But she would enforce God's will, regardless of Edlyn's desire, and she wisely chose the weapon to wield.

Would she throw Edlyn out of the abbey? Would she take Edlyn's sons away from her?

Edlyn knew the answer without a doubt. Hostility and despair mixed in equal parts, but she bridled her defiance, bowed her head, and whispered, "It shall be as you wish."

"As God wishes, child."

She couldn't dislike Lady Corliss, so she glared at Hugh with eyes that teared from the heat of her anger.

And like the cretin he was, he just said, "Wear something pretty."

"To our wedding, you mean?" She took great satisfaction in replying, "I have nothing pretty."

Having decided he had blundered enough, Lady Corliss shoved him away. "I'll find her something. Now go before you ruin all."

Like any good soldier, he comprehended retreat and the need for it, and he left without a murmur.

Edlyn stared at the door he'd closed behind him and said in despair, "You don't understand."

"Actually, I think I do." Lady Corliss put her arm around Edlyn's rigid shoulders and pulled her close. "But there are only the three estates to chose from."

Edlyn stood stiffly in Lady Corliss's embrace. "What do you mean?"

"Your betrothed said it, I think. There are men who labor, men of the church, and men who fight. A lady cannot wed a peasant who coaxes grain from the field, nor can she wed a man who has pledged himself to the church, so who else can you wed but a warrior?"

"Why wed anyone?" Edlyn burst out.

"Lady Edlyn, I have watched you since the day you endowed this abbey and asked me to come and lead it. You're a woman of passionate beliefs, of joys, of sorrows. You don't live life, you revel in it, and you draw people with your warmth. This last year has been difficult for you, not just because of the tragedy of your marriage but because you've had to conform to our order's rules." Lady Corliss chuckled. "I have been glad I didn't have to deal with you as a nun."

"Have I done so badly, then?"

"Not at all, but you've had to restrain the fires within you, and I see them dying from lack of fuel." Tightening her arm briefly, Lady Corliss said, "I've seen the fires raging in you in the last fortnight and wondered what ignited them. I believe it's that man."

"I'm not on fire for him," Edlyn muttered. What was she doing, talking with Lady Corliss about the fire between a man and a woman? The whole subject made her uncomfortable, and she squirmed like a guilty child.

"Marrying him will free you to feel the fire." Lady Corliss released her. "We had best go find something for you to wear."

"Would you really have thrown me out and kept my children?"

Lady Corliss ushered Edlyn out of her office, out of the church, and toward the abbey cloister. "What do you think?"

"I think you are as ruthless as any warrior."

"My thanks, Lady Edlyn." As they walked, Lady Corliss beckoned, and the nuns fell in behind them. By the time they entered the cloister, they were surrounded by ladies of all kinds. A widowed countess, the virgin youngest daughter of an earl, a baron's discarded wife, two ladies whose husbands, like Edlyn's, had chosen the wrong side in a battle fought long ago. The cool, dim common room filled with women, and when Lady Corliss asked for clothing that would befit a bride, their voices broke into a babble of glee. Before Edlyn knew quite what had happened, the door had been barred and she'd been stripped and placed in the tub for the ceremonial bathing.

As she was being scrubbed, the call echoed through the square. The first banns had been called.

The nuns pulled Edlyn out of the tub, dried her

body and her hair, and began the long task of combing the tangles out of the sweep of brown locks. As they worked, they exclaimed at her slenderness after bearing a child. Lord Hugh would want her fattened up, one suggested. Lady Neville, the widowed countess, laughed and said, "I saw him look at her in the square. He seems to find her well enough as she is."

Outside, another call echoed through the square. The second banns had been called.

The nuns brought forth the finery they had hidden away. They dropped a thin white linen shift over her head. It reached her knees and didn't tie. Instead it lay flat and wide against her chest, and a tracery of embroidered vines and leaves along the top etched her skin. After much serious discussion, they narrowed the choice down to two gowns—a cotte with light and dark green stripes that accented her eyes and another that was a plain sweep of delicate blue wool.

"Not green," Lady Neville said firmly. "'Tis a color for a woman of light morals, and there's been too much said about that this day."

Edlyn's ears and cheeks burned fiery red.

Lady Neville looked impatient. "Don't distress yourself, Lady Edlyn. Only the ignorant believed it."

The nuns murmured, some doubtfully, and Lady Corliss saved Edlyn from further embarrassment. "I prefer the blue. It is the color of Our Lady."

The nuns nodded solemnly.

Then she added, "And the open side lacing and center split skirt will surely render Lord Hugh helpless in her hands."

The young virgins gasped. The widowed and discarded didn't even try to hide their laughter.

Another call echoed through the square. All the

banns had been called. Only the ceremony of marriage itself remained.

They hurried now, placing a wimple of lace on Edlyn's head and leaving her hair down as a sign that, although she wasn't a virgin, she was still a virtuous lady. Quite a difference from a few hours ago, she noted bitterly. She had been rescued from her state of sin by a lord with unsubstantiated claims of loyalty and nobility.

The thin hose were white, the shoes of painted leather were too large but very tooled and detailed, so the nuns ignored her complaint and stuffed bits of cloth in the toes. Then she was ready for the ceremony that would mark her as a man's chattel once more.

As they had done in her two previous marriages, they gave her a bouquet of myrtle and rosemary to hold. This time, she threw it down.

"An inauspicious beginning," one of the nuns muttered.

"'Tis not flowers Lord Hugh wants of her." Lady Neville adjusted Edlyn's wimple. "But he'll have to work for what he wants. It's good for a man to have to concentrate on his woman."

The afternoon sun lashed at Edlyn's eyes as she stepped outside. She blinked and raised her hand to her face until she had adjusted to the glare, and when she lowered her hand, she wished she hadn't. Everyone stood in that square. They'd formed a path through the midst of them that led right to the church steps, where the abbot, Wharton, and Hugh stood waiting.

What irked Edlyn was that Hugh had obviously remained calm throughout the afternoon's preparations. He never had a doubt she would do what he desired, and it made her wish she'd held on to the flowers so she could publicly toss them in the dirt. Her impulsiveness had cost her a grand gesture.

Someone nudged her in the back. She didn't move, so someone pushed her, and she stumbled over her own feet as she started down the aisle of watching eyes and grinning mouths.

"I don't want to," she whispered to herself. "I don't want to, I don't want to."

Her rebelliousness reminded her of that first wedding to the old duke. She'd been young and frightened that day, aware she had no choice and helpless to stop the events. Now she felt the same except she wasn't frightened, but the helplessness drove her to glare at Hugh with all the venom she could muster.

His expression, one of carefully maintained affability, retreated to gravity, and he seemed to gain some sense of the task he'd set for himself. How would he placate his bride?

He wouldn't, because she was determined not to be placated. Mounting the stairs, she let her steps drag in obvious protest. He smiled faintly. When she reached him, he took her hands—empty of flowers—nodded to the abbot, and the swearing ceremony began.

When Hugh vowed to care for her even after his death, her toes curled in her too-large shoes.

A warrior. He was a warrior. And he would die like all the rest. Like all the young men Robin had gathered around him. Like Robin himself.

She whispered her vows, and they were wed. A cheer rippled through the crowd, growing as Hugh freed her hands, but only so he could wrap his arms around her waist and bring her close.

"Edlyn." He bent his head and brought his mouth close for the kiss of peace. "Stop pouting," he whispered.

She wasn't pouting. She was crying, and he saw the welling of tears.

"Sweeting, what's wrong?"

He could afford to croon now. He had won everything.

"Sweeting?"

The cheers had subsided to buoyant babblings, but one sharp voice soared above the rest. "My lord, I want to be the first to congratulate you."

It was Baron Sadynton, his meager mouth pinched into an affected smile, and Hugh raised his head like a wolf sniffing danger.

"It's extraordinarily compassionate of you to marry this woman, especially after your actions of last summer. The king must be proud of your peaceful overtures."

Edlyn didn't like Sadynton. Had never liked him. Thought him a whiner and a troublemaker, and she knew he held her responsible for denying him his syrup of poppies. But his satisfaction in this instance made her more than uneasy. It made her ill. She clutched at Hugh's arms, unaware that alarm encouraged her to hold him as he wished.

When Wharton headed toward Sadynton with his fists clenched, she clutched Hugh even harder.

Sadynton backed up and talked faster. "I never thought to see the day the widow of the earl of Jagger would marry the earl of *Roxford*."

Her hands fell to her sides.

"It's not often a woman will wed the man who hanged her husband."

8

Hugh, commander of the royal troops in the West, watched as Edlyn disappeared into the woods.

"Ye going after her?" Wharton asked.

"Nay." Hugh couldn't believe he was saying that, but Lady Corliss's reprimands clung to his mind. Not that he let a mere woman influence his decisions, but the abbess showed unusual wisdom in her decisions. Also—and he admitted this grudgingly—he suspected the abbess might comprehend the workings of Edlyn's mind better than he did. "Let her go."

"What?" Wharton danced around like a rooster plucked of its tail feathers. "But ye *didn't* hang him."

Hugh snorted. "Not personally." But he had captured Robin, earl of Jagger, and sent him into the prince's hands, where he'd been executed. That was the reason why, even after he'd regained enough strength to protect himself from assassins, he'd remained quiet. He'd hoped to lay claim to Edlyn before she discovered his identity.

A real claim. A physical claim. The kind of claim no woman could forget or dismiss.

He responded to the thought of placing that physical claim on Edlyn with a hard shudder of desire.

Nay, he couldn't let her wander alone in the woods as she wished. He had to make sure she would return to him, willingly or not. "Wharton, you know her best. Go after her. Keep out of her sight, yet keep her in yours. I'm not comfortable with her wandering the woods alone."

"If ye'd go after her yerself, ye wouldn't have t' have me sneaking around like a mole after a worm," Wharton protested.

"You flatter neither yourself nor the lady. She'll be better after a brisk walk, then I can explain my actions to her."

Wharton scoffed. "Don't explain t' women. Just give 'em a bop on th' head an' they're better fer it."

"I'll give you a bop on the head if you don't get after her," Hugh answered. "And I'll thank you to keep your marriage advice to yourself."

"Been married more often than ye," Wharton replied insolently.

Hugh knew his man well. "And how many of your wives are you still married to?"

Glancing at the abbot, Wharton lowered his voice. "Two fer sure. Mayhap three."

"I am reassured," Hugh said sarcastically. "Now go."

With a nod, Wharton started along the path Edlyn had taken in her flight from her new husband.

Hugh called, "Remember, she is my lady and the greatest treasure of my soul. Treat her as such."

Wharton raised his hand in acknowledgment.

The nuns stood at the back of the crowd, and Hugh heard one say plaintively, "But we didn't get to throw the wheat."

Wheat for fertility. Wheat for increase. Wheat for a son of his from Edlyn's body. Aye, he wanted that ceremony with the wheat, but Lady Corliss shepherded the nuns toward the cloister and they obeyed as good women should. By God's gloves, when Lady Corliss spoke, *he* would obey, too. The woman was an autocrat—and a holy woman.

Hugh's men lined themselves along the bottom of the stairs, and Hugh started toward them. They were his own personal troops, the men he had gathered around him through the years. A dozen knights, twenty squires, and the menservants for them all, they had remained in the area after the battle, hiding themselves and Hugh's possessions on Wharton's instruction for fear of giving away Hugh's position. Now they had gathered for his wedding and watched solemnly the scene that played before their gazes.

As he descended the stairs, he spotted Baron Sadynton watching him with a satisfied sneer. Without a thought, Hugh changed directions, planted his fist right in Sadynton's face, and before Sadynton had even toppled, strode into the crowd of his men.

They closed ranks and walked him toward his newly resurrected camp. The usual marital congratulations seemed inappropriate when the bride had abandoned the groom, and Hugh understood that. "Come, men," he called. "Let us go speak together."

"My lord." Hugh's squire, a young Welsh boy of thirteen by the name of Dewey, took Hugh's hand and kissed it fervently in a gesture of respect and relief. "We despaired of your life until Wharton arrived to reassure us of your good health."

"It was not my time to die yet." Hugh freed his hand, then ruffled the lad's hair. Turning, he glanced over the group. "Where's Morven?"

Dewey sighed and kicked the ground, and Hugh rubbed his forehead. "He was too young for such a fate. And Sir Ramsden?"

Dewey shook his head dolefully.

"A seasoned warrior, lost to us now." Hugh was well aware of the gap Sir Ramsden's death would leave in his small band. No one worked with the horses better than Sir Ramsden, and he had been a faithful companion for many years.

The youthful squire Morven hadn't been with them long enough to make an impression, but if anything Hugh mourned him the more. Sir Ramsden had lived a full life and had died with a sword in his hand. Morven had been nothing but a lad, all gangly legs and jutting arms, and Hugh muttered, "I should have worked with him more."

Dewey heard him, for he quickly replied, "Nothing could have saved him, my lord. Three seasoned knights attacked him. I tried to reach his side but was too late."

"Three knights?" Hugh's strides lengthened. "Why would they bother? The lad had nothing for them to steal."

Sir Philip, new in Hugh's troop but a seasoned warrior nonetheless, answered. "They attacked because he stung them like a persistent wasp, keeping them at bay when they would have taken your fallen carcass."

Dewey turned on Sir Philip with a hiss, but the knight lifted his hand to silence him. "The lord had to know. He would mourn Morven more if he thought he had died a useless death than to know he died for love of Lord Roxford."

Lord Roxford. That was he, although Hugh wanted to look around and see this lord of whom everyone spoke. He was new to this earl-homage and found it still staggered him on occasion.

"In sooth," he said, "Sir Philip is right. It helps ease the grief of his death to know the lad died helping our cause." Yet still he remembered Morven's big worshiping eyes following him everywhere, and he wished he'd left the lad with his mother. True, there had been nothing but poverty and starvation ahead of them, but at least Morven wouldn't now be rotting in the ground. "You did get him buried?"

"Aye, my lord. I took care of it myself," Sir Philip answered.

Another lad trudged with them, and Hugh called to him. "How did you fare in the battle, Wynkyn?"

"'Twas magnificent, my lord." His words were hardy but his tone faint.

Hugh lifted an eyebrow at Dewey.

"It made him vomit." Dewey answered the unspoken question.

Intercepting the nasty glance Wynkyn sent Dewey, Hugh asked, "Is that all? In my first battle, I sweated so much from fear I lost my grip on the sword and almost slashed off my own leg."

"I couldn't sleep for nights after my first battle." Sir Philip grimaced and smoothed his gray hair off his forehead. "I kept hearing the screams of the wounded, and I hated the crunch the horses' hooves made when they stepped on the bodies."

Hugh's chief adviser, Sir Lyndon, had made his way to Hugh's side, and he smiled with all his considerable charm. "Ah, to me it is the sweet sound of battle."

"Really?" Hugh shuddered. "I still hate that."

Wynkyn paled. "Does it get better? The abomination of it, I mean."

Walking over to the lad, Hugh wrapped his arm around Wynkyn's neck and tugged him off-balance while ruffling his hair. "It's always dreadful, but some-

how you get used to it. Unless it's really a bloody battle, of course. Then you're back puking your guts up."

He released Wynkyn. The lad would do. His father,
the earl of Covney, had been concerned that Wynkyn's
dreamy air would shatter at the first taste of combat,
but Wynkyn had held up well and Hugh would send a
letter of reassurance to the earl.

Forgetting Wynkyn, he looked at the looming fab-
ric walls of his tent with fierce gratification. He had
feared he'd lost it when he disappeared from the battlefield, but here it was. He'd seen chambers in a palace
with less room than his tent, but on the frequent occa-
sions when it rained and the wind blew cold, he hosted
strategy sessions for his whole troop. He kept a table,
camp stools, his camp bed, and trunks filled with blankets and clothes for the squires should they need them,
which as boys they frequently did.

Sir Lyndon stepped beneath the black felt roof that
protected the entrance and held the flap back invit-
ingly. "Would you care to rest while you await the
return of your bride?"

"Nay. I would have refreshment while you recount
all you know of the battle past and give me your
reports of our enemy's movements." Hugh needed to
know, and besides, he couldn't rest until he had Edlyn
within his grasp again.

Sir Lyndon tied back the flap. "When you disappeared during the battle, we were discomfited, my lord,
and I fear we failed to guard your possessions as we
should. After the battle, marauders stole much from
you, but I would offer my own camp bed for your comfort. It will be better than the hard floor."

"My thanks, Sir Lyndon, but of what use is a narrow cot to a newly married man?" Hugh accepted a
goblet of ale from Dewey and swallowed the liquid in

one long gulp, ignoring Sir Lyndon's lifted brow. He
knew what Sir Lyndon thought—that a warrior should
have better control over his wife. But while he had long
treasured Sir Lyndon's advice in battle or siege, he
remembered the pale, beaten aspect of Sir Lyndon's
wife and the suspicious aspects of her death, and he
dismissed any claim Sir Lyndon might make about
domestic peace. "Dewey will instead make us a wide
pad of skins and blankets on the floor."

Sir Lyndon snapped his fingers and Dewey hurried
to obey.

Hugh settled himself on a camp stool outside in
the shade of his tent's overhang. From here he could
watch for Edlyn's return. Around him, squires placed
stools according to each knight's rank and the confidence Hugh held in him, and his knights seated themselves.

There was a general clearing of throats, then Hugh,
earl of Roxford, demanded an accounting of his men.

"They fought like demons, my lord, especially
when they thought you were dead." Sir Lyndon flexed
his hand as if he recalled the agony of holding a sword
for too long. "But actually, 'twas all to the good, for de
Montfort's men overextended themselves and we were
able to divide the army and conquer those who didn't
flee."

Hugh sipped from his refilled goblet and looked at
Sir Philip. "We took hostages?"

"Aye, and shipped them off to the prince for justice
after stripping them of their armor and horses." Sir
Philip smiled, well pleased with their haul. "We've dis-
tributed the wealth evenly, my lord, and left you what
we thought you would desire. Should you decide differently, we'll give up whatever you wish."

Hugh smiled, too. His years as a landless knight

had given him an appreciation for the tradition of stripping defeated foes of their belongings. Many was the time he'd eaten off the money he'd made selling knightly trappings back to his enemies after a tournament or battle. This time, no such offer was made. Those who fought for Simon de Montfort had given up their rights to their property. And some, like the earl of Jagger, had given up their lives.

Hugh glanced toward the forest not far from the tent. Where was she? How long would she sulk? She wouldn't keep him waiting too long, surely; the sun rapidly approached its nadir, and night in the woods was a fearsome experience.

"We missed your leadership on the battlefield," Sir Lyndon said. "If not for your early wisdom in planning our maneuvers, we would have been sore pressed after you were wounded."

Hugh didn't answer. He didn't like Sir Lyndon's barrage of compliments. He didn't like that their friendship had changed from one between equals to one between superior and supplicant. When Prince Edward stripped Edmund Pembridge of both his title and his castle and bestowed them on Hugh, Sir Lyndon had begun to regard Hugh with an eye toward profit. Hugh found it disconcerting to be viewed as a cow to be milked.

"Who escaped the battle?" he asked.

"Richard of Wiltshire and his party of mercenaries." Sir Lyndon spit on the ground after saying that name. "Baron Giles of Cumberland. And the clan Maxwell." He would have spit again, but he knew better.

"The clan Maxwell," Hugh repeated. He didn't say so, but he was glad they had escaped.

"I can't understand what they were doing fighting on English soil." Sir Lyndon dared to grumble.

Hugh grunted. "They're Scottish, aren't they? The Scottish love to see the English fight among themselves, because the Scottish always make a profit off our wars. And why shouldn't the Maxwell take sides? If the prince wins and the king is freed, they can retreat over the border into Scotland and live off the plunder they've taken. If de Montfort wins, they'll have the pick of any loyal English lord's castle."

"You consorted with them, didn't you?" Sir Lyndon said.

"After they captured me in battle, I lived in Scotland for almost a year," Hugh acknowledged.

Swept by curiosity, Dewey didn't realize that a squire should never interrupt. "Did someone ransom you, or did you escape?"

"Neither." Hugh looked each man in the face as he answered. "They let me go."

Sir Philip stared in fascination. He hadn't been with them long enough to have heard this story. But Sir Lyndon avoided Hugh's gaze. Hugh's year with the Maxwells occurred before they met, and Sir Lyndon seemed to wish Hugh would forget it—or, at least, stop talking about it.

But Dewey pressed for an explanation. "The Scots let you go? I thought the Scots are barbarians who roast their captives if they can't make a profit off of them."

"So they are," Hugh agreed. "Although I never saw anyone roasted, they do make slaves of their unransomed captives."

Dewey knelt by Hugh's stool. "They made you a slave?"

"And made me turn the grindstone in their mill," Hugh said. "I was chained, and the man in charge told me I was better than a horse and dumber than an ox."

"He thought you were dumb?"

Dewey didn't wonder about the "better than a horse" part, Hugh realized, and that was a tribute to his strength. "Aye, he thought I was dumb. That was his first mistake. Letting me off the chain to fight in their championships was his second. I beat everyone there, and when the laird took me into his castle, the miller found himself buying an ox."

Dewey's eyes bulged. "Then what happened?"

"I served the Scottish lord—Hamish Maxwell, by name—until I rendered him such service he let me go." Hugh's men shuffled their feet and cleared their throats, embarrassed for him that he had served such a lowly creature as a Scottish lord. Hugh didn't care. To Dewey, he said, "That is why, to this day, I can speak Scottish, eat haggis, and sing every clan song from start to finish. 'Tis good to know your enemies, Dewey—never forget that."

"Aye, my lord."

"Now," Hugh said, "I smell meat roasting, and I've had too little of that this last moon. Would you bring me something to eat?"

Dewey jumped to his feet, chagrined that he'd had to be nudged into doing his duty. "As you wish, my lord. We've put together a wedding feast for you and your new lady."

As the squire disappeared toward the fires set among the tents, Sir Lyndon said, "Too bad your new wife isn't here to share in it."

Hugh ignored his counselor and looked again to the woods. Had he made a mistake by letting her go? Would pride make her stay longer in the forest than was wise? She'd already demonstrated an overabundance of regard for the wisdom of her actions.

In sooth, he could depend on Wharton to watch over her.

"So the rumors are true." Sir Philip combed his beard with his fingers. "You lived with the Scots. Are they truly the barbarians of legend, or are they nothing more than superb fighting men?"

Hugh grinned at Sir Philip's choice of words. "Nothing more than superb fighting men," he said. "Before you go into battle against them, have the priest give you last rites and pray you don't need them."

"I always do, my lord. I always do."

Hugh studied Sir Philip. He was a quiet man, older, and at his age nothing could make him Hugh's best fighting knight. He had lost his youthful quick reflexes and he had only one eye. Yet Sir Philip still lived, he still fought, and Hugh had come to treasure his thoughtful advice, both before and after battle. Hugh needed to raise Sir Philip's status in the hierarchy of his knights, but for now he said only, "Where have the enemy retreated?"

Sir Philip opened his mouth, but Sir Lyndon hastened to reply first. "The barons who support Simon de Montfort scattered. De Montfort himself is in the area of his stronghold at Kenilworth. Most of the others have moved to the north. Richard remains close—he's besieging Castle Juxon."

"I told Juxon to strengthen his defenses. I hope he listened," Hugh said dispassionately. The earl of Juxon was the kind of nobleman he most disliked. Juxon had been born with lands and through his own negligence allowed them to fall into ruin. He squawked loudly that the prince should protect him since he had remained loyal, yet he sent less than the minimum of knight service he owed while he lounged in his great hall impregnating his serving girls. Nay, he'd get no assistance from Hugh, who'd got his winnings the hard way.

"Easy pickings." Sir Lyndon dismissed Castle

Juxon. "Richard is the most ruthless mercenary I've ever had the misfortune to face, and the earl—he's a fool."

"I'll not argue with you there." A movement at the edge of the forest brought Hugh to his feet. Wharton approached at a run, and Wharton wouldn't run for less than an emergency.

Shoving Lyndon aside, Hugh met Wharton just outside the circle of his knights. Wharton panted in huge gasps, his great chest working like a bellows. "Master . . . master . . . they've got her."

Hugh grew cold at the ragged note of panic in Wharton's voice, and he wrapped his hands around Wharton's arms. "Who's got her?"

"Thieves. Rogues. Mercenaries. Got her. Took her. Headed south."

Hugh dropped Wharton as if he were a cold-blooded snake. Captured? Edlyn was captured? Impossible! She was a woman under his protection, and he would never have failed so fully.

"Master."

But he had. Fear exploded in his chest. His fingers tingled with it, his head swelled.

"Master."

And rage—God's glove, how he wanted to bellow his rage, to paw the ground and charge off after her.

"Master."

Hugh looked down at Wharton.

"Ye may slit me throat fer failure, if ye wish."

At the sight of Wharton's bared neck, Hugh gained control. Bellowing, pawing the ground, giving vent to his emotions would accomplish nothing. His men all stood now, staring at Wharton and at him, prepared to go to battle on his command. They'd done it before, this sudden preparation to attack or defend, and they all understood what Hugh would do, and their duty, without words.

As confidently as if emotion had never touched him, Hugh said, "Let's go rescue my lady, then."

They stirred into motion. Someone gave Wharton a drink and his stool while Dewey and Lyndon—usually it was Dewey and Wharton—brought Hugh his hauberk and weapons and prepared him for battle. Someone had gone to get his destrier, too, he knew, and the thought of settling into the saddle of that mad warhorse calmed him as nothing else could do.

But when they brought him his gentle traveling palfrey instead, he found the rage had not retreated so very far. In a tight, controlled voice, he asked, "What do you expect me to do with that?"

"Can't ride a destrier where we're goin'," Wharton said. His breath had been restored, but he kept his message brief. "Anyway, we lost your Devlin during the battle."

"Dead?" Hugh demanded.

"Aye, master."

Another strike against the rebels. Devlin had been the best destrier he'd ever owned, and he wanted to catch the worms who had murdered his magnificent beast. But since he couldn't, he would take out his ire on the men who had dared steal his wife.

His wife. His fists clenched. Edlyn.

As soon as Dewey had finished belting the sword around Hugh's waist, Hugh said, "Follow me, then, for I'm going to rip the hearts out of these renegades with my bare hands, and their bloody carcasses will warn all men not to ever steal a woman for fear she is *my wife.*"

*   *   *

The fire flickered in the clearing, burning bright in spite of the mist of rain that had descended with the night. Hugh crept through the underbrush, climbed over boulders, every sense on the alert, and focused on that one light in the dense dark of the forest. There he would find his wife, and he feared for her fate with a deep and abiding fear.

Would he find her raped by an endless parade of men who valued women less than sheep? Would he find her beaten, taken to task for her unending impertinence, and treated to the taste of a man's brutal fist?

Would he find her dead?

Around him he could hear his men moving with him, but he had instructed them to stay back until he had rescued Edlyn. He wanted a chance to shield her from the stares of his men—and if it was too late, he wanted the chance to kill each and every one of the mercenaries responsible for her death.

The clearing before him seemed unusually quiet for a camp of eight men. Wharton had reported that number, but a silence hung over the forest. Occasional moans sounded on the still air, and Hugh heard his men muttering as they reacted to the unearthly noises. These weren't fairies. They weren't anything he understood, but he didn't care. He cared only about Edlyn.

Close to the clearing, Hugh parted the brush. Wiping the drips of water from his face, he surveyed the area. He couldn't see any shapes moving close to the fire, yet the fire must have been tended recently or else it would have been smothered by the rain. The fire and the lack of visible targets made him even more uneasy. Had these men posted guards? Did the mercenaries know they were about to be attacked? And where was Edlyn?

Sweet mother of God, where was Edlyn?

The panic grew in him, dark and smothering. *He* had let her go. *He* had made the decision to allow her time to adjust to the idea of being his wife. If she were dead, it was his fault. No one's but his.

Those lumps at the far side of the clearing must be the men, lurking in the shadows, waiting in anticipation of his attack. He would give them what they wanted. Steel rang as he unsheathed his sword. With a roar of fury, he leaped out of the woods and into the light. Holding his blade high, he raced toward the unmoving shapes. Behind him, he heard his men, surprised by his unforeseen charge, fumble with their weapons and tumble out of the bushes. He'd never done something so stupid, so unplanned, but he'd never been responsible for the death of his wife before. He'd never lost the woman he sought to save.

As he reached the shapes, he swung his sword, then almost jerked his arm out of its socket as he tried to pull back.

Stones. They were nothing but stones. The blade nicked one boulder. The force of the blow sent a shiver up his wrist, and he heard the snap as he put a notch in the fine steel.

He swore, a long string of French and English curses, and swung back to face the fire.

His men milled about, but no enemy remained here to face Hugh's ire. Where were they? And where was Edlyn?

"They've moved on, I guess, master." Wharton stood off to the side, well away from the reach of Hugh's sword. "We'd best—"

A figure moved out of the shadow of the trees, and in unison every man there swung around and faced—

"Edlyn!" Hugh ran toward his wife, grasped her,

pulled her into him. He held his sword in one hand and kept her safe with the other.

She stood without swaying in his arms, patting him as if he were the one in need of comfort. He swung her toward the light of the fire and stared at her face. One long scratch marred the perfection of her cheek, and he wiped it with his thumb.

"A branch hit me," she explained.

"Are you . . . ill?" He was a plain-spoken man, but he found himself unable to do more than stammer. "Did they . . . ?"

"Nay."

He lifted his sword. "I'll kill them anyway."

Calmly she freed herself. Her torn cotte had dark splotches along the hem, but the lacing at the sides seemed to be intact. Grasping his wrist, she extricated his sword and handed it to Wharton. "Not while you're holding me, I pray you."

"How did you escape their . . . ?" Wharton asked. "Did you have to hurt . . . ?"

Embarrassed, he faltered, and Hugh noted that even his hardened man-of-arms couldn't speak of such intimate matters.

Edlyn tried to smile at Wharton and at the men who gathered around. "I made them sick," she said.

"What?" Hugh sounded as stupid as he felt.

"I convinced them I'm a good cook—which I am, you know. I make quite a good stew and have a light touch with the . . ." Something she saw in his face must have warned her to stop chatting. "They grabbed me in the forest and took me with them. They'd been waiting for days for the woman they wanted, they said, and they were half-starving, poor things."

"Poor things," Hugh repeated.

"I told them I was the herbalist at the abbey, and

not the lady they wanted, but they wouldn't let me go. They said they were under orders—"

A growl rumbled in Hugh's chest and was echoed by his men.

"Well, it doesn't matter what they said." Speaking as quickly as she could, she said, "I convinced them we would ride better on full stomachs. So one of them snared a family of coneys and I wandered along and plucked herbs and berries, and when we got here and they were satisfied we weren't being followed, they let me cook."

Hugh tried to answer, but he couldn't even form the words, so Wharton asked, "Is that how ye made them sick?"

"Aye, with elderberry bark and roots. Given in sufficient amounts, it causes a cramping of the gut followed by an uncontrollable release of the bowels."

Wharton looked around at the woods that pressed close. "Are ye saying those scoundrels are out there squattin' over a log?"

"Can't you hear them groaning?"

Incredulous, Wharton asked, "Why didn't ye come back t' us?"

"I thought you would come to recover me, and if you hadn't, I would have returned at first light. I didn't trust myself to find my way back in the dark." She turned to Hugh and rebuked him. "So you see, it's not necessary to fight at every opportunity. Sometimes guile will suffice."

Hugh couldn't believe it. He couldn't believe it. He'd charged a tumble of boulders to rescue his woman—and she'd already saved herself. He'd been in a lather of fear, and she'd been waiting for him to arrive! Alone, she'd routed her attackers.

He looked around at his men; their gazes were

glued to Edlyn in blatant disbelief. He looked at Wharton, who stood scratching his head with one hand while holding Hugh's sword in the other. And in a low, controlled tone, Hugh said, "Men, round up the knaves as they come in from the woods and take them to the constable. He'll know what to do with them."

"But they're hungry," Edlyn said as if that should excuse their villainy.

"Would you leave them free to capture some other poor woman and have them use her as they didn't get to use you?" Hugh demanded.

She faltered.

"I wouldn't worry about the fate of those men if I were you." He jerked her close against him. "I'd worry about your fate —and my revenge."

At the edge of the clearing, the noble knight sat on his horse and observed.

He was furious. Nothing, *nothing* had gone as planned. He'd patiently waited for her for a year. He'd had her watched from a distance. He'd been prepared to take her when the time was right —and instead he'd received a message from his men saying she had been wed.

And to his enemy! To Hugh de Florisoun! To the man who dared think he could take the place of his better.

He'd abandoned everything, all his schemes, and ridden as quickly as he could to the abbey, only to find rumors flying that the bride had been kidnapped.

By his own men. He'd laughed then, sure the devil himself was on his side.

But nay. Edlyn had defeated him, as she had

defeated him so many times before. She knew how he felt. This was a betrayal, nothing less.

He would have his revenge, and then he would have her—and Hugh de Florisoun would be driven to hell on the point of Edmund Pembridge's sword.

9

Edlyn didn't know a lot about Hugh de Florisoun, but she knew that right now he was angry. He tromped her through the woods in the dark, in the rain, keeping her close and holding the branches away from her face as if he could heal the mark on her cheek with his care.

Yet he was so unyielding she thought a good wind would topple him. Could she lighten the atmosphere? Would a few words, spoken in a normal tone, lessen his displeasure? She could try. "Are we walking back to the abbey?" she asked.

"You're not going back to the abbey tonight."

He hadn't answered her question, which was *how* they would be traveling, but he'd raised a lot of new ones. Yet his repressive tone made her hesitate, and while she did, he stopped and raised a hand to his mouth. An owl hooted, and if she hadn't felt the vibration of his chest against her shoulder, she would never have realized the sound had originated from him.

Guiding her once more, he moved toward a clearing. She heard the stomp of horses' hooves and their rumble as they blew a greeting, and a youth spoke right beside them. "My lord, I heard your call. Did you recover her?"

"Aye, I have her." Hugh's arm tightened. "The men are rounding up the mercenaries, and I'm taking her back to camp."

To camp. They were going to his camp. Edlyn tried to cheer herself. If she waited long enough, mayhap Hugh would answer every question in this roundabout manner.

The youth brought a palfrey forward, and Hugh released her long enough to vault into the saddle.

"Shall I give your lady my horse, my lord?" the youth asked.

"She'll ride with me." Hugh sounded gruff.

Well aware of the shape of the saddles, Edlyn tried to back up, but Hugh bent far down, picked her up with his hands under her armpits, and swung her in front of him.

She couldn't help exclaiming, "You'll hurt your back."

The only answer she got was muffled laughter from the youth on the ground.

It wasn't a good fit. She didn't know what to do with her legs—astride? to the side?—so Hugh arranged her, lifting her and placing her as he wished. She ended up sideways across his body and held up so the saddle wouldn't pinch.

The rain fell harder. The darkness loomed so thick she blinked and couldn't tell the difference. One of Hugh's arms lifted her bottom while his hand cushioned her from the thrust of the stiff leather. His other arm held her under her thighs. She wanted to ask who was guiding the horse, but his body moved as he controlled the palfrey with his knees. "Who trained this horse?" she asked.

"Sir Ramsden. He handled my horses."

"He does so no longer?"

"He is dead in the last battle."

His brevity convinced her of Hugh's displeasure with her. So she supposed if she wanted to lighten his mood, she ought to ask him about that battle. Men loved to talk about battle. They belabored every slash of the sword and every arrow's flight. And if they weren't talking about a battle past, they could be coaxed to talk about a future battle, or even a legend about a battle.

Unfortunately, she'd already heard it all, and she didn't care to hear Hugh's stories. She'd sworn she would never again listen to battle tales, and marrying a warrior—sweet Mother, another warrior!—only reinforced her determination.

There had to be another way. "Can your poor horse carry us both?" It was a stupid question; obviously it could. It was.

He ignored her.

"Your arm must ache from the strain of holding me. Would you like me to walk?"

He stopped her almost before she tried to free herself. "Save your breath," he said. "You'll need it."

She didn't like that. What did he mean? Was he going to beat her? Hugh didn't seem the type to beat a woman for being kidnapped and causing him trouble, but really, how much did she know about him?

Robin had hit her in anger when she'd complained about his tomcat habits. Her duke had hit her in frustration when he couldn't get his manhood to function. Hugh was her husband now, and he'd spoken of revenge.

Lights shone through the trees. When they broke out of the forest, she saw the abbey ahead. He'd said they weren't going to the abbey, but . . . he turned the palfrey toward the stable.

Of course. He had to get his horse under cover. The stable boy came running out and held the palfrey's head while Hugh eased Edlyn down. When her feet touched the mounting block, he dismounted himself and took her hand. Tossing a coin to the boy, he dragged her through the muck toward a community of tents. They hunkered down around a fire like fat maidens around a well, and Edlyn remembered seeing them in her flight into the woods. She'd been so upset she hadn't paid attention to them or realized they housed Hugh's men.

Another youth—the fire-tender, Edlyn guessed— stepped out of the shadows at their approach. "My lord, you found her! Is she well?"

Hugh ignored his query. "Put a light in my tent."

"Aye, my lord." The lad popped a quick bow and took off at a run.

Trying to reassure him, Edlyn called, "They didn't hurt me."

If Hugh had been a bear, he would have snarled. "He'll hear the story soon enough."

He moved toward the largest tent, a behemoth of felt and ropes. The youth walked through the front flap with a lighted candle and darted out empty-handed, and Hugh didn't even thank him. She'd have to take his manners in hand . . . if he didn't beat her.

Edlyn paused to take off her shoes before she entered the tent, but Hugh said, "There's no delaying your fate, my lady," and hustled her inside.

Her housewifely soul cringed at the marks his great boots made on the woven hemp rug.

The large room was spotless. Trunks lined the wall. A table held the lighted candle. A large pallet of skins lay on the floor in the corner, the edge turned back in invitation . . . she jerked her attention away.

Obviously someone worked hard to keep the area tidy for the master. Pointing to the mud, she said, "That's going to have to be cleaned up."

He barely glanced down. "Not tonight. No one's coming in here tonight."

He turned to her, and for the first time she saw his face.

He *was* angry. He was so angry. "Let us get this out of the way now," he said. "I captured your husband and sent him to London to be executed. 'Tis a piece of misfortune I was the commander to do so, but he was ripe for hanging. He took chances, Edlyn, that no knight should have taken."

"I know." She did know. Robin had thought himself invincible. He'd embraced danger much as he'd embraced women—indiscriminately and with great appetite.

"He almost threw himself into my clutches."

"I believe you."

He loomed over her so quickly she didn't even have time to stumble back. "Then why did you run away?"

Would he understand? "Because you're a warrior just like him."

He *didn't* understand. "I'm not just like him. I'm nothing like Robin of Jagger."

"Except that you live for combat."

"I don't live for combat."

"What would you do if you couldn't fight? If you'd lost a leg or an eye and could never ride into battle again?"

He flinched. "That won't happen."

"Even now, after you were so badly wounded, you

still can't wait to get back into the field, can you? Your hand itches to take up your sword. You could scarcely wait to attack those outlaws tonight!"

"Because they had you." He wrapped his hands around her chin and lifted her head. "It doesn't matter why you run or who takes you prisoner, I'll always get you back and I'll always take vengeance on those who hurt you. I'm sorry I captured your husband, but that's nothing between you and me, so tell me you're angry and let me soothe your ire, and then let us go on with our marriage."

He was right. Capturing Robin had nothing to do with them, and she didn't blame him for Robin's death.

And she was right. He didn't understand why she refused to lavish her love on him. "I'm not angry."

He was so big, and he smiled at her widely. "For tonight, I'll let you get away with that falsehood. Because—I am." Turning to one of the trunks, he flung it open, gathered up an armful of different kinds of cloth, and placed them on the table. Lifting the tent flap, he stepped outside.

She stood in the middle of the tent and shivered and wrung her hands. *Would* he hurt her? She couldn't contemplate the humiliation of going to the abbey and asking for help in bandaging her own wounds. Was there an escape from this trap?

A rush of fresh air alerted her to his return, and she looked at him with haunted eyes.

He was naked.

Huge and naked.

Ready and naked.

It wasn't his anger she should be fearing. It was his passion.

Her head whirled as she tried to adjust. She'd been dreading him, but from what she could see, he was just like any other man. He had nothing on his mind except a wedding night.

Well, not exactly like any other man. And not exactly on his mind. But she'd been married before. Why should she care? It was just an act, quickly over and pleasurable only to the man.

Her body tightened as she gazed at Hugh. He must have stood out in the rain, for all trace of mud had disappeared. The blond of his hair had turned dark with water, and moisture gathered on the sides of his face where his beard now showed one day's growth. Drops of water clung to the light dusting of hair that covered his legs and his arms. They collected at the top of the arrow of hair on his chest and ran in rivulets past his navel down to . . .

Who was she kidding? She loved this part of marriage. It had been the only thing she'd missed—and she'd missed it for longer than she cared to remember.

"Take off your clothes."

It wasn't a request; it was a demand. His rough voice betrayed anger still, and she didn't understand.

"My squire helped me undress. Shall I help you?"

He took two big steps forward and she stumbled back. "But you're furious!"

"Aye." She'd lost her wimple, so he went to work on her cotte, slipping the sleeves over her shoulders and letting the garment drop to the ground. "I almost got you killed today." He stepped back and stared, then smiled. "You're soaked all the way to the skin."

She looked down. The white linen shift had been transparent before; now, plastered against her skin, it showed every curve, every dimple. Her nipples, puckered against the chill, thrust themselves toward him like two blushing wantons begging for attention. The cloth had just slipped between her thighs, and the mound of brown hair struggled to free itself from entrapment. Independent of her volition, her whole body spoke, and too obviously he comprehended every message.

"'Twasn't your fault I ran off." She'd done better at other conversation gambits, but never under more pressure.

"I let you go." Reaching out, he molded her breasts in his hands. His forefingers rubbed the highest point, creating a sweet friction. "You're cold."

"Nay."

He chuckled, the first time she'd heard that common sound of mirth from him. "You're shivering, and your lips are blue."

Reaching down, he snagged the shift's hem. With his fingertips on her skin, he raised the shift. His eyes blazed with fierce pleasure and that strange fury. He liked making her uncomfortable, he liked stripping her, and she shut her eyes to seal out the sight of his intrusion.

As if that helped. She knew his every movement. His touch alerted her as he skimmed her thigh, then her hip, her waist. As physical as his touch, his gaze sought out her bare parts and relished them, and she didn't know now whether she shivered from cold or from embarrassment.

Suddenly with both his hands he stripped the shift off over her head. Her eyes sprang open as he cupped her breasts again.

"Look at them. They're beautiful, and they're *mine*."

His possessiveness brought the sound of choked amusement to her lips. "So you said."

Startled, he asked, "When?"

"When you were sick. You grabbed me and said, 'Mine.'"

Tilting back his head, he laughed out loud. "Did I? Did I indeed?" The water was drying on his skin, each drop evaporated by his heat. "If you were going to run, you should have done it then." He dropped to his knees in front of her.

She tried to scramble back. He caught her with one arm around her rear. In a soothing tone, he said, "I'm just going to take off your hose."

Her hose. The only things left between her and . . .

"I don't think I can do this."

"Aye, you can."

He looked up at her, and she cursed the stupid impulse that had led her to reveal her anguish when he was kneeling at her feet. Pressing her legs together didn't lessen her discomfiture, nor did staring out into space above his head. He was examining her, and he probably saw every flaw. After all, she wasn't fifteen anymore.

Then he said the same thing, but with a totally different intonation. "You're not fifteen anymore, are you? You're not that scrawny little lass who used to follow me around. You're a woman now."

She didn't answer. She didn't know what to say.

"Aye, you're going to give me what I want. Call it a debt fair paid."

He said that in a more businesslike manner, and she wondered how to get him back to that other, more worshipful tone.

He sat back on his heels. With both his hands behind her, he separated her legs, and before she realized his intentions, he tasted her.

"Hugh!" She shrieked his name as if she were calling on a saint. She tried to step back. He held her too closely and used her wild action to widen her stance.

"You taste just as I remember," he said, looking up

at her but obviously not interested in meeting her eyes. "That night you gave me the fairy remedy."

If anything, that appalled her more than his lascivious plans. "You remember—what do you remember?"

"The taste of you." Again his tongue flicked out.

"You didn't taste me!"

"I sucked some part of you." He burrowed closer, using his lips to open her and his tongue to torment her.

"My fingers." She gasped as pleasure tightened its grip on her.

He didn't answer. He had found a place in her flesh that made her try to escape and get closer, both at the same time. And when her legs started shaking, he took his mouth away. He was done, thank the saints. If he hadn't stopped, she would have humiliated herself by collapsing, by pulling him on top of her and begging. He'd given her a reprieve.

"Your fingers."

It took her a moment to remember what he was talking about.

Then he took her hand and sucked on her fingers. "A different savor, perhaps, but definitely you. But could you tell me why I thought we were in a barn?"

Her trembling legs almost betrayed her, but she stiffened her knees. "A barn?"

"I was making love and looked up, and you were above me, giving me such delight . . . "

He looked up at her. She looked down at him. He'd confused the memories, but somehow he'd placed them in her head. She remembered now—the heat, the scents, the motion, the excitement. She remembered something that had never happened.

"You made me a happy man," he said. "You gave me a taste of yourself, and with that taste, you told me what life could be. You saved my life, and I owe you for that.

And Lady Edlyn"—his hands had been resting on the back of her thighs, but no longer—"I always repay my debts."

His finger entered her from behind. His tongue lashed her from the front. She didn't want to be the first one to make a spectacle of herself as she climaxed, but his finger deliberately coasted in and out while his tongue, in a counterpoint of rhythm, touched and withdrew.

She couldn't stand up. She had to tell him. But she bleated, "I can't . . ."

"You can." He widened her legs. His finger plunged in her.

Too intimate. Too shameful. Too *good*.

She spasmed and cried out, and he pressed her with his open mouth, using his lips and tongue to prolong the exquisite sensuality.

When he had extracted every shudder, every moan, he removed his finger. He kissed each of her thighs and held her up with one hand on either cheek. He nestled his face against her stomach and waited, patiently, for the shaking to stop. And when it had, he asked, "Can you stand alone now?"

She couldn't. Right now, she didn't think she'd ever be able to stand alone again. But pride stiffened her spine. She clenched her teeth and nodded.

"Good," he whispered. "Good. I would hate to think I had wearied you before the night had truly begun."

What should she say to that?

Briskly, he untied her garters. "I have been a fool for you, Lady Edlyn." The wet hose clung to her legs, and he worked the material down each calf. "Step out," he instructed.

She had to rest a hand on his shoulder to balance on one leg, but he didn't seem to mind.

In contrast to the care with which the hose had

been chosen, Hugh tossed them aside. "You saved my life. I have paid you back and will continue to do so all our days. But no woman makes me a laughingstock before my men and gets away with it."

"I don't understand."

Standing, he grabbed a folded square of cloth off the table, shook it out, then twisted it around her hair. "Dry it."

A simple command, but she didn't want to raise her arms before him.

"Dry it," he said again, and shaking out another square, he went to work on her body. He rubbed it hard, without a shred of ardor, returning the circulation to her skin.

That commonsense approach freed her to tend to her hair, and when she had dried most of it, he handed her another towel.

"Now, dry me."

Her body still rang with the results of his seduction, and if she touched him, it would all begin again. As he no doubt knew, the wretched knave. "You're already dry."

"Not all of me."

She wouldn't look.

"Dry me," he said. "It will delay your fate a little longer."

He had that note of warning in his voice again, and she placed the cloth on his pectorals. Only his pectorals, but if she dried lower, her towel would become entangled, she would be trapped by curiosity, and she'd see what she'd scarcely glanced at.

So she dried his chest, then his arms, with slow sweeps of the cloth. "I didn't make a fool of you."

"I went to rescue you from the knaves who had kidnapped you. I thought you were raped or worse."

"So 'twas your imagination which played you false," she said, triumphant about shifting the blame that he seemed intent on placing at her doorstep.

Taking her wrists, he directed her hands downward. "You know how when your sons run off to play and get involved and don't come home?"

"Aye . . ." His lower belly demanded attention, and his hips. And she could stall by drying his upper thighs, although it was difficult to accomplish without looking. If only she could concentrate on the conversation.

"You're worried, the sun is getting low, and you imagine all kinds of dreadful things that could have happened to them."

"Aye." She was beginning to get his drift, and as she comprehended his words, she also comprehended his intention.

"Then they run in, dirty, scratched, without a care, and you're so happy they're safe you want to hug them and slap them at the same time."

She stuck out her lower lip. He didn't want her to dry him. He wanted her to stroke him, and mayhap, as he watched her squirm, he would get a little of his revenge.

"I rushed out and ruined my best blade on a stone for you—and you'd vanquished your captors yourself."

A bubble of indignation rose in her. He wanted her to caress him intimately, and he insulted her at the same time? Brusquely she circled him, moving with a speed he didn't think to counter, and began to dry his back. "Would you rather I had done nothing?"

"Nay. Oh, nay, I'm proud of you for your quick thinking."

He sounded sincere, and she relaxed enough to swipe at his rump. First one side, then the other, both covered with those fine blond hairs. He had a rather attractive behind, with the sucked-in, muscled cheeks of a very active man.

"But while I'm proud of you, you scared me to death."

He turned and faced her, and she once again got the shock of seeing him in all his glory. Funny how the back wasn't nearly as threatening as the front.

"I'll hear nothing but trouble from my men for this, and so you must pay now."

"Pay?"

His hands closed on her shoulders, and he brought her body close against his. He was warm and yes, a little wet in spots, but his intention was quite clear.

Completely rattled, she blurted, "Are you going to hit me?"

He stared at her, and his perception went far beyond their limited acquaintance. "I don't beat women. There are better ways to get their attention."

She relaxed.

Then he smiled, a toothy, rapacious grin that would have been at home on a hungry predator, and she realized she had relaxed too soon.

"Aye, you'd better be worried." He backed her over to the pallet of skins in the corner. "It could take me a very long time before I'm satisfied with my revenge."

She was in trouble. She was in big trouble. Brightly, she asked, "Would you like to tell me the details of your last battle?"

He just kept smiling.

10

"*We have them,* master. Eight good-sized rogues, ripe fer hanging."

Hugh took Wharton's arm and moved him away from the tent and toward the fire. "Did you have any trouble?"

Wharton's sharp cackle of mirth made the other men look as they prepared for bed. "Nay, yer lady fixed them up properly. The reavers could scarcely stand from th' cramps in their guts."

Looking up at the stars, Hugh decided the rewards of the marriage bed had eased his indignation, and he said proudly, "She's a clever lass."

"Aye, fer a lass." Wharton dismissed her ingenuity with scorn. "It wouldn't have happened if she hadn't gone haring off like that."

A smidgen of worry nudged at Hugh's mind. "How many women marry their last husband's executioner?"

"Ye didn't execute him. Not exactly. An' anyway, he deserved it. I don't suppose ye'll be wanting my services this night?" Wharton shook out his bedroll.

"Nay. I have no need of your services tonight." Hugh glanced back at his tent. He'd left Edlyn sleeping, but he had the urge to wake her again. For some reason, he needed to imprint himself on her, and he needed to do it tonight. With only half a mind on his words, he said, "Have the sheriff hang the reavers as soon as we leave Eastbury."

Wharton paused in the act of kicking the already sleeping squires. "Not first thing in th' morning?"

"'Twill upset my lady. She developed a tender place for those reavers."

"Move, ye varlets!" Wharton used his foot to clear a space for his bedroll. "'Tis odd. They seemed to know her more than simple reavers should know."

Alarm jangled in Hugh's mind. "Why do you say that?"

"When we said they'd hang fer trying t' rape a lady, they groveled. They said they never would have touched her."

"Flimsy prattle." Hugh dismissed that.

"I thought they meant it." Wharton scratched as he lowered himself to the ground. "They'd been watching her, I think. It sounded as if 'twas her they'd been planning t' capture. Not just any woman, but Edlyn, countess of Jagger."

The rumble of men's voices woke Edlyn, but her eyelids were so weighted she thought it would take a mill wheel to lift them. She thought about prying them open with her fingers, but that would involve moving her hand from wherever it rested.

She wiggled her fingers.

Ah, her hand lay beneath her cheek. Close to her eyelids. Very close. As the abbess always said—

Without use of mill wheel or fingers, Edlyn's eyes sprang open. Lady Corliss. The abbey. She observed the dim sunlight that entered the open tent flap. Morning Mass. She'd missed them all!

The men's babble died. A large shadowy shape stood up from the table where the voices had originated, moved across the tent floor, and knelt beside her. "You're awake." Hugh's voice. Hugh's now-familiar touch on her cheek. "I was getting worried."

"How late . . . ?" Her voice came out raspy.

Hugh snapped his fingers. "Mid-morning." Another shadowed figure came to his side and gave him something, then withdrew. Hugh lifted her head and placed a goblet to her lips. She drank greedily, and when she had finished, he said, "You're hoarse this morning. Too much moaning last night, I suppose."

She planted her hand on his chest and pushed, and he sat down hard. The men at the table laughed, but Hugh laughed too. This morning, he no longer cared if his troop mocked him. He'd extracted his revenge last night.

If only she hadn't enjoyed it quite so thoroughly.

"Go back to sleep," he said. "It's a misty morning, not good for anything but sleep."

"I have to go back to the abbey." Although how she was going to get dressed with all those men sitting around, she didn't know.

"Why?"

He didn't sound hostile, but that single brief word didn't bode well for her plans. "If I am to leave this place with you, I need to pack my belongings." Then it occurred to her she was assuming much. "That is . . . I am supposed to go with you?"

"You'll go with me." He gathered her hair in his hand and moved it off her shoulder, then covered her shoulder with his palm.

His silent gesture of possessiveness made her uneasy, and she asked pertly, "May one ask where?"

"To Roxford Castle. I am to take possession of Roxford's lands as well as his title."

"Roxford." A face flashed before her. Long and thin, handsome, intelligent, and . . . cruel. Edmund Pembridge, now the former earl of Roxford.

Robin's crony.

"Do you know him?"

"Nay." She denied it, although she didn't know why. It was, perhaps, the instinctive reaction of a woman made uncomfortable by the admiration of a man.

"I'm surprised. I thought you would have known such a leader in the rebellion."

Had Hugh seen something in her face? Or was it simply logic?

She feigned irritation. "I didn't know them all." Twitching her shoulder away from his touch, she buried it beneath the furs and did her best to change the subject. "Is that why you married me? To manage your new possessions?"

In a flat tone, he answered, "It is a sound plan, is it not?"

It *was* a sound plan. He'd never owned property. She'd managed Robin's, and successfully, too. And it certainly reduced the previous night to its rightful dimensions. "Then I must—"

"Wharton already gathered your belongings from your room at the abbey and brought them here in a sack."

She withered at the thought of Wharton pawing through the few pathetic things she'd managed to amass since she'd come to the abbey. But some of the items were important, and she asked, "Did he bring everything?"

"All of it," Hugh confirmed. "Although he might as well have burned it."

Appalled, she sat up. "Nay. Say you will not!"

The men at the table cleared their throats as Hugh lunged to cover her. As if she would be so stupid to show herself to them! She held a thin blanket before her and glared at Hugh, and he glared back. Jerking his head, he commanded, "Out!"

She wondered briefly if he meant her, then stools tumbled and men fled the tent, shutting the flap behind them.

Enough light leaked through gaps in the tent pieces for her to see Hugh's stern features. "Tell me why I shouldn't burn that pathetic pile of drab clothing and worn blankets," he demanded.

Tell him? Not likely. "Those are *my* possessions," she said firmly.

"I'm your husband," he answered. "They're now my possessions." He slipped his thumb along the ridge of her collarbone. "As are you, my lady Roxford."

He had an expression on his face she recognized, for she'd seen it often last night before the candle burned down and left them in darkness. She caught his hand as it wandered down her chest. "I submit to your dictate obediently, as a wife should, and will discard most of my previous possessions, as my lord demands. I ask only that you allow me to pick out two things before you burn all else."

His hand turned in hers, and his fingers tickled her palm. "Make me."

"Make you?"

"Enthrall me. Enchant me. Make me do your bidding."

She hated playing games like this. She'd done it before with the highest of hopes. She'd given everything, used every wile, and when she was done, Robin had praised her and promised to do as she begged, then he had forgotten or given the favor to another, better lover. No, she wouldn't give in to Hugh's challenge. "I'm not an enchantress," she said gruffly.

"Ah, but you are." He leaned into her, crowding her back.

She refused to fall easily as she'd done last night. She'd made everything too easy last night, but he'd taken her by surprise. She'd been too long without a lover. Or was it that he was too good to resist?

Her reward for constraint was a kiss bestowed upon the shoulder he'd earlier caressed. "See how you enchant me?" he whispered. "Even after a night such as last night, the sight of you stirs me."

She tried to inject a prosaic note into the rapidly heating atmosphere of the tent. "You'll get used to me soon enough."

"Will I?" He tried to twitch away the blanket, but she held on tight. "I have no experience with this. Do all men weary of their brides?"

"Sooner or later." His hands crept around to her back. As his fingers slid into the hair at the base of her skull, she fought to keep her sense of reality. "Probably sooner." But she said it with a sigh, and she let him ease her back on the pillow.

"Then they are bride and groom no longer." He massaged her scalp. "But husband and wife."

"And he's unfaithful."

"Not I, my lady." He leaned over her, an elbow planted on each side of her head, and he pleasured her with the slow intoxication of relaxation. "I pledged my troth to you, and I always keep my vows."

Eyes closed, she laughed weakly.

"Don't you believe me?"

His hands slipped away from her—in punishment, she supposed—and she wished for the moment of cherishing she'd lost. Then his hands were back, moving around her ears and among the roots of her hair. "You'll apologize to me for that one day," he pledged.

"By the saints, I hope so," she muttered.

"I'm not Robin of Jagger."

"I know that."

"I will not betray you with another woman."

She didn't answer, for she didn't believe him.

"I am nothing like him," Hugh insisted.

Sitting up in a sudden blaze of fury, she tore herself away from his hands, jerking strands of her hair loose in the process. "Oh, aye, you are! You're just like him. A warrior, going forth to right every wrong, to fight every foe." *You get out of your clothes as quickly, too,* she wanted to say. That she kept to herself, but somehow, he'd stripped himself while he caressed her. "And you'll end up just like him, too."

"I will not hang!"

"Mayhap not, but you'll be just as dead. Spitted on a sword, or bashed with a mace, or bludgeoned beneath the hooves of some other knight's horse. They'll bring you home to me on a slab, and I'll cry until I'm hoarse, and I'll be alone again."

He laughed. Laughed! "I won't be killed. Better men have tried many a time and haven't succeeded— why would they succeed now?"

The stupid oaf mocked her rage and her fear. She'd heard that braggadocio before, and once more, she tried to reason with something that couldn't be reasoned with—a man's brain. "As time goes on, the chance is ever greater that you will be killed."

"As time goes on, my skill in battle grows ever greater."

"Mere luck works against you." He still smiled, that patronizing "I know best" smile. He tried to take her hand, but she rapped his knuckles. She wanted to fight. He wanted to swive. He'd win, of course, but she'd challenge him anyway. "You want me. All right, you can have me. I'll warm your bed and keep your house and you'll never know what you're missing."

That made him stop. Moving closer, he stared at her face as if she would tell him a secret. "What will I be missing?"

"I won't give you any of my . . . my true affection." There was no use talking about love. She didn't still cherish him in her heart. She didn't cherish any man in her heart. "I'm not going to grieve for a man who looks for a fight when peace can be made with a smile."

He still didn't understand, and she guessed why. All he wanted was her efficiency and her body, and he would be satisfied. Fine and good; she'd give him both in generous portions and keep the important parts for herself and her sons.

Then he grabbed her, his face alight with comprehension. "Are you saying you'll not give to me what you gave to Robin?"

"Ah." She spoke to the air. "He's a clever lad, he is."

"That's what you think, my lady. That's what you think." He stripped the bedcovers away from her and pushed her down. He placed his hands one on each side of her hips and lowered himself to her, and his sword stood ready for combat.

She grabbed him by the back and put the mark of her fingernails along his spine. She was ready for him. Even the wildness of the night before couldn't extinguish her excitement.

She might not love this man, but she wanted him, and that was enough. "You'll not win this battle," she vowed.

"I win every battle," he answered, his hazel eyes flaming with conviction.

Wrapping her legs around his hips, she opened herself to him, determined to swallow him and leave him defenseless.

Without even directing himself, he thrust home.

She arched back, caught instantly in frenzied orgasm. He rose like a whale breaching in a wave. On his knees he caught her hips. He forced himself deeper. She couldn't take more, but he made a place for himself deep within her. Her womb welcomed him with ripples of demand and pleasure.

No finesse. Nothing but instant desire, followed by instant release.

He muttered, "I don't take you. You take me."

He admitted that, so she was winning. Winning! Another orgasm caught her, and she screamed from the heat and the fierceness.

He besieged her, thrusting again and again. The castle gate had fallen, the enemy was within, but he hadn't defeated her and he knew it. His hands moved over her; he pinched her nipples, then moved his hand down below her waist and slid his thumb between their bodies.

The result brought her right off the mat. She pushed with her hands under her until she, too, was sitting up. Until her bottom rested on his thighs and he caught her around the waist to raise her to his level. With her feet planted firmly on the floor, she used her legs to move, and this time he groaned, loud and deep, like a beast in its death throes. She set the rhythm, making him follow, and when he swore at her, she tilted back her head and laughed.

He tumbled them over and tucked her beneath him. She couldn't fight him. Her thighs trembled with the effort she had made . . . or was it the continuous, vibrant flow of life between them that weakened her?

"You're mine." He wrapped her legs high up on his back and began the final assault. "Mine. Mine."

She heard it as a chant.

"Mine."

As magic.

"Mine."

She grabbed the length of hair that hung over his shoulders and jerked until he opened his eyes and fixed his attention on her face. Fiercely, caught up in his demands, in the demands of his body, she said, "Mine," and dragged him down so she could seal his lips with hers.

It was nothing less than possession, and he recognized it. He freed his mouth, and with a shout, he gave himself to her. She felt his muscles strain and stretch through her skin. She saw his lips curl back from his teeth and the agony of pleasure that stamped every feature. As he finished, she heard him intone her name. "Edlyn. Edlyn."

They collapsed in an exhausted heap. This union, and all they had said, bore contemplation, but Edlyn didn't have the energy or the inclination. All she wanted to do was drift.

When he moved off her, she complained with a soft whimper.

"I'll crush you," he whispered and pulled the furs over her. They couldn't take his place, and she waited for him to come back and warm her. He didn't, and she opened her eyes just a slit to see him dressing.

Too bad, because she liked him better naked.

He saw her peeking, and as he adjusted his belt, he knelt beside the mat. "See? You are an enchantress." Burrowing under the covers, he kissed her breast, her navel, her chin. "You may have your two possessions before I burn the rest of that . . . matter."

He didn't think much of the effects she'd accumulated at the abbey, she could tell, but she didn't blame him.

His voice softened, and he coaxed, "Is there any other service I might perform for you?"

Give up your fighting. "Not unless you can bring my sons back from their pilgrimage," she muttered.

"They'll be back soon, won't they?" Hugh asked. "No matter, we'll wait for them."

Surprisingly, it never occurred to her Hugh *wouldn't* wait. "I know, but . . . I want them now." She wailed like a child, and she waited for him to laugh at her.

Instead, he tucked the blankets around her shoulders. "Just sleep. I'll take care of everything." And in a whisper, he said, "And I will win our battle, my lady. That you must never doubt."

Her sense of repose slipped away. "Not until the day you cherish peace as much as you cherish the clash of arms."

"Battle in a good cause is a noble thing," he insisted.

"There is more than one way to win a battle, my lord. Watch." She smiled. "And I will demonstrate."

"Ah." Edlyn dug through the sack of her belongings and pulled forth those two most precious mementos. She rubbed her face on the ragged pieces of cloth and breathed in their essence. Then, carefully, she folded them and placed them in a corner.

She had to have something with which to cover her bare body also. Something more than the surcoat she'd found tossed across a stool. Hugh had made her promise not to remove anything else from the sack, but Hugh didn't want her wandering naked, either.

Having made that sensible deduction, she dressed herself in the old brown cotte she'd worn every day in the dispensary.

Now she was clad and ready for . . . what? Midday had passed, so she broke her fast with the bread and ale waiting on the table. Then she stood, indecisive. Should she leave? Should she stay? If she left, would Hugh's men grin at her while she crossed the camp and tease her about her late rising? Worse, would they frown at her and think Robin's widow unworthy to wed their commander?

And what would she say when she reached the abbey? She'd stretched the formerly beautiful wedding dress over a trunk and picked at a stain on the hem. Worse, what would the nuns say? How was Edlyn going to explain the grass stains on the white hose and splotches of mud on the painted leather shoes? The nuns had loaned her those clothes cheerfully, in a charitable spirit, and she would be returning them in tatters. The nuns would lecture her. They might even shun her, and rightly so. The weaving of cloth, the sewing of clothing, occupied every spare moment of every woman's day, and she had ruined some of the fairest examples of the craft in her midnight rambles around the forest.

Hugh might have satisfied his need for revenge during the night, but she couldn't pay the nuns for the damage she'd done in the same coin, and she had no other. Just as before, she was poverty-stricken.

"M' lady?"

Wharton's rough voice outside the tent flap made her jump. She'd vanquished her fear of him, so she'd thought, but apparently the memory of his early threats lived on, and mayhap, just mayhap, her kidnapping of the day before had recalled those memories.

"M' lady?" He sounded a little impatient now. "I've brought ye something t' wear."

Shaking her trepidation, she walked briskly to the flap and pulled it back. Behind Wharton, the camp appeared to be empty.

He looked at her garments in disgust. "I thought ye promised t' keep only two things out o' that bag."

"I have to dress!"

"If ye can call it that." A wool sack, one that looked much like the first, sat at his feet, and he thrust it at her. "Here. From th' master, with his compliments." He sounded quite gallant, but then he spoiled it by adding, "Ye'd best shuck that ugly cotte an' throw me out that sack afore th' master gets back, or he'll do as I told him an' keep ye naked an' with child."

"You said that?"

"It'll be th' only way t' keep a woman such as ye out o' trouble, from what I can see." He turned away, muttering, "Not even one hour married an' ye got yerself stolen."

"It wasn't my fault," she called after him.

He shrugged.

"I got myself out of it!"

He made a sound with his mouth that would have been more appropriate coming from his arse.

"How childish," she said. She used her best mommy voice, but Wharton only jeered.

A head peeked out from behind one of the other tents, and she realized some of the squires remained. But where had the knights gone?

No matter. That obscure embarrassment still lingered, and she ducked inside. At the table, she dumped out the sack's contents. She gasped. Jewel colors glowed in the dim light. Somehow, Wharton had gotten his hands on clothes. Lovely clothes. Cottes of thin wool. Slim tubes of hose. Shifts, all of them as fine as the one she'd stained the night before. And shoes. Shoes of all sizes.

She backed away from them as if they were a slithering snake. "Wharton," she whispered. Then louder, "Wharton!" She ran outside, looking for Hugh's manservant.

She found him squatting by the fire, darning a hole in a man's rough black hose. Stalking up to him, she grabbed him by the front of his surcoat. "How did you get those clothes?"

"M' lady, why do you ask?" He smirked at her. He had been waiting for her. He knew just what she suspected.

"Did you steal those clothes from my *nuns*?"

He placed his hand on his chest in a gesture of innocence. "Steal from nuns? What a dreadful thought."

She leaned over until her face was level with his. "How did you get those clothes?"

He rose, keeping his eyes glued tight to hers. "My master gave me a purse full o' coins an' told me t' buy you a wardrobe."

"Oh." What else could she say? "Oh. Well . . . did the nuns *want* to sell their clothes?"

"Lady Corliss encouraged them t' open their trunks, an' th' gold convinced them."

She stumbled back. "Oh."

"Thanks would be appreciated."

"Of a certainty," she mumbled. "My thanks."

"Not me." He looked disgusted. "My master."

Glad to break eye contact, she glanced around. "Where is he?"

"Dress t' please him. That's th' thanks he wants."

That seemed reasonable. "But where is he?"

"He'll be back."

She wasn't getting anything out of this discussion, and besides, she could almost hear those clothes calling her. Trudging back to the tent, she tried not to look too eager. After all, she *had* worn fine clothes before. She'd been the wife of a duke and an earl. But oh, how she had missed the silks, the thin wools, the bright colors! It was odd how new clothes gave her such pleasure. She would have to consult Lady Corliss about her excessive vanity.

When she emerged from the tent, she wore the green striped gown the nuns had refused to let her wear on her wedding day. She liked it, symbol of easy virtue or not. Her hair was tucked into a net crispinette at the nape of her neck. She'd owned several before her eviction from Robin's castle, and she missed the convenience of confining her hair. Now she had three crispinettes as well as various headgear of all shapes and sizes.

Wharton and the shy youth who had peeked at her sat on camp stools set in the sunlight, and it seemed Wharton was instructing the young man in the art of hose repair.

Edlyn approved. She liked a man who could care for himself.

They didn't seem to see her, but without looking up, Wharton demanded, "Where are ye going?"

She stumbled slightly on the too-long hem. "I'm going to the dispensary."

"Why?"

She dumped the bag of old possessions at his feet, then showed him the bag he'd brought her new clothes in. "I have to gather some herbs for my travels and provide guidance to whoever is taking my . . ." In disgust, she exclaimed, "Oh, why am I explaining myself to you?"

"Because th' master told me t' keep an eye on ye an' keep ye out o' trouble. That's why I couldn't ride with th' men." Wharton's voice rose. "I'm playin' nursemaid t' th' master's wife."

"Oh." Clearly, he'd wanted to ride with the men. She looked at the youth. "Are you here to watch me, too?"

The youth scrambled to his feet. "Nay, my lady. I'm here to guard the tents against thieves."

He was taller and thinner than she'd realized, and she smiled in a gust of amusement. Just so her sons would appear in a few years. "What's your name?" she asked.

"Wynkyn of Covney."

"You're a long way from home," she observed.

His face twisted in that pained expression young men used for a smile. "Nay, my lady, this is my home."

A pang struck her, and she looked at the tents. "Mine, too, I suppose."

Sensing criticism, Wynkyn rushed into speech. "The men are kind, my lady, and the lord has the finest of everything."

Wharton lifted the black tube he held. "An' I'll show ye how t' darn hose if ye're nice t' me, m' lady."

"My thanks, Wharton, but I already know how to do that." Wharton made to hand her the hose, and she jumped back. "I trust in your skill completely."

Rapidly she turned toward the abbey, and Wharton called, "'Tis yer husband's."

"And you know how he likes them," she called back, grinning at the rude word he used in reply.

She approached the dispensary tentatively, already feeling alienated from this place where she had been poor, chaste, and struggling for resignation. All the windows were open and the door gaped wide, and she could hear someone muttering. She tapped on the sill, and the muttering stopped.

"Aye?" The strong, impatient voice identified the speaker at once.

Edlyn stepped over the threshold. She smelled the black, disgusting odor of wet charcoal and saw the boxes and herbs that cluttered the tables. "Lady Neville, what are you doing?"

The widowed countess pulled her head out of the oven and glared. "I'm trying to start a fire; what does it look like I'm doing?"

"Did it burn out?" Edlyn went and peered in the little door. "Why don't you have your servant start it?"

"Because when it burned out, you used to start it, so I thought, 'How hard can it be?'"

Lady Neville's obvious exasperation made Edlyn burst into laughter. "It took me months to learn to do it, and believe me, if I'd had a servant, I would have given the job to her. The main thing I learned was never to let it go out." Peering inside at the firebox, she scraped out the ashes, then crumpled a handful of punk. "Decayed wood works best as tinder," she explained. "I can never get it started with aught else." Taking the steel from Lady Neville's limp hands, she struck it against the flint until it sparked, sparked again, and finally caught the tinder. Carefully she blew on the flame, then fed it slivers of wood until it burned enthusiastically.

Lady Neville snatched the firesteel and the flint from beside Edlyn and put them on the table. "I can do the rest," she snapped.

"I know you can," Edlyn said soothingly.

They looked at each other, and Lady Neville gave in and laughed. "I'm supposed to take care of the dispensary now that you're going. Why do you suppose my lady abbess decided that?"

"Probably for the same reason she decided I should be in the dispensary. I have no patience with men like Baron Sadynton with their spurious ills and their petty complaints, and I tell them so."

"That could be it," Lady Neville acknowledged. "After your wedding yesterday, he ran into a fist."

Appalled and surprised, Edlyn asked, "You hit him?"

"Not I." Lady Neville smiled. "'Twas your husband who did that honor. I merely loudly expressed the opinion he should lie in the dirt of the square and bleed from the nose until his head ran dry."

In admiration, Edlyn stared at the tall aristocrat who looked like a cat presented with a fat mouse. "I have always liked you."

Sarcastic, abrasive, Lady Neville didn't make friends easily, and she stiffened at this confidence. Then, sensing Edlyn's sincerity, she relaxed. "And I, you. But after my comment, my lady abbess asked that I visit her in her office, and she gave me this task."

With mock sincerity, Edlyn said, "The patients will be relieved, I'm sure."

Lady Neville bit her lip to subdue a smirk. "You have the right of it, I'm sure, but I'm of an age to say what I like, and no sop of a baron is going to stop me." She fed a few more twigs onto the growing fire, then straightened. "I know you didn't want to marry that man, but 'twas the best thing for you and your children."

Edlyn blinked. Did every man and woman think they had the right to express their opinions of her affairs?

"I've offended you, I suppose, but without patients

to abuse, I must make do with you." Lady Neville ignored Edlyn's startled laugh. "When you're gone from this place, remember me occasionally and give your husband an extra roll in the blankets in my name."

"You didn't have to take vows when your husband died, you know," Edlyn observed.

"I didn't have children, I had no dower, and I had no desire to live with my pitying relatives as a nurse-maid for their brats. Lady Corliss took me in without a dowry, and I'm grateful. I will become a good nun if it takes me the rest of my days." Lady Neville sighed as she looked at the mess of boxes and herbs tossed about the room. "Which it will."

Pride had placed Lady Neville here, and pride Edlyn comprehended. "I can't help you become a good nun, but I can show you the herbs and what they're used for. Then I'll take enough to carry me through to my new home."

Lady Neville brightened. "A fair exchange, indeed."

For the remainder of the afternoon, Edlyn explained the duties and the remedies to Lady Neville. At the same time, Edlyn discovered the other reason why Lady Corliss had chosen Lady Neville to take Edlyn's place. Lady Neville might not be able to start a fire, but she knew many herbs and quickly grasped the uses for the rest. At last, Edlyn straightened and rubbed her aching back.

Lady Neville surveyed her with a twinkle in her eye. "My barbette looks good on you."

Edlyn touched the yellow linen band that passed under her chin and was pinned at the top of her head. "This is yours?"

"It was, but when that man came offering gold for clothes for you, I gladly gave it up. Better it should entice your husband than rot in my trunk."

Edlyn couldn't repress the chill of anticipation the thought of Hugh's lovemaking brought her. "Do you think it will entice him? I had not thought the head covering would do so."

"For a man like your husband, a head covering is a challenge. He'll muster all his weapons, defeat your headdress, and win his way to your uncovered tresses in a flurry of triumph." Lady Neville lined the herb boxes straight against the wall to avoid Edlyn's gaze. "I know these things. My husband was a pigheaded fool of a knight, just like yours."

"Do you miss him?" Edlyn asked.

"Every night," Lady Neville answered.

Edlyn pulled the cork from a clay bottle and sniffed the contents. "I don't miss Robin."

"That's not surprising," Lady Neville said flatly.

Edlyn swung around and stared.

"Well, really, my dear, did you think his exploits were known only to you? The man couldn't walk past the knothole in a tree without fornicating with it. He had bastards from one end of England to another and stupid girls lining up for their chance in his bed." With a sly smile, Lady Neville said, "I met him once."

"Did you?" And had she bedded him, too?

"I didn't climb in his bed, but if it weren't for my Neville, I would have. And I knew better! I knew his reputation, and I despised all the women who twittered about him. His charm, his masculinity, his handsome features. Pah!" Lady Neville sneered. "A grown woman like me should know better. But when I met him . . . "

"I know." Lady Neville's recollections had started an ache in Edlyn's gut. "Who better? When he came along, I was a new-made widow, a virgin, far from anyone who loved me, but so cautious. I'd been knocked about almost all my life, and I didn't trust anyone." She shook her head at the memory. "I tumbled into his bed the first night."

Lady Neville looked around for a chair, and when she couldn't find one, she hoisted herself up on the table. "At least he wed *you*."

"I had dower lands."

"Nonsense!" The dignified lady's feet dangled, and she swung them. "There were heiresses all over this land waiting to lay their hearts—and their wealth—at his feet."

Edlyn eyed the distance from the floor to the table-top. Lady Neville was taller, but she was also older. Surely Edlyn could pull herself up, too. Placing her hands flat on the table, she jumped—and missed.

"You're soft," Lady Neville observed. "That's what you get when you don't handle the patients, I suppose."

Exasperated, Edlyn wiped her palms on her skirt. "Then you'll be soft soon."

"God grant." Lady Neville put her hand on Edlyn's elbow. "Come on, I'll help you."

This time she made it. The tall table gave her a different view of the dispensary she thought she knew so well. Was there more than one view of her marriage, too? "'Tis true, Robin could have married any number of women," Edlyn acknowledged. "After the birth of our son, he scarcely bothered me for more than money, but at the beginning I think he loved me."

"I think he always loved you, as much as his immaturity allowed him to love anyone."

"He had so many gifts."

"And he wasted them."

"Aye. Always chasing after something better when the best waited at home. By the time the prince's men came to throw us out of the castle, I was done with waiting. My love for him was a flame, and it went out for lack of tending."

Edlyn thought she'd said it well, but Lady Neville shrieked in consternation and jumped off the table so fast, Edlyn thought she'd offended her.

"The fire." Lady Neville laid her hand on the oven. "I forgot about the fire!"

"It should be fine." Edlyn assured her.

"It's warm," Lady Neville said hopefully. Kneeling, she stared in the door. "It's glowing."

"Put some twigs on it and blow gently. You'll see; they'll burst into flame."

Lady Neville cocked her head and peered at Edlyn. "So put some twigs on the fire of your feelings for Lord Hugh and see if they don't burst into flame."

Edlyn made a face. She'd started this silliness; now Lady Neville turned it on her.

Lady Neville laughed at Edlyn's sour expression. "Don't forget to blow gently," she teased. "'Tis blowing which fans the flames."

"You're wicked." Hearing a commotion outside, Edlyn jumped from the table. "No wonder Lady Corliss wants you to work by yourself." But she couldn't resist a grin as she opened the door.

Two lads in miniature monks' habits bowled her over. "Mama," they caroled, "we're home!"

11

Hugh wanted to rush forward and rescue her, but Edlyn lay underneath two squirming lads with every evidence of delight. She hugged them, ruffled their hair, kissed them, wiped her kisses away when they groaned, and generally acted as delighted to see her sons as he hoped she would someday be delighted to see him.

Then Parkin started asking questions. "Are we really going to a castle to take possession of it? Are we going with Hugh and his fighting men?"

"Aye," she said. "That's because—"

He didn't wait for explanation but launched into a new series of questions. "Are we going into battle? Will I get to fight? Will Allyn get to fight? Can we use a sword?"

Rolling him over, Edlyn muffled Parkin with her hand. "We'll talk about this later," she answered with a frown.

Hugh moved so his shadow fell on her, and she looked up, startled. He extended his hand, and she stared at it without accepting his help.

What was the matter with the silly woman now?

He'd brought her sons back, just as she wished. Leaning all the way over, he grasped her wrist and pulled her to her feet. He smiled warmly into her face.

She didn't smile back.

Not many women could look dangerous, but Edlyn did right now. He hadn't noticed before, but in the slanting light of the westering sun, her face stuck out with all sorts of weird angles, jutting and unrelated. Her chin was wide, and she had a habit of pushing it forward as if she were challenging his superiority. Her cheekbones rose at such an angle they pushed the outside corners of her eyes up and gave her an odd, witchy glare—a glare she now bent on him as if he were one of her sons she could reprimand.

Then Parkin bounded to his feet and put the finishing touches on her irritation. "Are we really going to train for the knighthood?"

"Nay," she snapped, and Hugh remembered guiltily her determination that her sons should be men of peace.

"But Mama, Hugh said so," Parkin whined.

She turned that glare on Parkin and said, "Hugh's not in charge of you. I am."

Allyn rose off the ground and nudged her arm with his head until she hugged him to her. Even at eight, the top of his head already reached her shoulder. In his quiet voice, he asked, "Is it true you wed Hugh while we were away?"

Stricken, Edlyn could only stare at her lad.

Hugh answered for her. "Aye, she really did, but she didn't want to."

Allyn fixed his thoughtful gaze on Hugh. "Why not?"

"I wanted to wait for you." Edlyn shot Hugh a warning scowl, one he didn't understand, and followed it with a warm smile at Allyn. "But we couldn't wait any longer, so we wed yesterday."

Jealous of his brother, Parkin snuggled against his mother's other side. He wasn't quite as tall as his brother, but Hugh had seen twins like this before. They didn't quite look alike, and their personalities showed little resemblance, but they shared the same father, of that there could be no doubt.

"Why couldn't you wait longer?" Parkin asked.

"Sometimes people have to do things they don't want to," Hugh explained. "You'll find that out when you're grown."

"Oh." For the first time since Hugh had met Parkin, the lad calmed, and it seemed he donned the weight of added years. "I know about doing things you don't want to."

Like being thrown out of your father's castle, Hugh could almost hear the boy add.

Edlyn walked toward the bustle in the square, taking the boys with her. As she stepped away from the protection of the dispensary's fence, she spotted a distraction. "Look, lads, there's Sir Gregory who took you on your pilgrimage. Let's go and thank him."

Her sons groaned, and Hugh thought Sir Gregory must be groaning also. When Hugh found him trudging along the road with two lads in tow, he had been pathetically grateful for the offer of a ride to the abbey.

But the monk valiantly smiled when Edlyn hugged him and said, "I hope they weren't too much trouble."

"Not at all, Lady Edlyn." Sir Gregory twitched as he lied. "They were exemplary lads and an honor to your name."

"Do you think they're ready to start the novitiate?"

Parkin said, "Ma-oh-ma!"

She pulled a lock of his hair. "Are they?"

"Mayhap in a few more years." Sir Gregory faded back toward the monastery. "Not just yet, but soon."

Edlyn looked frustrated, the boys looked relieved, and Hugh had to pinch himself to stop from laughing. Unfortunately, Edlyn knew his mirth without seeing it, and she started toward the camp at full speed.

Hugh had no trouble keeping up. "Aren't you going to thank me?"

"For the clothes? Thank you." She kept walking. The boys bobbed along beside.

"For fetching your sons," Hugh said.

She glanced at him, then slowed reluctantly. "You fetched them?"

"Where do you think I've been all day?"

"I didn't know. Your close-mouthed servant wouldn't tell me."

"He found us at the crossroads." Parkin contributed his part cheerfully. "It would have taken two more days to get here because Sir Gregory walked so slow."

"Maybe he was tired," Edlyn suggested.

"Why?"

The boys couldn't comprehend the stamina it took to keep up with them, and Hugh shared a grin with Edlyn. Then she wiped the smile from her face as if such mutual amusement had somehow betrayed her.

Hugh walked close to her and bumped her gently with his arm. "It's hard to stay angry at me, isn't it?"

"Your charm is much overrated." The heat had gone from Edlyn's voice. "But my sons are not training to be knights."

"We'll see." Hugh knew how to use irritating phrases just as well as she. "For now they're going with us."

"I wouldn't ever leave them behind!"

Hugh found himself confused. "I never suggested

so. I simply thought you wished them to be fostered by the monks, and for that they would have to stay here."

"Not yet," she answered decisively. "They're not old enough to leave me yet."

"They're past the age when most lads leave their mothers," Hugh said with what he thought was irrefutable logic.

"Most lads . . ." She stopped and stared at the whirlwind of activity around the tents. "What's happening?"

"We're breaking camp."

"But why?"

Because I want to get you away from this place and off to myself. "I've lingered here too long," he said.

"This doesn't make sense." She tried to sound reasonable and succeeded in sounding exasperated. "It's evening! How far can we get tonight before we must set up camp again?"

Now he grinned. "I travel quickly."

"Not when you're burdened with two children, you don't!"

"Ah, Mama." Parkin shook with humiliation. "We're not children. We can keep up."

Allyn's embarrassment, though quieter, struck just as deep. "No one will have to delay for us, Mama."

Hugh turned a smug face on Edlyn. "If someone can't keep up, I suppose it will be you."

He had to give her credit; she didn't suggest that her sons might be overestimating their endurance. But she did glare at him. Then she glanced up and saw Wharton supervising the breakdown of Hugh's tent, and she picked up her skirts and ran. "Wait! Where are the contents of the tent?"

Wharton jerked a thumb toward the packhorses and carts. "There."

"I left two blankets on the table."

"Ye mean those two rags?" Wharton's scorn could have curdled milk. "I flung them in th' scrap bag."

"Those were the two things I kept out of my possessions!"

"Ragbag's in that cart." Going back to his duties, Wharton said loudly enough for all to hear, "Women!"

Curiosity held Hugh in place as Edlyn climbed in the cart and began to excavate the contents. What bits of cloth had she bargained for so determinedly? What memories did they hold? Edlyn jumped down from the cart, waving faded bits of cloth, one in each hand, and her sons leaped toward her with a shout. Each grabbed the tattered remains of a blanket and furtively touched it to his cheek. Then Parkin shoved his beneath his surcoat while Allyn rubbed his with his hand. Edlyn watched with the kind of smile mothers get when they've sacrificed much and found the reward ample.

"What are they?" Hugh asked her.

"Blankets made for them before their birth. They were swaddled in them, carried in them. They've slept with them every night of their lives, except during this pilgrimage, and they're the only things I managed to secure from Jagger Castle when we were thrown out."

Hugh had heard of things like this, but his warrior mind could scarcely comprehend. "You saved their blankies?"

"It's their one link to their former lives. Their one contiguous link to their babyhood. It gives them security."

"They're too old for things like that."

She turned her head and looked at him with a comprehension that made him shudder. "You're too old to suckle, too, but when you were ill, you certainly seemed to enjoy it."

She walked away before he subdued his chagrin enough to shout, "It's not the same thing at all."

She just waved a mocking hand, and he knew he'd lost. The boys would keep their blankies.

"I ain't takin' ye across tonight." The ragged peasant faced Hugh's whole troop with exasperation. "Are ye mad? 'Tis time fer sleep, not fer travel."

Edlyn agreed with him wholeheartedly, but she could see Hugh took his criticism personally and ill. For some reason, Hugh wanted to get as far away as possible from the abbey, and he wanted to do it quickly. But faced with the River Avon swollen with spring floods, he had no choice but to use the ferry to move men and horses. The ferryman wasn't having any of it, and she followed the conversation in this rough English as closely as she could.

"Th' master wishes t' go across now." Wharton clearly expected that the ferryman would see the good sense in getting this knight and his retinue far away from his pitiful house of mud and twigs.

The scrawny, cantankerous ferryman didn't seem concerned with the knight, or his men, or how they could render their malice on his belongings. Mimicking Wharton, he said, "Th' master'll have t' wait."

"There's time before the light fades entirely to get us across, and it would be in your good interest to do it." Hugh sat tall in the saddle and used his deepest, most commanding voice, but it was still a threat.

The boil on the ferryman's cheek darkened to crimson. "Aye, ye'll get across in th' light, an' I'll have t' come back in th' dark, an' th' river currents is treacherous enough in th' day. I'd not do it fer th' prince if he came abeggin'."

Part of the problem, as Edlyn saw it, was that Hugh didn't like having a common old peasant challenge him in front of his new wife and his men. Challenges were for knights and noblemen. Peasants did as they were told—except for this one. Unused to riding, Edlyn had dismounted to ease the cramps in her legs. Now, as she removed her riding gloves, she sidled closer. She didn't like the nature of this confrontation.

Wharton eased a coin out of the hem of his surcoat. "There's an extra shilling in it fer ye t' do it now."

"Nay!" The ferryman hobbled toward his hut. "Just settle yerselves down an' I'll take ye in th' morning."

Edlyn saw the exact moment Hugh lost his temper. He dismounted with a swirl of his cloak, marched up to the ferryman, swung him around by his arm, and glared, a warrior at his most ferocious. "You'll take us *now*."

The ferryman thrust his face right back at Hugh. "I'll take ye in th' mornin' . . . if I'm feelin' charitable."

Hugh fumbled for his knife, and Edlyn ran. Grabbing Hugh's arm, she murmured in Norman French, "Would you kill an old man for this?"

Hugh answered her in the same language. "Nay, but I'd sure frighten him a bit."

The old man showed his canniness when he answered Hugh in his rough English, "Ye can't frighten me. I've fended off greater men than ye."

"I'm sure you have." Edlyn interposed herself between the stubborn dolts.

Hugh tried to shove her aside. "Woman, mind your needle and let me manage this."

She used his impetus and her weight to bring Hugh around to face her. "How? By hurting him? He's not going to yield, and in the morning we'll have a ferry, all the light we want, and no ferryman to take us across.

By the saints, Hugh, some things can be handled without violence!"

If his most docile bitch had nipped at him, Hugh couldn't have looked more astonished. Edlyn turned her back on him and threaded her arm through the old man's. Speaking slowly, wrapping her tongue around the unfamiliar English words, she said, "Come. I'm chilled with the onset of night, and you've got a fire. Would you object if a mere woman warmed herself there?"

"Not at all." The ferryman, who smelled like dung and reached no taller than her shoulder, patted her hand and shot a smug glance over his shoulder at the astonished and horrified men of the troop. "It has been many a night since I've had such a pretty lady sittin' at me fire."

"I can hardly believe that." She smiled into his face and ignored the rank breath that bathed her. "A handsome man like you."

He responded well to that kind of teasing, if only to annoy Hugh.

"What's Mama doing?" she heard Allyn ask from the cart where he rode.

"Making a nuisance of herself," Hugh snapped.

That made her smile at the ferryman all the more.

"Aye, I was handsome in me day, but since I lost me last wife, women have come only t' board th' ferry."

"Aye, to board the ferry." Edlyn winked at him as she gave the phrase a salacious intonation, and the old man almost collapsed from pleasure. "What's your name, if I may ask?"

"I'm Almund, m' lady." He reached up to pull his forelock and had to settle for touching his bald head. "At yer service."

With a flourish, he showed her his place on the log.

He'd worn the bark away, he'd been there so long, and she seated herself, ignoring the men, the horses, the carts, her sons, and her new husband, all lined up on the road and waiting for attention. She had none to give them right now. She needed it all for Almund. Stretching out her hands to the feeble fire, she said, "I noticed, Almund, you have a boil on your cheek."

He touched it gingerly. "Aye."

"It looks painful."

"I've tried everything. Killed a toad by th' new moon an' slept all night wi' it on th' damn boil, an' all that toad did was make it worse."

Edlyn touched the pouch that hung at her waist. "I'm an herbalist of some renown. If you would permit me, I would be glad to try one of my poultices to draw out the poison."

"If th' toad doesn't work, why would yer poultice?" Almund asked.

"No harm in trying."

Almund would have refused, but Hugh took that moment to appear next to the fire. "Woman, go back to your palfrey."

"She can't," Almund snapped. "She's goin' t' fix me a poultice."

Hugh groaned and spread his arms wide to the skies where the evening star shown above the horizon. "God grant me patience."

The old man cackled wickedly, and Edlyn said tartly, "I prayed for release, and God granted me you, Hugh of Roxford, so be careful what you pray for." Standing, she asked, "Are we carrying mead?"

"Are you going to drink with him, too?" Hugh asked.

"Temper," she chided. "The mead makes a good base for the poultice, and the rest of my herbs are in the cart with the lads. If you kind men would excuse me?"

She moved away, and Hugh glared at her back.

Almund squatted down and poked the fire. "Women. Can't live wi' 'em, can't make 'em do a damned thing worth sense."

It was the first thing Hugh had heard from the ferryman he knew to be the truth. "We just got married," he found himself blurting.

"Guessed that. Ye look at her as if she is a foreign country ye need t' conquer."

"Oh, I've conquered her." Hugh remembered how she looked as she slept after he'd swived her into oblivion. "How many times do I have to conquer her before she stays that way?"

"Why would ye want that? She's got that beauty that goes bone deep. I mean, look at her. She wants t' make sure I stay alive, so she steps in front o' yer knife. An' she wants t' make sure ye get what ye want, so she offers t' cure me boil." He nodded wisely. "Me guess is I'll be takin' ye across at moonrise."

All of Hugh's masculine pride rose in indignation at the old man's words. "You know she's manipulating you and you don't object?"

"Why should I? I get me boil cured, ye get yer way, an' she gets t' think she created peace from strife. Which she did, God her soul bless."

Hugh stared at the old man in silent admiration. Almund saw more than Hugh himself, and despite Edlyn's opinion, Hugh considered himself insightful.

"Sit down, ye're givin' me a kink in me neck."

Hunkering down, Hugh experienced a pang of discomfort. He grunted and stomped one foot until grains of wheat showered out of his garter and planted themselves on the ground around him. "She lived at the abbey, and they gave us a proper send-off as we left late this afternoon. They rang the bells and banged pans and threw wheat.¨

The old man didn't look nearly as surprised as Hugh felt. "'Tis a proper thing t' do after a weddin'."

"The wedding was yesterday. That was the proper time to do it, but I let her go off and get captured and . . ." Why was he confessing his failure to this old man? "Rather than throwing the wheat yesterday, they did it today when we left the abbey. I think they did it because they liked her." Grimly, Hugh remembered the circle of leering people who had tried her for promiscuity as the result of his deception. "They hadn't treated her well before the wedding."

"Yer fault, I wager."

How did the old knave know that? And why did Hugh feel this pang of guilt for his actions? He had done the right thing, he knew it. Edlyn needed a husband, and no one owed her reparation as much as Hugh himself. She had refused to accept his help, so he had coerced her. That was as it should be. A man made the decisions. A woman respected them.

If only she hadn't told him she would never give herself completely into his keeping. He never refused a challenge, and he allowed himself no doubt, but . . . he'd never faced a woman unwilling to give him her body and her soul. Worse, he never imagined he would care.

He rubbed the tight muscle in his chest. It was that challenge, that was all. He cared only about the challenge.

"If th' wheat slides into yer curlies, it means yer plow's goin' t' plant early an' often."

Startled, Hugh stared at the old man and fought the desire to lift his own surcoat and check for kernels.

"If 'tis in her curlies, she's quickening already."

The ferryman considered, then shook his head, and a few wild hairs waved on the top of his bald head. "Nay, but she's not got th' glow about her."

"Doesn't she?"

"That one'll not conceive until she's taken ye fer husband in her heart."

Hugh settled carefully on his rump, pulled off his boots, and peeled down his hose, trying not to give the old man's statement too much importance. "How do you know that?"

"When ye get a little smarter, ye'll know some things, too."

Hugh could scarcely argue with that. He'd only in the last day begun to realize how much he didn't know.

"Where are ye off t' in such a hurry?" the ferryman asked.

The cramped sensation in Hugh's chest eased at once, and he answered proudly, "To our new home. To Roxford Castle."

"Just got yer lands, did ye?" The old man wiped his nose on the long sleeve of his shift. "Worked hard fer 'em, too, I trow."

No one knew how hard, except perhaps Wharton, and maybe Sir Lyndon, but not even they could comprehend the desire that gnawed at Hugh's insides at the thought of a castle, his castle, and a demesne, his demesne.

"Here we are." Edlyn's light, musical voice broke into his reverie, and Hugh looked up at her.

A wife. His wife.

He wanted her there, in his home, a symbol of all he had achieved. He didn't need that affection she withheld from him, as long as he had her physical body to maintain his castle and his lands.

Then unbidden, the thought of her naked body in a

tall bed slipped into his mind, and he knew he needed
her physical body for more than just its abilities to
work. He wanted it for pleasure—his pleasure, and
hers.

The ferryman started cursing as soon as she
applied the steaming poultice to his face, and he kept
up a steady stream of blunt English words that should
have made a woman who'd lived in an abbey blush.
They didn't seem to faze Edlyn, but mayhap she didn't
understand them. Hugh dumped wheat from his hose
and wiped it off his feet as he listened, and he grinned.
Regardless of the conversation they'd just shared, he
still wished for the old man's discomfort. After all, he
had defied Hugh in front of his own men.

He had the satisfaction of hearing the ferryman
howl in pain as she lanced the boil and seeing him shuf-
fle his feet as she gave him ointments and lectured him
on their use. Finally, she patted the old man on his bald
head and promised him the boil would be completely
drained and feel better in the morning so all his secret
admirers could lavish him with their love.

"Ain't got no secret admirers but ye, m' lady, an'
that's enough fer me." The old man touched the bandage on his cheek. "But it throbs so much I couldn't
sleep tonight anyway, an' th' moon's arisin'. Could be I
would ferry ye across now."

Edlyn shot Hugh a triumphant glance, then said to
the old man, "You are generous indeed."

Disgusted, Hugh pulled on his hose and boots and
shouted for his men. It took three trips to get everything across. Most of his knights went first, and with
them Edlyn's sons, still awake and so rambunctious it
was decided they could frolic on the far side while the
ferry made its remaining trips. Wynkyn was put in
charge of the lads, and Hugh felt sorry for his page.

Parkin and Allyn, he thought, could use a man's discipline, and when they were settled at Roxford Castle, he would see to it.

About half of their possessions went second, guarded by Wharton and the squires, who moved from place to place under Almund's direction to keep the ferry in balance.

Last came Edlyn, Hugh, the remaining knights and the rest of their gear. As they bobbed along, the moon shining on the river, Almund pulled Hugh aside. "Part o' th' reason I would bring m' lady across in th' night is because o' that knave."

Hugh's mind leaped to the claiming of his castle. "Edmund Pembridge?"

"Who's Edmund Pembridge?"

"The former earl of Roxford," Hugh answered.

"Ah, him. Nay, not him, although I hear he's a right wretched knave, too. Nay, I'm talkin' about him what took Castle Juxon."

Hugh's pulse quickened. "Richard of Wiltshire took it?"

"Aye, an' from all accounts, a more feckless brigand never lived."

"I'll not quarrel with that," Hugh said. "He's lacking in honor."

"Honor?" The old man laughed until a cough racked him. Grasping the paddle, he leaned over it until he got his breath, then said, "He's nothin' but a thief who speaks wi' yer fancy tongue an' entertains travelers while pluckin' them clean o' every bauble an' coin."

Hugh scowled. "He's a knight, a younger son thrown out into the world to seek his fortune. Not a pleasant prospect, of course, but common. Most men don't immediately turn to robbery."

"He's good at it."

"Aye, he had plenty of practice." Hugh had met Richard of Wiltshire and despised him with all his heart, and that had done nothing more than amuse Richard.

Richard's reputation as a merry master had attracted a troop of disaffected knights, and they hired themselves out as mercenaries. They fought for whoever paid them. They had nothing to lose and everything to gain, and now they'd gained a castle. When the rebellion was over, the king would reorganize and recover those lost lands, but until then Richard and his men would laugh and swive and drink the castle cellars dry.

"There's been a few he let go wi'out their fancy clothes or their gold, o' course, an' they've come through here. I wouldn't like t' think o' m' lady—or any lady—in his hands, if ye know what I mean."

The old man cast a meaningful glance at Edlyn, and Hugh vowed, "I will keep her safe from him."

12

The tug of the current on the ferry felt like the hand of God to Hugh. Almund grabbed for the paddle, but the handle twisted right out of his hands. The ferry lurched, then slowly, inexorably, it tilted up on its side. Hugh fought to grab the rail, but the rotten wood broke when he leaned on it and he went over the side with a shout.

"Hugh!"

He heard Edlyn cry before the water closed over his head.

He fought for the surface, but something floating knocked him back down. The second time, he came up and stayed up, and he saw the ferry breaking up in the water. "Edlyn," he roared, treading water and looking frantically around him.

"Hugh."

Her voice sounded from the side. She was climbing up on the bank, assisted by his knights.

"Hugh!"

She pointed at something off to his left, and he saw a jumble of their belongings floating by.

Did she expect him to save them? With this current,

he'd be lucky to save himself. The river took him in a swirl, and he saw a thin shape floating not far away.

"Hugh, 'tis Almund."

He heard Edlyn at the same moment as he recognized the limp figure of the old man and started swimming toward him.

"You've got to save him," she called.

Of course he would save him, Hugh thought with irritation. Did she think him incapable of a compassionate intention without her teaching? Reaching Almund, he wrapped his arms around him and towed him to shore. The treacherous currents spun them in circles several times, and once a trunk floated up behind Hugh and gave him such a blow on the head he almost lost consciousness.

One thing kept him going, though—anticipation of Edlyn's gratitude. When he towed the old man to shore, she'd see him for the hero he was, and that would be the first step to capturing her affection. Her *true* affection.

Hands stretched out to him as he neared shore, but he shook them off and reached with his feet for the bank below him. Gasping, he dragged Almund behind him, then picked him up, placed him on his shoulders, and carried him to a soft place in the grass. Carefully he lowered him, then straightened, waiting for his reward.

Just as he'd hoped, Edlyn ran right for him. He opened his arms wide—and she dashed past to kneel at Almund's side.

"Is he breathing?" She rolled the old man over. "Push the water out of him!"

Hastily, Hugh lowered his arms and hoped no one had noticed his disgraceful bid for Edlyn's attention. "He's a tough old bird." He stood dripping until

Wharton handed him a linen towel from the supplies already on the shore. "He'll survive."

Edlyn pressed on Almund's back until he vomited up river water. "If he doesn't, it is your fault," she scolded. "If you hadn't been in such a hurry to get across the river at night, this would never have happened."

Through the haze of his own outrage, Hugh heard Wharton say, "Don't ye talk t' th' master that way! 'Tis not yer place t' question his commands!"

"If someone questioned them occasionally, mayhap he would think before he made them!" Edlyn answered back, as spirited as Hugh had ever heard her.

In some way, Wharton's indignation and Edlyn's anger soothed Hugh. He *had* made a stupid decision, and he'd hear about it from Edlyn. That was as it should be; a wife claimed the right to educate her husband, and Edlyn clearly had settled into that matrimonial role. "I won't do it again," he said meekly, and all conversation stopped.

He looked around at his gaping men. "Well?" He snapped his fingers. "Have you retrieved everything from the river?"

The squires scrambled down the riverbank. With a shout, Parkin and Allyn went with them, and Wynkyn hurried after. Hugh addressed the still-dry Sir Lyndon. "Did everyone escape the river?"

Sir Lyndon opened his mouth, but it wasn't his voice that answered.

"I certainly hope so." A strange man stood in the shadows at the edge of the road that led away from the landing. "It will make the ransom for you so much more lucrative."

Hugh swung around in surprise and dismay. A row of swords glinted in the moonlight, and they pointed right at him.

"Who dares threaten the prince's commander in the west?" Sir Lyndon shouted.

Wharton growled, and Hugh felt the sharp flick of exasperation. How stupid of Sir Lyndon to identify him to this enemy!

A warm laugh from the stranger confirmed Hugh's unease. "The prince's commander? I have captured Prince Edward's commander?"

Hugh's heart sank as he recognized the familiar voice.

"Hugh de Florisoun himself." Richard of Wiltshire stepped into the moonlight and gave a flourish of his sword. "It *is* you, Hugh! It's been many a year since I've had the honor of your acquaintance, but I admire you and your vaulted honor now just as much as I ever did." His voice turned soft and cruel. "That is to say—not at all."

"Did they capture everybody?" Hugh sat in the dungeon at Castle Juxon surrounded by his men and interrogated them as briskly as if he could see them—which he couldn't. The sun shone outside, but in this dank and vile cell beneath the very ground, no beam of light had a chance of ever penetrating.

"They got everything and everybody," Sir Lyndon answered, sounding dreary and discouraged. "My tent. My armor. My destrier."

"My wife." Hugh didn't appreciate Sir Lyndon's litany of his lost belongings when Edlyn's purity and her life were at risk.

"Your wife," Lyndon agreed, but he said it in such a lackluster tone it was clear he didn't comprehend the magnitude of Hugh's loss.

If only Richard of Wiltshire hadn't pounced on

them while they were still in disarray from the sinking of the ferry.

"They didn't get all th' servants," Wharton said.

"Well, I'll be expecting them to besiege the castle and rescue us at once," Sir Lyndon snapped.

"Shut your yap, Lyndon." Hugh listened to the stunned silence with a sense of gratification. "You've given up, and I don't like that. What kind of knight gives up just because he faces overwhelming odds?"

"One with good sense," Lyndon answered defensively.

This imprisonment had shown Hugh a new side of his chief knight, and he didn't like it. He didn't like Lyndon's easy acceptance of defeat, especially when it had been Lyndon who had failed to set a guard. He didn't like Lyndon's attitude about women, and really he didn't like Lyndon's disrespect to his wife.

Hugh's men shuffled and coughed as they tried to make themselves comfortable among the rats and the leavings of other prisoners, and Hugh wished he had started his sojourn in dry clothes, for the dampness of the dungeon seeped through to his skin and shivers racked him periodically. "Where's Wynkyn?"

No one answered.

"He had orders to watch Edlyn's sons. Could he have saved them from capture?"

"I didn't see those lads anywhere in th' line o' prisoners," Wharton said thoughtfully. "M' lady would have kept them by her if she could."

"It would have been better," Lyndon said, "if she hadn't told Richard she was your wife."

That, unfortunately, was true. Richard of Wiltshire had ordered Hugh stripped of all weapons while he unerringly found his way to the side of the only woman among the company, touched her under the chin, and asked who owned her.

Hugh wouldn't soon forget that haughty little answer. "I am the wife of Hugh, earl of Roxford, Sir Knight, but no one owns me."

"They do now." Richard had linked his arm with hers and smiled quite wickedly into her face. "They do now."

If Edlyn had understood the implications of that, she had given no indication. She just instructed Richard's men to lift Almund onto a cart so he could be carried to a bedchamber, and after a nod from Richard, his men had scrambled to obey.

Hugh dropped his head onto his knees and muffled a groan. All the scorn he had heaped on Richard in previous encounters returned to haunt him now. What nefarious activities would Richard force Edlyn to endure as vengeance against Hugh?

The tiny door creaked open, and a flickering light stabbed the room with little blades of agony. His men stood, almost in unison, shading their dark-accustomed eyes, but Hugh remained on the floor leaning against the wall. A man-at-arms stuck his head in the low opening and said, "Me master wants Hugh o' Roxford, an' he wants him now."

Hugh's men turned and looked at him, and Hugh waited a few beats of the heart to show his indifference before he rose.

The man-at-arms stepped back, holding a sword on him with capable hands, and said, "I have orders t' kill ye if ye do anything out o' place, an' I'd love t' kill an earl, so please, m' lord, try an' rush me an' me men."

Hugh held up his hands to show his defenselessness and bent to exit the dungeon. Straightening, he looked around at the narrow, short corridor that led to the stairway, then at the dozen men who stood at various intervals with swords, maces, and quarterstaffs, all pointed at him.

Hugh found cold comfort in knowing Richard respected his fighting ability.

The men-at-arms placed him in the middle, then paced upward toward the cellars, which were on the windowless ground floor. Here servants scurried, tapping the casks of wine. They all stepped back as Hugh and his guards came through.

Up the spiral staircase they went, moving toward light and warmth and noise. Hugh could smell roasting meat and bread and the sharp, shrill odor of spilled ale, and his stomach rumbled noisily. The man-at-arms in charge laughed at the sound. "If ye please th' master," he said, "mayhap he'll let ye eat— wi' th' dogs."

Hugh waited until they entered the great hall before he replied. "The dogs would be better companions than my present company."

The man-at-arms stopped short, then whirled and raised his sword.

"Halt!" Richard's voice rang out over the babble of voices. "You'll not kill that man while he lives on my charity!"

Hugh allowed himself a nasty smile as the man-at-arms lowered his sword. On one thing he knew he could depend—on Richard's sense of fair play.

In this massive great hall, the rough trestle tables were set up in a U-shape, with the diners seated around the outside for the servers' convenience. As usual, the bottom of the U was the raised dais where the noble folk ate, and there he saw Richard, sitting in the place of honor—with Edlyn at his side.

Hugh lunged toward the head table.

Blades gleamed as they flashed out of every scabbard in the hall.

Silence quivered as challenge met challenge and everyone awaited the next event.

"By the saints, you men are such children."

Edlyn's voice broke the tension, and she rose gracefully from the bench beside Richard. Richard grabbed her arm, and she glanced down at him. "I must go greet my husband and escort him to his place at the table."

Richard watched her with a scowl, then she smiled at him, and he softened. "Go on, then."

Hugh ground his teeth at the sight of ravenheaded, wicked Richard of Wiltshire yielding to the charm of Edlyn, *his* countess of Roxford.

The sunlight streamed in through the thin arrow slits that cut through the massive stone walls. It fell on the dark heads, light heads, knightly heads, and servants' heads with equal grace. The packed chamber vibrated with masculine ribaldry and rivalry, and Hugh expected one of these men to reach out a hand as Edlyn passed and pinch her rump or fondle her breast. He prepared himself to leap like a wolf to her defense.

No one did. Most of them turned their gazes away. A few of them responded to her smiles. A few blushed bright red and buried their faces in their curved horn mugs. And Hugh found himself wondering what the woman had done to tame this bunch of cutthroats.

She reached him before he could even begin to speculate. She held out her arms to embrace him, then stopped short and plugged her nose. "What have you done with yourself?"

He glanced down at the filth that covered him. "The river and the dungeon are a lethal combination, my lady."

"Too true." She flapped her free hand at him, then

turned to the aggressive man-at-arms with his ready sword. "How can you bear to stand so close?"

The man-at-arms stared at her, then at Hugh. "I didn't notice anything lackin'."

Edlyn laughed, a carefree trill that sounded quite unlike her normal merriment. "You are too diplomatic, my man." Plucking Hugh's sleeve between two fingers as if he were a slug she disdained, she said, "Step back and I'll take him to Richard."

"Richard?" Hugh rumbled. "You call that black-guard by his given name?"

With a slight tug, she urged him forward. "I call him as he wishes. I do whatever he wishes. I told him of my skill in storytelling, and he wishes to hear a story this night."

Hugh didn't hear the significant note in her voice. He only heard *I do whatever he wishes*, and he snarled, "If he wishes your tongue to entertain him in private ways, will you rush to do that, too?"

The knights and yeoman who lined the tables heard him and started to laugh, until she slapped him. Once, hard, across the face.

Silence fell again, an amazed and anticipatory silence this time, and everyone waited to see the direction his anger would lead him.

It led him nowhere. He was blank. Stunned. She'd hit him. Edlyn had hit him, and he would have sworn this woman never hit anyone, ever, as long as she lived.

So why . . . ?

"I hate stupid men," she said.

Stupid. He'd been stupid. She'd been telling him something, and his jealousy had led him astray.

Bending his head in apology, he worked to recall the bent of her conversation, and after drawing a breath, he said, "You're going to tell a story."

A tension relaxed in her. It told him she had a message to impart, if only he would listen.

"Richard wants me to entertain him with one of my famous tales of yore, and I have assured him I will so fascinate him and all the men they will be captivated"— she glared at him meaningfully—"and helpless."

Richard vaulted up and over to them before Hugh could reply. He picked up her hand and kissed it. "Are you scheming to escape, my lady?"

She stared around the great hall, filled with brigands, thieves, and blood-thirsty mercenaries. "Escape? Not even my lord is strong enough to battle this army alone."

"I'm glad you realize it." Turning to Hugh, Richard clapped his hand on his shoulder. "My friend! Welcome to my castle."

Hugh didn't know how to respond, and he didn't like it. If he answered in a civil manner, Richard would be pleased, for it would be a tacit acknowledgment of his illegal possessions. Yet to spit in his eye would endanger Edlyn and his men.

Richard understood Hugh's dilemma, and he reveled in it. His bright white teeth flashed, highlighted by the sooty beard that covered his face, and Hugh hated him anew. Lifting the hem of his surcoat, now dank and dirty, Hugh said, "Your welcome is one I will always remember."

"Next time," Richard said, "dress a little better."

Edlyn got between them so quickly Hugh didn't even have time to raise his fist. "Lads. This is a civilized meal, remember!"

The only satisfaction Hugh got in bridling his anger was seeing Richard's expression when he realized he'd been addressed in that motherly, admonishing tone Edlyn used so effectively.

"Get used to it," Hugh advised.

Richard showed a flash of boyish defiance before turning an enchanting smile on Edlyn. "I do as you command, my lady. I'll even bring the offal up out of the dungeon."

"If you kept your dungeons cleaner, you wouldn't have to worry about offal." She crushed his pretensions with a snap. "Now be civil."

Hugh noted a swollen purple bump on Richard's forehead on the fringe of his bangs that hadn't been there earlier. Was that how Edlyn taught him respect? And what had Richard done to deserve such treatment? The two men exchanged glares, each wishing the other would break the bonds she had set on them and attack.

Then they noticed Edlyn had walked away. They leaped after her, each competing for her attention, but she ignored them until she reached the head table. There she waited, regally indifferent, as they struggled to pull out her bench. She sat, then they sat, one on either side of the only noble lady in the room.

They might have remained locked in silence, but Edlyn leaned away from Hugh. "You have a greater stench than Almund at his ripest." She turned to Richard. "I'm not eating next to him while he smells this way."

Richard leaned around her and grinned. "You heard the lady. Move."

Hugh could scarcely comprehend her impertinence. "You want me to leave you here at the table with this thief?"

She waved her hand. "Just move back a little so the odor's not quite so fresh."

What was she doing? Was she mad? Hugh stared at Edlyn, but she pushed at him. "Go *on*."

Richard gloated and his men jeered as Hugh shoved back his part of the bench and slowly rose.

"Oh, stop looking like a beaten dog," she scolded. She rose, too, and stepped away from the table with him. "The knights won't mind if you sit with them." She lowered her voice. "And while I have them interested in the story, I want you to steal their weapons and get us out of here."

Relief and indignation mixed in his chest. Relief that she had reasons for chasing him away. Indignation that she had humiliated him. Indignation that she planned to use him. Indignation . . . well, the indignation far outweighed the relief. "You want me to get us out? With a sword? Not everything can be solved with violence."

His sarcasm scorched her, but she did no more than pinch him as she pointed at a bench at the far end of the head table.

"Parkin? Allyn?" he asked.

In a low tone, she said, "Not captured."

He was reassured. Women and children were notoriously difficult to rescue, and the less he had to worry about, the better.

Seeing the anxiety that briefly etched lines on her face, he knew she saw it otherwise, and he touched her hand.

She gripped him hard for one brief moment, then stepped back. "Almünd is recovered and roaming the castle. He will free the rest of your men."

"That's a help," Hugh said encouragingly as he seated himself.

She nodded and smiled, then returned to the head table.

He'd lied, though. A wizened old man had no chance against the dungeon guards.

Still, Hugh had to admit she'd come up with a plan. Not a good plan, but a plan. Unfortunately, it hinged on her storytelling ability, and as he stared around at the rough bunch of mercenaries who made up Richard's troop, he hadn't much faith in their willingness to listen.

His neighbor, as seedy a knight as any he'd ever seen, turned to him and on a wave of mead-sour breath said, "Great little light skirt you got yourself, my lord." He stared hungrily at the sweet sway of Edlyn's hips as she walked away. "We'll all get a bite of that later."

In silence, Hugh stood, grabbed the lecher by the throat, and lifted him off the bench. The knight kicked and tried to squeal, but Hugh towered above him and his grip on the cur tightened as he struggled.

In a great mass, Richard's men leaped to their feet and started for Hugh. Hugh swung the offensive knight in a circle. The limp and booted feet knocked half a dozen warriors down. They scrambled to stand. They swung their fists. They pounded each other by mistake, then on purpose. Shrieks of wrath and pain rang in Hugh's ears—his shrieks, others' shrieks, he didn't know. He didn't care. He went down in a pile of tackling bodies. He wanted to kill this rabble. He crunched his knuckles into their faces. He dodged some blows. Others slammed his face and belly.

The battle shifted somehow. He heard bellows of rage and saw bodies lifted and flung—away from him. He struggled to his feet and found himself back to back with someone, fighting like a madman.

They were winning. Winning!

Then the shouted words of the man at his back suddenly made sense. "I'll kill you, you asses! He's mine!"

Hugh spun on his heel, and Richard did the same. They stared at each other, enemies who despised each other.

Fighting equals.

Then Richard grinned through split lips. "Besides," he said, "he'll bring either a great ransom—or great amusement."

His knights muttered and wiped blood from their faces. Right now, they didn't care about the ransom. Left on their own, they would have battered Hugh to death, but they'd been trained to obey Richard, and that put a rein on their tempers.

The servants dragged away unconscious warriors, and when the knight who had started it stirred, they kicked him into submission and hauled him away, Hugh knew not where.

Hugh wiped blood off his face and winced at the swelling his fingers explored. Edlyn would have to examine this. Edlyn . . . she stalked toward them with her herb bag in hand.

She didn't look happy.

Prudently, Hugh stepped back and pointed at Richard. "Take him first."

"I will," she answered. "You deserve to suffer a little longer."

Richard sat docilely for her ministrations, but he addressed his knights the whole time. "Sheep aren't as stupid as you men. Think! The earl of Roxford is the royal commander. The prince will want him back. Simon of Montfort'll want him hanged. We can make as much money off of him as we could in a year of fighting."

He winced away from Edlyn's unexpectedly brisk hand as she applied salve to his broken nose. "And what do you intend to do with me?" she asked.

He looked startled.

"You never thought beyond tonight, did you?" She grabbed him by the ear and twisted it. "I'm nothing but a thing to use to even the score—whatever that score is—with my lord Hugh."

"Ouch," Richard said. "Ouch, ouch, ouch." His voice rose in a crescendo as he slid off the bench and onto the floor trying to escape her cruel hand.

Hugh had never seen her look more magnificent. Lit by the flame of fury, she incited worship, like a goddess from the old religion.

Richard had needed this kind of discipline for years, and Hugh cackled when he heard Richard whimper.

A mistake.

Edlyn let Richard go and rounded on Hugh. "If you think that's funny, wait until I clean *your* wounds."

"I am well." Hugh's jaw ached and the skin over his ribs— that newly healed wound—rang like a church bell, but his eye throbbed the worst. Cupping his hand, he covered it. "I am well!"

She pried his hand away and gazed at the magnificent bruise. "Put your head in a bucket of water. It'll take down the swelling."

She walked back to the head table, and no one stepped in her way.

"If you do that, you'll drown." Richard spoke from his place under the bench.

Hugh stared down at his nemesis, brought low by a lady's hand. "And you wanted to own her."

"She goes with you." Richard chuckled and crawled to his feet. "She can't be an easy woman to live with." He scratched his chin. "Especially if . . . "

His voice trailed off, but he got such an expression of fiendish delight on his face that Hugh clutched. What was Richard up to now?

With a speculative glance at first Hugh, then Edlyn, Richard took his place beside Edlyn at the head table. Hugh was braced for disaster, but although he observed them closely, he saw nothing untoward in Richard's behavior. They ate from the same trencher but never touched. They spoke but never smiled. They might have been miserably married for years, for all the coolness they showed each other, and Hugh found himself pitying Richard of Wiltshire.

Halfway through the meal of venison culled from the king's forest, Edlyn rose and from beneath the table drew a lute. Every eye observed her as she strode into the center of the great hall and strummed a note. All conversation died, and Hugh thought the thieves waited almost nervously for Edlyn's next move.

She strummed again, then played a dramatic series of notes. "On the request of my host, I tell the tale of Fulk Fitzwarin the outlaw."

Not that tale! Hugh wanted to shout. *Anything but that one.* He didn't need Richard and his men encouraged in their struggle against the king's authority.

But as her sweet, low voice began the tale, Richard's men leaned forward, prepared to listen to the tale of the outlaw so like themselves.

It seemed Edlyn knew what she was doing.

Moving slowly, careful not to draw attention to himself, Hugh slipped back into the shadows, prepared to grasp what weapons he could and steal the others. Edlyn might be irritated with him, but she needed him to save her from the fate that awaited her.

Slowly, accompanied by occasional dramatic strummings on the lute and an innate sense of drama, Edlyn spun the story of Fulk Fitzwarin and his mighty struggle against evil King John. She told how he lost his birthright through treachery.

Hugh slipped sword after sword from the scabbards that rested on the floor beside each mesmerized knight.

She told how Fulk always maintained the highest standards and never robbed except from the king.

Hugh picked up a carving knife from one of the platters of meat.

She told how Fulk married the lovely and gracious Lady Matilda to save her from King John's lecherous intentions.

Hugh found a shield propped up against the wall and hid his stockpile of weapons beneath it. Then he grasped the sword and dagger he'd chosen as his own. He would attack at a propitious moment—but first he wanted to hear about the deliverance of Sir Ardulf. It was his favorite part.

The men around Hugh forgot to eat, they forgot to scratch, they forgot to fart. They did nothing but stare at Edlyn as she jerked their heartstrings. They laughed when she described how Fulk used the king's fine cloth to make outfits for merchants, then sent the men to the king to thank him for his generosity. They held their breaths when she described Fulk's daring rescue of his brother. They cried when two of his faithful followers fell to the king's arrows.

They listened to the end, so intent on Edlyn's tale they were transported through time and space to walk in the shoes of noble Fulk Fitzwarin.

And when she finished, they paid homage to her skill in stunned and worshipful silence.

Hugh paid homage, too, until she stared into his eyes and he woke from the spell with a start.

He looked at the sword he grasped tight in his hand.

It was even his sword.

He'd taken it from the scurvy wretch who had

stolen it from him—and he'd forgotten to use it. Edlyn had used her voice, her skill, her cleverness to bind the thieves, and she'd bound them so tightly he could have slit every throat and each would have died with a smile on his face. But she'd bound him at the same time.

He'd never felt so foolish in his life. By the saints, he'd never *been* so foolish in his life.

From the head table, he heard a quivering sigh. Richard of Wiltshire was recovering.

Both Hugh and Edlyn snapped their attention to their host and saw him wiping his eyes on the edge of the grimy tablecloth. The other men, sniffling and clearing their throats, lifted their cups in silent tribute.

Standing, Richard inclined his head humbly to Edlyn. "My lady, you have indeed followed through on your vow to entertain us most nobly. I put my hand, my heart, my possessions at your feet."

She swept him a curtsy. "Good Sir Knight, I thank you for your praise of my feeble efforts."

"There is nothing I would not do to give you your heart's desire, and that desire, I believe, is for . . . freedom." He winced a little as he said it, but when he saw that dismay made Hugh's jaw drop, his voice strengthened. "Aye, freedom for you, for your men, for your possessions." His men interrupted with shouts of complaint, but he laid about him with the flat of his sword and cowed them into silence. "Your possessions," he repeated. "And your husband." His gaze shifted to the sword Hugh held, then he smiled mirthfully at Hugh. "Aye, let your husband know he owes liberty and life to his bride."

13

Edlyn waited in horrified anticipation for Hugh to reject Richard's offer. She could see the pride working on him and could see, too, Richard's waiting with confident expectation for Hugh's challenge.

This was not about her or her skill at storytelling but about two men who saw the chance to settle an old rancor.

But she had children lost in the wilds outside Castle Juxon, and Hugh had allowed himself to be intoxicated by her telling of a legend. She cleared her throat meaningfully, and Hugh tore his furious gaze from Richard. She mouthed the words. "Thank him."

Hugh curled his lip. "We accept with gratitude, Richard of Wiltshire." He bent as if to bow in low obeisance and instead swept a scabbard off the floor.

Richard stepped back in sudden alarm, but when Hugh made no hostile move, he grinned mockingly. "You didn't get to be the prince's commander by being stupid, did you?"

Hugh looked at Edlyn. He knew how he must behave, but like a child he appealed to her for sympathy.

She did understand his distaste. When Richard grinned like that, *she* wanted to do him an injury.

Staring at Richard without expression, Hugh buckled the scabbard around his waist.

"Hey!" The knight sitting near Hugh pointed. "That's *my* scabbard and *my* sword. I stole it honestly!" He dove for Hugh and attempted to snatch it back.

Hugh used the knave as a substitute for Richard and took the opportunity to beat him half silly.

The grunts and shouts of the brawl assaulted Edlyn, but she pretended not to notice.

Meanwhile, Richard shouted to his men until they started moving, very slowly, to bring out the goods they had stolen from Hugh's company. What had been packed away was now heaped together with other loot taken from other travelers, and Edlyn moaned softly as she considered the coming task of repacking the carts.

Satisfied he had been obeyed, Richard appeared at her side. "My lady." He took her hand and kissed it. "Should you ever have need of any kind, send a message and we will come at once." He kissed her palm, then lapped it with his tongue.

She jerked her hand free and slapped him.

Richard didn't even flinch. He just flashed his usual cocky grin and indicated the still-fighting Hugh. "Too bad he found you first. You would have made a fabulous outlaw."

"I doubt that." She nursed her stinging palm and wondered at herself. She had never hit anyone—now, in the space of one afternoon, she'd slapped two men. Not that they didn't deserve it. "My sons would disapprove."

Both black eyebrows lifted. "You have sons? Not in my dungeon, I hope."

"Somewhere in the forest," she answered.

The outlaw wasn't stupid. He read her anxiety, and for the first time since she'd met him, all trace of humor vanished from his countenance. "I'll send my men."

As he gave instructions, Hugh came to her, picked up her hand, looked at it, then glared at Richard. She didn't know how, in the midst of his fight, he'd seen Richard kiss it, but now he scrubbed her hand between both of his as if to erase the contact.

At his touch, she relaxed. A silly relief, really, to think that if he held her, he still liked her. He probably didn't; he'd looked so chagrined when she finished Fulk's tale, and she knew how men thought. Probably he blamed her for capturing his interest so thoroughly he forgot his duty. But the warmth of his skin seemed to tell her that with Hugh she would be safe, and she leaned into him and rested her forehead on his chest.

Hugh caught her neck with his big hand and pressed her closer, turning her head so she rested against him and his arms could enfold her. His voice rumbled in her ear. "I'll not doubt your storytelling abilities again."

She detected a note of self-deprecating humor in his voice and raised her head. His face had been battered. His lips were split. His cheek puffed out. One eye was almost swollen shut, but the other eye twinkled at her. Her fingers stopped clutching his waist and slid up his chest, up his neck, and touched each bloody place gently.

He caught her hand and kissed her fingertips.

This bore no resemblance to Richard's kiss. It wasn't like anything she'd ever experienced. It was a spark created by two simple points of contact, like a firesteel and flint. Then his body pressed ever more tightly against hers, and their union was more than a spark. It was the whole pile of wood in flames. It was the forest fire ignited by lightning.

"If I don't get you alone soon . . . "

Beside them, Richard cleared his throat. He'd caught them entwined like two illicit lovers, and Edlyn stepped quickly away. Then she wished she hadn't. They were, after all, married. Only . . . not for long. Not long enough for them to be comfortable with each other.

"My lady." Richard took her hand, the same hand Hugh had kissed.

She bunched it into a fist.

He held up the fist for Hugh's inspection. "A message, do you think?"

Hugh held up a fist, larger, mangled, and bloody, and said, "A message you would be wise to heed."

"But let us observe the courtesies for the time we have left together." Richard placed her fist on his arm. "We'll go release your lord's men from the dungeon."

"Go with our host, dear wife," Hugh said. "I'll be right behind you."

It would be silly to object, she knew. Richard could still, after all, change his mind and keep all of them prisoners. Still, the men could fend for themselves. "I would rather find my children."

"My men will find them," Richard said. "If your children are anything like their mother, they probably already have a plan to assault the castle and free you."

"Saint Mary forbid!" she cried but wondered if it was true.

Leading her toward the stairs, Richard called, "You come, too, Lord Roxford."

"I wouldn't miss it."

When Richard's man-at-arms opened the dungeon door, a blast of stale air struck Edlyn.

"Come," Richard called congenially. "'Tis time to take your leave of my hospitality."

Cautiously, one by one, Hugh's men staggered out. They stared and blinked.

Wharton rushed toward his master. "Ah, yer face!" Standing on his toes, he examined Hugh. "How fares th' other man?"

In a solicitous tone, Sir Lyndon asked, "The bastards have been beating you, haven't they, my lord?"

Beneath the touch of her hand, Edlyn felt Richard jump. She clutched at him and said, "We don't have time for another brawl." Pointing at Richard's bruises, she told Lyndon, "If anyone's been beaten, it would seem Richard of Wiltshire came in for his share."

Sir Lyndon stared pointedly at her hand resting on Richard's arm and tried to speak again, but Almund crawled out of the dungeon on his knees.

With an exclamation of horror, Edlyn rushed to assist him.

"What's he doing down here?" Richard asked. "The last I saw of him, he lay upstairs moaning, complaining he would die while coughing up his lungs."

The man-at-arms in charge said, "That man tried t' crack me on th' head wi' a battle ax."

"Did he?" Richard looked at Edlyn knowingly. "An amazing feat for one so enfeebled."

"I woulda done it, too." Almund let Edlyn prop him against a wall.

"Aye, except ye tipped over when ye lifted it," the man-at-arms said.

Everyone laughed. Everyone except Sir Lyndon. He glared around in vexation. "The old ferryman said Lady Roxford schemed for him to rescue us. Trust a woman to plan something so asinine."

"Ye're out, aren't ye?" Wharton said sourly.

He didn't like Sir Lyndon, Edlyn realized. Of course, she didn't like Wharton, so where did that leave them?

"My lady Roxford's schemes have worked well for all of you," Richard answered. "Line up against the wall. Line up!"

Hugh's men looked to Hugh, and he waved them along.

Rubbing his hands, Richard announced, "I want you all to know I am letting you go, and I want you to know why. Your lady won you your freedom. She, and she alone, convinced me to return your belongings and allow you to go on your way."

Hugh's men said nothing. They stared at her up and down, then at Richard, and Edlyn shriveled as she realized what they thought.

Richard realized, too, and she acquitted him of trying to dishonor her name when he added, "She won your freedom with her skill in storytelling."

"Storytelling?" Sir Lyndon sneered. "I've never heard it called *that* before."

Richard and Hugh almost collided trying to get to him, but Richard was closer and he got there first. The knife appeared in his hand so easily he must have had it up his sleeve, and he pressed it against Sir Lyndon's throat. "You're insolent, my man, about your betters."

"Betters?" Sir Lyndon said. "She's just a woman and a—"

Richard shaved a piece of skin off Lyndon's Adam's apple. "You're stupid, too." Blood spurted in a dreadful crimson stream. "But you're not my man, praise God, and it's not my place to kill you." He looked at Hugh. "May I slit his throat, my lord?"

"Hugh." Edlyn bumped him, and when he looked at her, she shook her head.

"Nay." Hugh agreed reluctantly. "My wife wishes to grant him his life." His voice strengthened. "But you can leave him in your dungeon until the rats have devoured his contemptuous tongue."

"Should anyone else feel the desire to insult my lady Roxford, let me announce I would take it poorly." Richard threw Sir Lyndon at his guards, and they bundled him back toward the open dungeon door. "All my compassion has been consumed by this ill-met villain, so I will only tell you once—Lady Edlyn told us the tale of Fulk Fitzwarin with such skill she trapped us in her spell, and as a reward for her kindness, I am releasing you all. All!" He gestured extravagantly, knife still in hand, and Hugh's men shrank back. "*With* your possessions. So thank your lady and get out of my castle."

They did thank her. They thanked her as they filed past her on their way to the bailey. They thanked her as they filled the carts with their tumbled belongings. They thanked her until Richard smirked at Hugh. They even thanked her after Richard left to supervise the distribution of goods.

Standing with Hugh on the steps of the keep, Edlyn scanned the open drawbridge.

"I know what you're thinking," Hugh said.

"I haven't said a word." And she hadn't. She had more important things on her mind.

"Wharton! That trunk is *mine*." Hugh shouted at his man as the knights shoved half-packed possessions into the carts. Wharton gestured that he'd heard and directed it toward Hugh's cart.

Turning back to her, Hugh said, "But I can hear what you're thinking."

"I doubt that." Men milled and shouted as they led horses from the stables and fought over saddles. Stupid men.

"You're thinking I failed you in there. That you can't depend on me."

"Not at all." She clipped off the words.

"I swore I would protect you, and I will. I swear—"

She turned on him fiercely. "Will you stop babbling?"

He froze.

"I'm thinking about my sons. That's all. My sons. I want my sons back, and I want them back now. So if you must worry about something, worry about that."

"Your sons. Aye." A half-smile curved his mouth. "I've brought you your sons once before. I can do it again."

Hugh captured his palfrey, found his saddle, and was halfway to the gate when Richard caught up with him. They spoke together, then Hugh rode out.

Richard appeared at her side, scowling. "He said he's going to get your sons."

"I pray 'tis true."

"I wanted to go look, too."

Gently, she answered, "I don't think that would be wise."

"That's what Hugh said. Ah, but I'd best call him Lord Roxford now, hadn't I? He said I'd better stay here or fights will break out." Richard rocked back and forth on his heels. "He's right, damn him."

If she hadn't been so troubled, she would have laughed at this little boy rivalry.

"Of course, if you ask him, he's always right," Richard said. "How do you bear it?"

Loyalty kept her tongue silent.

This man *did* read her thoughts. "Aye, 'tis irksome," Richard continued. "'Tis why I can scarcely be with the man without trying to shatter that imperious attitude."

"That's why you let us go." It was so easy to comprehend the simple workings of a man's mind. "You didn't care about the story. You just wanted Hugh to know he owed his freedom to me."

"I liked the story. Besides, it'll make him grateful." Richard winked.

"You're a man." Exasperation made her sharp. "Do you really believe that?"

He looked down at his shoes and shuffled his feet.

"Oh, fine. You know better."

"I know your lord is a fair man." He spoke strongly and stared her in the eyes. "Owing his freedom to you might grate on him, but he'll never take it out on you. He'll just do his best to repay you. You'll see. He'll find your sons."

"I know," she said softly. "I know."

Stepping down into the muddle of bodies and belongings in the bailey, she went to work organizing and packing. Richard forced his men to give up the big things—horses, saddles, tents, armor. But never would Hugh regain all the possessions from the trunks.

As she tried to place everything in Hugh's cart, she heard a shout. Hugh rode across the drawbridge with only one figure clinging behind him. Edlyn dropped everything and ran across the bailey. Wynkyn clutched Hugh's belt, and his white face frightened her more than the absence of her boys.

Before he even came to a halt, Hugh called, "They're both fine. They're coming behind with the outlaws."

"Thank the saints." No prayer had ever been more sincere, but she recognized now the signs of pain in the page and the way he rested his arm on his knee. "What's wrong?"

"He broke his collarbone," Hugh said, "falling out of a tree trying to reconnoiter the castle. They were planning an assault."

Behind her, Richard choked off a chuckle and called for a stretcher. Edlyn heartily approved of it when it appeared; a blanket stretched between two poles, it was similar to the stretchers the nuns used in the infirmary.

"In our business, we get a lot of wounded men," Richard explained. "And we're constantly moving them."

"Help me get him down," Edlyn instructed, and the two men maneuvered Wynkyn until he rested flat on the ground on the stretcher.

Hugh and Richard held Wynkyn as she examined him, then with strips of bandages forced the bone back in place. Wynkyn cried out, then a startled expression transformed his face. "It feels better!" he said.

"It always does." Edlyn dressed the outer skin with boneset, then wrapped the bone and his arm to restrict movement. "But he can't go on tonight."

Clearly disgruntled, Hugh nevertheless said, "Of course not. We'll have to stay until the morrow."

Richard refrained from cackling, and Edlyn gave him full credit for that. "If you would accept my hospitality further," he said, "my men and I would be pleased to have you stay."

Edlyn wanted to see how Hugh would react. Would he accept as graciously as Richard had offered? More horsemen crossed the drawbridge at that moment, though, and she heard the call, "Mama, Mama."

Picking up her skirts, she ran toward the two boys perched behind two of Richard's men, and Hugh and Richard watched her go.

"I steal what I want," Richard said. "But if I stole her from you, I still wouldn't have her."

Richard was going to talk! Hugh trembled with

anticipation. His adversary was going to tell what had happened during the long hours Hugh had been incarcerated in the dungeon!

Hugh waited, breathless, and Richard scowled. "Oh, stop looking so avid. You know she cleaves to you only." He rubbed the bump on his forehead as if remembering how he got it. "You'll be safe here tonight, and so will she, although she's expressed her opinion of the condition of the solar, so I doubt she's going to want to sleep there."

Hugh lifted his eyebrows.

"Juxon was a pig," Richard said bluntly. "This demesne deserved better than a man who fed his belly and twanged his tool and let everything else go to the devil."

Remembering the squalor of the great hall, Hugh asked, "You mean it was this bad before you got here?"

"It's better than it was. We've done much work." Richard took Hugh by the elbow and turned him to face the keep. "See that loose stone on the second-story wall? We filled it in. Juxon apparently wanted a window, so he knocked out part of the wall in the great hall."

"Nay." Hugh couldn't believe the man had been so stupid.

"Aye." Richard confirmed it. "'Twas good for us when we besieged. Once we made it through the gate—rotted wood and no problem at all—we tossed some ladders against the keep and took it through the window."

Hugh staggered at the idiocy of it. Even a small castle such as this was worth holding. "He didn't deserve this place."

"None of them deserve anything." Richard's lips drew away from his teeth in a terrible parody of his usual grin. "The older sons, they toss away their inheritance while we younger sons starve."

Hugh didn't answer. He didn't approve of Richard. How could he? Yet he comprehended Richard's ire only too well.

Richard shook Hugh's arm. "When this rebellion is over, I have no doubt the royals will have won. The king will be released, and he'll send somebody—you, probably—to take this castle back from us. He'll give it to Juxon, and the place'll be a ruin in twenty years."

It was true. Hugh knew it was true.

"My lord Roxford, you have the prince's ear. Speak to him." Richard shook Hugh again. "Speak to him! There are worse tenants than I and my men, and we would swear loyalty to the king and never waver."

"The prince would never give a demesne to a gang of outlaws," Hugh said. "He wouldn't trust you to do his will."

"You trust me." Richard grinned with true mirth this time. "You trust me to let you and your men and your riches go in the morning."

Hugh looked again at the hole in the keep to avoid admitting anything to Richard.

"Talk to the prince," Richard said. "That's all I ask."

Wynkyn slept soundly on the floor beside the fire in Castle Juxon's great hall, despite the little moans of discomfort he gave in his sleep. Edlyn tucked a rug closer around his neck and stared into his face, so smooth even in the shadows of the night. Allyn and Parkin slept one on either side of him. He was their new hero, and they couldn't stand to be separated from him.

He was her new hero, too; he had protected and

cared for her sons, and he would always have a place at her side.

Around the fire in concentric circles lay snoring, twitching bodies. Closest to the heat were all the men who had been wounded or who were ill. Beyond that were the healthy, the young, and the vigorous. For some reason, there seemed to be few of those among Richard's men. When earlier in the evening she had told the sick to line up and she would treat them, a constantly increasing number of men had complained of head pain or chest pain or joint pain—all inexplicable, of course.

She should have thought of them as knaves and rogues, evil men who preyed on helpless travelers and relieved them of their worldly goods. Instead, they reminded her of her sons. Those pathetic eyes, those well-guarded whimpers, those tales of discomfort they would tell only her. And no matter what she gave them—an herb, a warm drink of wine, or just a cool hand on their forehead, they proclaimed themselves cured and thanked her with gifts.

They presented bolts of cloth, rings, and a lady's saddle. All stolen from those unlucky travelers, but precious nonetheless, and all given with sincerely stammered gratitude. She accepted everything with thanks and a smile. The plight of these men she understood too well. They had no women who cared for them. They'd cut themselves off from their mothers and sisters by their plundering ways. They had no place in society, so they made one for themselves, and this place, she feared, would be the eventual home of her landless sons—if they were allowed to train as knights.

Hugh and Richard, united in their disgust of such unmanly behavior, had held court on the far end of the great hall, and Edlyn would have given much to know what topic so animated their conversation. Politics probably. She snorted. To men, such matters took precedence over the welfare of their knights.

Over their own welfare, too, for Hugh still bore the marks of battle on his face and he never sought her services.

But now everyone was abed: Hugh in the solar, Richard in a corner of the great hall. She should be in bed, too. She should go into the solar, with its broken door and its musty bed, and climb in beside her husband and sleep. Only she was too tired to swive, and Hugh was too new a husband not to want to.

"M' lady."

A hoarse, quavering voice called her, and she stepped over the boys to reach Almund's side. The old ferryman concerned her. His gallant attempt to rescue them had only worsened his condition. "What can I do for you?" She laid a hand on his overly warm forehead.

"I just wanted t' tell ye, I won't be going wi' ye tomorrow."

"What do you mean?" He still shivered, regardless of the number of rugs she piled on him. The honey she'd poured down his throat had only slightly eased his cough.

"I'm too ill t' go on, an' I'll have t' be staying here."

She looked around at the rotting reeds on the floor, the boarded-up hole in the outer wall, the dogs that snacked on cast-off food scraps, and the cat that leaped from body to body, a dead mouse in its mouth.

He said, "'Tis a fine castle. I never been in one before."

She closed her eyes. If he thought this castle fine, what must his hut look like?

"Sir Richard came t' me an' told me I was welcome t' stay, too."

"Did he?" That surprised her.

"Seemed quite concerned about an ol' man."

"I wonder why."

"Ah, m' lady, I've been around many a year, an' that Sir Richard is no' so bad as folks say. He's got a good heart—he just keeps it well hidden."

Funny, but when Richard wasn't irritating her, she thought much the same thing.

"These brigands know enough t' give me me medicine, an' ye know yerself I'm not well enough t' be moved."

She did know, and she'd been worrying about it. She thought that with God's grace he could survive this illness, but only if he stayed put with someone to tend him. Now his cheerful resignation lifted a weight from her shoulders. "Mayhap it would be best," she acknowledged.

His bony hand caught hers in a surprisingly firm grip. "Aye, but if ye ever have need o' me, ye have only t' think it, an' I'll know an' come t' yer rescue."

His bright eyes looked black and bottomless, catching the occasional lick of orange flame from the fire and dousing it. Here, in the quiet of the night, she could almost imagine he had the power to read her mind. "If I ever have need, I'll think of you."

As she walked across the great hall toward the solar, she told herself she wouldn't have need, because she was married. Married to a great warrior who thought himself invincible.

It seemed she attracted men like that.

At the door she hesitated. Dark filled the chamber with only the light from the distant fire to illuminate the gloom.

"Edlyn?" Hugh didn't sound sleepy at all. "Come in."

Of course he wasn't sleepy. He'd been waiting. He'd told her earlier how he wanted her.

Men. Who did he think had been applying ointments, soothing brows, and praying for the recovery of the wounded? Hugh probably thought the elves came and took care of all that. He certainly didn't value her labor or her skill in anything but the bedchamber.

She jumped when his hand encircled her wrist.

"It is dark, isn't it?" He led her toward the bed. "Be careful of the step. Did you finish caring for the men?"

"Aye."

Lifting her, he sat her on the mattress. "It's smelly, I'm afraid. If the prince gives Richard the right to keep the castle, he'll need a wife to set things straight."

She murmured agreement as he slipped her shoes off her feet and turned her lengthwise on the bed. He scooted in beside her. The pillow was nothing but a bag filled with feathers from a goose that had no doubt expired from old age. The covers, she feared, crawled with vermin. It was cold and damp, and she braced herself for Hugh's kiss like a true martyr. Instead she heard a hiss of steel from beside her head as he drew his blade from his scabbard.

"Who's there?" He shot off the mattress.

"My lord, don't hurt me." In the dim light, a man stood with upraised arms. "'Tis Sir Lyndon, come to plead my case."

"Why did they let you out of the dungeon?" Hugh asked, and Edlyn shivered at the chill in his tone.

"They wanted to put me out of the castle." Sir Lyndon took a few steps in, and Hugh moved between her and the knight. "But I hid and came to you here. Please, my lord, don't turn me out. I've been with you for years, fighting at your side, and you wouldn't scorn me for one slight misspoken word."

"Slight? You slander my wife and you call it slight?"

Both men were silhouettes now, blocking the square of light from the doorway, shifting from foot to foot, showing by their stances who was the penitent and who the master.

"Nay, 'twas not what I meant." Sir Lyndon stammered, and Edlyn would bet he had broken a sweat. "'Twas the heat of battle and the embarrassment of defeat combined to make me thoughtless in my discourse. I would never speak ill of the woman you have chosen to take as your own."

Hugh didn't answer.

Sir Lyndon tried to cajole him, to become the jolly companion. "We've had good times, Hugh." Then, with a little more desperation, "I have saved your life more than once."

"As I have saved yours. Are we not even?"

"It's good to have someone to watch your back whom you can trust."

Hugh seemed hard, immovable, without pity.

Edlyn couldn't stand it. "Hugh," she whispered. "Let him stay."

She thought neither man heard her.

Then Hugh glanced back at Edlyn. "Will you take compassion from the hands of my lady?"

Sir Lyndon turned his head to the side, and she saw his silhouette as he licked his lips. Hugh had made it as difficult for him as he could, and that she hadn't intended. She should have let Hugh handle this rather than interfere. Didn't Hugh realize how much Sir Lyndon must resent her?

Slowly, as if each word hurt him to say, Sir Lyndon answered, "I will take your lady's compassion."

"Very well, then. You can go on with us to Roxford Castle, but Sir Philip is my lead knight now."

Sir Lyndon leaped toward Hugh. "But you promised—"

"I know what I promised, but I promised it to a man I deemed worthy." His hand fell on Sir Lyndon's shoulder. "When you have proved yourself again, I will compensate you fairly."

Sir Lyndon's indrawn breath was audible, and Edlyn wondered how Hugh could be oblivious to his ire.

"How long will this trial take?" Sir Lyndon asked in a strangled voice.

"Not so long. As you said, you have been my faithful comrade for years." He shook Sir Lyndon, then released him. "'Twill not be so long. You'll see."

"My thanks. I'll not disappoint you again." Sir Lyndon walked out of the room, and Edlyn thought that in the middle of his dark silhouette a fire glowed.

"That went well." Hugh sounded cheerful as he slipped his dagger into its sheath beneath her pillow and climbed into bed.

"It did?"

"Aye. He's back in the fold and knows he must defer to you as my lady."

"I don't want to be the cause of discord between you and one of your trusted knights."

"You're not that." Hugh lifted her so she rested against him. His warmth assailed the chill of the rugs around her, and she tried to move closer still. "An unease about Sir Lyndon has been growing in my mind, and this insolence on his part has only strengthened it."

"Have you been friends long?"

"Aye, for many years. We met on the tournament circuit and threw our lot in together, and we've traveled the roads together since. He was happier then, before it became obvious that—"

His hesitation made her curious. "Before what became obvious?"

"He didn't realize at first I was the more powerful knight. Some men, less tactful than me—"

She smothered a laugh in his chest.

"—made it clear through word and deed they considered him a knight in my service."

"Is he not?"

"Not then! How could he be in my service when I didn't have a pot to piss in or a window to throw it out of?"

"But you always knew you would win a lordship, and he always knew he couldn't."

Hugh's silence condemned Sir Lyndon's lack of ambition.

"So he went from companion to supplicant," Edlyn continued.

"He is not beyond redemption, I think. He was always a man of honor."

A man of honor, Edlyn thought, who had grown bitter with the passing years as Hugh's star shone ever brighter and his own dimmed and faded. But she kept that thought to herself as Hugh's fingers raised her chin and his head came close to hers. She braced herself for a kiss, but he did no more than touch her lips with his.

He made no further move, and she asked, "Are we going to—"

"Nay!" He denied her swiftly and with a vigor that meant, mayhap, he wished otherwise. Then more moderately, he said, "You're tired."

"Well, aye, but . . ." When did a woman's condition ever matter to a man? As far as she knew, all a woman had to do to pleasure a man was to be there.

"I'm sorry." He touched her head briefly. "I

know you want me, but you have worked long today. For tonight, at least, you'll have to abjure your desires."

A soldier can sleep anywhere, anytime, and Hugh did so, leaving Edlyn awake and unsure whether to laugh or curse.

14

It was big. Bigger than Hugh ever imagined, even in his most magnificent dreams. Castle Roxford stretched across the lush green countryside like one gigantic blot of hostile stone. The dry moat bristled with sharpened stakes pointed outward. The drawbridge, when lowered, would allow ten men to walk abreast. The gatehouse crouched around the drawbridge like a mother wolf over a vulnerable cub. Its crenelations bit the sky with gray teeth, and every inch of the outer walls had been built for ease of defense.

It was the best endowment the prince had ever given.

"I wonder if there's a feather bed anywhere in there."

Hugh turned his head and stared at Edlyn. A feather bed? She could look on that imposing castle and worry about a feather bed?

She rubbed her back. "I am tired of sleeping on the ground these last few nights. Not that I blame you for hurrying away from Castle Juxon, but to spend a night with a roof over my head and clean furs covering me will be pleasant." She glanced at Hugh. "Aren't you going to send your herald to ask for admittance?"

His herald? Did he have to? He'd taken so many castles over the years, it just seemed that announcing himself and walking in was too easy. He wanted to fight for this estate. Only in that way would he truly make it his own.

Edlyn got tired of waiting and said to Dewey, "Go up and proclaim that Hugh, earl of Roxford, has arrived to take possession of his new demesne." Dewey hesitated and looked to Hugh, but she urged, "Hurry. Hurry, lad."

Hugh nodded his permission, and his squire rode forward. In a voice that broke in the middle of a word, he shouted his message to the top of the wall.

The chains on the drawbridge squealed as the toothed wheel fed them out, and the wooden gate landed on the opposite side of the moat with a thump. Not a sound came from inside the walls.

"What's wrong with them?" Edlyn wondered.

Hugh looked around at his men. Wharton, veteran of too many campaigns to count, shrugged. He'd seen everything and made no judgment now. Sir Lyndon mingled with the other experienced knights, who watched the keep with narrowed eyes. The squires and pages imitated them, even Wynkyn, who walked beside a horse rather than ride and jar his shoulder. Parkin and Allyn kept him company, and like Edlyn, they seemed bewildered by the silence that greeted them.

"They're frightened." Gesturing to his men to maintain their positions, Hugh urged his horse forward. "And rightly so."

He moved toward the gate, but he watched for treachery. This was, after all, the former earl of Roxford's primary holding. Edmund Pembridge's family had held it since William had conquered England,

and everything inside would be stamped with his possession. If one of Pembridge's men-at-arms were more loyal to his former lord than to his king, a chance-met arrow would end the problem—if only momentarily.

Hugh crossed the drawbridge without incident. The walls of the gatehouse closed around him. It had been constructed as a corridor of death for attackers who had somehow breached the moat and shattered the drawbridge. The walls contained arrow slits where men-at-arms could safely dispatch the enemy. Murder holes through which boiling tar could be poured pocked the ceiling.

Hugh approved.

Yet the back of his neck twitched, and he wished he could see someone, anyone, from within who offered a peaceful gesture.

Then he broke out into the outer bailey. The large, open area between the outer walls and the inner walls contained an orchard, numerous gardens, and more buildings than he could guess the use of. Yet nothing moved. Nothing except . . .

Behind him, he heard the clatter of hooves over the drawbridge. Edlyn broke out of the gatehouse corridor and glanced around. "Where is everybody?"

"I don't know, and I don't want you here."

His stern tone didn't seem to impress her at all. "Surely you don't expect an attack?"

"I don't know, and until I do, I want you to remain in safety."

"Look."

She pointed toward one of the outer buildings, and Hugh drew his sword as he turned.

"I saw someone peek out the door. They don't know what to expect."

"That makes two of us," Hugh mumbled. He'd never claimed a castle for himself before, and his tension and uncertainty surprised him.

"If they were going to attack, they would have done it by now," Edlyn said decisively. Going back to the opening to the gatehouse, she waved through the corridor and called, "Come on. They won't hurt you."

Unwillingly, Hugh grinned. He could imagine how his knights felt about a woman assuring them of their safety.

Now that she had pointed out the signs, he could see the furtive movements as the servants sought a glimpse of their new lord. With greater confidence, he moved toward the second gate. Another gatehouse protected this much smaller passage through the inner curtain wall. He had to stoop almost to his horse's neck to enter, and when he could straighten, he almost dropped the reins.

Nothing had prepared him for the grandeur of the inner bailey. Years of tender care had created a lush vista of gardens and stables and trees, and in the middle, rising with turrets and towers on every corner, stood the keep. He'd never seen a keep like this, so great and tall, softened by the green drape of ivy that reached to the very highest stones, yet imposing enough to awe him with its majesty. Beside him he heard a shaky exhalation of breath.

"The prince must love you dearly." Edlyn craned her neck around like a yokel visiting a cathedral. "This is even finer than George's Cross."

Hugh tried to suspend his awe and deal with realities. "Defense might be a problem."

"Defense?" She stared at him. "You are taking possession of this noble estate, and you're worried about defense?"

"I would hardly need to worry about it if it weren't mine, would I?" he asked coolly. "There's no way in at the ground, of course, but the stairs to the second floor look quite sturdy."

Edlyn dropped her head into her hands.

"There may be a way to disconnect them from the building." He scanned the keep some more. "There are windows, too, although not many and they're high. Mostly it's just the size that's the problem. Where would I concentrate my defense?"

"I don't know." Edlyn's voice became diplomatic. "Why don't we ask *them*?"

A man and a woman, richly dressed, had stepped onto the second-floor landing and stood looking down at Hugh and Edlyn and the trickle of men and carts now clearing the inner gatehouse. The woman bowed her head, but the man took her by the hand and, with a whispered word, led her down the stairs.

"Who are they?" Hugh's hostility must have transmitted itself through the reins, for his palfrey danced until a whisper of dust rose beneath its hooves.

Edlyn leaned over and patted his animal's neck until it calmed. "The steward and his wife, I suspect. They've come to greet us and surrender the castle."

She removed her riding gloves and dismounted, but Hugh did not. These people were Pembridge's servants, the managers of this great estate, the supervisors of both house and fields.

They would have to go.

Clearly they both knew it. As they drew near, the woman fought back tears and the man clenched his jaw tightly. They weren't young people; both were of an age to have grandchildren and probably did. The grandchildren would have to go, too. Every last relic of Pembridge would have to be wiped from the estate so

Hugh could start over with his own people, loyal only to him.

"My lord." The man's voice trembled. "I am Burdett, the steward of Roxford, and I extend a welcome from the inhabitants of Roxford Castle."

"Burdett." Hugh boomed the man's name and saw Edlyn jump. His interfering wife started to walk forward, but he placed his horse between her and the steward and effectively blocked her path. "Burdett!" he boomed again. "You have held this demesne for the traitor Edmund Pembridge, and for this act of treachery, I exile you from my lands."

"What?" Edlyn sounded indignant.

Hugh paid her no heed. "Get out. Take your kin and get out with nothing but the clothes on your back, and be grateful I don't hang you from the highest tree."

Burdett lost all color, and his wife wept openly.

Edlyn said, *"What?"*

She spoke loudly enough this time that heads turned. The wife sucked back her tears, and Burdett craned his neck to see.

"Have you run mad?" Edlyn grabbed Hugh's stirrup. "You can't throw these people out!"

"I can." Hugh backed his horse away. "I have."

She hung on to his stirrup. "They'll starve—or worse."

"They served a man disloyal to our king and prince."

"They kept their vows to him. For that they should die?"

He couldn't believe his wife confronted him before his men and—he looked around—the bravest of the castle servants. He wanted to reach down and slap at Edlyn's fingers until she let go, but that didn't fit with the dignified image of the king's justice. In what he considered a reasonable tone, he said, "I'm not sentencing them to death. If I were, they'd be swinging already. I am simply—"

"Tossing them out into the world with only the clothes on their backs and without a way to live. They'll die, or they'll turn outlaw." She lowered her voice. "They're older, and they'd be no good at it, and then they'll die."

"That's not my concern." He tried to back up his horse again.

She followed. "Look around you, Hugh. This castle is perfect. Every bit of it is well maintained, and it has to be because Burdett and his wife have worked to keep it so. It's not the earl of Pembridge who did the labor—all he did was choose the steward, and wisely it would seem. Burdett and his wife have taken pride in Roxford Castle, a pride far beyond the usual, and they deserve a chance to prove themselves to you."

"It's not possible." He jerked the reins and wheeled the horse away.

The stirrup jerked out of her hand, and she balled her fingers and cradled them as if he'd hurt her. But she came after him, her features alight with a flame. "Don't tell me it's not possible. You're the lord. Anything is possible for you."

Angered in his turn, he snapped, "The prince expects a swift demonstration of justice."

"You sit on your horse in all your glory and you revel in your ultimate power." She stared at him as if he were an unusually large form of vermin. "In all your years of fighting, you have never contemplated anything but victory. But the world is littered with knights who never contemplated anything but victory, and just because they lost a leg or an eye, they're reduced to begging on the streets. The graveyards are full of stewards who served their masters faithfully only to have their masters abandon them. Is that justice?"

"What do you want? Did you want me to change the way of the world?" He forgot about his men and the watching servants. He forgot about everything but Edlyn and her simple notions. "And while I'm at it, I could make the sun rise in the west and the tides run once a day."

"I want justice!"

"The prince decides what justice is!"

"The prince." She said it in the kind of voice a priest used to speak of Satan. "The prince's justice had its way with me. I've sat in the dirt outside my home and hated the intruder who threw me out. I've watched over my children in the wilderness and feared for their lives. I've wondered if I would have to turn outlaw or prostitute to feed them on the trek to the abbey. I've begged for a crumb and humbled myself for a blanket. I've felt the prince's justice, and it didn't feel just to me."

Hugh didn't know what to say. He didn't know what to think, except that he'd been stupid beyond all belief. Edlyn was being stubborn and maddening because she'd faced the same trial the steward and his wife now faced. He could dismiss womanly compassion—as he had with the outlaws who had kidnapped her—but this was personal.

Yet the prince expected Hugh to do his duty thoroughly.

He looked at Edlyn's set, furious face.

The prince was fighting far away and she was here, and she could make his life hell forever.

He dismounted slowly, giving her a moment to think about her insolence. He walked toward her, his step measured.

She didn't retreat. She just glared at him through those witchy eyes.

He took her hand. He looked at it. A fingernail had been torn back, and the skin on the insides of her fingers had been scraped away when he'd jerked the stirrup from her. She hadn't cried and tried to get her way by making him feel guilty. She'd made him mad and tried to make him feel compassion. Well, he didn't. He didn't care about Burdett and his wife, but he did care about his comfort. And . . . well . . . he cared about Edlyn.

How odd to realize how little he valued the worship knights and squires lavished on him, yet he wanted Edlyn to think well of him. He wanted her to worship him as everyone else did, only Edlyn didn't care about his fighting skills, and fighting was the only thing he knew.

"It shall be as you wish, my lady." He kept his voice low. "I give you Burdett the steward and his wife to run my estate."

A smile broke across her mutinous face, and she sprang to hug him.

He stopped her with a grip on her arms. "But lady, should they betray us, I will take the payment out of your hide."

She still grinned even though he held her away. "I'm not a fool, Hugh. I know how to read and balance books. If they've been cheating, I'll know immediately, and you can throw them out. And if they try to cheat us"—her chin firmed—"they'll only do it once."

He believed her, and he felt a little better. Now if only he could keep this from the prince . . .

"Good people," he announced. "I yield to my wife's plea of compassion and will allow Burdett the steward and his wife to remain until they prove their worth."

Burdett's wife collapsed into Burdett's arms. Burdett tried to speak but couldn't be heard for the cheering of the servants.

"They like them," Edlyn said. "'Tis a good sign."

Burdett's wife broke away from her husband, ran toward Hugh, and flung herself at his feet. "My lord, my lord! I thank you." She grabbed his boot and kissed it. "God will bless your generosity. I will pray for your body and your soul every day. We will never betray you. Never."

15

"Neda kissed your boot."

"Aye."

"That's *disgusting*."

Hugh stopped and considered. "I rather liked it."

"You would." Edlyn clearly loathed the idea, but Hugh grinned.

He and Edlyn had been following the steward and his wife about the keep for hours, smiling, nodding, and all the while Edlyn had been bubbling with indignation. He'd been glad to let her. She deserved it after that scene outside. But at last she could contain herself no longer, and her ire had burst forth.

She deserved that, too, and he mocked her. "You're just angry because she didn't kiss *your* boot."

"I didn't want her to kiss my boot!"

"My lady?" Neda stopped when she realized they had fallen behind.

Hugh glared at Neda, but when she shrank back, he pasted a smile on his face. He resisted showing his chagrin at bowing to Edlyn's demands, but he had to needle her.

Burdett hurried to them. "Is there a problem, my lord and lady?"

The steward and his wife were going to have to learn not to interfere before he'd extracted his full revenge.

"I think my lady said something." Neda's voice trembled with worry.

Edlyn patted Neda's hand. "Nothing of importance. Pray continue the tour."

The steward and his wife exchanged miserable glances, then the steward nodded and Neda held the next door open. "This is the buttery."

Burdett gestured them inside. As with everything, the chamber for serving drinks was in perfect order. On the other side of the corridor was the pantry, with all the accoutrements for cutting the trenchers out of bread.

As they left, Hugh caught Edlyn and turned her to face him. "You may not have wished her to kiss your boot, but I saw the look on your face. You were jealous."

"I was not."

Her sharp chin stuck out, her cheekbones stretched her skin, and her eyebrows formed two slashes of brown across her forehead. She wasn't a pretty woman, but those angles challenged a man much as a quintain challenged an untried squire.

Hugh felt challenged, but he wasn't untried. He knew just how he would bury his lance in her. They'd been celibate since they had left the abbey's grounds, and he'd been almost too busy to care.

He wasn't busy now.

"But she might have thanked me!" Edlyn said.

Her resentment made him blink. "For what?"

"For what? For talking you into letting them stay."

That made no sense to him. "It wasn't your decision."

"I know that, but they would have been thrown out without coin or goods if I hadn't insisted."

"Insisted?" Nothing could dent his good humor, and he wrapped his arm around her shoulders. "You begged."

She tore herself away from him. "Aye, I'm good at that."

He blinked at her back as she swept away. What did she mean?

He tried to remember. The only time he heard her beg was in bed. He stroked his chin. Was that what she meant? He watched her walk ahead of him using that sway that so attracted him. That *was* probably what she meant. She knew he liked it, that's why she walked that way, and that's why she'd mentioned making love to him.

Although why she sounded bitter, he didn't understand.

Probably it was a woman thing. Probably she was remembering how good it had been on their wedding night. The saints knew he was remembering.

Especially when she walked like that. And she'd removed her cloak too. She said it was warm enough without it, but now he knew better. Probably she wanted him to see her in that traveling gown he'd bought her. She wore it for him, so he'd know he possessed her just as he possessed the gown and everything she had. And he deemed that important. He believed it was better to have a woman who depended on him for everything. He'd seen too many noble marriages where the wife owned land and was related to great men, and the husband never knew if she'd remain with him should he have troubles.

Edlyn did depend on him for everything, and look—she now sent out clear signals she wanted him. This was a right and proper arrangement.

Neda had moved ahead, but he lagged behind and now she hurried back. "You're tired after your journey."

Hugh blinked. Tired? He thrived on traveling. He'd done it his whole life.

"I should have realized it at once." Neda made a "tsk, tsk," noise. "My lady is drooping, too."

If the steward and his wife were to remain in their present positions, Hugh had to break them of the dreadful habit of interrupting when Edlyn was deliberately enticing him.

"Follow me and I'll show you the bedchamber."

On the other hand, perhaps Burdett and Neda could have some intelligent ideas.

Burdett spoke now. "We've had our servants work with your squire—Dewey, I think his name is—and your possessions have been moved into the solar, my lord. I apologize for anything that is missing. We'll do our best to locate it, of course, but your man Wharton told us of your incident on the road, and most things seem to have been repacked in a most haphazard manner. Neda will see to it in the morning."

"Aye." Hugh didn't care about that right now. Edlyn had kindled a fire in him, and he longed to let it burn him. "Does the solar have a door?"

Burdett didn't seem to understand that. "Aye, my lord, it . . . it does." Trying to anticipate any other odd queries, he said, "It's spacious, as I think you will see, with a fireplace, many fine tapestries to block the drafts, and glass windows of which we are particularly proud."

"Does it have a bed?" Hugh asked.

Comprehension dawned on Burdett's face, and he exchanged a conspiratorial smile with his wife. "A very large one, my lord, and it has been aired and is ready for occupancy."

With a spring in his step, Hugh followed Edlyn up the spiral stairs to the story above the great hall.

The long, wide landing held a single large wooden door. Neda flung it open and asked, "Will the lord and his lady wish to eat in the privacy of the solar?"

"Nay," Edlyn said.

"Aye," Hugh said.

Neda bent her head to Hugh. "It shall be as my lord commands."

Edlyn stepped inside and muttered, "I'm sorry I ever interceded for her."

Hugh didn't answer. He was too busy staring.

Burdett hadn't begun to describe the solar. It was as large as many a great hall. Gold cups and pitchers waited atop polished wood tables. The diamond-shaped windows glittered even when the rain splattered them, as it did now. The fireplace opening yawned in the wall like a dragon's mouth, spewing warmth and light. The bed . . . ah, the bed. It rose on a dais, its great posts pointing to the ceiling and each finished with an eagle. The bed curtains were a fuzzy red material, thick and heavy enough to keep out the winter breezes, and they were pulled back to reveal furs of every color and thickness scattered across the mattress.

Hugh considered the furs, then considered Edlyn, then considered the furs on Edlyn.

Edlyn didn't appear to be following his train of thought. She still gaped around her. "What a magnificent chamber."

Her veneration freed Hugh to say, "Edmund Pembridge chose poorly when he decided to support Simon de Montfort."

He thought he heard Burdett say, "Damn fool," but when he looked, Burdett was turning to his wife.

"Let us leave our new lord and lady to their devices and find places for the rest of their retinue."

Edlyn stepped forward. "Where will my sons be?"

"They have refused to leave the young man Wynkyn and are sleeping with the squires and pages in the great hall." Neda smiled. "I'll watch over them, my lady, and personally see to their safety."

"Just where they should be," Hugh said. "With other noble lads involved in the noble endeavor of fighting."

Edlyn didn't answer. Apparently she thought she'd challenged him enough that day, and that suited Hugh fine.

She did answer Neda, though. "If you would keep an eye on them and bring them to me should they ask, I would be most grateful. Change frequently makes them . . . anxious."

Neda looked surprised. "I hadn't seen any sign of that, my lady. They're just excited to be here and to have the care of young Wynkyn, and they're taking their duties very seriously."

"Well"—Edlyn pursed her lips—"good. Good, I'm glad."

Burdett and Neda backed toward the door, bowing as they went. Before they shut the door, Neda said, "If you have need of a maid, my lady, call me and I will perform the service."

"She won't need a maid." The door had already closed, but Hugh didn't care. He stalked toward Edlyn. "I'll see to her needs myself."

As if she didn't know just what he was talking about, as if she hadn't been deliberately enticing him, she gave him a startled glance. Then she sighed loudly. "Hugh, I'm sore from riding."

"I'll ride you carefully."

She didn't struggle as he discarded her wimple and crispinette and pulled her cotte over her head. "Do you want me to beg for . . . for . . . "

"Swiving?" He finished her sentence while staring at the darker place on the linen where her nipples rippled the material. He found himself suddenly, violently aroused, as if his body had been saving itself for this moment. "You can if you like, but there's no need. I'll give you what you want, and more."

Her breasts rose and fell quickly, and crimson rinsed each of her cheeks. Was she only angry, or was she aroused, too? He picked her up by her waist, and she remained stiff. Her hands clenched in fists at her sides, and her toes curled. She had that stubborn, you're-a-man-and-you're-swine look on her face, and he wondered what he'd done to deserve it this time.

More than that, he wondered what he could do to erase it and replace it with that soft glow of passion.

He'd never begged anyone for anything in his whole life, but he was desperate. "Edlyn," he whispered. "I beg of you . . . please."

He could scarcely believe it, but it worked. It worked! She placed her hands on his shoulders and stared at him with suspicion. He didn't know what she saw—agony, maybe, or his cock trying to fight its way out of his breeches—but she said, "Aye," and wrapped her legs around his waist.

"God." He threw her on the bed, lifted his surcoat, and dropped his drawers around his ankles. She struggled to remove her shift, but he had to have her *now*. He jumped on her. Just jumped on her with no finesse, like a boy with his first woman. He got the shift out of the way and her legs spread, and he looked. "God." It was the prayer of a sinner seeing his heaven. "Can you take this?" he asked frantically while sinking between her legs and probing for entrance. "Sweeting, am I going to hurt you?"

"Nay." She placed him just right. "Give to me."

Just like before, he worked to enter her. She was tight, cupping him, yet her body must be saying *yes* because she was slick and, oh, so hot. He could feel his pubic hair singeing.

Then she bucked, taking him all the way in and he couldn't feel anything. Or else he felt everything. He plunged and rocked, holding her thighs so she opened to him all the way.

She moaned deep in her throat, like a dove that had found a treat. The scent of her pampered him, roused him from the drowsy austerity of his former life and into the world of the senses. Harnessing her fire as if it were some beautiful, temperamental animal, he muttered in her ear. "More."

There was nothing more they could do. There was nothing he knew of beyond this poking and thrusting.

But his body seemed to be hearing something from her body. With her, he knew there was more than just physical movements. If he could get it just right; if he could hold her tight enough, give her enough pleasure, he could conquer her. He could possess her.

Reaching between them, he found the pouting lips that protected her from too much delight and opened them so each thrust rubbed his pubic bone against her.

She reacted with a frantic scrambling. She called his name, and her voice contained a sob. She strained against him.

Still he said, "More."

His body reacted as if he were fighting the greatest battle of his life. His heart beat half out of his chest. His lungs burst from strain. His legs shook from the pleasure. He wanted to collapse. He wanted to go on.

He wanted.

"You're . . . mine." He buried himself in her.

"You're . . . mine." He sucked at her neck.

"You're . . . mine." He rubbed his chest over hers until her nipples peaked.

He was throbbing, waiting, knowing he couldn't wait, giving her so much of him he might never find it all again.

Then heat blasted like that from a kiln around him. She rose beneath him with a shriek. She clawed at him. She sucked at him, but not with her mouth.

And the same heat engulfed him. He burst into flame, pumping his life into her, so deep inside her they melted together and were fired into one.

But he couldn't relax and revel in that moment. He had to tell her now. He had to hear her admit it.

Letting go of her legs, he pushed his hands into her hair. He held her head so he could look into her eyes. "You're mine."

"Nay."

That single word doused his fire like a splash of icy water. She dared to say nay? After the most fabulous experience of his life, she dared to deny him? Didn't she understand with whom she dealt?

He swung off her so fast half the furs on the bed landed on the floor. He landed on the floor, too, his feet beneath him. He tugged the rug beneath her toward him until she lay beneath his standing wrath. "Nay? After what we just did, you can say nay?"

Her eyes had an exhausted slant to them. Her wide lips were swollen, as though, before she gave in to them, she'd fought the sounds of pleasure. Her hair trailed halfway across the bed. She looked the epitome of exhausted sexuality. But she still said, "Nay."

He needed to take her again. He realized that now.

He should never have left her so abruptly. If he stayed inside her, if he kept making love to her, he could make her say she was his. She'd admit it when he'd possessed her often enough, he knew it—and, praise the saints, his body was willing.

She sat up on her elbows and pushed the hair off her forehead. "I told you I wouldn't give all to you. Be satisfied with what you've got." She looked at his face, saw something that vexed her, and pushed her hair back again as if exasperated. "I should have never told you what I withheld. You would have never known."

Wouldn't he? He stared at her. Perhaps not. Not at first. At first he would have been satisfied with the dance of bodies that she performed so well. And he hadn't ever been married before. Probably he hadn't even been loved. How could one miss what one had never had?

But he would have. He wasn't a stupid man, no matter what she thought, and he had memories of Edlyn . . .

"You were in that barn, weren't you?"

She sprang clear of the bed so quickly she pulled the rest of the furs off the bed. "What?" Scrambling on the floor, she snatched at her cotte. She held it in front of her as if she were afraid to lift her arms and pull it over her head.

Her reaction convinced him those vague recollections were the truth, and he stalked toward her. "You were in the barn. You were spying on me, and you saw me swiving that woman."

"Her name was Avina," Edlyn snapped. Then she blushed a ruddy red.

"I remember now." Memory fragments floated to the surface of his mind. Fragments that tugged at whole rafts of thoughts, amazing thoughts, thoughts so suffused with lust and magic he could scarcely contain his excitement. "I was sick, and I remember hearing your voice. You called up the old times. You told me about Avina, and watching us—"

She tried to skitter to the door. He raced ahead and slammed his arm across the wood like a living bar to escape. "You said you loved me."

She raced back across the chamber toward the window, as if its opening far above the bailey offered an exit. "You were dreaming."

He followed her. "Nay, I wasn't."

She tried to get the cotte over her head now, and he stopped her just in the way she feared—he snared her with her arms up and her head covered. Carefully he uncovered her head and looked into her face while keeping her trapped. "I heard you. You told me that when you were a girl, you loved me."

"You were ill."

"I was more than ill. I was dying." She folded her lips tightly to seal in any response, so he shook her. "Wasn't I?"

"I don't know." Tears sprang to her eyes, although whether of annoyance or distress, he didn't know. "I'm not God."

"*I* know. I saw the other side, and only one thing called me back." His hands slid up and down her arms as he held them over her head. "'Twas you, Edlyn. 'Twas you."

She trembled now.

"So you see, I can't resist you." He still smiled, but tenderly now, as if he sympathized with her embarrassment. "Nor can you resist me."

His face lowered to hers, and she slithered down until he held her cotte and she sat on the floor. "I can, too."

She tried to crawl away, but he caught her shift by the back and held her until he could wrap his arms around her waist and lift her.

"You asked for a feather bed," he said, "now let us enjoy it."

Was she going to give him all he wanted again? Was she going to collapse like some feeble, wanting female who thought she needed a man to complete her life?

She was not. Not when she knew he didn't need a woman to complete *his* life. Not when she was nothing more than a useful tool he possessed.

He held her backside pressed against his loins as if he were a wolf panting for its mate and walked toward the bed.

She shrieked, "I won't!" and tried to spring away even before he put her down.

He put his knee in her back and knocked her onto her stomach. "I say you will."

She gave the most hateful intonation to the word she could call up. "You . . . *husband*."

"I'll make you like it."

He wasn't laughing. He wasn't mean. He sounded as calm and as determined as she imagined he would when faced with a siege. He'd promised her before he would win this battle between them, and now it seemed he had decided on his choice of weapons.

It wouldn't work, of course. She couldn't let it, not without letting the pain back in when the prince called him to war.

"I won't do this." She twisted, trying to swat at him, and he used her momentum to flip her onto her back. Placing his hand on her belly, he held her down and wiggled around while she lashed out at him. One foot landed painfully close to his groin, and he caught it just in time.

"Our unborn children," he chided. He grabbed her wrist and stretched it toward the headboard.

"What . . . ?"

He whipped one of his garters around her wrist and secured it around the post.

"What!" She took a swing at his head with her other hand.

He grabbed it and tied it above the other hand.

She stared at her wrists, tied securely to the bedpost, and tried to understand. She'd heard of men who did things like this. It was one of the things women whispered about—husbands who tied them and hurt them unbearably. But Hugh?

She swung around and looked at him. Hugh wouldn't hurt her.

Then she really looked at him. He sat on his heels, surveying his handiwork with the satisfaction of a dedicated artisan.

Nay, Hugh wouldn't hurt her. There might be torment involved, but it wouldn't be painful torment.

He slid his hands under her shift and touched the top of her hose. "Now," he said. "Let us begin."

"Begin what?"

"First, let's talk about that barn and why you followed me in there."

16

"*I'll have to have a new* shift made for you." Hugh ran his fingers down Edlyn's belly. She liked that, he knew. She said it felt like a trickle of water, and when he did it right, her stomach collapsed. He stared in satisfaction.

"Why?"

She sounded drowsy, just as if she hadn't spent the entire evening and all of the night in bed, and that warm drowsiness made him lean forward and kiss her. She rubbed his shoulders with her hands—he'd freed them long ago—and he stretched with pleasure. He liked her to touch him, but he liked to torment her by making love to her when she was tied, too. It had been a most enlightening, a most enjoyable, experience, although she'd proved unusually intractable.

"Because I cut the other shift off."

"I have another. In fact, I have several others."

"Oh. The ones I bought you at the abbey."

"Nay."

She hadn't said she loved him yet. She hadn't even admitted to loving him when they were both growing up at George's Cross. Yet while wrapped in the passion of the night, he'd become resigned. Trying to convince her to say it was almost as much fun as hearing her say it.

She stretched and pulled the covers up. "I'm hungry."

"Me, too."

He rubbed his legs against hers. She had loved him when she was a girl, and that made sense. All the village girls had doted on him, and more than one noblewoman had lured him to her bed. And she must love him still, for he'd not changed much. If anything, his body was stronger, and other women said the scars on his face added character. He still lived to win, and if his focus had changed from winning a fortune to winning a woman . . . well, that was what men did.

He thought about the shifts again, then frowned. "What do you mean nay?"

"I don't think I got any more shifts from the nuns, but I got several from Richard's men."

He sat up, contentment flying away with the covers. "From *Richard's* men? Richard of Wiltshire?"

She made a soft sound of complaint and tried to retrieve the furs. He stopped her with his hand on her arm.

"What do you mean, Richard's men gave you shifts?"

She stared at him as if he'd lost his mind, then chuckled and touched his cheek. "There's no reason to be jealous. It wasn't just shifts. They gave me everything. They gave me fans and gloves and rings and the cutest gold toy ball with a bell in it. I don't know who they stole that from, but it must have been someone very wealthy."

A great up-welling of some emotion, he didn't know what, made him ask sharply, "*Why* did they give you gifts?"

"They claimed it was gratitude for the story, but I think partly it was because I talked to them as if they were normal men rather than just outlaws." She sat up, raised her knees, and wrapped her arms around them. "Oh, and I gave the sick men tonics and patted them on the cheek and promised to pray for them."

Hugh didn't even have to think before he said it. "I want you to send it all back."

"What?"

He didn't like the way she was staring at him, as if he were being unreasonable, when in fact some louts had blatantly usurped his responsibilities. He jumped off the bed and padded toward his trunk. "I want you to send everything back. Everything that they gave you."

"I can't do that!" She sounded uncertain, as if she didn't understand his mood. "They'd be hurt."

"Hurt? They're a bunch of thieves." He flung open the trunk and dug through his clothing.

"Hugh." She took an audible breath. "I know what I have is stolen, and mayhap that makes it tainted, but the poor women who lost their possessions will never get them back. Some of that stuff had been hidden away in the trunks for years. The linen was yellow in the creases, and the men were blowing dust off the shoes!"

He dressed as rapidly as he could. He didn't want to talk about it. "Send . . . it . . . back."

"I'll tell you what." She was coaxing him, trying to make him see sense. "I'll send monies to the abbey to offset the sin of owning stolen goods."

He didn't want to see sense. She had gone from owning nothing just two days before to owning more than her heart desired.

He hadn't planned it this way. He'd wanted a wife

thoroughly bound to him, a woman who knew that by advancing his cause she advanced her own. When Edlyn came back into his life, he'd told himself she was the one.

Setting his boot on the floor, he stomped his foot into it, then grabbed the edges and pulled it all the way up.

Perhaps he'd been foolish. He'd ignored the fact Edlyn had managed to survive—nay, thrive—in conditions that would have ground most women into the dirt. He'd pretended he didn't notice her competence, her defiance, her tenacity. He'd assured himself that she had found her way to the abbey with the grace of God, that Wharton had been directed to bring Hugh there through God's direction, and that their union had been part of a heavenly plan. God wouldn't have given him an inappropriate woman.

He set his other boot on the floor and slammed his foot toward the gaping hole.

Would He?

Hugh didn't hit the boot squarely. The sole skidded away and stumbled sideways.

"Are you hurt?" Edlyn walked toward him, trailing a woolen blanket.

He glanced at her. Her dimples shone, one in each cheek, like swirls in thick cream. Her right leg stuck out through the parting in the blanket, and her calf flexed in a way that reminded him of how she clasped his hips when he . . .

That was just what he needed right now. Another cockstand.

He put out his hand in a gesture that brought her to a halt and, in an aggravated tone, said, "I can put on my own boot."

She pursed her lips in that exasperated manner

that so irritated him and said, "I think I'll get dressed now."

As if that would help.

He grabbed the edge of the boot and held it this time, and his foot slid in.

The trouble was, with Edlyn *he'd* wanted to give her everything. He wanted to be the one to give her pleasure. He didn't want her lavishing her smiles on other men. He certainly didn't need to know that she could charm the plunder out of an outlaw. For if she could survive on her own, what need did she have for him?

"Are you going to put that on?" she asked.

She sounded only mildly curious, but he realized he'd been standing there, clutching his mantle and staring at it.

"It goes over your shoulders," she said helpfully. Fully dressed, she stood before him, feet apart, arms akimbo. "So. Do I have to insult my friends and return those gifts?"

His mantle swirled as he swung it over his shoulders. "Keep them." He walked toward the door, determined to ignore her, then walked right back. "I just want to know one thing." He held up his index finger. "Did you truly love me when you were young?"

She stared at the finger with a mutinous expression, then looked into his face. A little smile tilted her lips. "Aye. Aye, I did."

"Then you can damn well learn to do it again."

"Is the kitchen not to your satisfaction, my lady?" Neda asked in a tremulous voice.

"Aye, aye, it's wonderful. One of the best I've ever seen." Edlyn stared with discontent around the kitchen hut with its large fire pit, its clean utensils, its expert cook. "I just had forgotten how pork-brained and stubborn men are."

The cook, a large, brawny man, looked horrified, and Neda said, "That's a difficult thing to forget. Are we talking about any man . . . in particular?"

Her delicate pause made Edlyn realize the cook's discomfort, and with an effort, she smiled at him. "The kitchen is clearly the home of an artist."

He sighed with relief, and Edlyn told Neda, "I was speaking of husbands in particular."

"The cook is roasting an ox for the celebration of your coming." Neda pushed Edlyn forward with one hand on her back. "Would you like to approve the menu?"

Edlyn didn't care. The food thus far had been excellent, but the kitchen crew stood lined up for her inspection and she recognized their need to be greeted and given the approval of the new countess. It wasn't as if she hadn't done this before, although never under the guidance of such an expert as the steward's wife.

She greeted every turnspit and learned every name, and when they left to walk across the bailey to the cow barn, Neda said, "You've charmed them forever, my lady. They'll serve you gladly."

"That *is* the idea," Edlyn said impatiently, then returned to the subject that occupied her mind exclusively. "I've been living in an abbey. I've hardly seen a man for a year, and then only monks."

Neda adjusted her cloak against the rain. "I see your difficulty. Not seeing any but monks for a year, one would forget what men are truly like, for by the saints, I've never met a monk I considered a normal man."

"Normal?" Edlyn didn't like that word. "They're normal."

Neda said hastily, "They're holy! They're great men. They perform a wonderful service. But . . ." She opened the door to the barn and the milkmaid bustled up to them. "Greetings, Judith, this is our new lady who has come to inspect our milk cows."

Edlyn didn't want to inspect cows. She wanted to hear what Neda had to say about monks. Instead she had to run her hands over each cow's hide and look in every scrubbed wooden bucket.

But as soon as she and Neda stepped out of the barn, she stopped and said, "But what?"

"I'm not trying to offend you, my lady. I'm sure you have many monks of whom you are quite fond. I have an uncle who is a monk and a brother, too, and I adore them."

"But?" Edlyn insisted.

"I've lost them both. They're not dead, but they've suffered to become one with God. They're good monks—as they should be—and they have nothing left over to care for me." Neda stared across the bailey. The rain dripped off the barn's thatch roof and splashed at their feet, and she backed up until her spine rested flat against the wall. "I am selfish, but I remember how close my brother and I were when we were children, and sometimes I want him back."

"If your brother had become a knight, you wouldn't have him, either. He'd probably be dead."

"As God wills." Neda tucked her hands into her sleeves. "But maybe he would be alive, and sometimes he would come to visit, and he'd hug me as he used to. In addition, he surely would have married, so even if he'd died, I'd have his children who would grow up in his image."

In the middle of the bailey, some peasant lads were playing in a mud puddle, and they looked no older than

Edlyn's sons. In fact, if Edlyn hadn't specifically forbidden Allyn and Parkin to play outside, she would have thought they *were* her sons. One of them picked up a stick and challenged the other. They fought as if the sticks were swords, as busy and rambunctious as any two boys.

Edlyn's hand crept to her heart. She didn't want her sons to be knights. She wanted them to be monks, to be safe. But did she want this for their sake or for hers? Did she want this so she wouldn't have to suffer the agony of knowing they were in battle and perhaps would never return to her?

If what Neda said was true, there would come a day when all their boyish fire would be quenched. All their love would be for God, and she'd never see Allyn's face light up at the sight of her or feel the butt of Parkin's head as he requested a hug in his own inarticulate way.

"We've got to go on, my lady. We'll never get done at this rate, and the servants we've put off will imagine a slight when the ones we visited first hold it over their heads." Neda went first as they picked their way across the mingled mounds of grass and slicks of mud. "As for the men we marry, they are indeed pork-brained. Your husband . . . well."

If Neda was going to malign Hugh, then Edlyn knew she liked this lady. "What about my husband?"

"'Tis nothing, of course. Nothing more than any man would have done." Neda walked a few more steps and burst out, "But would any *woman* have tried to throw the steward and his wife out, especially when the estate showed such obvious signs of tending, without first asking about their loyalties?"

Edlyn leaped to agree. "My thought exactly!"

"Burdett told me what would happen. I said not

necessarily. If the new lord had intelligence—and I had investigated your husband, our lord, and from all accounts he was a canny man—he would retain us, or at least give us a chance."

Edlyn egged her on. "What did Burdett say to that?"

Neda stopped in the middle of the bailey. "Burdett laughed at me. At me! We've been married thirty years, and he told me I was a foolish woman. What's foolish about keeping on the experts to make money for you, I ask?"

"I tried to tell Hugh that."

"And he didn't listen, did he? Logic means nothing to these men. Only this cosmos of tangled loyalties had significance. And they say we're irrational!"

Edlyn liked Neda more and more. "I had to stoop to a womanish appeal to get him to keep you."

"Oh, my lady"—Neda grasped Edlyn's hand—"I do thank you for that. I don't know what we would have done if you hadn't helped us. I kissed his boot, but I know who was truly responsible. We will never fail you, I swear!"

"I know you won't." Edlyn returned Neda's clasp firmly. "Although Hugh is worried about any lingering loyalty you might have to . . . Edmund Pembridge."

Indeed, the way Hugh spoke of Pembridge, Edlyn feared for her own safety if he discovered she knew him. Why had she lied when Hugh asked if he had been a visitor at Robin's home? It would have been easy enough to say aye. But then Hugh would have questioned her about him, and she would have had to admit that Pembridge had been Robin's dearest friend.

His dearest friend and, if she had allowed it, his wife's lover. Even now, her mind veered away from the memory of Pembridge's admiration. He had composed poems to her beauty, sang about her grace, and, most dreadfully, praised her steadfast devotion to her husband while all the while his gaze had ridiculed her.

Pembridge, she thought, lived in a confusing welter of emotions. Love for Robin, love for her. Veneration for her fidelity, mockery every time Robin took another mistress. He had waited for her to fall into his arms, yet at the same time she knew he would have despised her for betraying Robin.

"Pembridge." Neda invested scorn into the name, and Edlyn jumped with guilt. "Always out for his own profit. Never thinking of what would happen to his people if he supported Simon de Montfort and he lost."

"Simon de Montfort hasn't lost yet." Like an aching tooth that disturbed Edlyn's concentration again and again, the knowledge that this was only a temporary respite from the rebellion returned to her.

"The rumors say that his support among the barons has eroded." Neda nodded wisely.

"Nevertheless, he'll have to be finally defeated," Edlyn said. To accomplish that, Hugh would have to return to battle, and Edlyn would be alone to fret and cry once more.

Only, she'd sworn not to love Hugh. She'd sworn she would never look in the mirror again and see her own eyes bleak with foreboding. She hadn't broken her own vow yet.

Had she?

Neda said briskly, "But Pembridge has already lost this holding, and that loss must grate on him. This demesne is his primary source of income, and I expected him to protect us with a little more wisdom."

Curiosity forced Edlyn to inquire, "He didn't marry in the past year?"

"Nay. He didn't want to marry, he said, although he indulged himself where he would."

"'Twas his duty to marry and carry on his line."

"He was a single-minded man. He wanted who he wanted and no other, and I believe the one he wanted was unattainable. Although"—Neda shooed Edlyn toward the shelter of the blacksmith's open-faced shop—"the last time he visited, he said he'd be bringing his wedded lady home within the year."

Had Pembridge been watching her at the abbey, waiting until her time of mourning was over?

That was stupid. He wouldn't have believed any one woman was worth so much trouble. Edlyn stilled the slight tremble in her hands. "Where is Pembridge now?"

"Chasing around after de Montfort, I suppose."

Edlyn sighed in relief. She didn't cherish the idea of Pembridge skulking in the forest, brooding over his dispossession. Brooding because he'd lost her.

Neda added, "Unless he's regained his senses and gone to the prince to pledge his undying loyalty."

"It's too late for that." Edlyn prayed it was so. "Hugh is in possession of this holding and of Pembridge's title, and the prince wouldn't be so foolish as to change his mind. He'd have Hugh in revolt then."

Neda's mouth quirked with a humor that flashed a previously unseen dimple in her cheek. "From what I've seen of your lord, that would indeed be foolhardy. Nay, Pembridge has lost Roxford, just as he deserved, and my husband will not hesitate to pledge his fealty to Lord Hugh."

"I will so assure my lord. He'll be pleased to know that." She groaned as the realization struck her. "Oh, Neda, we're going to have to organize a ceremony for Hugh's vassals to swear fealty."

"I can do that."

Neda's casual dismissal startled Edlyn. Every lord

knew the importance of the ceremony of fidelity. Every vassal, every servant came to their lord, offered gifts, and swore before the priest and witnesses to support and obey their lord. Once that was done, any betrayal could be rewarded with condemnation and death.

Hugh worried Burdett would break faith with him, for despite the fact the prince had commanded Pembridge's subjects to cleave to Hugh, some men took their own vows more seriously than the dictates of the prince. Hugh had no way of knowing if Burdett was one of those men.

Speaking slowly and seriously, Edlyn said, "This most important ceremony should be honored with a clean keep and copious feasting to bind the vassals to us with reverence and gratitude. You can organize the ceremony for the whole estate?"

"'Tis my duty, my lady."

Edlyn took a breath to argue, but Neda stood imperturbable, like a woman who had organized hundreds of ceremonies. As she probably had. Edlyn let her breath out with a long sigh. Neda's promise relieved her of another anxiety and left her free to concentrate on her new position of lady—and her new position of wife. "What day would be best?"

"The village reeve will have to be there, as well as the sheriff. Does the lord have other estates he wishes to involve?"

"Nay. No other estates." Although with Hugh's ambition . . . "Not yet."

"Then . . . shall we say . . . in four days?"

"Four days." To prepare enough food for the hundred hungry people who would come to stare at the new lord and his lady.

Even now, Neda seemed unconcerned. "Step back, my lady." She clucked her tongue in disgust and pointed at a green shoot that curled up and around the supports of the blacksmith's shop. "'Tis blister vine, and a pest."

"Wretched stuff." Edlyn stepped away from it. She'd suffered its effects more than once in her search for herbs.

Neda gestured to the keep. "It creeps up the walls of the castle all the way to the top of the battlements, finding root between the stones. I fight it constantly. We'll tear it out and have it burned."

"Be careful," Edlyn warned. "Even the smoke is tainted and blisters the skin and claws at the eyes."

"Then I'll be sure to do it before the ceremony." Neda smiled. "We don't want to poison our guests before they can swear their fealty."

17

"*We'll go to the* blacksmith next."

"Aye, let me see the man who will shoe my horse." Hugh said it heartily, but in his wildest imaginings, he'd never thought he'd be following his steward, a dozen of his curious knights on his heels. So far, he had inspected muddy fields, village huts, storage barns, and all the while, rain dripped down his neck. Was this the life of a lord?

He walked slowly until Sir Lyndon had caught up with him. "This could wear on a diligent knight quickly."

It was just a quip, a quick word to try to lighten Sir Lyndon's displeasure, but it didn't work. The corners of Sir Lyndon's mouth lifted briefly, and he said distantly, "Aye, my lord, 'tis true."

Hugh walked on, trying to think of something else to say, but Sir Lyndon sulked like a woman. No, like a child, because Hugh had never seen Edlyn behave so perversely.

"Ah, let th' new earl alone, ye ol' mule!" a woman's voice brayed.

Hugh looked up and saw her standing in the doorway of one village hut, her generous bosom lightly laced into a flimsy shift.

She gestured at Burdett. "He wants a drink o' me ale." She grinned at Hugh and showed several missing teeth. "Don't ye, m' lord?"

"Ale."

Hugh heard Wharton exhale the word like a man's dying prayer. Wharton was no doubt bored, and all of Hugh's men wore similar glazed expressions. Only Sir Lyndon looked polite, and Hugh couldn't wait to escape his company.

Hugh made a decision of which Burdett would disapprove. "Aye," he said. "I want a mug of ale to wet my throat."

As Hugh anticipated, Burdett looked shocked. "But we're not done with the inspection of the village, my lord, and after that—"

"Ale." Hugh headed for the alehouse, his big feet squishing the charcoal-colored mud that Burdett claimed was so fertile. "Now."

The warm rush of bitter air from the hut smelled like heaven to Hugh. He'd not been in an alehouse for too many moons, and he chucked the alewife under the first of her chins and said, "Bring us all a mug."

"Aye, m' lord." She hustled away, her ample shape jiggling, while the men sidled around the table in front of the fire and relaxed with a sigh. They left the end for Hugh. He took a stool and straddled it, then pointed at the far end. "Sit down, Burdett."

The steward found a stool. He wasn't yet comfortable in this tight-knit company of knights and squires.

Wrapping his arm around the alewife as she placed a handful of mugs on the table, Wharton asked, "What's yer name, ye fair young thing?"

The alewife let go of the handles and slapped his fingers. "I'll not tell ye. I'm savin' meself fer th' lord."

"Fer Lord Hugh?" Wharton burst into laughter. "Ye'll wait a long time fer Lord Hugh, me pretty. He's newly wed, an' him an' his bride fair shook th' rafters all last night while they beat th' mattress."

The men rocked with raucous laughter while the alewife leaned back, arms akimbo, and inspected Hugh. "Does he speak th' truth, m' lord?"

Hugh pulled a horn mug across the rough wood of the table. "I'm newly wed," he allowed.

"Then," she said, wrapping her arms around Wharton, "me name is Ethelburgha."

The knights roared this time, and Burdett joined in. "Easy Ethelburgha, we call her in the village."

Ethelburgha shook a finger at Burdett. "Don't be tellin' all me secrets."

"It's no secret." Burdett took the mug Sir Philip passed him. He waited until every man clutched one, then he rose. "I propose a toast. To Hugh, earl of Roxford, with my thanks and my eternal gratitude."

Hugh laid a hand on Wharton's arm when he would have stood to second the toast. He wanted to know his steward's mind, and he decided to learn it now. "Gratitude? Why, pray tell, are you grateful to me?"

"For allowing me to remain as steward of Roxford Castle." Burdett lowered his mug and spoke earnestly. "My lord, I am truly grateful."

"But are you loyal?" Hugh asked.

"To you, my lord? You can be assured of that."

"Why should I trust you?" Hugh challenged him. "Didn't you pledge fealty to Pembridge? Don't you have a passing pang of distress over his loss?"

Burdett looked down. Picking his words carefully,

he said, "The former earl was my master for many a long year, and I have served him well and faithfully. Thus I would never scorn him in my speech." He looked to Hugh over the watchful gazes of the knights. "Yet Pembridge freely sacrificed Roxford, and it is to Roxford Castle I am truly committed. My father was steward here and my grandfather. If Prince Edward had commanded I remain faithful to Pembridge, so I would have done. But the prince commanded I change my fealty to you, and so I do."

Hugh liked the sincerity in Burdett's tone. He liked that Burdett was committed to Roxford above all things, but— "That doesn't bode well for me should I fail Roxford in any way."

"I do not know you well, my lord, but you don't seem to be a man who disregards the source of his title and nobility for ambition and greed."

"When the prince calls, I will go," Hugh answered.

"That is your duty, my lord." Burdett leaned his knuckles on the table. "Mayhap I am but a quaint relic, but I believe in duty above ambition and loyalty above greed. In short, if Edmund Pembridge had kept his vows to King Henry and Prince Edward, I would not be sitting here drinking with you now. I would be holding you at bay outside the gates, and you would never take Roxford while I breathed."

"Well spoken." Hugh agreed and released Wharton's arm, and Wharton tumbled Ethelburgha aside and rose to join Burdett.

"So I'll join ye in yer toast t' Lord Hugh, long may his line increase!" In a more personal tone, he said to Hugh, "'Tis glad I am I lived t' see this day."

The rest of the men stood also and clicked the mugs, and while they drank, Hugh found himself blushing as red as any maiden on her wedding night under the barrage of good wishes. Luckily for him, it was dark and smoky, or he'd be teased as if he were a maiden, too. "My thanks, good men." Hugh lifted his mug in return. "It would never have come to pass without your stalwart company."

He took care not to show Sir Lyndon extra favor, and all accepted the tribute with equal grace. Again they clicked their mugs, and again they drank. Then it was time for a refill.

Still on his feet, Wharton raised his mug. "To Roxford Castle, may it always be prosperous and the cornerstone of our good fortune!"

The men drank, and Dewey let out a belch loud enough to make Ethelburgha giggle.

Sir Philip raised his mug. "To our king, may he escape Simon de Montfort to reign again!"

A few heads turned to Burdett to see if he would drink, but he cried, "To the king!" with the rest of them.

They drank again, and Ethelburgha poured them another refill.

Still standing, Sir Philip said, "And to Prince Edward! May he triumph over the royal enemies with the help of Lord Hugh, and may we all live through the battles unharmed!"

"To the prince!"

Most of the men had subsided onto the benches by now, but Burdett managed to retain his footing. Lifting his mug, he toasted, "To the lady Edlyn. May her womb be ever fertile and her belly ever full, and may she continue in grace and compassion forever!"

Hugh's men cheered, and Hugh lifted his mug with the rest.

Then he slammed it on the table. "Are all women so imprudent?"

The laughter and camaraderie stumbled to a halt, and the knights looked around at each other in bewilderment.

Only Burdett, flushed now with drink, seriously considered the question. Seating himself, he said, "I don't know how imprudent the lady Edlyn is, my lord, but in my experience, women are usually . . . difficult."

Sir Philip nodded wisely. "My wife was more than difficult. She was impossible."

With a snort, Wharton said, "Me wives have been nigh t' hopeless. Talking, talking, talking, even when we were humping, an' then they were complaining about it being too short, or too long, or not often enough." He noted the amazement that marked each face turned toward him and subsided into his ale.

Ethelburgha patted his head and filled his mug.

"My father always used to say he would have never married but he tired of his own hand." Every head turned toward Dewey, and his fair skin turned red. "Well, he did!"

Hugh said, "Edlyn was angry because Neda kissed my boot."

"Whose boot did she want her t' kiss—hers?" Wharton laughed briefly, then read the answer in Hugh's face. "Naw, ye're jesting!"

Burdett groaned. "Women. Always making a man's business their business."

"Trying to take credit for the lord's generosity," Sir Lyndon said, and he sounded surly.

"But you wouldn't have said they could stay if Lady Edlyn hadn't begged you," Dewey said. Everyone turned and looked at him again, and he turned redder than before. "Well, you wouldn't!"

"'Twasn't her decision," Wharton said.

"Don't you worry, my lord." Burdett watched as

Ethelburgha refilled the pitchers and set them on the table, then he poured ale into every mug he could reach. "My wife'll set your lady straight. She said she would."

Hugh lifted his brooding eyes from the swirl of ale in his cup. "How?"

"Well . . ." Burdett clearly squirmed on his stool. "My wife's a proud woman. When she kissed your boot, I was surprised. I wondered if she . . . ah . . . I wondered . . . that is, I thought she did it for . . . me."

No one laughed. If anything, they were horrified at the emotion his unchecked phrases revealed.

Burdett hurried his speech, and he slurred a few words. "Her public demonstration of gratitude would be supplemented by a much warmer, sincerer demonstration of gratitude in private to Lady Edlyn, and I pray, my lord, that that will ease Lady Edlyn's chagrin, and thus your discomfort."

"That's not fair!" Wharton objected.

"Ah, leave it." Sir Philip turned his mug around and around. "Women are powerless. None of them have a man's good sense, but it still can't be easy."

"What would a woman do with power?" Sir Lyndon demanded. Then he answered his own question. "Squander it, that's what."

Wharton stood on the bench, and he pointed his finger around the small room with a scowl. "A woman doesn't know what t' do with power. Most women don't know what t' do with a cooking pot. I tell you, when we let women rule our lives, they create nothing but havoc. We've got t' start treating them like they deserve, giving them an occasional smack, using th' stick fer—"

Hugh heard the thunk before he realized anything was amiss.

Wharton flew up. His feet whipped around. He hit the ground on his back, and all of the breath left his lungs with a grunt.

In the place of Wharton, Ethelburgha stood. She bristled with indignation, like a hedgehog at the sight of a wolf pack. "Ye're all a bunch o' asses an' lickspits."

"Ethelburgha!" Burdett staggered to his feet.

Ethelburgha pointed at him, and as if her finger contained power, he sat back down.

She said, "Every time yer armies march through this village an' burn me alehouse, I wish men'd learn what every woman knows. Th' sense is peace at all times an' in all places, not yer eternal squabblin'. If one o' ye had th' brains God gave every girl-baby, ye'd go thankin' yer women fer teachin' ye all ye know about kindness."

Dewey muttered something.

Hugh thought it sounded like respectful agreement.

"What her ladyship's askin' is but credit fer her wisdom, an' ye men're too blinded wi' pride t' give it."

Sir Philip could scarcely speak for choking. "You can't talk to the earl like that."

"I suppose she can." Hugh stood and wrapped his cape close around his shoulders. "What am I supposed to do, kill the village alewife for insolence on my first day here?"

"Some men might," Ethelburgha said.

"You gambled well," Hugh started for the door. "Whatever your opinion of me, I'm not so asinine as that."

"So go an' give yer lady thanks fer doin' what ye wished when she married ye, an' that's givin' ye th' benefit o' her experience managin' estates."

Hugh's head snapped around, and he stopped before exiting. "How did you know that?"

Burdett sat with his hand over his eyes. "Ethelburgha knows everything."

"Not everythin', but I know who yer lady is an' what she was t' me old master," Ethelburgha retorted.

Hugh heard her and he kept walking, and Ethelburgha kept following him. As soon as she cleared the door, he grabbed her fleshy arm. She tried to twist away, but he clutched the fat that jiggled there. "My lady didn't know your old master."

She walked sideways when he pulled her away from the alehouse so his men wouldn't hear them.

She never stopped talking. "No one knew th' master, but he had a way o' stalkin' a woman that sucked th' goosebumps up on th' flesh."

He didn't believe it. He'd asked Edlyn if she knew Pembridge, and she'd denied it. Yet he remembered the way her eyes fell away from his when he questioned her, so now he asked, "What makes you think he stalked my lady?"

"He used t' go t' Jagger Castle an' come back wi' that wild look in his eye." Ethelburgha jerked herself free and rubbed her arm. "An' all th' maids wi' brown hair an' green eyes would tremble an' hide."

"That's hardly proof of wrongdoing by my lady!"

"I'm no mean gossip, m' lord." Ethelburgha's eyes snapped, and she poked him in the chest with her pudgy finger. "I didn't say there was wrongdoin'. If there'd been wrongdoin', I wouldn't have told ye. 'Twas a wandering minstrel who gave me th' gossip, m' lord. He said th' folk at Jagger Castle buzzed about their lady's virtue in th' face o' her husband's adultery, an' when I said I didn't care about folks so far away, he laughed an' said I ought, since 'twas me own lord who sniffed after her."

"Why wouldn't she tell me?" Hugh asked, half to himself.

"Because havin' Edmund Pembridge lurkin' behind ye is nothin' t' brag about, m' lord." She lowered her voice. "I'm tellin' ye this because Burdett wouldn't listen. He says I'm just a woman an' t' stir me kettle an' leave th' thinkin' t' th' men, but I tell ye, m' lord, Pembridge never let anythin' go that he wanted. As long as he lives, I fear fer Roxford, an' ye should fear fer yer lady."

Sincerity shone from her, and Hugh took her words to heart.

Then she raised her voice. "A little public gratitude wouldn't go amiss wi' yer lady. Try it, m' lord, an' ye'll see."

Hugh glanced up. His men stumbled out of the alehouse. Ethelburgha didn't want them to hear this scandal.

He didn't either. Raising his voice to match hers, he said, "Mayhap I will."

"Try givin' her th' same loyalty ye espouse fer th' king."

Hugh glared and stomped toward the castle.

"Or more!" she yelled.

He pretended not to hear.

Hugh and Edlyn met at the foot of the stairs going into the keep. They stood, two wet, miserable people who happened to be married, and stared at each other as if unsure what to say. Behind them were Burdett and Neda, Wharton, Dewey, Sir Philip, Sir Lyndon, and all the men of Hugh's retinue, and they stared at the couple with an interest heightened by the recent revelations.

Edlyn wanted to speak, then wondered if she should allow Hugh to speak first as a gesture of respect.

Hugh wanted to speak, but he didn't know what to

say to a wife he'd been alternately fighting with and making love to since the day of their wedding.

Finally, driven by the west wind, the increasing rain, and a strong sense that someone had to do something, he stepped back with a slight bow and indicated the stairs.

She smiled, a slight curve of the mouth, and started up ahead of him.

"Mama! Mama!"

The boys' shouts spun her around.

"I fought Allyn with a sword and won!" A mud-covered boy—was that Parkin?—danced in the puddle at the side of the stairway.

"He did not!" Allyn, just as covered, kicked water at his brother. "I let him win."

Edlyn stood immobile. The two urchin boys who had fought in the mud with sticks were her sons. Hers!

"Yeah?" Parkin said.

"Yeah," Allyn answered.

"Liar."

"Tattlemonger."

"Lads!" Edlyn might not know what to say to Hugh, but she knew what to say to her sons. "Stop right now."

"But—"

"He said—"

"Not another word." She started to descend the stairs, but Hugh stood in her way, and he didn't budge.

"Do you mind if I handle this?" he asked.

His deep voice startled her, and the concept startled her more. Since the day of the boys' births, she'd had sole responsibility for their behavior and their discipline. Now this man, this husband, had offered to help.

"I have trained many a page and squire in my day."

He seemed to read her hesitation as more than surprise. He seemed to think she didn't trust him. "I will not hurt them, but I'll end this squabbling and have them clean with no trouble to you."

She stared at Hugh and saw him, not as husband, lover, or foe, but as a knight able to curb her sons where she could not. To allow him to chastise and instruct her boys would be more than a gesture of faith. It would be an unconscionable relief. Making an abrupt decision, she said, "With my blessing."

The boys had fallen silent. They stared at her with wide eyes as if she had betrayed them. Aye, let them realize how the upheaval that they'd so welcomed would topple their expectations of unlimited freedom.

Hugh snapped, "Get out of those clothes! Bathe yourselves in the rain! Wash your clothes in the horse trough!"

The boys began to sputter, then to cry.

"My lady." Neda took Edlyn's elbow. "Let us go inside."

Edlyn didn't object. She turned away from the sight of her wide-mouthed, bawling lads with no sensation of anything but contentment and climbed the stairs to the keep. Hugh wouldn't abuse them, but he would teach them.

With Neda's help, she changed into dry clothes—nothing from Richard's men, she made sure—and when Hugh entered, she was sitting by the fire in the great hall, spinning thread from a spindle while the servants hurried to set up the trestle tables for dinner.

She rose at once from her chair. "Praise the saints you have returned, my lord." She stripped off his wet cloak and handed it to the maid who appeared at her elbow. "You saved me from a fate I detest. My spinning skills have not increased during my time at the abbey."

"Then leave the spinning to the maids," he said, obviously bewildered by her offhandedness. Glancing around at the scurrying servants, he added, "There are enough of them."

"Perhaps I will." She smiled at him, determined not to ask what he'd done with her sons.

Hugh didn't wait. He just told her. "They're clean, they're getting dry, and they'll be along to beg your pardon for going out without your permission and for quarreling."

"My thanks to you." She'd never meant it as much as she did now. He'd lifted a weight off her shoulders, a weight she'd never hoped to share, and she was grateful. "If you would like, my lord, I took the liberty of laying out your dry clothing in the solar."

Steam began to rise from his clothes as the fire heated him. "Not yet. First I think we should talk about your sons . . ." He peered down at her, almost embarrassed but completely determined. "Our sons."

She had indicated to herself her willingness to share her children, and now he took responsibility for them and called them his own. That bond between them—the bond of parenthood—helped demolish the sense of helplessness she'd experienced since the time of her marriage. Curious, she said, "You could easily enforce your will about Allyn and Parkin, but you do not. Why is that?"

He stared as if she had openly called him a bully. In shocked tones, he said, "You are their mother, while I have come late to the role of father. I bow to your greater experience."

He *was* a bully, of course, but not one prompted by cruelty or meanness, and he'd changed without even realizing he had. "I was previously a wife, while you came late to the role of husband, yet you forced me to marry you as if I were a child in need of guidance." She thought she detected movement from Hugh— could he be fidgeting? "At the time I thought you truly believed it."

He looked her in the eye. "If I had it to do again, I wouldn't do it any differently. Although, mayhap, I would do it for different reasons."

"You would still force me to wed you?"

"I had no time to court you, Edlyn, and as you have said, I thought you showed a remarkable lack of intelligence in not wishing to wed me."

She wanted to laugh, but he seemed to be serious.

"Now, however, you've proved your superior wit time and again, and so I have to suppose your hesitation was nothing more than a woman's natural caution when faced with a momentous transition."

He could irritate her even as he sought to compliment her! "Could it not be, as I said, a sincere desire to avoid the grief that accompanies a marriage to a warrior?"

"That wouldn't make sense, and you are a sensible woman."

Another compliment, another irritation. Didn't he understand that some emotions didn't respond to reason?

She stared at him, so solemn, so earnest.

Of course he didn't. He lived in his man's world as the ultimate specimen of success, and illogical emotions had no place there. Edlyn could talk until next week, and until he experienced the pain of worry when a lover stood in the way of danger, he would never understand.

Recognizing defeat, she sank down on a bench and indicated the place beside her. "Tell me what you think about our sons."

Instead he dragged a stool forward and placed it facing her. Seating himself, he took her hands. Immediately, the work in the great hall slowed and all the servants found a reason to linger close.

Neda's voice called them to attention. "Get you to your chores!"

They scattered, and Hugh spoke. "I think little of your plan to place the lads in the monastery." She tried to interrupt, but he said, "Let me finish. While I know you have your reasons, I see the fire and spirit of Robin in each of the lads. Parkin's a wild man, and he needs to be trained to control that wildness. Allyn's kind and thoughtful, but he has a temper he must learn to control. I fear if they were placed in the monastery, their father's fire and spirit would be extinguished forever. Certainly their father's line will be extinguished, and I know you loved Robin too much to allow that to happen."

She knew what he was saying, and she spoke around the lump that formed in her chest. "You want them to be trained for the knighthood."

"It is the right and fitting thing to do."

She didn't know what was right and fitting anymore. She'd made her decision to have them become monks, but Allyn and Parkin had hated the idea. Although she had previously rejected Hugh's counsel in this matter, his sincere horror at that fate, even for the sons of his enemy, had given her pause. And the monks themselves seemed to have reservations about the boys' fitness for the contemplative life.

Her indecisiveness made Hugh eager. "Let them settle here," he said, "and know this place for their home. Then when they know we will be here when they return, we'll send them out to be fostered."

Hugh didn't comprehend the impossibility of what he proposed. Picking her words with care, she said, "Noble sons are sent away to strange households to be raised and trained by other men for one reason, and one reason only—to strengthen the ties between those two families. Once a knight has fostered a lad, he's almost a godfather. The families are close. Their influence is as one."

"That's true."

"Allyn and Parkin are sons of a traitor to the king."

When Hugh realized she was actually discussing this in a reasonable manner, his eagerness knew no bounds. "You place too much importance on their being the sons of a traitor. Because of my position, we can get anyone in the kingdom to foster our sons."

Her head buzzed as she strove to move old prejudices and paralyzing fear aside and act as a mature woman would. "I have no doubt you can use your influence and get Allyn placed, but who's going to foster Parkin? Who'll take care of my rambunctious lad?"

"Just because he's high-spirited—"

"Not because—" She took a breath. She had to tell him, but such confiding went against the years of reticence. "They'll take a traitor's son perhaps. But a traitor's bastard?"

Hugh just stared. He acted as if she were speaking a different language suddenly, or as if she had changed the parameters that ruled the world. "A bastard?"

"Parkin isn't truly my son. He's the son of my . . . of the earl of Jagger and my maid." She saw the moment it all made sense to Hugh, and she couldn't bear his shrewd expression.

"A bastard off a commoner," he said.

"Robin got bored waiting for me to calve, as he so charmingly put it, and she was sleeping beside our bed anyway, so he . . ." She hadn't felt this pain for a long time. She thought it over and done with. But Hugh's reaction brought it back.

He dropped her hands and rose. He circled her,

water dripping from the hem of his surcoat as he walked.

She appreciated his need for movement. Right now she would have given anything to hold that spindle, to have something to occupy her hands and her eyes while Hugh stared at her. But the spindle remained on the other side of the fireplace, and she didn't think she could rise.

She hated that Hugh pitied her, yet the woman she was now also pitied that lass she had been. Robin's wife, with the swollen ankles and the distended belly and the mate who found her so repulsive. She had been young and so grateful to Robin for marrying her, but the gratitude had faded when his grunts of pleasure had combined with her virgin maid's sounds of pain. Her maid's shame and guilt had made Edlyn look at Robin in a new light, and her love had begun its slow death.

In sooth, Edlyn had been a poor, odd creature when he'd wed her, but even *she* deserved a husband who went outside their bedchamber to ease his overfull loins. So she cringed as she remembered her early anguish, but she kept talking. "So I knew the baby was Robin's right from the beginning. When Parkin's mother died in the birthing, Allyn was only four months old."

"They're not twins." Hugh still wrestled with reality.

"I had milk, and Allyn wasn't well. Every day I feared he wouldn't wake from his sleep. I kept remembering how she'd suffered in the birth, and I couldn't condemn Parkin when death hovered so close to my own child." She glanced up at him. He'd stopped pacing and just gazed at her now. "That's what would have happened if I'd given him to one of the other women to nurse."

"Is Parkin the only bastard that Robin has?"

She laughed. "Heavens, nay. He scattered his seed everywhere, like a farmer standing in the wind. But as far as I know, all their mothers live still."

"Do the lads know? Does Parkin—"

"Of course. Did you think anyone who lived in Jagger Castle would keep that quiet?" Hugh's amazement had faded, and she explained as much as she could as quickly as she could. "That's why Parkin demands attention, and why Allyn lets him. The busybodies have told Parkin he's not truly mine, and he worries. Allyn is more secure, and he loves his brother."

"You treat them alike so they won't grow to hate each other like those nuns. Like Lady Blanche and her sister Adda." Hugh swiped his damp hair off his forehead. "No wonder your trust is a flimsy thing."

"I trust you," she answered immediately. "Am I not listening to your counsel about my sons?"

He sat back down, facing her once more. "Aye, you trust me with your sons, but not with yourself."

Did she? Was that true? What kind of mother would trust a man with the well-being of her sons but not with her own happiness? Or did she trust him, and was her defensiveness nothing but a frail bulwark that she longed for him to breach?

"You could tell me anything, Edlyn, and I would understand."

He sounded strangely compelling, as if he knew her secrets.

He whispered, "What must I do to prove I will never abuse your love when you give it to me?"

"I . . . you . . ." She glanced around, seeking escape.

He glanced around, too, and saw a dozen faces

peering at them. "If you don't have anything to do, I'll give you something to do!" he roared, sounding so much like Sir David of Radcliffe, Edlyn broke down and giggled. Disgusted, he said, "They've done it, now, haven't they? They've distracted you."

Neda was scolding, the servants were fleeing, and Edlyn tried to pretend she didn't know that he wanted a task to perform, a way to make her trust him. He didn't realize he'd shown strength and honor, which she valued above all things. Faintly, she said, "Our sons. We need to settle our sons."

He sighed but addressed the topic as she desired. "I have influence among the nobles, 'tis true. But more than that, I have friends. I've saved men's lives and been saved by them. I've drunk with barons and dukes and earls. I've accepted their hospitality, and I've given them mine. That is one of the reasons the prince remembered me when Roxford Castle was free for the claiming. My friends in court reminded him I was deserving." He indicated the head table where Wynkyn filled the goblets and inspected the trenchers. "My page is the earl of Covney's son, given to me to foster. If nothing else, I can give Parkin to Covney and know he'll be properly raised, and Allyn will not be the first traitor's son to go forth and make a name for himself." He studied Edlyn. "Does that satisfy you?"

Satisfy her? Nay, it didn't satisfy her. Her head buzzed when she thought of it, and the blood drained from her face. She'd sworn this would never happen. She didn't want her boys to become knights, to break her heart when they were carried home on boards.

Yet Neda, all unknowing, had had a reply for that. If they were good monks, they would eventually be lost to Edlyn in their devotion to God. And how could she give them to God and then pray they fail in that devotion?

"Aye." She said it before she could change her mind. "That is acceptable to me."

As she spoke, her eyes cleared and she saw the big smile Hugh gave her. "That's my lady!" He slapped her on the shoulder just as he would one of his knights, then grabbed her before she could topple. "Edlyn! I beg your pardon."

She held her aching arm and began to laugh.

"You're not hurt?"

She shook her head. "Not at all, but I see why you understand the lads' minds so well. You're nothing more than an overgrown lad yourself."

"Well." He smiled at her meaningfully. "Sometimes." Before she could reply to that, he turned her, his hands on her arms. "Here are our sons to apologize for causing you grief."

Allyn and Parkin, with that prompting, could scarcely fail in their duty. Edlyn studied them as they stood before her, dry and clean, stammering their expressions of regret. They were both so much like Robin, and that frightened her. But with Hugh as an example, they could learn consistency, integrity, and all the virtues of knighthood. Relaxing, she knew she had done the right thing.

"I have decided . . ." She stopped, then caught one of Allyn's hands and one of Parkin's hands. "We have decided both of you should train for the knighthood. Would you both like that?"

Parkin came right up off the floor. "Train now? With a sword? Can I have armor? When do we start?"

Allyn, more quiet but with his face shining like a newly polished stone, repeated, "Oh, Mama. Oh, Mama!"

"If they are to be knights," Hugh said, "they first must be pages." He snapped his fingers, and Wynkyn, his arm still in a sling, and Dewey, large and stern-looking, materialized behind the boys. "Take them and train them to properly serve the table."

"The table?" Parkin couldn't have looked more horrified. "Why do we have to serve the table?"

"Because that is what pages do," Allyn said. "And when we become squires, we'll have to polish the armor. *You* wanted to be a knight because you thought it would be easier than being a monk."

"Did not."

"Did, too."

"You don't fight in front of your betters." Dewey cuffed them both, and as they stood rubbing their heads, he said, "Come with me and I'll tell you what to do."

Hugh and Edlyn watched as they were led away. "They're good lads," Hugh reassured her. "They'll settle in and learn their duties."

"I know."

He took an audible breath and made his voice deeper as if to impress her with his earnestness. "As I toured the demesne this morning, I could see that I, too, have much to learn." He scuffled his feet in the reeds. "There's more to this than just sitting on my arse waiting for a maid to bring me ale."

From the smell of him, she thought he'd had plenty of ale. It didn't seem to be affecting him adversely, except for the way he squirmed. "Hugh, I will gladly excuse you to use the garderobe."

"I don't need to bleed my sausage!"

He seemed totally indignant, and she murmured an apology.

"At least, not much."

She grinned.

"I'm trying to . . . that is, I wish to thank you for . . ." he stammered.

His uncertainty made her serious. What did he want?

"My thanks for helping me make the . . . proper decisions about Roxford Castle."

"Louder!" someone stage-whispered, and Edlyn glanced around. All the servants had paused to listen again, but this time Hugh didn't chase them away.

"Without your gracious guidance"—he boomed so loudly she flinched—"I would have made a serious mistake by dismissing the steward and his wife, and it is with great good cheer that I thank you and encourage you to continue to lend me the wisdom of your expertise."

"Oh, Hugh." She blinked back tears and impulsively leaned forward and kissed him. "You are too good."

He caught her when she would have retreated. "Not good enough. Not yet. But I will be, and you'll give me all soon."

She hugged him, and the servants cheered quietly, then hurried about their business as if expecting Hugh to yell again.

He wouldn't. Not now. Not while he was feeling so cocky.

"Edlyn?"

And sensitive. Somehow, for some reason, he'd sensed the temblor that rocked Edlyn to the soul. The girl who'd fallen in love with Hugh had been buried, and Edlyn thought her dead. Now it seemed she had only been sequestered by the insulating walls that she'd built to block the pain of experience. One wall had already fallen this day; would another tumble?

"Edlyn?" he said again, his voice eager and his body expectant.

She pulled back, just enough to see his face. If she gave her heart into his keeping, it would be the biggest gamble of her life. For if he failed her, she would wither. And if she didn't give her heart into his keeping, wouldn't she wither anyway?

"Hugh." She cupped his face in her hands. "Hugh . . ."

"M' lord!" Wharton's shout brought a chorus of shushes, but he persisted. "M' lord, 'tis th' prince's messenger." His eyes gleamed with anticipation. "He brings news of the war. We'll be fighting again soon!"

18

She'd almost made a serious mistake.

Edlyn moved through the bustling great hall, directing the packing.

She'd almost declared her love for Hugh.

She glanced across the huge, vaulted chamber at her husband. He sat at the table on the dais, directing his men, scribbling notes, listening to the messenger, and generally acting like the commander of the royal troops in the west.

She'd almost given her love to Hugh, and that would have been worse, for the other was only words but the love itself formed part of her soul.

She caught one of the pillars as a spasm of pain clutched at her.

She hadn't given him her love.

"We'll leave tomorrow morning," she heard him say. "The rain has stopped and the sun is out."

Was the sun shining? Edlyn hadn't noticed.

He continued, "Obviously, God favors our cause."

For that bit of ludicrous nonsense, he got a snort from Edlyn. She'd heard *that* before. Before Robin had marched off to his last battle, that was what he'd said.

But Hugh didn't care what she thought. Hugh just moved to do his duty and never mind that she was dying inside.

Or she would be, if she loved him.

"Edlyn."

He called her from across the great hall, and she needed to brace herself before she could look at him. To give herself a moment, she instructed the maidservant. "Air the rugs well before you put them in the trunk lest they mildew."

"Aye, my lady." The maid, caught in the middle of airing the rugs, curtsied without expression.

She no doubt thought Edlyn mad, but Edlyn didn't care. She'd indicated her indifference to Hugh by waiting a little too long to answer.

"Edlyn?"

His hands closed on her shoulders, and she jumped.

"Come and meet the prince's messenger. He's an old friend of mine." He pushed her before him toward the dais. "Ralph Perrett of Hardwell."

A conciliatory-looking man, Ralph Perrett stood and bowed before she even reached him.

She hated him. All that courtesy oozing from him. That polite murmur of gratitude for her hospitality. That inoffensive, yet appreciative gleam in his eyes as he gazed at her.

Who did he think he was fooling? She knew him for what he was. The prince's stooge.

Ralph Perrett subsided onto the bench when she gestured, and she found herself placed beside Hugh with a firmer hand than she cared for.

"He has brought me information about the troop movements across the countryside. Prince Edward and the Marcher barons hold the Severn Valley. Simon de Montfort and his forces have been driven back into

South Wales. His son is bringing forces up from the southeast." Hugh's eyes gleamed. "We'll meet the rebel barons soon and defeat them completely."

"With God's blessing," Perrett said.

"That again," she muttered. She jumped when Hugh poked her with his elbow.

Edlyn supposed she was acting much as her children had acted earlier, but she was tired of being mature. She was tired of settling in, thinking she comprehended her situation, adjusting accordingly, and then having everything knocked arse over hedgehog. She was just tired.

"We have everything arranged now," Hugh said. "There's nothing more for me to do tonight except feast and soak in the warmth of a hearth fire."

When it became clear Edlyn wouldn't answer, Perrett said, "Aye, that's true. 'Twill be autumn before you sit before anything but a campfire's feeble flame."

"I need to arrange the meal." Edlyn tried to rise.

Hugh's hand on her shoulder pushed her back down. "Neda is doing it. This rain has been a curse for the rebellion, but a blessing for me. It gave me a chance to heal after that wounding at Eastbury."

"I heard you were killed." Perrett allowed Allyn to refill his cup of mulled wine. "The rumors were flying!"

Hugh smiled grimly and took the cup Dewey offered. "De Montfort must have thought he'd had a stroke of luck."

"Why is it luck if the battle goes well with Simon de Montfort and God's grace if the battle goes well with you?" Edlyn asked.

Hugh shoved the cup under Edlyn's nose. "Drink."

As if she had a choice! He almost slopped the liquid down her chest to fill her mouth—and stop what it was saying. Well, if he didn't like it, he could let her go.

"It's hot!" she complained when he finally let her come up for breath.

"It's likely to get hotter," he warned in an undertone. To Perrett, he said, "My own dear lady wife cured me of that wound. I took that as a sign I should wed her."

"A sign from God, of course?" Perrett asked smoothly.

Edlyn almost laughed. If Perrett was going to be amusing, she would be hard-pressed to dislike him.

"Of course." Hugh must have felt her shudder of suppressed amusement, for his grip on her relaxed.

"How long will you be gone?" She hoped for an answer, that kind of solid reply on which she could depend.

De Montfort's troops are in tatters, she imagined Hugh saying. *All I'm going to do is chase them into the ocean.*

She could almost hear it. *I'll be back before the new moon,* he'd say. *Don't try to take all the responsibility for Roxford on yourself. Leave some for me.*

Best of all—*I couldn't stay away from you. If I did, my step would falter and my eye would dim. Nay, Perrett, you must go to Prince Edward and tell him. Tell him I wish only to stay with my wife who has stolen my heart.*

Instead he said, "We have to find the enemy first. Mayhap we will meet up with the prince and fight a battle with him. That battle will only last a day, but we must kill or capture de Montfort and his son. We'll have to chase them as they retreat and engage them in another battle."

He relished the thought, it was clear. His eyes

twinkled, his smile, lavished on her so seldom, appeared and stayed.

Wharton slapped a loaf of bread on the table. "Then ye'll free th' king an' then ye'll have t' go t' court." He shuddered. "I hate court."

He would, Edlyn thought. No man could be more out of place than Hugh's servant.

"Simon de Montfort has lost most of his support among the barons," Perrett said.

"Then I'll be back before the first snow flies." Hugh leaned back with a sigh of what sounded like dejection.

Edlyn came off the bench so fast that his hand, when he reached for her, closed on nothing.

"Edlyn," he yelled. "Come back right now!"

Edlyn didn't want to cry. She wanted to beat on somebody. She wanted to go hide. She wanted to . . . to . . . cry. No instinct told her where to go. She hadn't lived at Roxford long enough to seek refuge blindly. But she ran toward the stairs that led outside, heard Hugh's steps behind her, and plunged instead up toward the solar. That bar on the door could be used to keep Hugh out as well as any intruders on marital privacy, and anyway, how hard would he try to get in? What he really wanted to do was talk battle strategy with Ralph Perrett, the royal weasel.

She darted up the stairs and hit the door with all her strength, then shoved it closed. She reached for the bar only to stumble back when Hugh smacked the door with all *his* strength.

He didn't even notice when she sat down hard among the rushes. He just stomped over and stood above her. "What did you think you were doing down there? You broke every rule of hospitality."

"Oh, hospitality." She scooted back. "He doesn't deserve my hospitality."

"He's a guest. Our first guest." He paced away. "And my friend!"

Standing, she rubbed her sore rump and wondered what exactly she should say. The rules of hospitality were firm. With few inns, and those louse-ridden, and with men like Richard of Wiltshire on the road, the castle owners always opened their pantries and offered a place to sleep to the weary traveler. She knew the rules. She'd lived by the rules, even enjoyed the rules, for all her life. But being polite to Ralph Perrett had been more than she could do.

"Well?" Hugh tapped his foot.

For the first time, she realized why he got so irritated when she treated him like one of her sons. "I didn't feel like welcoming Ralph Perrett."

"Why not?"

Because he came to take you away.

The thought blasted through her with the chill of a winter storm, and she jumped away from it.

"Why are you so nervous?" Hugh demanded. "I told you before, I don't beat women. Although you have tested that resolve sorely this night. Now come back down and—"

"I will not." She moved to the fire and warmed her hands. "You go down and make my apologies to your friend. Tell him I will rise to see him off. Him, and you, and . . . are you taking my sons?"

Her sons? Hugh heard that like a crack across the knuckles. What did she mean, her sons? Only this morning, they had been *their* sons. "I wouldn't take two untried lads into battle. They don't even know how to carve a roast, much less spit a knight!"

"Thank you for that, at least."

Her voice had grown quiet, down from that high-pitched squeak of anger and dismay. It sounded better on the ears, but somehow he suspected it wasn't better for him, or for her.

"This is about my going into battle for the king, isn't it?"

"Your depth of comprehension astonishes me."

No one dared mock him, but he recognized this nonetheless. "Did you think I wouldn't go when the prince called?"

"Oh, nay. I always knew you would go."

"Then why are you angry?"

"I'm not angry."

She really didn't seem to be, but something was wrong, and he knew what it was. "The king is my sworn lord and in need of help from all true English lords. I cannot abandon him!"

"Your duty calls. I'm not stopping you."

But she was. She was holding back some powerful emotion, and when he recalled that moment of the morning, that moment when he thought she was going to gift him with herself, he felt sick. Had it all been a lie? "You told me you didn't care anymore when he died. You said he'd killed your love."

"Who?"

"Robin. That's what this is all about, isn't it?"

"Nay!"

"I captured your husband, your one true love, and sent him to be executed, and you thought you could sway me from my duty to the king by promising to . . . to . . . "

"Love. The word is love."

He girded his loins. "By promising to love me."

"That's not true."

"Then what is true?"

"I loved Robin once. That love is dead. Was dead when he died. That has nothing to do with this."

"Then why are you acting this way? A lesser man would feel guilty for leaving you in the performance of his duty."

"And you're not a lesser man."

She was sneering, and he didn't like that.

She tried to speak, and words seemed to elude her. At last she said, "You might be killed."

She had sounded matter-of-fact, so he tried to, too. "We've talked about this before. I won't be killed."

Her sensible facade cracked. "Robin said that, too."

"I . . . am . . . not . . . Robin."

"I've met the widows of other men who marched off to battle with like minds."

"Then this *is* about Robin. The shade of Robin haunts our marriage."

"Nay!"

"What other reason could there be for you to wish me to stay behind when men are joined in battle?" She glared and twisted her hands, and he dared something he would never have tried before this morning. "Are you saying," he asked carefully, "you don't want me to go because you're afraid of Pembridge?"

"Pembridge?"

"Aye, Pembridge. You did meet him when you lived with Robin, didn't you?"

She widened her eyes so much the whites shone all around, and her horror spoke for itself. She had lied to him. He had asked her if she knew Pembridge, and she'd said nay. What was she hiding?

"I met him," she admitted.

He almost staggered from the pain of her betrayal. "Have I been wrong all along? Is this about *him*?"

"Nay!" She shot to her feet and stood, visibly shaking. "I didn't tell you because he . . . I didn't like the way he . . . I am afraid of Edmund Pembridge."

"Afraid?"

"He never hurt me, but I think he is a cruel man."

Hugh thought she was right.

"I was always faithful to Robin."

"But did you want to be?"

"I never wanted Pembridge." Her shaking increased.

"What about me?" His dissatisfaction and sorrow increased with every anguished moment. "Then do you want me?"

Her eyes sparked; she began to answer.

He'd asked the wrong question. "Nay, wait—do you *love* me?"

"I . . . you . . ." She seemed to be wrestling with some great emotion that weighed on her mind and turned her eyes a sluggish green.

He wanted her to say yes. She would say yes, he knew it.

"I . . . nay."

He let out his breath. "Well. That is that, then."

"Nay." She said it again—in case he didn't hear it the first time, he supposed. "I don't love you. But I am your true and loyal wife, and I swear, my lord, that I would never betray you."

She looked at him without hesitation or fear, and he remembered what Ethelburgha had said. That no woman would brag about having Edmund Pembridge lurking behind her. Remembering the man and his sly habits, Hugh hoped that might just be all the truth. With a sigh, he said, "Thank you for that, at least."

Hugh's step faltered as he trod the stairs down to the great hall. He didn't know what to believe anymore. He couldn't despise Edlyn, as much as he wanted to. She'd proved herself to be capable, clever, and kind, and he wanted her. By the saints, he did want her.

He almost turned back and climbed those stairs once more when he saw Wharton, Sir Lyndon, Sir Philip, and Ralph Perrett sitting around the trestle table, waiting for him. It should have been a council of war; from the expressions on their faces, he knew it was a lecture, and he was the one who would hear it.

Wharton smirked. "Is she going t' let ye go?"

Placing his hands on the table, Hugh seated himself.

"She is overwrought." Sir Philip obviously disapproved.

"That woman needs discipline." Sir Lyndon clipped the words off.

In soothing tones, Perrett said, "I've seen it a dozen times. When the wife hears the husband goes to battle, she must go and cry."

Hugh found himself biting his tongue. For most of his life, he had been the best at everything—at riding, at combat, at commanding. This day he had shown his ignorance to Burdett time and again with his stupid questions. While Burdett had hidden his astonishment well and answered patiently, Hugh chafed at his own incognizance.

Now these men, his companions, thought to give him advice on the handling of his wife. As if he were some inexperienced boy with his first woman! The reduction to student galled and humiliated him, and he could scarcely contain his impatience.

Worse was the knowledge he had invited their comments with his remarks in the alehouse that very afternoon. And tonight he might be listening to these men's opinions—aye, he might—except for the memory of

Ethelburgha and her righteous indignation. She had scorned Sir Philip, Sir Lyndon, and Wharton—Wharton still sported a lump over his eye from her scorn—and gave Hugh different advice. Advice that he'd put into action and that had almost given him the desired results. Edlyn had almost told him she loved him. Almost. So close.

Maybe women knew what they wanted more than men knew what they needed.

"So you'll leave me in charge," Sir Lyndon finished.

"What?" Hugh had missed something, and he narrowed his eyes as he considered Sir Lyndon.

"You'll leave me in charge of Roxford Castle while you go into battle," Sir Lyndon repeated obligingly. "It only makes sense. I'm the knight who has been with you the longest, and someone has to remain behind in case of treachery."

"Whose treachery?" Wharton asked.

Sir Lyndon twitched toward the place where the steward and his wife worked.

"Humph."

Wharton didn't seem impressed with any suspicion against Burdett and Neda, and Hugh noted that. Wharton had proved to be an astute judge of character over the years.

In fact, Wharton had never liked Sir Lyndon.

Hugh still smarted with the knowledge that Edlyn had lied to him about Pembridge, so he leaned close to Wharton. "Do you like Lady Edlyn?"

Wharton reared back, affronted. "*Like* her?"

Hugh tried again. "Do you trust her?"

"Oh." Wharton nodded. "*Trust* her. Aye, I trust her."

So did Hugh. Mayhap he was a fool, but he trusted her. She said she didn't love Pembridge, and he believed her. "I will leave my lady in charge."

Sir Lyndon almost fell off his bench. "Your—"

"My lady. That is why I married her."

"She just went wailing upstairs because you're leaving her. She's a stupid little—" Someone must have kicked him under the table, for Sir Lyndon jumped, then visibly regained control.

"She has much experience with directing a castle while her husband is away." Hugh shook his head when Wharton offered ale. He needed his wits about him.

Sir Lyndon had gotten over his first shock and now applied logic. Or what he thought was logic. "I've been around your lady for quite a while now, my lord, and she is overflowing with emotions. She's always blubbering or laughing out loud. She has no dignity. What kind of control would she have over the servants? Over the men-at-arms?" He leaned forward and pressed his hand on Hugh's arm. "Hugh, you need a man here. A man like me!"

"I do need a man here." Sir Lyndon's gesture didn't impress Hugh, any more than his use of Hugh's first name. "Sir Philip will perform that service."

"I, my lord?" Now Sir Philip had trouble maintaining his seat.

Sir Lyndon stared at Sir Philip as if he wore a beetle for decoration. "He's nothing but a one-eyed old knight!"

"Ah." Sir Philip stroked his mustache. "I understand now. In sooth, Sir Lyndon, that is the reason my lord chose me rather than you. You have a place at his side during the vigor of battle, while I perform my duty at home."

"Does that offend you?" Hugh asked Sir Philip.

"It is a little odd to be left behind after so many years of combat," Sir Philip said. "But I cannot complain about the reasoning or the duty."

Sir Lyndon lost control. He stood and towered over the rest of them and pointed his finger at Hugh. "I was to be your commander in your castle. You promised me!"

"I need you in the battle."

"I deserve—" Sir Lyndon caught himself, and the words hung on the air.

"You have no experience in domestic matters." Hugh didn't address Sir Lyndon's expectations, but as Sir Lyndon spoke, he became more and more sure of his own wisdom. "You should do as I do and learn from the people who have experience."

"Who?" Sir Lyndon snapped.

"Lady Edlyn," Hugh answered.

A vein in Sir Lyndon's forehead swelled and beat with his agitation, and Hugh thought he would leap over the table and strangle him.

Instead he took several deep breaths and sank down into his seat. His chin dropped, and he spoke to his lap rather than to Hugh. "Then leave me here to learn."

"Sir Philip—" Hugh began.

"Sir Philip is a warrior, too. He knows not about the direction of a castle, especially a castle so large. I would place myself under his direction, learn as he learns, and prove myself to you once more." Sir Lyndon looked up and smiled persuasively, reminding Hugh of the joyous, rash young warrior he had once known. "And as you yourself said, my lord, Sir Philip is an old man. I doubt he would object to knowing there is someone here to carry out his orders."

Hugh hadn't thought of leaving both of them behind, but he would feel better knowing two minds, two hearts, were dedicated to protecting Edlyn and his home. They would serve as a check on each other, and knowing the other was watching, each would be forced to obey Edlyn as if she had always been their lady.

Sir Lyndon sensed Hugh's weakening. "And my lord, I would like to point out that no one has seen Edmund Pembridge or any of his men since the battle last fall."

Hugh jerked in surprise. "He's with Simon de Montfort."

Sir Lyndon shook his head.

"Then he's with de Montfort's son."

Sir Lyndon smiled grimly. "He is not with either of them, nor is he dead, my lord. 'Tis said he wintered in his castle in Cornwall and with the spring went on the march against his enemies. Mayhap it would do well to zealously fortify his former home against him."

Did Hugh think Edlyn was a fool? She would have declared love, affection, need, anything if it would have kept him at her side, but nothing would do that. She could have wallowed in love, tempted him with her body, strung a thousand kisses across his form, and he still would have ridden off to do his duty.

Duty. It made her ill. She'd done her duty too often and too well, and what had it got her? An empty bed.

Of course, some people might say it didn't need to be empty. Hugh had slept elsewhere last night, but only because she'd locked the door against him. He'd been furious, if his poundings and his shouts had been any indication, but she'd just pulled the covers up and ignored him, and eventually he'd gone away. He hadn't even burned down the door as she half expected. He'd just . . . gone away.

Gone away.

She shoved the rugs off her head and sat up. An

early morning light beamed in through the glass, and she stared at it in blatant incredulity.

If she didn't get downstairs, he would leave without her pledge of love.

She scrambled out of bed fully dressed and ran to the door. Remembering, she ran back to her trunk and pulled out a white linen shift. Hands trembling with haste, she returned to the door and pulled the bar out of its brackets. Her bare feet made no sound as she descended the stairs, and the cold of the stone made no impression on her. She only knew she had to find Hugh before he left. She skidded on the reeds as she raced into the great hall and found it abandoned.

So all the servants had gone downstairs to bid the warriors farewell. She would join them.

The outer door hung open, and from the landing she saw the great gathering of servants, just as she expected. But rather than facing outward to wave good-bye, they walked toward her as if that duty had already been carried out.

She looked at the gate, but no troop of knights remained within.

"My lady?" Neda stood on the bottom step and looked up at her. "They're gone."

Stupid with dismay, Edlyn stared at the older woman. They were gone? She'd sent Hugh off, probably to his death, without a word?

Something of her anguish must have shown on her face, for Neda said, "If you wish, I know a place where you can watch him ride away."

Edlyn rushed down the stairs, Neda took her arm, and together they hurried through the gate into the outer bailey, then up the stairs to the top of the battlements. On the broad wall walk, every man-at-arms leaned out and watched some event off in the distance.

Edlyn rushed to a notch in the stone and stared out also. "There they are!"

They were close enough that she could still distinguish each knight, and Hugh himself towered over the others. They weren't looking back though. They all faced forward, moving away from this home that had sheltered them briefly and toward the fighting they knew so well.

"Hugh." Edlyn whispered his name. Then she screamed. "Hugh! Hugh!" She stepped up into the embrasure between the tall stone merlons. "Hugh!"

He couldn't have heard her, but his head turned suddenly and he stared back at the castle as if imprinting it into his brain.

Frantically, she waved the shift she still clutched in her hand. "Hugh. Hugh!"

Attracted by the flailing white garment, his gaze lifted to the place where she stood. He stopped, staring, and turned his horse. Then she saw the flash of his teeth, and he waved an arm in reply.

The knights around him took in the situation in one glance, then rode on. Only Wharton remained by Hugh's side, and even from the distance Edlyn felt the disgust in his glare.

She didn't care. Hugh was smiling and waving, and she continued to signal with the white shift even after he'd gone on.

Behind her, Neda said, "He's out of sight in the forest, my lady."

"Aye." He was. She knew it, but she didn't want to face the emptiness of the castle behind her. Oh, people filled it, of course. She had many duties to attend, and her sons required she reestablish her discipline now that Hugh had left. But knowing she would not catch a glimpse of Hugh, not hear his voice or have the opportunity to touch him, made her obligations almost too heavy to bear.

Dear lord, she did love him.

She'd sworn not to. She'd been hurt so badly by Robin she had sincerely thought her capacity to love had been destroyed. But Hugh had resurrected an old love and built on it, and now all of her—her past, her present, her future—was saturated with the desire to be with him. She loved him. She loved a warrior.

"You should come down now."

Edlyn felt a tug on her cotte, and she saw Neda held her hem in both fists as if she feared her lady would fall.

"You've signaled your desire for truce to your lord."

"Truce?"

"The white flag," Neda said gently. "He understood, I'm sure."

The white flag? Edlyn stared about her. Ah, the shift in her hand. She'd waved it, and Hugh had thought she had declared her submission. Well, she hadn't. She might love the man, but she was far from submissive.

Hugh stood on a hill and stared across the open meadow turned golden in the setting sun. There, on the morrow, he would meet and defeat one army of rebels who fought for Simon de Montfort's cause.

The breeze lifted Hugh's hair and cooled his cheeks, and the sky showed no hint of rain. Aye, it would be a good day for battle. Not so hot that men would broil within their armor, but dry enough so that the horses could find footing.

Yet the armies were a mere eight days' march from Roxford, and that made him uneasy. In this terrain and in this weather, a lone man with changes of mount could ride to Roxford in two days. That was too close. There would be vagrants after the battle, men who had captured horses and armor and looked for other plunder. Worse still, the armies of Simon de Montfort and his son could easily move in that direction. Then Edlyn would be besieged.

Edlyn. He took a breath of fresh air and remembered the sight of that white flag she waved from the battlements. Trust Edlyn to signal defeat when he couldn't claim his reward. She had left him with an itch he couldn't scratch and strengthened his determination to get back to her so he could subdue it.

Edmund Pembridge might have besieged her heart, but Hugh de Florisoun had won it.

If only they'd had time to have the fealty ceremony! If he could have held the hand of each knight and each servant in his own and looked into his eyes as he swore to obey and serve Hugh as his master, Hugh wouldn't be so anxious now.

Where was Edmund Pembridge? Hugh had thought him in Simon de Montfort's army or even with de Montfort's son. To hear that Pembridge had disappeared into the English countryside made Hugh want to watch his back—and to beg Edlyn to watch for treachery, too.

For really, how much did he know about the men he'd left to guard Edlyn?

Oh, aye, Burdett had said he would gladly transfer his loyalty to Hugh, but would he really? He had been Pembridge's man for years; was he still?

Sir Philip he didn't know well either. He was a private man, not given to confidences, and while Hugh thought him reliable, he couldn't help but wonder if any man was reliable enough to trust with Edlyn.

That was why, he told himself, he'd left Sir Lyndon at Roxford Castle, too. If only Sir Lyndon had fulfilled the promise of their early years together. If only he would acknowledge his mistakes and leave his bitterness behind. His offer to remain behind as second-in-command was a beginning. But now, as Hugh waited on the eve of battle, it occurred to him that if Sir Lyndon wished to make mischief, he had placed himself in a prime position.

The fears preying on Hugh's mind only strengthened his resolve. He had to defeat the rebel forces.

His hands ached to hold a sword, yet across on the opposite hill, he could see the tents of the enemy lined up in colorful rows. Before each tent waved a flag with the symbol of its owner sewn on in bright silks. Lions, griffins, and eagles reared their heads, but to one Hugh's gaze kept straying.

A stag on a background of black and red proved one thing. The Maxwells were here.

"My lord." Dewey stood at his elbow. "Sir Herbert wishes to know where he should place his archers."

Hugh's gaze never left the tents. "I already told him."

"I know, my lord, but he seems nervous."

With a sigh, Hugh turned and went toward Sir Herbert's tent. A good knight and one of the king's faithful barons, Sir Herbert was inclined to fret on the eve of battle, and Hugh knew it was worth his while to reassure him.

Then Hugh returned to his place on the hill. The sun had set while he calmed Sir Herbert's fears, and now he could see aught of the other camp but the fires of the enemy.

Many were the flames, and many were the knights squatting around them. It wouldn't be an easy fight, not at all, and he looked forward to it.

About that, anyway, Edlyn was right. He did like to fight. What man wouldn't? The scent of destrier between his thighs, the sight of an armored knight charging him, the clash of arms all around . . . ah, it roused his blood. No mere woman could understand.

Still, an intelligent man did what he could to ensure victory, even if his actions didn't involve killing.

His gaze returned to the place where he knew the Maxwells waited.

"M' lord, I got a group o' foot soldiers who've never seen battle before, an' they're making themselves half ill with fear." Wharton's voice came from the dark void beside Hugh. "Could ye come an' put th' fear o' deserting into them before they flee?"

"I'll come," Hugh answered. It was always thus the night before a battle. Every man looked up at the stars and feared he would never see them again. Every man feared he would end a legless beggar on the street, reminding passersby of a long ago battle and pleading for a few pence. Every man feared he'd left his wife for the last time.

Edlyn . . .

Hugh calmed the foot soldiers easily. They were good men, but untried, and when he demonstrated a few tricks with the quarterstaff and the lance, they stopped quaking and began practicing. He left Wharton supervising their training and walked through his camp, greeting his knights, speaking with his lords, reassuring everyone the royal commander was there and knew his duty.

But even as he walked, his mind returned to the camp across the way.

The Maxwells.

He'd lived in their drafty, primitive castle in Scotland for over a year. They'd taught him Scottish tracking techniques. He taught them English fighting tricks. He'd drunk their ale and learned their songs, but tomorrow he would face them on the battlefield and kill them.

It was part of a knight's life and nothing new. So why did he think there could be a better way?

He couldn't help but remember Edlyn, captured by the bandits and feeding them noxious herbs. And Edlyn, trapped in Richard's castle, singing her way to freedom. Edlyn didn't understand fighting, but she did understand how to weigh the balance in her direction.

He liked not such womanish tricks, yet the sight of that white flag haunted him. He had to defeat this army so his forces could rescue the king and place him once more on the throne. He had to get home for Edlyn.

Hugh heard Wharton's hoarse voice calling him and swerved away. Dewey spoke not far from Wharton, and Hugh swerved again. He made his way to the supply wagon, and while the man in charge gossiped with his helpers, he hoisted a barrel of ale onto his shoulders and tromped off into the night.

19

"*You cannot send* to my lord to tell him of our dilemma." The evening rushlights were lit as Edlyn spun a thread from her spindle.

Beside her, Neda watched and muttered in disgust as the thread got fatter, then thinner, then fatter again.

Edlyn ignored her critique and said, "It would distract him from battle, and that I cannot allow."

"But my lady, our situation is dire!" Burdett paced across Edlyn's bedchamber and ignored his wife's murmured instructions to his lady.

Burdett's agitation had been growing every day since Pembridge and his knights had shown themselves at the gate of Roxford Castle. Although the steward was efficient in every other way, Edlyn had found him ill suited to warfare. His wife dealt with the disquietude of this siege much better than her husband, and Neda glanced between Burdett and Edlyn in obvious worry as she wound her own finely pulled yarn into a colorful ball.

"Pembridge knows this castle too well," Burdett said. "He knows our weaknesses, he knows our vulnerabilities. He breached the outer walls through a nefarious trick, and he came so fast we lost the villagers to him."

Such a point rubbed Edlyn sore. It was the duty of the lord and lady to protect their people, but she'd had no time to give the villagers refuge. Pembridge had been at the outer gate almost before they could shut it, then even as they'd amassed the castle workers, he'd attacked through a hidden gate and captured the outer bailey. Now, every day, she watched from the wall walk while Pembridge used the villagers as labor, and at night she listened to the screams of the women as the knights used them for enjoyment.

No wonder the villagers had been ready to change lords. Yet what must they think of her as they suffered under Pembridge's hand?

Burdett was oblivious to Edlyn's dejection. "The loss of Sir Philip as commander has sore crippled our defense."

Edlyn could have groaned at Burdett's indiscretion. A glance at her bed showed that Sir Philip, propped up on the pillows and ruddy with fever, had been angered by Burdett's thoughtless comment. "Crippled? Crippled?" Thrusting back the covers, he lifted his bandaged leg in both his hands. "I can still give orders."

"But you cannot lead!" For a steward, Burdett showed a rare lack of tact. "You cannot walk on a foot with the flesh seared off, and the herbs my lady gives you to ease the pain have—"

Edlyn interrupted. "Sir Philip well knows his shortcomings, yet the men still trust him." She gladly dropped the spindle and pointed a finger at Burdett when he would have spoken again, and the steward silenced himself. "And we still have Sir Lyndon."

"I am not so wounded I don't know what's happening," Sir Philip snapped.

Edlyn walked to his side. "In sooth, I do not know what I would do without you." Covering the knight again, she smiled into his face. "You may not be able to walk, but your battle wisdom has proved invaluable to me."

"Damn that Pembridge." Sir Philip seemed calm, but Edlyn didn't doubt the sincerity of his curse. "He got his men in through that gate before I even knew there was a gate."

"How could you know?" she said.

"*He* might have told me." Sir Philip glared at Burdett.

Burdett defended himself hotly. "I would have if I'd had a single suspicion that an attack force lurked in the forest just waiting for Lord Hugh to leave."

"Sir Philip knows that." Neda tried to soothe him.

"'Tis almost treason!" Sir Philip shouted.

"Burdett is trustworthy," Edlyn said.

"The gate was blocked up years ago!" Burdett shouted back.

"And reopened when?" Sir Philip roared.

"I know not!" Burdett tapped his chest. "But I am not a traitor to your lady. If I were, would I not have simply opened the gates and allowed Pembridge and all his henchmen free entry? Perhaps 'tis you, and that was why you were wounded."

Sir Philip sat up straight for the first time in three days. "Are you saying I'm so stupid I couldn't even open the gate without injury to myself?"

"That is enough!" Edlyn rapped out. "I will direct the defense without either of you if you won't stop insulting one another."

Both men subsided.

"What was done is in fitting with Pembridge's character," Edlyn said. "He ever skulked and waited for the right opportunity. I simply wish he hadn't found his opportunity here."

Sir Philip's heavy gray brows curled with his interest. "Do you know him, my lady?"

What was the use of denying it now? "Aye, I know him. He was a friend of my husband's. A friend of Robin of Jagger." Neda and Burdett exchanged startled glances, but Edlyn didn't want questions. In the tone she used to upbraid her sons, she said, "I called you here, Burdett, to assist Sir Philip in preparing his defense." Sir Philip looked smug until Edlyn said to him, "Which I wouldn't have if I believed Burdett was a traitor. Give me the credit for that much sense, anyway!"

The two men alternately glared and looked sheepish.

"It seems, my lord husband and my lord knight, you have forgotten to whom you speak." Neda verbally rapped their knuckles. "Lady Edlyn has displayed a rare good sense in her sojourn here, and for you both to so disdain her judgment shows a lack of it in you both."

Burdett looked as if he would like to smack his wife, but before he could deal with her in the way he thought proper, Sir Philip asked, "Where *is* Sir Lyndon? Shouldn't he be here to consult with us?"

"I sent for him," Edlyn answered. "He didn't come."

Sir Philip's silence spoke loudly, and Burdett turned away to the window.

Finally, Sir Philip said, "He has ever treated me with courtesy."

"Would that he were so polite to my lady," Neda said.

Edlyn picked up the spindle once more and bent

her head to the task of spinning thread. "He has never been rude to me."

"It's not what he says, it's how he says it," Neda snapped.

The truth of that was what made Edlyn's position so untenable. How did she complain about a man who not only spoke fairly, but was given to such extravagant refinement he made her cringe with discomfort? What could she say? *He's too polite?* She was glad he'd failed to attend this meeting, for it freed her from the uncomfortable sensation of being the object of some incomprehensible amusement. "We'll have to do without Sir Lyndon. No doubt he discovered something which needs his attention," she said. "Pembridge holds the outer bailey, and we have no chance of retrieving it. But the inner wall is strong, the gatehouse is impregnable, the keep is stocked, and the water well is fresh. We could hold out until winter, and my lord Hugh will surely return by then."

"Aye," Burdett conceded. "Unfortunately, I know not what other dastardly tricks Pembridge has prepared."

"He is right, my lady," Sir Philip said. "In addition, I have my orders from Lord Hugh. I was to send to him at once if I suspected any threat to you."

"To Roxford Castle, you mean," she said smoothly.

"That, too, was in his mind," Sir Philip agreed. "But it was of you he spoke, and I must obey."

She squared her shoulders and didn't answer.

"My lady, you must think of your sons!" Burdett said.

Think of her sons? She thought of nothing else. "Do you really think Lord Hugh will come if we send for him?" She couldn't help sounding sarcastic. "He has sworn to rescue the king from the rebels, and if we send word that his castle is under siege, all that will do is distract him from his duty. He will not abandon it, but he will worry about Roxford, and perhaps that worry will weigh his sword arm down when he has need of it. Nay, Allyn and Parkin will benefit only from Hugh's life, not from his death. So until I see a chance of defeat from Pembridge —and I see no such chance right now—we will keep Hugh in ignorance."

Sir Philip said, "My lady, normally I would agree a man should not be distracted in battle, but Lord Hugh is no normal knight. He has the strength and courage of ten men, and defeat is not a word he comprehends."

"Would you say death is a word he comprehends?" Edlyn asked.

Burdett answered, having decided to join with Sir Philip to sway her. "Nay, never, my lady."

"Yet I saw death lay its hand on him." A sight that had haunted Edlyn ever since he had left for battle, although she'd not say so to these men. "He's not going to be undefeated forever. Every knight has a finite number of years to fight, and he's already sustained one wound that almost killed him."

Burdett and Sir Philip exchanged a glance that clearly expressed their dismay. They reached some unspoken male decision, and Sir Philip answered in a tone clearly meant to soothe. "Every knight has only so much time to seek his fortune, and if he's good enough and lucky enough, he can find it. Lord Hugh did find it, and now he has a whole new life opening before him."

"That's why he married me," Edlyn made haste to point out. "Because I have experience with this life and I can help him."

"Aye, that's one of the reasons, although—forgive me my boldness—it seems to me it is not the primary reason." Sir Philip grinned for the first time since the tarred arrow had pierced his foot. "Nevertheless, your experience is not in fighting, and with all respect, I would point out mine is. I like not this Pembridge and his knowledge of this castle. I like not his confidence or the way he demands we surrender, and—again, forgive me, Burdett—I fear he might have a conspirator within. Please allow me to send a messenger to Lord Hugh."

"They've done their damage," Edlyn said stubbornly, "and I don't believe we are in danger. Nay, Sir Philip, send no messenger. We are safe. I assure you."

The two men watched in silence as she and Neda gathered up the spindles and the finished balls of wool and departed.

When the sound of their footsteps had faded, Burdett turned to Sir Philip. "I wish you would send a messenger to the lord, regardless of my lady's wishes."

Sir Philip looked long into Burdett's face and clearly debated his answer. At last he said, "I sent a messenger the day of the attack, and again yesterday. I pray one of them got through."

Alternately amazed and pleased, Burdett finally found his voice to say, "God grant that they did. God grant them both speed."

Down the hill, across the meadow, and on silent feet, Hugh moved into the enemy's camp.

He was a fool. He knew he was. But he wanted to visit with the Maxwells one time before he had to kill them all.

He made it all the way to the Maxwells' tent before rough hands grabbed him from behind.

"State yer business, laddie, or 'twill go ill with ye."

Hugh grinned and relaxed. He knew that voice. Moving with a care he hoped would not alarm his captor, he put the barrel down on the ground. Then, grabbing the man's knuckles, he twisted them and turned out from underneath. "I'll state my business, laddie, when ye can beat me at tossing stones without cheating."

Malcolm Maxwell was silent for one astonished moment, then he roared, "Hugh! Hugh, me lad, how are ye?"

Hugh dropped the big man's fingers and clasped his shoulders instead. In the Scottish he'd learned while turning the millstone, he said, "Good to see ye, Malcolm! Although in this light, there's not much seeing to be done."

"Come in then! Come into the light where we can—" Malcolm stopped talking, then pushed Hugh's chest with all his might. As Hugh stumbled back, Malcolm said, "Wait. We were told ye were the commander of the English prince's troops."

Hugh righted himself. "Aye, so I am. Did ye think that would keep me from the best hospitality now in the south of England?"

Malcolm maintained a suspicious silence.

Hugh kicked out and connected with the barrel, and the dull sound of its laden richness spoke loudly of his intentions. "I brought a barrel of stolen English ale to prove I've not forgotten what ye taught me."

Malcolm roared with laughter. "Ye learned well— for an Englishman. Aye, 'tis the night before battle, and we'd best have our drink together now before I separate your head from your body."

"Aye, or before I teach ye proper respect for an English lord." Hugh hooked his thumbs into his belt. "I *am* a lord now, ye ken."

Opening the tent flap, Malcolm bowed low. "Enter our humble abode, then, English lord, and let us show ye a Scotsman's awe for all things English."

Which was none, Hugh knew, else they would not be there. Blinking in the light of candles, he had the impression of a tent full of large, hostile men before another rough Scottish voice spoke. "Did ye capture one of the king's Englishmen already, then, Malcolm?"

"Better than that, Hamish." Malcolm pushed Hugh forward so the light shone on him. "He came to surrender when he heard we were here."

One moment of stunned silence greeted Malcolm's announcement, then the laird himself, Hamish Maxwell, came to his feet and rushed forward. "Hugh! 'Tis glad I am to see ye, lad!"

The other clansmen, the ones who had been there during Hugh's tenure in Scotland, surged forward, following the lead of their chief. Angus and Armstrong and Charles and Sinclair, and some he recognized but could not remember, surrounded him and pounded him on his back. The others, the ones who were too young to remember him or who had been elsewhere, stood up and watched in ill-concealed amazement.

Passing from hand to hand, Hugh got tweaks and slaps and manly punches, and he returned them in fair measure. He'd forgotten how much he enjoyed the company of these men, barbarians though they were. They never pretended false friendship, nor did they break oaths given long ago. He was safe in their midst until the next day, when they would meet on the battlefield and try, as Malcolm said, to separate heads from bodies.

At that thought, he could almost hear Edlyn's voice in his ear. *There had to be a better way.*

"I've brought ye ale"—Hugh lifted the barrel above his head—"and wonder if ye have something to offer in return."

The men quieted, and Hamish eyed the barrel.

"'Tis a bold guest who brings a gift in hopes of receiving one in return."

"Ah, but most of your guests haven't gone twelve years without the fine flavor of Scottish haggis," Hugh answered.

The tent erupted into wild masculine laughter, and Hugh found himself pushed onto a stool. He was relieved of his barrel. An oat scone was placed into his one hand, and a wooden platter of haggis steamed in his other. It was, he assured them, enough to bring tears to an adopted Scotsman's eyes.

They used a tap—"just happen to carry one with us, lad"—to break through to the ale, and before a single drop had been consumed, the Scots heartily toasted him. Then he ate, and he toasted them. Then they toasted each other, then Hugh wiped the brown liquid off his upper lip and said, "I have a longing to sing a song I've not heard for too many years." In a hearty, booming voice, he started singing the song he'd heard so many times while a guest of the Maxwells. It was the song that boasted of every Maxwell's courage, strength—and the length of his claymore.

The Maxwells, caught by surprise, sputtered for only moments before joining in. One song led to another, and other adventuring Scots from other clans pushed their way into the tent. They sang their songs, too, and drank the ale until the tap ran dry. After that, different barrels, most with mysteriously English markings, were brought from their hiding places and cracked.

Hugh had forgotten the camaraderie of a Scottish evening, where every man drank all he could and spoke his piece and each wrestling match begat another. When Hugh found himself on the ground beneath a pile of smelly Scotsmen, he proved the truth of the adage that the wildcat on the bottom always won.

Late into the night, the party broke up with laughter and cheers, and Hamish Maxwell himself clapped his hand on Hugh's shoulder to show him the way out of the camp. Malcolm walked on Hugh's other side, making sure, Hugh supposed, that he would go right back to the king's camp and not loiter to cause trouble.

But Hugh didn't plan to physically attack the rebel army. Oh, nay, he had a different plan, and Hamish Maxwell knew it. The joviality left him, and he asked, "So, lad, why did ye really come to see us this night?"

"'Tis scarcely night, now," Hugh said. "See? The morning star is low on the horizon, and the sun will be rising ere long."

"So it will," Hamish said agreeably. "And then I will take your head from your shoulders."

"Ye will try." Hugh corrected him. He stretched hugely, hoping to work the aches out of his muscles that the night's work had put in. "'Twas a good cause for any Scotsman, I think, to join with Simon de Montfort and his son and all the barons who are fighting the English prince. 'Tis a good chance for a Scotsman to raid English towns and sack English farms. I imagine ye filled your coffers with goods and gold."

"And if we did?" Malcolm asked.

"'Tis no more than an Englishman expects," Hugh answered. "We all know the Scots like to fight, especially when there's profit to be made and especially when it's not on their land. But I wonder"—he cracked his knuckles, and the sound snapped through the predawn like a lance breaking—"if the Scots will be smart enough this time to escape with their plunder."

"The Scots always escape with their plunder." All geniality had escaped from Malcolm's voice.

But Hamish still sounded no more than curious. "Why wouldn't we?"

"The rebellion is about over. Simon de Montfort is in retreat, and 'tis a long march to the border from here."

"We swore to support him," Malcolm said.

"De Montfort?" Hugh laughed. "An Englishman? Since when does a Scotsman swear to an Englishman and keep his word?"

"Scotsmen have been known to keep their words." Malcolm was openly hostile now.

"Aye, to other Scotsmen, and to their adopted brothers, as ye have proved to me tonight." Hugh clapped his hand on Malcolm's back. "But to the English? Who often as not swear brotherhood to the Scots and then slit their throats?"

Neither Hamish nor Malcolm answered for a moment. Then Hamish asked, "Do ye think we're going to get our throats cut?"

"The losers always get their throats cut. Especially . . . foreign losers who are far from their homes."

The silence now was thoughtful. Hugh thought that Hamish and Malcolm were communicating without words somehow, and he wasn't surprised when Malcolm said, "It *is* a long march to the border from here."

"And a long walk to your camp, Hugh," Hamish added. He shoved Hugh forward. "So go on with ye or ye'll be fighting your battle tomorrow with your eyes only half open."

"I'm going." Hugh opened his arms and wrapped both men in a sudden hug. "Until we meet again."

He released them and ran down the hill to the meadow, then back up to his own camp. The lookout challenged him, and when he answered, Wharton himself came hurrying to his side.

"Where have you been?" Wharton scolded. "We've been scouring the camp for you."

"I've been preparing for today's battle." Hugh staggered in a sudden onset of tiredness compounded by an overabundance of ale. "And I want to go to bed now."

He did, and when he rose, Wharton came to his side and in a most peculiar tone told him that de Montfort's Scottish mercenaries had packed their gear and slipped away.

The rebels would be easily defeated on this day.

Almund stood on the outskirts of the forest that surrounded Roxford Castle and observed the activity with consternation. He'd heard the rumors as he rebuilt his ferry out of logs stolen from the king's forest, and he'd come at once. After all, any tale that concerned that sweet Lady Edlyn deserved notice, and he was glad he had listened.

The outer gatehouse had clearly been breached. Black smoke spiraled up from different places inside the bailey. The place smelled charred and a few bodies, peasant women from the village, rested in the moat. Worse, the demons who sought to dispossess his lady carried buckets of tar and great stones inside, and he heard pounding and much masculine laughter.

Whoever it was was very sure of his victory.

Almund turned and ran to get help.

"They're running, master." Wharton stood a little distance from Hugh's destrier and pronounced victory in this battle. "They'll not stop until they reach th' sea."

Hugh de Florisoun, earl of Roxford, removed his helmet and grinned as the last knights fled the battlefield. "'Twasn't much of a fight after all."

"Not without th' Scottish mercenaries." Dewey wiped the sweat from his brow. "What do ye suppose made them leave?"

"I wonder." Hugh turned his horse toward camp.

"Aye." Wharton sounded suspicious, and he stared long and hard at his master. "I wonder, too."

Hugh shrugged.

"Aye, ye're innocent," Wharton said. "Innocent as a wolf stampeding th' sheep."

Hugh threw back his head and roared with laughter.

He felt *good*. What a lesson he'd learned. What a wife he had! He'd routed the enemy, and he'd be returning to Edlyn intact and long before she expected him. Oh, aye, he'd have to join the prince in defeating de Montfort's main army, but with the addition of his forces, that should be accomplished with ease. And the king would be rescued, and the prince would be pleased with him! Perhaps Hugh would take Edlyn another estate as a gift for her forbearance.

And he'd take the defeat she'd signaled with her white flag as his gift.

A smile curled his lips. Aye, his homecoming would be all he'd ever dreamed. Edlyn would hold him to her breast as she'd done that other time when he was so sick, and she'd tell him of her love. She'd swear never to hide anything from him again. She'd caress him with her cool fingers and confess her every emotion: tenderness, caring, a deep, abiding passion that would never end, no matter how often he rode to battle. That was what she would do.

And him. He would hold her and kiss her, and when he was done making love to her, he'd say . . . what would he say? She'd expect him to say something. Something about love or commitment.

Aye, that was it. Commitment. He was committed to her, for she was his wife. She'd be satisfied with his commitment. Surely she would.

As Hugh tried to decide why he didn't believe that himself, one of Hugh's young knights rode up, half-wild with excitement. "My lord, there is a messenger waiting back at your tent."

"From the prince?" Hugh asked.

"From Roxford," the knight replied.

That wiped the smile from Hugh's face. Why had Edlyn sent to him? Was she worried about him? Would she nag him? Would she humiliate him by insinuating she feared for his life? "Roxford? What has my wife to say?"

"It's not from your wife, my lord, 'tis from Sir Philip."

"Sir Philip?" Wharton sounded as dismayed as Hugh felt. "Not good news, if it's news from Sir Philip."

Hugh spurred his destrier, and the beast bounded forward. He reached the tent and called, and the messenger, thin and fatigued, dragged out.

"My lord, Edmund Pembridge has besieged the castle. The outer wall has fallen by trickery. They occupy the bailey, and Sir Philip fears another ruse will win them all."

"Edmund Pembridge?"

Hugh imagined that he saw Edlyn's proud expression again as she said, "I am your true and loyal wife, and I swear, my lord, that I would never betray you."

Pride. He'd once told Edlyn she had too much pride, but still he'd demanded she surrender everything to him while he gave her only things—a castle, her shifts, his body. If he'd been willing to surrender *his* heart, she would have gladly abandoned her pride.

Then he imagined that white flag waving on the battlements and knew she had done just that. She'd abandoned her pride for him, and this was everything Hugh feared and more. "Why didn't my lady send for me? How goes my lady?"

"She is well, my lord, but unwilling to summon you." The messenger staggered back, still weak with exhaustion. "She refused to distract you from your battle, but Sir Philip begs that you come. Come at once, or all may be lost."

20

"My lady, I don't know what they're doing, but I like it not."

Against Edlyn's orders, Sir Philip had had himself carried to the top of the wall walk on a stretcher. She accompanied him, she told herself, to make sure he didn't overexert himself. In truth, she'd come because she had to know if she'd made a mistake. She didn't like the sounds of jubilation that came from the outer bailey. Pembridge and his men were too confident, and she feared Sir Philip was right. Either Pembridge knew of a way in, or he had an accomplice, or both.

"Mama, what's that shed doing leaning against the outside of the wall?" With his hands gripping the stone merlon that rose like a wolf's tooth out of the battlement, Parkin climbed the stones and hung far out on the other side.

She reached out and grabbed him by the hem of his surcoat, then eased him back to safety. "Don't do that," she admonished while lifting a questioning brow to Sir Philip.

"Grims?" Sir Philip couldn't rise from his

makeshift bed to see, and so he relied on the report of the chief man-at-arms.

"They built a shed and wheeled it against the wall." Grims spoke in English, then glanced around at the small knot of men-at-arms who surrounded them, and they all nodded.

"Why there?" Edlyn did what she'd just reproved her son for doing. She hung out of the battlement and stared down at the clumsy structure of wood and hide.

Grims shrugged. "I don't know, m' lady. Would that I did."

"They're not using a battering ram," Sir Philip observed.

Allyn stood off to the side, but he made his eight-year-old opinion known. "We'd *hear* that."

Sir Philip didn't seem offended, and Grims said, "'Tis a good, sturdy place in the wall, too."

"Do you hear the sounds of digging?" Sir Philip asked. "Are they tunneling beneath the wall in hopes of making it collapse?"

"There's no sound at all." Grims, a veteran of other campaigns, seemed as puzzled as Sir Philip.

Edlyn's attention wandered from the mysterious hut to the wreck of what had been a prosperous bailey, and she marveled at Pembridge's capacity for destruction. The milking shed, the dovecote, and the henhouse had all been put to the torch. The abandoned cows had been slaughtered and left to rot and swell in the sun. The horses had trampled the vegetable garden and fed on the greens. The wood from the trees, green though it was, had been used to light the bonfires that burned late each night, and around one mighty oak fagots had been placed in ceremonious care. The fagots had been lit and the tree reduced to a blackened skeleton that remained ominously erect.

Sir Philip tried to get up but sank back after the attempt. "Set the shed on fire."

Uncomfortable, the men-at-arms stepped back. They scratched and cleared their throats.

"What's the problem?" Sir Philip answered. "A flaming arrow or a cauldron of boiling tar—"

"Pembridge is using our villagers to work there, I believe." Edlyn looked at the men and in her inept English asked, "Is that not right?"

Grims nodded. "Aye, m' lady. 'Tis my wife who works within, an' th' people that I know."

"By the cross!" Sir Philip swore. He knew, of course, that the use of the villagers handicapped his soldiers in a way Pembridge could not have improved.

"Set the shed on fire anyway." Sir Lyndon walked up from the far tower where he taken up residence.

"They can't kill their own people!" Edlyn said.

"They're just a bunch of peasants. It's not like they have feelings." Sir Philip shushed him furiously, and he said, "Oh, they scarcely even speak a civilized tongue."

He was wrong about that, Edlyn thought, if the expression on Grims's face was anything to go by.

"What does Pembridge hope to accomplish?" she wondered aloud, hoping to change the subject before a fight began. "Should Pembridge take it, the prince will have this castle back before the end of summer."

"He's a jealous lord, is Pembridge," the chief man-at-arms explained. "'Twas not ever a good time when Pembridge came here t' live. I remember one time when he wanted t' bed th' cook's wife. She was a pretty thing an' sweet. Pembridge gave her flowers, an' her own cow, an' a lady's frock trimmed in fur. Th' way he looked at her, I thought he truly loved her." Grims rubbed his shield to keep his gaze away from Edlyn, as if the story was too intimate to share. "She didn't want him, nor did her husband want t' share, so she fled int' th' woods t' hide until Pembridge left." Grims stopped suddenly.

"Well?" Sir Philip demanded. "What happened?"

"Well, he hunted her down an' killed her." Grims managed to sound matter-of-fact. "Had th' dogs tear her apart. Said if he couldn't have her, no one could."

Edlyn's blood congealed as the man-at-arms fin-ished his tale. "He would destroy Roxford rather than allow Hugh to have it?"

"He'll not leave one thing that belongs t' Lord Hugh alive," Grims said.

Edlyn looked around at the inside of the crowded inner bailey. Every servant and villager who had escaped lived here now. Cattle bawled as they fought for grass. Chickens danced in and out between their hooves. Children tended their goats, and women sat in groups and discussed their situation as they spun. Ethelburgha stood over a fire and stirred a mixture of what would be ale. The keep rose in the middle of it all, and inside babies slept, toddlers played, mothers nursed. Burdett and Neda had their hands full keeping peace and spent their days hurrying from one crisis to another. They all, every one of them, depended on Edlyn.

And she'd been too proud to summon her husband to defend them.

Allyn hugged her. "All will be well, Mama."

Parkin danced up to her other side. "We'll save you! Wynkyn is teaching us everything about fighting."

Edlyn looked around at the men, a crooked smile of gratification on her face. "I feel safer now."

The men-at-arms grinned back at her. They under-stood motherly pride.

Sir Lyndon snorted.

"Hey, up there!"

Edlyn heard the cultured man's voice clearly, and she recognized it. Releasing the boys, she moved back to the wall. "Pembridge."

"'Tis he," Grims agreed.

"I see you peering at us," Pembridge called. "Is that the lady?"

She stepped out so those below could see her clearly.

Her appearance seemed just what Pembridge had waited for. His voice hardened. "Is this the lady who was once the wife of Robin, earl of Jagger? The lady who betrayed his memory by marrying his executioner?"

She could see the little knot of noblemen, but she recognized Pembridge by his gaudy raiment and his great height.

"I have something to show you, lady." Pembridge bowed low to her, and his mockery rang clear. "Let me show you what I can do." He stepped aside, and a poor, pathetic creature was shoved forward to fall at Pembridge's feet.

Sir Philip struggled to his feet, looked out, and muttered, "God help him."

She asked, "Who is it?"

"I sent a messenger," he admitted.

"A messenger?" Sir Lyndon turned pale. "You never told me you'd done that."

"What difference does it make?" Sir Philip asked. "They caught him, it seems."

"A messenger to my lord?" Edlyn's anger flared as she watched them put a noose around the broken figure below. "When I instructed you otherwise?"

"Lord Hugh instructed me first," he said.

She bit off the comment she would have made. He

looked miserable enough as he watched Pembridge's henchmen drag his messenger toward the blackened oak. The messenger choked and struggled as the noose cut off his air.

The end of the rope was tossed over the biggest limb, the messenger was hoisted up, and his feet kicked frantically. When he began to flag, they brought him down, let him recover, then took him up again.

"You see, my lady," Pembridge called. "I will have my castle back, and when I do, you and every one of those misbegotten servants of mine will suffer, just as this messenger suffers."

Drawing his sword, he walked up to the struggling figure hanging on the limb and hacked off one foot. The man's shriek, released from a throat constricted by the rope's pressure, sounded clearly in the morning air.

Pembridge wheeled around to the wall. "All except your sons, my lady. You do still have Robin's sons, don't you? You haven't discarded them, have you, as you discarded Robin's memory?"

"God save us all," she whispered, and when the lads tried to show themselves, she held them off.

"Your sons, my lady, I will keep and train up in my image and teach them to curse your memory every day of their lives."

"I will not!" Parkin shouted. He was fighting her restraint, trying to show himself to the demon-man below. "I'll never curse my mother."

Allyn slipped around her and tackled him. They tumbled to the graveled floor of the wall walk. "Shut your maw, you idiot," he said. "Can't you see he wants you to defy him?"

Parkin pushed Allyn off him and wiped the trickle of blood from his neck. "We *will* defy him."

"We're not going to give him anything he

wants." Allyn looked at his palms. "Ick, I skinned my hands."

The messenger below shrieked again, and Edlyn didn't have to look for sickness to bubble up within her. Through lips that seemed suddenly numb, she said, "Shoot him."

Grims signaled an archer to come near.

"Shoot the messenger," she said. "Put him out of his misery. Then, if you can, shoot Pembridge."

Obedient, the archer sent an arrow into the messenger. Mercifully, it hit its mark, and the struggles, the shrieking, stopped at once. Even as Edlyn started her prayers for the man's soul, Pembridge scampered back out of range, and the second arrow whistled uselessly through the air. "You'll pay for that, lady," Pembridge shouted.

Aye, she would. Of that she had no doubt. Turning away from the spectacle below, she asked Sir Philip, "Is there any way to send another messenger to my lord and tell him of our dilemma?"

"He's on his way," Sir Philip answered.

She stared at him, not comprehending.

"I sent two messengers." Color swept from Sir Philip's face. "The second one must be safe."

She took a hard breath in. Hugh. Hugh was on the way. Hugh would save her.

Then she breathed out, and despair swamped her. Hugh was fighting a battle for the freedom of the king. Hugh would be distracted. Hugh might be killed.

"He's fainted!" Sir Lyndon's rude voice intruded on her confusion.

It was true. Sir Philip flopped back on the stretcher, his mouth open and his eyes rolled back. Edlyn dropped to her knees and examined him. His clammy skin and chalky color proclaimed his weakness. Even this outing had taxed his strength to the limit.

"Take him back to the keep," she said. "Put him to bed."

She watched unhappily as the knight she trusted was taken down the narrow stairs.

Sir Lyndon blew out his breath in disgust. "He's no good to you. You'll have to depend on me."

Depend on him? But he despised her. He might show respect when Hugh was in residence, but now that he was gone he didn't hesitate to undermine her decisions with mockery. She didn't want to depend on him—but surely the men-at-arms needed a knight in charge.

Especially since Pembridge had proved that he knew her identity and carried a grudge.

Grims didn't seem to agree. "Don't fret, m' lady, we'll keep ye safe."

Her? She stared at him through glazed eyes. If she lost this castle and Pembridge razed it to the ground, nowhere would be safe for her. She would have destroyed Hugh's dream as surely as if she'd moved the stones with her own hands, and he'd want to kill her.

Nay, worse, he'd think it nothing more than what he expected from a woman, and he'd never trust her again.

Or . . . or he'd imagine that she'd done it for revenge, because she still loved Robin or because she was in collusion with Edmund Pembridge.

A woman's screech down in the bailey brought the men-at-arms to the edge of the wall walk. "The knaves are coming through the wall!"

"Nay!" Edlyn couldn't believe that. If Pembridge's men were tunneling beneath the wall, they could get through but not so quickly. Such an operation took months . . .

Grims muttered words in English, then began shouting to his men.

Sir Lyndon grabbed her upper arm and squeezed it tight. "You need me, lady. Give me command!"

"Let go!" She didn't have time to worry about him. Allyn and Parkin rushed to the edge of the wall walk overseeing the inner bailey, and she lunged to bring them to safety. Holding them struggling, she strained to see for herself.

Armed knights wearing Pembridge's device burst through the thin lining of stone that separated them from the inner bailey. Long ago Pembridge had somehow built a tunnel beneath the wall, lined it with stone, and shored it with timbers, then covered it with stone that matched the wall that rose above it. The workers on the other side of the wall hadn't been tunneling. The villagers had been simply removing the chiseled stones.

Now she stood far from the safety of the keep. Burdett stood below, directing the castle folk and villagers with frantic gestures. Her sons tried to push her behind them in the valiant manner of lads who'd never seen battle but knew their duty.

"You need me," Sir Lyndon said again.

The knight wanted to be in charge, but she didn't trust him. She refused to answer, refused to give him her blessing.

"Nothing's going to stop them, and who else is going to defend you?" he asked contemptuously. "You don't understand combat!"

It was true. She didn't. Always she'd depended on her wits, but they failed her now.

Oh, why had she never learned to fight?

*   *   *

The first time Hugh heard the woman scream, he ignored her and leaned over the neck of his destrier to urge it on. What was one more woman's shriek compared to the blood and agony of battle that he'd just witnessed? He glanced off into the forest. It was probably just some shrew yelling at her husband.

But she screamed again, loud and shrill, and even his horse checked. There was no anger in the sound, only pure terror. Edlyn would have demanded that he stop and check on the woman.

But Pembridge was after Edlyn, and if what Ethelburgha had said was true, Edlyn was in great danger. In this instance, at least, she would beg that he disregard the plea implicit in that shriek.

The woman screamed again.

Who was he trying to fool? Edlyn would have gone off to check on the screamer herself if he had refused. Somehow, without his realizing how, Edlyn had begun to ride with him everywhere.

As he slowed his destrier, the cloud of dust from the road caught up with him. It coated his clenched teeth as he asked, "By Christ and all the saints, what's wrong with that wench?"

His men rode around him and glanced at each other.

"What wench, master?" Wharton asked.

They hadn't even heard her. "That woman," Hugh said. "The one who's screeching."

"Oh," Wharton said stupidly. "Her."

"Would you have me see, my lord?" Dewey asked.

"Nay." Hugh turned his horse and headed in the direction of the noise. "I have to do it myself."

Caution urged him to reconnoiter the situation, but he didn't have time and he didn't have the patience. The hut stood close to the road in a protected glade, and as he burst out of the trees, he took in the situation at once. Two armed knights and their squires, no doubt mercenaries who had served in the battle, held a woman to the ground and prepared to rape her. Worse, another knight held a whimpering girl-child and prepared to do the same. The woman's screams weren't for herself; she was straining, trying to get to her child to rescue her.

"A pox on you!" Hugh cursed them as he drew his sword and urged his destrier forward to do justice. The knight with the child, caught with his breeks around his ankles, could do no more than try to waddle toward his weapons as he saw a large, clearly infuriated knight on his charger bearing down on him.

Hugh removed the knave's head with one swing of his sword. The others he hacked where they stood and crawled. His men, astonished by his sudden attack, hurried to join in but could do no more than finish the task Hugh had so ably started.

Then he galloped away, pursued by the mother's cried thanks and his once again startled men. Hooves pounded behind him. Roxford Castle remained leagues ahead. And time, like an impenetrable fog, tightened its grip around him. He wanted to be at Roxford now. If all went well, he wouldn't be there for two more days.

So he prayed. "Please, God. I rescued that woman and her child. I'll give an endowment to Eastbury Abbey. I'll do anything! Just smite my enemies and keep Edlyn safe."

At that moment, there was a great roar. Men shrieked their dismay.

Edlyn heard the cry, "Their tunnel is collapsing!"

It was true. Great stones tumbled to the ground. Gravel and fill from the inside of the wall showered on

Pembridge's astonished men, obliterating them in a billow of dust.

The wall above cracked from top to bottom as the foundation that held it weakened. Then it settled. All slipped into silence.

All except Pembridge's screaming injured as they futilely struggled to free themselves from the tons of stone.

The people of Roxford gave a ragged cheer. Burdett assessed the situation, then ran up the stairs where his mistress still stood on the wall walk. Edlyn cast a triumphant glance at Sir Lyndon.

"Do you think it's over already, you silly woman?"

The way he said the word "woman" was the worst insult he could cast at her. He was false clear to the bone, she realized. All his previous protestations of devotion had been nothing but a wind to bring Hugh back to his side. He hated her. He hated Hugh's marriage. He hated the changes it had wrought, and now that Hugh had gone, he saw no reason to conceal that hatred.

He was a dangerous man.

She pretended not to notice, pretended to be as stupid as he thought her. "It's not over, but it's given us a moment to regroup."

Apparently he perceived her courtesy as weakness, for he stepped close enough to loom over her and said, "If Hugh were here, he would order you to put me in charge!"

"I do not presume to know my husband's mind, but if he were here, Pembridge would not be within the castle walls at all."

It was a reproach, and Sir Lyndon's eyes narrowed as he considered her.

Then her son, her Allyn, piped up, "Aye, he would have kept them out, not let them in."

Sir Lyndon stepped back so swiftly Edlyn feared he might tumble off the edge of the wall walk. "I didn't let them in."

"No one said—" Edlyn began.

"Someone did," Allyn said.

Parkin chimed in. "We saw him."

Grims bore down on the lads with purpose. "Did you see his face?"

They shook their heads, but their young faces didn't hide their suspicions. Grims looked at Sir Lyndon in open speculation while the knight glared at her sons with a malevolence that chilled Edlyn. She tried to defuse the situation and sound firm at the same time. "Fight on, Sir Lyndon, but I leave Grims in charge of his men. He knows them, and the castle, better than you."

Sir Lyndon pushed around her and stormed down the steps to the bailey.

"There's trouble, m' lady," Grims said. "Shall I set a watch on him?"

She looked at her sons. "Why do you think it's he?"

The lads exchanged glances, then Allyn said, "He's tall and he's thin, and he's got such black hair."

They were hiding something, she could see that. "Why didn't you tell me sooner?"

Parkin wiped his nose on his sleeve. Allyn stared at the sky.

Edlyn wrapped her arms around them and held them firmly. "Tell me true—have you been out of the castle by the postern gate?"

"Once," Allyn admitted.

"After Hugh left?"

She had to lean down to hear Allyn's whisper. "Aye."

Her knees quaked as she considered the peril they'd been in. That was the problem with being a mother. A mother could always imagine the worst, even when the danger was past.

Parkin sounded choked with tears. "Do you think we showed that man the way to betray us to the enemy?"

The man-at-arms turned the boys around by their arms to face him. "Did you tear boards away to open the gate? Did you move stone aside?"

They wiped their noses on their hands and shook their heads.

"Then 'twas not you who opened the postern gate to the enemy. 'Twas done by another." He looked meaningfully at Edlyn.

He suspected Sir Lyndon, and she feared Sir Lyndon. "Put surveillance on him," she said.

Moving to the stairway, Grims met Burdett coming up and they spoke, giving the order to watch Sir Lyndon. Burdett nodded and bounded away.

Grims came back to the top of the wall walk and called down to the people, "God's grace has spared us. Now do your part. You women—get the children into the keep. Men—prepare defenses before they break through again. They'll take down the curtain wall if they can." He looked at the crack above the tunnel. "God grant it hold."

Everyone in the bailey scurried to obey. Taking her sons by the hands, Edlyn joined the other women and ran for the keep. In the only doorway, an opening on the second floor, Burdett stood waving them inside. Edlyn stood beside him until all had entered, then watched with approval as he took an ax and hacked the stairway down.

"It'll not be easy to take this keep, my lady," he said.

*   *   *

The rhythm of the hooves on the packed dirt road accompanied the chant in Hugh's mind.

"*Please* God. *Please* God."

A priest would have been more eloquent, but Hugh was a fighter, not a poet, and if sincerity counted for anything, God would hear his prayer.

Hugh had never begged before. He'd said his prayers and trusted that God would realize the good sense of them. He hadn't seen the need to grovel. But this—this was different. Edlyn's well-being was too important for such overweening assurance. He had no pride where she was concerned.

Wharton kept pace with him, and now he shouted, "Roxford Castle is just ahead, master."

Reluctantly, Hugh reined in his mount—the fifth in two days.

"Listen," Hugh said.

The sounds of battle were muffled rather than clear as they should have been. Hugh glanced at Wharton, hoping his man would scoff at his foreboding.

Instead Wharton looked grim. "The enemy is within."

But how far within? They needed to know details, so Hugh nodded at Dewey. "Scout out the situation."

His squire dismounted. Hugh and his men followed suit, but Hugh's gaze never left Dewey until the lad had disappeared into the surrounding forest. He was swift and had proved himself in the battle just past, but Hugh wanted to be with him, to see for himself what Pembridge had done.

Instead, he allowed Wharton to help him don his chain-mail hauberk and his helmet. He watched as his men let their squires do the same, then all freed their weapons from their travel cases. They rested their destriers—and they waited.

The waiting was the worst. It gave Hugh time to count the number of knights left with him. He'd lost men on the trip, mostly to lack of fresh horses. They promised to follow as they could, but they wouldn't come soon enough. Hugh fidgeted with the strap holding the helmet to his hauberk. He'd slept during the dark hours of nights when not even his horse could see to run and eaten when his men demanded a rest. Each moment when he'd not been riding had been sheer torture, and even the riding had been torture of another sort.

All he could remember was the white flag Edlyn had waved as he rode off and his arrogant plans to accept her surrender.

Who would be accepting her surrender now? She'd called Edmund Pembridge a cruel man, and Hugh feared she would find out the truth of it. Now Hugh would give anything to have her whole and healthy, secure in her pride. Secure enough to tell him that she loved him.

And he—what would he say? Would he offer her his commitment and think that was enough, or would he . . . ?

"My lord!" Dewey slipped back through the brush.

"That was fast!" Wharton said.

"Aye, I hurried," Dewey answered.

Had they both run mad? Hugh thought they'd been waiting forever.

"Pembridge has well established himself within the outer bailey." Dewey didn't have time for details, but his bleak face told the tale. "The outer gatehouse and drawbridge are intact. There was no battle to get inside."

Hugh and Wharton exchanged glances, and Wharton said, "Treachery then."

Dewey said, "That's what I thought, too. Already they've broken through to the inner bailey, so I thought perhaps more treachery. I didn't dare go farther, but I saw the smoke of burning and heard fierce fighting. I fear much of the castle is damaged."

"The castle?" Why was Dewey blathering about the castle? Hugh wondered.

"And, my lord, he has dozens of knights." Dewey blushed as he spoke, but he said honestly, "We haven't a chance against them."

Hugh glanced around at his men, then remounted. "Every man must choose his battles. I have chosen mine. If you have no heart for it, then go with my blessing."

His men stared at him. Then Wharton said stiffly, "There's no need t' insult us, master."

The armor of every one of his knights clattered as they mounted their horses and stood awaiting instructions, and Hugh's fervent "Please God" became "My thanks, God."

He moved to the front to speak to them as their commander in this fruitless battle. "We have no reinforcements and no hope of getting them, so we'll attack from the rear. There's a chance they've become so accustomed to cutting down men-at-arms that they'll be unprepared to face other knights."

Hugh and his men rode across the drawbridge and passed through the gatehouse—undefended. That pleased him. It meant he faced an overconfident enemy. Then the outer bailey opened before him. "Pigs!" He spat the word, furious at the wanton destruction.

A few of Pembridge's men milled around the inner gatehouse, so sure of their victory they took a rest from the fighting. One of them saw Hugh and his men; he pointed. Before he could shout, Hugh scythed him with his mace. His men did the same until not one living creature remained erect.

From above, Hugh heard cheers as Roxford's men-at-arms realized their salvation had arrived.

Hugh only wished that were true.

21

"They're here, my lady, they're here!"

Edlyn put the kettle of boiling lard down on the floor of the roof and let the breeze dry the sweat from her face. As her eyes adjusted to the sunlight, she could see the glow on Neda's face and on the faces of the other women. "Who's here?"

"The lord! Lord Hugh! We heard them shouting outside, and we looked. 'Tis he!"

"He's alive?" Edlyn staggered back. "He's alive." God had heard her prayers. Nothing could defeat her now.

Then she heard the clash of arms below and the screams of a dying man, and reality returned with a flourish.

Pembridge had had that treacherous hole at the base of the curtain wall reexcavated. The gatehouse defense had been overwhelmed not long after, and Pembridge's men had thundered into the bailey on horseback. Roxford Castle's men-at-arms fought valiantly, but they were essentially defensive fighters, and against the knights' superior position and power they had little hope.

Yet against all odds, Hugh had come, and Edlyn couldn't quash the optimism that lit the women's faces, nor could she halt her own exuberance. Running to the battlements that enclosed the roof, she would have leaned out.

"Be careful." Neda stopped her with a hand on her arm and pointed at the green vine that rooted between the stones and curled around the merlons. "That's blister vine."

"Aye, m' lady." Ethelburgha held out her reddened, swelling hands. "Look at this. I'll not be brewing ale for days."

Edlyn winced but didn't touch. Without her herbs, she couldn't help Ethelburgha, and she had no wish to be stricken with the rash.

Stepping to a different embrasure, Edlyn leaned out and took in the sights of the battle below.

Astride his destrier, Hugh struck out at the enemies who dared to capture his property, and at the sight her heart trilled like a lark in the morning. Then she saw how hard those enemies pressed him. "Does he have enough men?"

The steward's wife lost her smile. "I don't know."

What she meant was nay, but Edlyn said, "No matter. It's our best chance."

"Curse Pembridge and all his kind." Neda pointed. "They've lit bonfires in the bailey. They're readying the arrows. They're going to shoot them into the door and burn us out, and the lord can't defeat so many."

Fire was the only thing that they truly had to fear, and fear it they did. Edlyn looked back at the pot by the trapdoor. The serving women had been boiling lard at the fire in the great hall, carrying it up the spiral stairs to the roof and dumping it onto Pembridge's men. The bubbling grease had sent knights flying to pull off their armor, and each time that happened the women gave a cheer. It wasn't much—some would call it a feeble effort—but it kept the women occupied and out of Burdett's way as he worked to prepare the keep for the final siege.

And who was to say what might turn the scales of battle?

Edlyn's eyes narrowed as she considered the three fires below. The wind within the bailey created little eddies and cast the smoke every which way. The cluster of archers who surrounded each fire coughed and flapped at the fumes, but the men couldn't go far; they had a duty to perform. "Go down to the great hall," Edlyn commanded Neda. "Start dousing the inside of the door, the lintels, and the threshold with water. Soak the wood, if you can, and Neda?"

"My lady?"

"Can Burdett shoot an arrow?"

"Is he not an Englishman?"

Edlyn smiled at the pride in Neda's voice. "Then send him to me with his bow and his arrows and an ax and a good sharp knife."

Shooing the women before her like a flock of wind-blown geese, Neda moved to obey.

"Have him bring yarn, too, and my riding gloves."

Neda turned back. "I'll return with him."

Edlyn looked around at the open roof. The stone battlements had protected them, but if the archers were successful, that protection would be no more. They would shower the roof with arrows, and any person foolhardy enough to remain up there was in danger. Edlyn had to do it. It was her castle. But to expose both Burdett and Neda to danger . . . "Nay," she said. "Send Burdett alone."

Neda wanted to argue, but Edlyn firmed her chin,

and the steward's wife bowed and followed the serving women down the stairs.

The battle still roared below, but up here alone she could hear the wind whistle. It was an odd sensation to know that men were dying below her and she could do nothing. It was even odder to know she would do anything—incapacitate a man with boiling lard, drop stones on their heads, shoot arrows, or lift a sword—to protect her children and her castle.

And it was her castle, in a way that Robin's castle had never been hers. In Robin's castle, she had always been the scorned wife, holding her head proudly erect while her husband dallied with other women. Here she was the chosen one, the mistress Hugh had endowed with all authority, and no one dared to ask how long his favor would extend. All knew that Hugh took his vows seriously.

All except the traitor who dared betray him— indeed, who dared betray them both—during Hugh's absence.

Who was he, this limping maggot of a man?

"My lady?"

She jumped and turned to Burdett. He'd come up through the trapdoor on silent feet. His long bow and quiver hung from his shoulder. In his hands he held a short-handled ax and a knife. He started toward her, and suddenly all the doubts about the steward returned with a rush. She was alone up here. Burdett could cut her throat and fling her over the edge, then go down and murder her children.

She took a step back when he swung the ax up. She lifted her arms to protect her head. He flipped the ax and caught it by the blade, then extended it. "My lady? What did you wish to do with this?"

Slowly she lowered her arms. He stared at her, the

handle outstretched, and she reached forward and grasped it. He let it go easily. He dropped the knife at his feet and waited, helpless, should she decide to strike him. And she blushed for her own stupidity. But with one sentence she could banish the hurt from his gaze.

"Give me the gloves," she said. "We're going to save Roxford Castle."

Blood from his wounds trickled into Hugh's mouth. His sword dragged at his arm like a bag of milled flour, and he used it, he thought, with no more than a miller's expertise. His chest rose and fell like a bellows, and still he couldn't get enough air. Worse, his destrier showed the same exhaustion.

His best knights were battling against impossible odds, each man pressed by at least three of the enemy. He had ordered Dewey to abandon them early in the battle, but whether the lad had made it out, he didn't know. Wharton had stayed close to Hugh, defending his back, until the sheer weight of numbers had separated them. Hugh himself wanted nothing more than to strike the death blow to Pembridge, but Pembridge stayed well behind his bodyguard and fought only with a mocking lift of the visor on his helm. Sure of their victory, Pembridge's archers tended their fires and prepared to plunge the tar-tipped arrows into the flames.

It was only a matter of time until the keep fell. It was only a matter of time before Hugh and his men lay dead. Only a matter of time until his dreams had died. Dreams of a castle of his own, tended by the wife he loved . . .

Glancing up, Hugh caught sight of her on the battlements of the keep.

Amazing, when she looked so much like other women, that he knew her from a distance even while in the heat of battle. Yet the woman he knew to be Edlyn met his gaze and waved a long, leafy branch. She showed the same exuberance waving that plant as she had shown waving her white flag, and he wondered at the significance.

Out of the corner of his eye, he saw a sword swing toward him, and he barely blocked it with his shield.

Staring at Edlyn would get him killed. Better he should fight for her.

Lost in the blood lust of battle, he scarcely noticed a sudden stirring among the group of Pembridge's archers who clustered around the nearest fire. Not until Pembridge started shouting in febrile denunciation did he lift his head long enough to notice them fleeing. They rubbed their eyes, coughed, and blundered toward the gate as if they could tolerate no longer the winds of war.

Curiosity poured a measure of his old strength into his veins, and Hugh dispatched the two knights who fought to capture him and moved toward the fire—a fire abandoned already by the men who should be tending it.

It appeared to be nothing but a smoldering pile of ill-lit logs and still green branches, but as he watched he thought he saw a feather rise on a heat current, then curl into ash and blow away.

Plunging through the melee of bodies and weapons, a knight on horseback crashed into Hugh's destrier with all his might. With a snarl, Hugh turned to fight—and beneath the open-faced helmet, he saw his old friend, Sir Lyndon.

He recognized betrayal.

"Lyndon." The name whistled from between his tightly pursed lips.

The rapid journey and the previous battle had fatigued Hugh.

Not so Sir Lyndon. He grinned with fresh eagerness. "Well met, dear lord! Did you not expect to find me lift a sword?"

"Not against me."

Sir Lyndon's smile disappeared. "Then you're a fool. I stayed at your side like a faithful dog for years, waiting for the day you would win your reward and share the bounty with me. Instead, you married that woman and turned your back on your faithful companions."

Sir Lyndon just didn't understand, but Hugh wanted to make him. He didn't want to kill the man who had fought at his side through so many battles. "I told you that should you prove yourself of penitent mind—"

"Prove myself? To you? I had proved myself too many times to allow you to test me again."

Sir Lyndon's sudden tension foreshadowed a blow, and Hugh deflected it easily with his shield.

"You're a knight. Your honor—"

"Honor is for those who can afford it." Sir Lyndon swung his sword.

Hugh moved to deflect it, but he mistook the object of Sir Lyndon's ire. The sharp blade sliced through Hugh's destrier right at the neck, severing the artery. The great beast sank to its knees, and Hugh scrambled to free himself from the stirrups.

"You see? Only noble fools can afford honor"—Sir Lyndon's voice rang with mockery, and he grasped his mace—"my lord."

As Hugh watched, the stallion died in a crimson pool, and Sir Lyndon urged his destrier closer. The smell of blood maddened the stallion, and maddened Sir Lyndon, too, it seemed, for both struck out. Hugh clumsily dodged the flying hooves, and the studded iron ball swung with deadly intent. Hugh didn't want to die with his skull crushed by a mace. He didn't want to die by being trampled by a horse. Not in the bailey of his own castle. Not defeated by his old friend turned bitter enemy.

Hugh was the better warrior, but Sir Lyndon held all the advantages. Coming at him, Sir Lyndon used his superior position ruthlessly. Guiding the horse with his knees, he shoved Hugh back toward the fire. Hugh was caught between the mace wielded so deftly and the flames that licked at his heels. When the fire was right at his rear and Sir Lyndon was right at his front, he knew only a miracle could save him.

Sir Lyndon lifted his arm to deliver the death blow. Hugh went to his knees, raised his shield, and braced himself—and heard a whistle and a thump close by his calf. He glanced down. An arrow had buried itself deep in the wood. He had no time to worry about the twisted growth of green leaves and twigs that clung to it. Sir Lyndon and his destrier lurched back, and Hugh used the distraction to rise and put distance between them.

Recovering from his surprise, Sir Lyndon taunted him. "Like everything else in this wretched castle, the archers are damn poor."

Another arrow zipped through the air and landed directly into the fire, casting a spray of sparks into the air.

Alarmed by the flames, Sir Lyndon's horse pranced out of control.

Another arrow struck squarely into the flames, and Hugh seized his chance. Lifting the burning log, he waved it under the destrier's nose. The animal screamed and reared. Sir Lyndon dropped his mace and shield and clutched at the saddle. The horse bucked forward before Sir Lyndon could regain his seat, and with a clang of armor, Sir Lyndon hit the ground.

Now the battle was even. Hugh advanced on his former friend, the flaming brand still outthrust. As the arrow ignited, smoke began to rise, the kind of smoke green wood and fresh leaves would cause.

"Get it away." Sir Lyndon flailed his arms. "For the love of God, Hugh, take it away!" He tried to rub his face with his hands and brought his metal gauntlets back bloody.

Hugh stood astonished. What was wrong with the man?

"Whatever you say, Hugh. I'll do whatever you want." He ran backward crazily, like a dog stricken with a foaming mouth. "If you ever loved me, spare me now."

Hugh hesitated, not understanding the source of Sir Lyndon's anguish.

Sir Lyndon brayed in agony, his eyes closed as if he dared not open them. "Remember our battles together. Remember and give me another chance."

"Oh, I'll spare you!" In disgust, Hugh cast the log into the fire. "But what is wrong with you?" Then he forgot his own question. A riderless horse stood nearby.

Opportunity. He recognized it well. He ran, gathering speed, and leaped into the saddle. The animal bucked; he fought it to a standstill, then turned back to take care of Sir Lyndon.

But Sir Lyndon was nowhere in sight. And another laden arrow whistled through the air and landed in the fire.

Hugh glanced up at the keep and saw Burdett

adjusting his aim toward the second fire where archers still stood and waited to do their duty. Then, as if Burdett spotted danger, he ducked behind the battlements with his long bow in hand.

Just in time. An arrow dispatched from the area of the second fire struck the place where he'd been standing. Now only Edlyn leaned out, pulling at the vines that twined around the stones, presenting the perfect target.

For the first time in the battle, Pembridge rode out from behind his bodyguard. He shouted at his archer. "Shoot her!"

The archer raised his arrow and narrowed his eyes.

Hugh roared at Edlyn, then raced his destrier toward the archer. He wouldn't make it in time. He knew he wouldn't make it in time, but he had to. He had to.

But before he could loose the arrow, the enemy archer fell in a drift of smoke.

Burdett leaped out of hiding and dragged Edlyn down.

Deprived of his prey, Pembridge galloped toward the fire and seized a bow, aiming it right at Hugh. From so close a distance, the arrow would pierce the chain-mail armor that protected him. Hugh braced for the impact, but before Pembridge could strike, a swirl of wind encircled Pembridge with smoke.

He shrieked as if the devil had him by the throat. Dropping the bow, he directed his mount toward the gatehouse.

What mischief was this? Hugh wondered. Then a random gust spread the noxious fumes over the men who fought and over to him.

Without any instruction from Hugh, his untried destrier pranced backward. "By our lady!" Hugh sawed at the reins as the smoke crept into his helmet. His chest burned. His skin stung. His eyes itched. He wanted to rub the pain away, but his chain-mail gloves made it impossible. He tried to get away, but it was too late. The poison clung to his skin and filled his lungs. If any able warrior were to attack now, Hugh would be lost.

But there were no able warriors. Those wretched arrows had fed agony into all three fires, and the smoke spread it throughout the bailey. Men were running, yelling, crying like newborn babes. Hugh guided his horse through the low, narrow gatehouse entry and out into the scorched outer bailey. Gratefully, he took a breath, then another and another. "Air." He coughed and squinted, trying to see through eyes raw and running with tears. "Fresh air."

Then the tears cleared his vision, and he saw him— Pembridge, alone, with only his weapons and his wit to defend him.

That wouldn't be nearly enough.

Pembridge saw Hugh, too, through eyes just as swollen, and he grinned with mad delight.

"A resourceful trick, my lord of nothing," he called. "My Edlyn has ever been resourceful." He gestured with his arm like a wizard conjuring his demons. "But not as resourceful as me." On his summoning, fresh knights rode through the outer gatehouse and filled the bailey.

Hugh stared.

Richard and his gang of thieves returned his stare, and at the very back of the pack was that skinny old ferryman, Almund, glaring at them all.

"You see," Pembridge said, "when you want allies to do evil, you must appeal to the lowest of creatures, offer them plunder, and they will do your will."

Something inside Hugh, some fragment of faith and honor, broke with a snap. He didn't want Richard to be the Judas. He wanted to believe the man when he insinuated he would forsake his thieving for a chance to start anew. He thought—dear God, he really thought—Richard had given Edlyn her freedom because he saw the beauty and innocence in her and wanted to nurture it.

And now here he was, prepared to strip Hugh's castle and rape Edlyn until she died.

Roaring like a wounded bull, he lifted his sword. "Nay!"

Richard lifted his sword, too, and in a clear voice he called, "Nay, indeed. We've come to protect Lady Edlyn and all she claims as hers—and you, Lord Hugh, are hers."

Hugh halted his charge before it began. Hope struggled into being. With Richard's men on their side, there was a chance they could defeat Pembridge.

From the look on Pembridge's face, he knew it.

"Will you fight?" Hugh called. "Or will you run?"

Pembridge swung savagely on Hugh. "I'll fight, and if I die, I'll see you in hell beside me."

22

"*He almost did it,* master."

Hugh looked up from his mat by the fire in the solar. Wharton stood above him, still ashen and shaking. "Who almost did what?"

"Pembridge almost took you to hell with him."

"He was a good fighter." Hugh shrugged, testing the binding on his broken collarbone. "But he wasn't fighting for what he loved."

"And you were?" Edlyn's soft voice sounded on the other side of the mat, and Hugh turned his head to gaze on his wife.

She had the soft, gentle bearing of an angel who brought surcease to the suffering and health to the ill—a bearing at odds with the woman he knew her to be. "That ill-begotten knave was right about one thing," he muttered. "You *are* a resourceful woman."

No one had to tell him that it had been Edlyn who had thought to shoot stems and leaves of blister vine into the fires to drive the archers away. Her strategem had totally disrupted the battle, and with the addition of Richard's men on Hugh's side, Pembridge's forces had been defeated.

It had taken an hour before the fires had burned away the blister vine's dreaded miasma and the winds had cleared the air enough for Hugh to reenter his own castle. He had used the time to thank Almund and Dewey and Wharton, and all of his men and even Richard's thieves. But the delay had seriously dampened his victory celebration, especially when, on hearing of the success of Edlyn's herbal warfare, Richard had laughed so hard he collapsed unconscious on the ground.

Further investigation had proved the man was suffering from broken ribs administered by a well-swung mace, but his chortle still rang in Hugh's ears.

Hugh's grimace didn't go unnoticed. "Why won't you let me move you into our bed?" Edlyn asked, not for the first time. "It's huge. There's more than enough room for you and Richard, and it would be so much more convenient for me to care for you both."

"I am not sleeping with that man," Hugh declared.

"Amen." Richard's voice, while determined, was weak. He lay propped up on the pillows, almost as white as the linen under his head, but not even pain could undermine his insolence. "I can sleep on a mat instead. There's no need for me to deprive the master of the castle of his bed."

That sarcasm made Hugh want to smack his former enemy and new ally.

But he didn't have to. Edlyn flattened Richard's pretensions of health. "Nay, you can't," she said. "I don't like the look of that chest wound, and you're not moving until I say so."

Only Richard wouldn't stay flattened. He merely sounded amused. "She is a tyrant, isn't she, Hugh? When *I* marry, I'll wed an obedient woman."

Hugh remembered similar fantasies of his own. "In my experience, you get what God gives you."

If a voice could be described as strutting, Richard's could be now. "My bliss will be the envy of all my *new neighbors.*"

Hugh grunted. "You assume a lot on the basis of one battle."

But Richard assumed correctly, damn his eyes. Hugh *would* ask Prince Edward to give Richard his castle. Then Richard would have to gain the acceptance he sought among the nobility, and it would be no easy thing to get from barons and earls who had been held at sword point and stripped of their possessions by that grinning shallow-pate in the bed.

More uncomfortable than knowing he would do his best for Richard was having Edlyn know it, too. She thought Richard was a good man given to kind deeds, and Hugh couldn't bring himself to disillusion her—even when he thought she was manipulating him. Now she smiled at him in a manner that reminded him most restively of the empty days since their last mating and mocked the empty nights until they were alone once more. Sinking down on her knees beside him, she arranged the pillows under his head.

He was baffled by her charm and couldn't help smiling back. "So, wife, how did you like your first taste of battle?"

"It was as ugly and as dreadful as I imagined." Still she smiled, her expression belying her words. "And if I'd had a weapon, I'd have fought those mercenaries with my own hands."

Hugh's own smile faded at the terror that thought brought him. "Why?"

"When I saw what Pembridge did to the outer bailey and knew what he planned for the inner bailey, the keep, my sons, and my people—by our lady, I still want to kill him." She clenched trembling hands in her lap. "And he's dead."

How odd to feel a sense of kinship with his wife because she wanted to kill someone.

Oh, he knew she'd been swept away with the fury of battle. She didn't really want to do violence, but now she understood, a little, the satisfaction that drove him when he fought well and won against the forces that would rend the nation.

"Th' master took care o' killing Pembridge," Wharton said matter-of-factly.

"I did do that duty and would gladly do it again. 'Twill take months of hard work to undo the damage he caused to Roxford Castle."

"He was ever like that." Edlyn reminisced with an ease that reassured Hugh that she had indeed never wanted Pembridge. "He carried a blight with him, and in every place he walked happiness died."

Her words reminded Hugh of an old friendship, equally touched by blight, and he stirred uncomfortably. "Has anyone seen Sir Lyndon since the battle?"

Wharton shook his head sadly. "Sir Lyndon was killed, master. We found his body among th' stacks o' other traitorous stiffs when th' priest was giving his blessing."

"Don't talk so disrespectfully," Hugh chided sharply. "He was a good man."

"A good man? Then it wasn't him I saw fighting fer Pembridge? An' it wasn't him I saw try t' kill ye?"

"But he repented his behavior."

"Ye're too soft." Now Wharton chided him "Wasn't it him yer sons say opened th' postern gate t' th' enemy?"

"Allyn and Parkin told me they couldn't be sure."

"Perhaps not before th' battle, but now th' evidence sure looks gruesome. I wouldn't have trusted him t' turn me back—or me wife's—t' him again."

"I'm flattered." Edlyn looked down to veil the amusement in her gaze.

"No need fer that, mistress." Wharton's sour face would have sucked the juices from a peach. "I don't know why th' master wants a woman as stubborn as ye, but I do his bidding always."

"Except that you do not trust me when I say Sir Lyndon was willing to try again!" Hugh said, exasperated.

Wharton shrugged. "I knew ye'd take his part, but it doesn't matter. He's dead, an' there's no use in arguing."

And after all, Hugh knew better than to think Wharton would admit to slipping a knife through Sir Lyndon's ribs. "Well," he muttered to himself. "'Tis done now, and I cannot undo it."

Indeed, he didn't know if he wanted to. Wharton was right. Hugh would never have trusted Sir Lyndon again, and if Sir Lyndon had lived, there would have been nothing but grief between them.

"Other than a tendency t' trust where trust is not warranted, th' master is good at what he does. Why, he cleared out half o' th' rebel army even before th' battle was joined." Slyly now, Wharton asked, "How was it ye did that, master?"

Hugh wasn't offended by Wharton's teasing, and he gladly gave credit where credit was due. "'Twas a trick my wife showed me."

Edlyn's eyes grew round and pleased. "Really?"

"I'm not a stupid man," Hugh said. "Twice I saw you win out over great odds by using the means available to you. I decided I could do that as well."

To his horror, big tears welled into her eyes.

Crying! She was crying! He didn't know anything about crying women. Hell, if he could have, he would have run. Instead he said, "Hey! I was giving you a compliment!"

"I know. It's just that"—she pulled a strip of bandage out of her bag and wiped her nose—"this is the first time I've been sure you approved of me."

"Approved of you?" Hugh tried to raise himself and found her arms wrapped around his shoulders. "What do you mean, approved of you? I'm in your bed every chance I get."

"I don't want to hear this." Richard started humming loudly.

"In my bed? So what?"

"So what?" He couldn't believe she'd said that.

"What happens in bed is not what's important."

Apparently Richard hadn't been humming loud enough, for he stopped so abruptly it proved he had heard her. Wharton stood frozen. Hugh stared at his wife's tear-stained face, and in the silence the men fumbled to comprehend this evidence of female simple-mindedness.

Faced with three incredulous men, she said, "Well, it isn't. It's the affection and trust between a man and a woman that's important. *You* weren't happy when you left the bed the last time we shared it."

"I'm covering my ears," Richard called, and he wrapped one pillow over his head in a slow motion that coddled his broken ribs.

All Hugh remembered about sharing her bed was the driving need to master her, the satisfaction when he did so, and the smug knowledge that she'd mastered him as well.

She must have read his face, for she said, "You weren't. You were angry because of that shift you wanted me to return to Richard."

Richard lifted the pillow a little. "That's a lie! I never gave her a shift."

Having Richard listen to a private discussion between him and his wife was like the scratch of a wolf's claws on granite, and Hugh snapped, "You should cover your ears better."

With elaborate circumspection, Richard rolled so they could see nothing of him but a mound of rugs.

"One of your men did." Edlyn spoke to the mound, and the mound groaned. "And Hugh wanted me to send it back." Now her gaze dropped to the floor, and she looked as shy as a maid. "I tried to catch you the morning you left to give it to you."

Right then, Hugh truly knew he didn't understand women. "To give it to me?"

"Aye. As a token from me to carry into battle."

He remembered the sight of her, silhouetted against the morning sky, waving at him. "Was that the white flag you used?"

"White flag?"

"To signal your surrender."

"I didn't surrender!"

"I saw the white flag."

She thrust her chin forward in exasperation and pushed a stray lock of hair out of her eyes. "I will never understand men. I just told you—"

"*What* were you going to tell me?"

"What?"

"What were you going to tell me when you came running with that shift?"

Her expression of embarrassment entertained him.

"Heh, heh." Wharton gave a most dreadful cackle. "She's starting t' comprehend she can't fool ye, huh, master?"

Hugh never took his eyes off Edlyn as he spoke. "Wharton, shut your maw and get out."

"Aye, master." Wharton inched toward the door sideways, like a crab easing its way toward the sea.

Richard had crept around in the bed so that he could stick his head out of the covers and listen.

Hugh wanted to throw them both out, but Edlyn was as nervous as a half-tamed falcon and just as flighty. He dared not take his concentration off her.

She moved her lips in a parody of speaking and finally squeaked, "I was just going to say that you should stay alive."

"Every one of your husbands has brought you nothing but grief." Maybe a man could understand a woman if he worked hard enough—and lived long enough. "Why would you want me to stay alive when your life would be so much easier if I died?"

Pulling the jumble of rag bandages out of her bag, she started to rewind them. "I wish no man ill."

He rubbed his broken collarbone with a grieved expression.

Glancing at him, she said, "You're not gulling me. I know what you're trying to do."

"What?" With gentle fingers he explored the scabs and bruises that covered his face.

She wound faster. "You're trying to make me think you're in agony so I'll tell you what I was going to say."

"You could have told me that morning when I was leaving. Why can't you tell me now?"

"Because then I was afraid you might die, and now—"

He winced when his fingers pressed on a particularly painful bruise.

"Now you're only in danger of me killing you." He put on a pathetic face, and she sighed in exaggerated disgust. "I wanted to tell you that you'd won me."

He snatched at her hand and got a fistful of linen

strips. In disgust, he threw them away. They caught on
the rough skin of his palms, and he cursed until Edlyn
took the bandages away from him and put them carefully in her bag. She took his hands in hers, and he
thought, for just a moment, that this was her sign of
surrender. Instead she looked at his blisters with an
exclamation of concern. "Did you get these from your
sword work?"

"Edlyn . . . "

She reached into her bag. "Just let me put some
ointment on them and wrap them up."

"Edlyn, I love you."

She froze.

He was appalled. He'd just blurted it out, in front
of Wharton and Richard, without planning or poetry or
song. He could have said, "You are the wife of my
soul." Or "Beloved, you are more beautiful than the
sun in all its glory." Lovers said things like that. He'd
always thought it stupid, but the women seemed to like
it, and he wanted Edlyn to be happy.

If he'd had the time to think, he could have come
up with some nonsense, but suddenly it had just
seemed unfair that she had to declare her love before
he did. After all, she'd loved before and seen that love
treated like goose droppings. That was the reason, he
knew, for her backward-stepping caution and for her
fierce defense of her own heart.

So now he'd insulted her with blunt speaking, and
he had to try to mend his mistake.

He mumbled. "Robin said it better, didn't he?"

She pressed her fingers to his mouth. "Robin was
most eloquent, but then Robin said it to so many
ladies." Smoothing his lips with the ball of her thumb,
she said, "I like your version better." She leaned forward until she could replace her thumb with her lips,

and her breath caressed him. "I think that when we have rebuilt Roxford Barn, we should go out and enact a girlhood fantasy of mine."

"What fantasy is that?" Talking like this was a kiss made audible, and he cherished the movements, the warmth, the anticipation of more silent—and more passionate—kisses.

"Of you. And me." Careful of his breaks and bruises, she stretched herself along his length. "Locked in an embrace."

Two bodies could not get closer, but he felt a niggle of dissatisfaction. With his hand on her chin, he pushed her head up and looked into her eyes. "I say you waved a white flag."

"It was a shift."

"It was a sign of surrender."

"It was a token of love."

That was it. That was what he had waited to hear. "Which I would have taken." He tightened his grip around Edlyn. "At least I have you safe."

Wharton's gaze met Richard's, and Wharton grinned. He didn't blame Richard for looking appalled. He didn't want to stay for this pottage of love words either. Too bad Richard couldn't leave.

Wharton walked to the door. Richard glared balefully.

Hugh touched Edlyn's lips. "And I have your love."

Edlyn slipped her hand over Hugh's heart. "As I have yours."

As Wharton shut the door behind, he heard Richard make muffled gagging noises.

The couple on the floor didn't notice.

CHRISTINA DODD

Winner of the Romance Writers of America
Golden Heart and RITA Awards

ONCE A KNIGHT

Though slightly rusty, once great knight Sir David
Radcliffe agrees to protect Lady Alisoun for a price.
His mercenary heart betrayed by passion, Sir David
protests to his lady that he is still a master of
love—and his sword is swift as ever.

*"This love and laughter medieval romance
is pure delight."* —Romantic Times

MOVE HEAVEN AND EARTH

Fleeing the consequences of scandal, Sylvan Miles
arrived at Clairmont Court to nurse battle-worn
Lord Rand Malkin back to health. The dashing rogue taunts her
with stolen kisses, never expecting her love to heal his damaged soul.

" An unforgettable love story that will warm your heart." —Arnette Lamb

OUTRAGEOUS

Sent by the king to spy on the lovely Lady Marian, Griffith ap Powel is determined to discover her secret. Yet as Lady Marian's defiant deeds make his
blood boil with fury, her beauty draws him beyond any hope of escaping her.

"A fiery medieval romance." —Romantic Times

Let HarperMonogram Sweep You Away

SIREN'S SONG by Constance O'Banyon
Over Seven Million Copies of Her Books Are in Print!
Beautiful Dominique Charbonneau is determined to free her
brother, even if it means becoming a stowaway aboard Judah
Gallant's pirate ship. But Gallant is not the rogue he appears,
and Dominique is torn between duty and a love she might
never know again.

THE AUTUMN LORD by Susan Sizemore
Time Travel Romance
Truth is stranger than fiction when '90s woman Diane Teal is
transported back to medieval France and must rely on the
protection of Baron Simon de Argent. She finds herself unable
to communicate except when telling stories. Fortunately she
and Simone both speak the language of love.

GHOST OF MY DREAMS by Angie Ray
RITA and Golden Heart Award-winning Author
Miss Mary Goodwin refuses to believe her fiancé's warnings that
Elsbury House is haunted – until the deceased Earl appears.
Will the passion of two young lovers overcome the ghost, or is he
actually a bit of a romantic himself?
